DAVID BALDACCI
The Mighty Johns – His New Novella

LAWRENCE BLOCK
The Ehrengraf Reverse

JAMES CRUMLEY
Semi-Pro

BRENDAN DuBOIS
A Sunday in January

TIM GREEN
Whatever it Takes to Win

COLIN HARRISON
Good Seats

DENNIS LEHANE
Gone Down to Corpus

MIKE LUPICA
No Thing

BRAD MELTZER
The Empire Strikes Back

CAROL O'CONNELL
The Arcane Receiver

ANNE PERRY
The End of Innocence

GARY PHILLIPS
Hollywood Spring and Axle

PETER ROBINSON
Gone to the Dawgs

JOHN WESTERMAN
Rumors of Gravity

1 Novella & 13 Superstar Short Stories
From the Finest in Mystery & Suspense

Edited By Otto Penzler

NEW MILLENNIUM PRESS
Beverly Hills

First published in 2002 by
New Millennium Press
301 N. Canon Drive, Suite 214
Beverly Hills, CA 90210

Text Design by Kerry DeAngelis, KL Design
Printed in the United States of America

Library of Congress Cataloging-in-Publication Data available upon request.

CONTENTS

THE MIGHTY JOHNS

BY DAVID BALDACCI

"You know," said Tor North, "if one really thinks about it, this field is logically comparable to the cortex surrounding the brain. The cortex, as I'm sure you know, is one-tenth of an inch thick and has vertical columns running from top to bottom that are roughly two-thousandths of an inch in diameter." Tor bent down and plucked a few blades of grass and showed them to the young man next to him whose name was Jimmy Swift. An east wind careened over the strange topography that surrounded the pair, wrapping the two young men in, at best, a precarious embrace. An east wind here was never kind or coddling, sometimes it barely left you standing as it carried the foul smells of the nearby manufacturing plants and mining operations into the lungs of the folks here. The confusing gusts could do you serious damage if you weren't careful or respectful enough. Swift studied this visible air current, apparently very intent on the beast's artful maneuvering or whimsical ways, depending on how one looked at it. It was easy to see that Swift respected that east wind and understood its potential for deceit.

Tor continued, "Now, those cortical columns could be the blades of grass on this field, Jimmy. Each column contains one hundred and ten neurons. There are six hundred million such columns and thus there are roughly fifty billion neurons in the cortex." He eyed his friend closely to gauge his interest and understanding for what lay ahead. For Tor North something inevitably lay ahead of one of his science-charged homilies.

"So what are you trying to say?" said Jimmy, who had other things on his mind as his gaze caught and held steady on the flagpoles due west of him. "Left to right," he muttered to himself, and then he marched two steps to his left and one long step back. He and Tor agreed on one point. It was all in the details, what they did. Anyone who said otherwise was a fool.

"Aren't you listening?" asked Tor, who then followed his friend's gaze to the poles and their accompanying flag erections. "The wind's fine. I calculate about six to eight knots, roughly east to west, not that significant really, though it is swirling, but then it always swirls because of the manufactured depression we're standing in coupled with the natural lay of the land outside of this concrete and steel bowl. And he's got a strong leg, and you're very fast. You're aptly named. So what do you think about my theory?"

Jimmy glanced at Tor and the expression of confusion could be said to be more weary than profound. Swift often looked puzzled when Tor was lecturing him. And, at least to Jimmy, Tor North held forth on the most arcane, impossibly useless subjects at the most inappropriate times. Last week, during a particularly rugged drill, Tor had grilled him on Carl Jung's theories on individuation, synchronicity and the existence of archetypes, when weighed against modern string theory and neuron consciousness with a dollop of quantum psychology thrown in for no extra charge. As opposed to quantum *physics*, Tor had been quick to point out. Never confuse the two, he had warned Jimmy, though they were obviously somewhat linked, what with each depending to an ever-exacting degree on the "quantum perspective" on life, death, planet earth and beyond to the farthest-away galaxy, this dimension, that dimension, and just about everything in between, including sex, politics, sports, religion, all things Americans loved, despised and feared. If you do mix them up, Tor had warned, you'll find yourself the butt of endless jokes by science geeks, and there was nothing more humiliating than being the butt of jokes by *them*. This was something Tor could well appreciate, since he happened to be one of their numbers.

"I'll be sure to remember that," Jimmy had said doubtfully at the time. Now he just looked blankly at Tor. Quantum theorizing obviously did not jazz Swift's motor to any appreciable degree. In his defense he had many other things on his mind, the wind for one. It was swirling, and swirling was not good. It also was gusting, and gusting was even worse than swirling as far as he was concerned.

Tor let the blades of grass drop back down to the ground where they were caught in miniature cyclones of that stubborn and treacherous east wind. "It's obvious, isn't it?" said Tor. "Come on, think, *Swift*."

Tor referred to him as Swift at such moments of divine ignorance on Jimmy's part, mostly out of good-natured joshing. If they hadn't been such close friends, Jimmy might have decked Tor. Yet the timing was no good. Right now he really needed the man, what with the grumpy wind and the darkening skies. It would be tricky, even for someone as skilled as he. The pulverizing of his friend might come later, though. That could have been Jimmy's unspoken thought as he glared at his companion, his concentration now completely broken by Tor's ill-timed pedagogical taunts.

"Not to me," said Jimmy, and he licked his fingers, just as he did every few seconds, to improve the traction there. "Look, I need to clear my mind, okay, not fill it up with stuff I'm never going to use once in my life. Particularly right now."

Tor tapped the bottom of his shoes clean and said, "Never use! The unmitigated arrogance of human beings truly is astonishing. Let me spell it out for you. We could be standing on a creation of nature with an intellect perhaps surpassing our own and we're stomping all over its neurons, Jimmy, the delicate yet critical canopy over its nuclear engine, so to speak. Where's the respect in that? Where's the inter-species diplomatic relations there? Do you truly believe that such a profound, life-altering concept has nothing to do with you? Are you that clueless?"

"Looks like grass and dirt to me, Tor, but then I'm just a dumb poli-sci major." Jimmy looked up into the bright lights that surrounded them and he stiffened when he saw what was coming. "Forget the cortex, Tor, time to go to work." Jimmy performed a little jig to get the circulation going in his legs and licked his fingers a final time. He cast one last look at the flagpoles which were barely visible now, what with the low cloud cover and the rapidly failing natural light, and then he set himself to wait for it to commence as the screams plummeted down upon the two men

3

like August hail, and the ground shook like a six-point continental plate-basher was barreling their way. A smile eased across Jimmy Swift's face.

Tor looked up, saw what Jimmy saw, strapped his helmet tight, inserted his mouthpiece and squatted low like a man about to do some serious personal business. His heart rate had just doubled, and he knew Swift's had too. And yet Tor had a relative calmness about him that came from the most basic of all endeavors: preparation. In fact he was never more ready in his life. And he was about to do something that, if it played out as perfectly as it had in his mind the last week or so, would literally rock the world, in his humble opinion, or at least make the powers-that-be sit up and take a good, hard look. And yet maybe not, for people were so obtuse and, unlike a carefully controlled science experiment run through to its final logical outcome, so maddeningly unpredictable.

The football descended upon them from out of the lights. Overcast skies pregnant with rain had further aged a gloomy Saturday afternoon into an early, melancholy dusk. It would have been difficult to see a plane coming at them from out of the blinding crest created by the banks of thousand watt stars that ringed the stadium. Yet, as usual, Jimmy fielded the small brown blob of leathery pigskin that plummeted from the sky with an athletic grace he possessed in envious quantity. For his part, the blocky, slower-footed, and yet extremely capable Tor eased back on his right foot and established a firm center of gravity on the possible cortex of a potentially large intellect lying beneath them. He silently counted to three as he eyed screaming barbaric young men charging at him and Swift. This fanatical—some would say infantile—group had somehow been transported into the "civilized" world for four quarters every Saturday in the fall across the length and breadth of America's college football empire. The cries from the stands echoed the brutes' battle hymn as blood-lusting spectators, now mere ghostly outlines in the diminished light—silhouettes of Johnny Rebs or Union Blues hunkered at the fogged tree line moments before the deadly clash—leaned forward and awaited with indefatigable glee a violent collision of young, strong bodies that was bare seconds from occurring. Not even patrons of the Roman bloodbaths snorting their fix of human pain and cruelty had ever witnessed anything quite so spectacular in its potential for glorious mayhem.

With an explosive burst, Tor North took off running. He said not one word, uttered not a single reciprocal scream, for he was saving every ounce of energy he had in order to transfer it on to others. As Newton's Third Law of Motion dictated with a majestic certainty, when an object exerts a force on a second object, the second object exerts an equal and opposite force on the first. And, at least for now, E did approximate MC squared, though Tor was working on alternative theories that were holding some promise. Yet, for his purposes right now, all that mattered was angle, speed and weight displacement, and the use of power against itself to maximize effect beyond all reckoning, for the sum of the parts was very often not so great as the entire throbbing whole. Tor had lectured Jimmy on this time and again, and the boy still was not getting it. Yet Tor North completely and absolutely understood each and every wonderful theoretical possibility, each tantalizing conundrum of secular faith and omnipotent science. What was rushing headlong at Tor North was a living, breathing physics experiment, and the young man did not intend to screw up such a magnificent display of infinite beauty.

With Jimmy dancing and juking behind him, awaiting any crevice he could slide through, Tor counted off his steps and simultaneously calculated axis rotation, curvature of the earth, mass, speed, and possibly most important for his purposes, angle of impact. When he reached the count of five Tor hit the wall of men at what seemed like the speed of light, or, as Tor would later say in his inimitable way of pedantic embellishment, actually at the speed of a subatomic particle tunneling under a quantum barrier, or at approximately four point seven times the speed of light. So fast, in fact, that the particle would exit the tunnel before it even entered it. Try explaining that to a layperson and one would observe eyeballs slowly glaze over for an interminable duration! Tor knew because he had tried. Tack on to that the morsel of knowledge that at the speed of light time stands perfectly still, like the hands of a stalled clock fittingly enough, and that traveling at a rate faster than that of light would actually carry one backwards in time, then one would see the entire body of the unscientific dunce recede into a state the coroner would conclusively term "rigor mortis," with the attendant physical rigidity and intellectual perception of a cinder block.

Of course one had to extrapolate out to the heavens and beyond to reach such a level of intergalactic thrust as that entailed by multiples of 186,000 miles per second, or six trillion miles per year, from something as relatively slow as a college football-playing science major. Yet extrapolation, even at extreme levels, Tor believed, was a necessary part of life if one was ever really going to get to the truth, which was always far more complex and even chilling than most humans dared to confront. Scientists possessed courage, Tor knew, far beyond the comprehension of most people. And the physicist, more than all the other disciples of pure, raw science, realized that humankind was simply one modestly evolved, often chaotic (and perhaps low-level) organic species existing in a single puny dimension on one truly unremarkable—some called it middling—planet among billions like it and unlike it. The authentic disciples of science could take the truth; the rest of humanity was blissfully ignorant, or as Tor often said, existing in a permanent state of self-denial of what actually could be out there; the very real possibility that mankind would not be anywhere near the top of the intelligent life heap. What terrified others, enthralled him.

Tor took out six men with his masterfully timed and placed flying body block that dropped the orange and black like dominoes in exact accordance with the formula of mass displacement at precisely angled high-speed collision on tortured playing field that Tor had so painstakingly devised. He had worked it all out the previous week, in between molecular analysis labs. Jimmy Swift exploited his enormous gash in the kickoff team's heart, flashing by as Tor lay in the dirt and grass, his facemask bent, his mouthpiece knocked out, a spot of blood on his cheek. All around Tor sprawled a sextuplet of young men in orange and black uniforms stunned by the impact of a quantum tunneler who had exited before he had entered. Not one opposing player had a good shot at Jimmy until he was at the opponent's forty-yard line. A very fast cornerback, Leon Panders—who had given Jimmy fits for three years—had selected a decent angle of attack as he raced after his streaking opponent. However, this time Leon had underestimated both Swift's speed and determination. Right as the cornerback went in for the kill, Jimmy kicked it into a higher gear, and Leon ended up eating grass, or billions of neurons, if you believed Tor. Jimmy sped untouched into the end zone to complete his one hundred-and-three yard trek, and then respectfully tossed the ball to the waiting official and jogged to the bench where he was mobbed by his frantically delighted teammates.

Tor rose among the bodies of the fallen enemies, snagged a few precious blades of grass, and mouthed a mea culpa to the great mind that might or might not be lurking below the football field at Draven University. The school sat in a drab, manufactured valley of perpetually darkened hues among the squat, hollowed and stripped coal hills of western Pennsylvania, and was home to the Mighty Johns football team. As Tor gazed at the berserk crowd, the metal and concrete stands shaking under their collective mass times energy, he knew these emotion-charged plebeians hadn't a clue as to what really had just taken place on the field. Tor had *only* displaced the almost century-old blocking stratagems of X's and O's by using the principles of modern quantum theory that most people would never be able to comprehend to any measurable degree, much less consciously use in their lives. Still, Tor had to smile at the mad party going on over at his team's bench. What could be better than an extravaganza of science coupled with the exuberance of raw, young men in all their beastly pomp and pageantry that co-existed for at least sixty violent minutes on Saturday afternoons in the fall at the universities of the best and brightest all across the land? Where else could you see smart, educated people physically wreck one another for nominal cost that included food, drink and even a place to sit? Perhaps it was worth tramping all over the brain sheath of a new species of intelligent being. At least for now, Tor would assume it was.

He jogged to the bench and slapped skin with Jimmy. His teammate also whacked him on the helmet with his hand. "One for the old cortex," Jimmy said, and the two friends sat down next to each other. Then it was dramatically announced over the PA that Jimmy Swift's run was actually a yard longer than originally thought. The rollicking, delirious crowd grew still and quiet at this momentous and stunning proclamation, for the truly unthinkable had just occurred.

Jimmy Swift had broken the forty-year-old record for kickoff returns held by the immortal Draven alumnus, Herschel Ruggles.

Jimmy, at the prompting of his coaches and teammates, was persuaded to run out onto the field to acknowledge the crowd's applause that cascaded down like towering waves of blue as men, women and children, many of them weeping uncontrollably—the sight of men with large exposed beer bellies heaving was particularly memorable—flicked their Mighty Johns' aquamarine towels back and forth to show their immense gratification at being a part of this momentous, once-in-a-lifetime occasion. At least a half-dozen married and God-fearing women in the stands would gladly have sacrificed themselves by engaging in a monstrous orgy with Jimmy Swift right there on the playing field, with the complete understanding and even blessing of their tearfully joyous husbands. It was truly worth that much to them. Here college football was not just loved by these folks, it was their faith.

Swift took Tor with him to acknowledge the crowd's appreciation, despite his shy friend's protest. "Like you didn't get it for me," replied Jimmy as he pulled the far larger Tor out with him. They both took awkward bows at the fifty-yard line while a stretcher crew carried off the six young men who had had the misfortune to wander into Tor North's laboratory at the Mighty Johns' twelve-yard line.

Tor and Jimmy returned to their seats on the bench as play resumed. Jimmy hunkered down and ostensibly began going over in his mind the wonderful run that had just made him a legend. Even the vicious, sneaky east wind could not dislodge Swift from his private and triumphant revelry.

Tor, motivated perhaps by being a part of the record-breaking feat, started contemplating for the hundredth time or so, the mysterious disappearance of Herschel Ruggles all those years ago. It had happened right on this very field, in front of twenty-four thousand, six hundred and twelve rabid Mighty Johns fans, including Tor's father, Peter North, who had been a teammate of Ruggles. While a man vanishing into thin air during a football game was not a physics conundrum per se, it was still a dilemma, a solvable dilemma, Tor thought, yet one that would take as much serious thinking as he could give it. And now, after helping to break the man's longstanding record, Tor North was finally prepared to do so. Tor was a scientist, but, as strange as it seemed, he was something of a superstitious one. This shattering of the record was an omen, a signal of unmistakable importance. It was finally time to tackle the mystery that had bedeviled Draven University, the commonwealth of Pennsylvania and the entire country for four decades.

What had happened to Herschel Ruggles?

After a practice that had left him drenched in a chilly sweat, yet not very tired, Tor walked out onto the Mighty Johns' football field. There was no crowd, no opposing team seeking to crush him, no Jimmy Swift and his complete indifference to the logical, if arcane, ways of science. Now he could think even as the wind nudged him here and there, like a fox lazily trolling the underbrush for easy prey. Other than the wind and the university there wasn't much of interest this secluded western wedge of the Keystone state had to offer a prospective tenant, and the constant wind—that when it wasn't cold and biting, was heat-filled and suffocating—was not much of an enticement.

However, Tor had come to Draven University because it

offered an excellent science program at a location not all that distant from his hometown. Jimmy Swift had come here because the school had offered him a full football scholarship and overlooked a grade transcript containing nothing but mediocrity. Through the odd ways of the world, these two very different men had become good friends and supportive teammates.

Swift had chosen political science as his major and then ascertained, too late, that it involved far more reading, writing and thinking than he had expected. He had tried to switch to history, but then discovered that discipline had similar if not even more onerous academic requirements. He decided to stick it out with poli-sci until better prospects happened along. They never had and he decided to await graduation and then determine what he wanted to be.

Tor hated history, though he had read far more of it than most. And yet he had once thought seriously of becoming a scholar in that field, until he started to delve more deeply into what was often passed off as history. He had found most of it to be revisionist drivel, intentionally misleading at best, outright fraudulent at worst. Tor would have none of the lies and deceits, the imagined imagery, the bankrupt soul. He could never be part of such a franchise of the apocryphal. He had, instead, turned to science, where equations and formulas of exacting precision could be relied upon and pursued alongside an opportunity for new discoveries at a level that had absolutely no peer in the universe. For instance, every scientist knew what mass was, yet no scientist had ever seen energy, only the effects of it on mass.

History and fields like it were too easily manipulated and colored by biased human hands gripping their own agendas. Science was not as susceptible to those types of influences. When one did A and then B, then almighty C would result virtually all of the time. Therefore it was upon science and not upon history that Tor had decided to wield his massive intellect. It was actually the best of both worlds for him: a foundation of iron upon which to plant his feet, and a sky without limit for which he could reach. He would need both of these attributes of the modern scientist to solve the problem that lay before him right now.

Tor knelt in the grass and studiously surveyed the exact spot where Herschel Ruggles had fielded that very special kickoff forty years before. Long before he and Swift had broken the record, Tor had read every available account of the incident, and there were many, of varying reliability and accuracy. One troublesome aspect, though, had been the almost complete absence of official police records regarding the disappearance, eyewitness accounts, that sort of thing. Thus, Tor had spoken with anyone he could find who had actually been in attendance that unforgettable day, including his own father. From all these sources, Tor had pieced together the events leading up to Ruggles vanishing. Tor also had Ruggles' entire touchdown run that day diagrammed in his mind.

Ruggles had fielded the ball three yards deep in the end zone. The Howling Cougar kicker at the time had possessed quite a leg and actually went on to play professional ball, first with the Packers and then with Unitas and the Colts. He routinely kicked the ball into the end zone and he had never had one taken back all the way on him.

Carrying the ball as he always did in his right hand, Ruggles had cut to his left, picked up his blocking wedge, and ridden it to the Johns' thirty-one yard line, where his protection finally had broken down. At that critical point Ruggles did something that had characterized his entire football career at Draven. Tightly scripted offensive schemes went out the window and pure instinct took over. Ruggles reversed field, running naked, for all the Johns had committed to the left side. The fact was most of them were down on the ground already having sacrificed their bodies for what had been a respectable return. Given the time on the clock and the Johns only down by four, thanks to a missed two-point conversion by their opponent—the Howling Cougars from Appalachian Valley Tech—things were looking pretty fair for the Johns and their high-powered offense, headed up by none other than tailback Herschel Ruggles, their only bonafide All-American gridiron legend. Yet what was respectable to ordinary mortals was far from acceptable to a man of Ruggles' ability and drive. It was known across the conference that Ruggles' ambition, if not obsession, was to score on every single play. And while of course he didn't, some Saturday afternoons it seemed like the man accomplished this lofty goal. Yet he had scored at least two touchdowns in every collegiate game he had ever played, and once had scored six times in a single half. Against Nebraska! Fully two-thirds of the season ticket holders at Draven were there solely to watch him perform. And Ruggles well knew it, from everything Tor had been able to discover about the man. Herschel Ruggles was not a man who lacked confidence. It was often that way with demigods, reasoned Tor, particularly those of the athletic kind.

Tor stood and then started to pantomime the remainder of Ruggles's legendary run into the records book. He cut from the left sideline and began a race to the middle of the field near the thirty-five. Before he got there, however, an ambitious Howling Cougar had launched what should have been a successful low tackle on Ruggles at the left hash mark. Truth was, he should have had Ruggles dead to rights, according to a fan who had seen it, and who Tor had interviewed. What he ended up with, said the now very elderly man, was an armful of nothing but crisp Pennsylvania air as Ruggles leapt right over him. Leapt right over him! By a good two feet, declared the man. Not even Michael Jordan could have done that, the old-timer added, not with all the bells and whistles athletes these days get. Back then, after a game all the players would sit around smoking and drinking beer and eating fattening food. There were no strength trainers, no weightlifting rooms, no dieticians, not one shoe contract, just towering men who played the game with all their big hearts because they loved it more than they loved their own mothers. Herschel Ruggles was just such a man, pronounced the old fan. Hell, he had leapt over that Howling Cougar by damn good *three* feet!

Tor attempted such a jump himself, and through there was no opponent seeking to take out his legs, he almost fell. Agility

had never been a strong suit of his. The next player who had had
a shot at Ruggles was a starting middle linebacker carrying thirty
more pounds than his target and who also had decent wheels. A
stiff arm the likes of which no one had seen outside of a Bronko
Nagurski bone-crushing jaunt had left the determined linebacker
flat on his back and the crowd stunned, according to several
other fans Tor had spoken with. Tor also had succeeded in track-
ing down the former Howling Cougar who actually had been the
recipient of this violent if legal blow. The fellow had remembered
every second of it, he had told Tor with seemingly bountiful
pride. Indeed, the man had remarked that it was one of the high
points of his life. The former Howling Cougar linebacker was now
a successful automobile dealer just across the state line in Ohio,
so he presumably had had his share of sacred triumphs in life. Yet
being pounded into the earth by Ruggles apparently ranked right
up there with all of them. From all Tor could learn from that fellow and others like him, Herschel Ruggles seemed to inspire such
devotion in those who crossed his path, however painfully.

Tor belted his imaginary foe and kept right on going. The
next two obstacles were a pair of Howling Cougars who had been
slow coming down on the kickoff and thus, ironically, were in a
position to make the key stop on Ruggles. The mightiest Mighty
John, however, had other plans. Ruggles had thrown a damn near
perfect Crazy Legs Hirsch scissors move, split the pair of defenders and then was gone like a flash of ship's light in a vicious,
unforgiving fog. The two Cougars ended up colliding and probably each one thought he had made the tackle on Ruggles. After
that Ruggles burst through two more tacklers, knocking both men
unconscious with the ferocity of his attack, because even though
he was carrying the ball, and was the presumptive target, that
was not how Ruggles played the game. When he was running with
the ball, and it was your task to stop him, *you* became the target
for him to destroy, which he often did, with complete and unassailable finality.

Finally, the kicker himself had the last legitimate shot at
Ruggles yet missed badly after biting on a feint and falling flat on

his face. Some said that during his long professional career after-wards, this same kicker never again attempted another tackle, due solely to his total embarrassment at the hands of Ruggles that day. After that it was a mere foot race, and the Olympian speed with which Ruggles was endowed left absolutely no doubt as to the outcome. Tor mimicked that race, albeit far slower than had Ruggles, and as the greatest of the Mighty Johns had done four decades ago, Tor crossed the goal line, arms raised, heart pounding with vicarious triumph.

The next movements were critical and Tor took a few min-utes to ponder them. The truly extraordinary fact was that Ruggles had not stopped there. He had not merely tossed the ball to the waiting referee and trotted back to the bench as Jimmy Swift had done. Ruggles had continued running, ball in hand, into the passageway that led deep underneath Herschel Ruggles Field and to the Mighty Johns' locker room. The stadium had been renamed from simply Johns Grounds ten years prior when Tor's father, a wealthy businessman deeply involved in the steel indus-try that predominated the area then as now, had given a large sum of money to the school. A decent two-way lineman with a heart far larger than his physical talent, and a former teammate and friend of Ruggles, Peter North had said, at the time of the field's christening in Ruggles' memory, that it was the proudest moment of his life, and a way that would forever keep alive Herschel Ruggles, wherever he happened to be, and regardless of whatever had happened to him. A great man, an athlete of near mythical proportion, a scholar of outstanding reputation, and a young man as compassionate and giving off the field as he was predominate and prolific on it, had said a truly moved Peter North. It was a speech that had also driven the crowd to tears, including Tor, who had only been eleven at the time. Not yet fully aware at the time of his mental prowess, that chilly fall day Tor had made a silent promise to his father that when the time was right, and he felt his skills were suitably developed, the son would once and for all discover the truth of what had happened to a man his beloved father had described as "Someone who even more than my own father had the greatest and most positive influence over me, and without whom I would not have achieved the success I have today. God Bless Herschel Ruggles, and all those like him, though they would most certainly have to be few in number." The crowd had cheered even as it had wept.

As Tor stared at the opening down which Ruggles had run and then never returned from, a slight chill hit him. Certainly, only a few at the school would know all the twists and turns, nooks and crannies, rooms and passageways, that lay under the stadium. It had been originally built in the 1930's, as had the entire college, by the coal mining baron, John Milton Draven; thus both the source of the school's name and the identity of its athletic teams. Draven had been near maniacal in his college building plans, and the earth had been gouged open to a great depth by the large machinery from the mogul's mining company. To such an extent, in fact, that what had been carved out beneath the ground could be said to be almost as elaborate as what lay above it.

Most folks attributed that architectural foible to Draven's background. He had started as a humble miner, digging out the black rock with a pick and later dynamite. Shrewd and ambitious, he had parlayed his skill at pinpointing enormous veins of coal into enough money to purchase a few choice tracts of land in the Alleghenies. One of these parcels had turned out to be lying above the largest geological trap of both coal and natural gas ever discovered up to that time, and had propelled its fortunate owner into a league with the Rockefellers and Vanderbilts. Yet Draven had never forgotten his roots and his money cascaded down not upon the underprivileged of America's metropolises but on the poor and disadvantaged of the country's Appalachian coal mining regions. Draven, forever remembered as tall and regal, white-haired since the age of thirty, and bearing a striking resemblance to George Washington, had explained the rationale behind his construction of such underground labyrinths by stating that the basis of his fortune had originated from there, and the happiest times of his life had come when he was beneath the dirt. Thus, he had added to great humorous effect, he, of course, not only did not fear his death, he was actually looking forward to it, as he would be returning to the very place he cherished most in the world, and that had so enriched him.

His inevitable detractors claimed that Old Draven was a wily man, most interested in his own well-being and adding to his already deep purse—despite his outward philanthropy that was not so nearly as great as reported, they claimed. These same sources also alleged that the real reason Draven had dug the earth out so much when constructing the college was that he believed there to be precious minerals buried there, just waiting for a nimble hand to pluck them. Whatever the truth actually was his enemies had the last laugh for a very elderly John Milton Draven had been buried alive during a visit to one of his Pennsylvania mines, the Gloria No. 3, named in honor of his wife of the same number. His body, and that of his entire party of twelve, not including the fortunate Gloria who had stayed home, was recovered several weeks later. They had, the evidence showed, lived for perhaps a week, until their air and presumably their hope had given out. Although there was some indication, as culled from the results of Draven's autopsy, that the rich man had actually been strangled. Those who had spent considerable time with the hot-tempered Draven—though not in nearly such close quarters as a small pocket of life a hundred feet underground— did not rule such a fate out of the question.

Tor felt the gaze upon him before he heard or saw anyone. The existence of a sixth sense was something he had grown up to accept as fact. It was an issue of other dimensions and the continuing saga of runaway energy colliding and transforming itself in various ways and places, of course, and thus fell within the domain of bedrock physics rather than charlatanic purveyors of psychic phenomena.

"Something on your mind, young man?"

The old fellow staring at Tor was badly stooped, though it was clear he had once possessed an impressive physique. In the bent torso Tor could sense pain incapable of being recorded by medical instrument, and yet the man's features betrayed not a trace of the agony being signaled to Tor by this potentially dangerous curvature of spine. The man's hair was a carpet of straggly, mottled gray and white with little lumps of black here and there, as though someone had carelessly dripped ink on dull-colored paper. The face was a jumble of seemingly mismatched parts. The eyes were too large for the face and the forehead was too short and spare in dimension when aligned against the slope of nose and width of skull. By contrast, the jutting chin was a shelf of intimidating proportion and the jaw was so geometrically perfect it seemed carved by jeweler's wheel. His long, stained fingers were wrapped around the handle of a broom. He held the tool, it seemed to Tor, like it was a part of him, an appendage of planed maple to go with the deformed body; perhaps it was necessary support for legs that looked too spindly to be of much practical use.

"Something on your mind, young man?" this organic shipwreck asked again as he took a few steps forward.

Tor rose and headed over to the man, who was just outside the entrance of the immortal passageway through which Ruggles had raced to his apparent doom. As Tor drew near, something caught his eye. When the man moved Tor could see the outline of his defined quadriceps push against both his blue pants legs. It was like the silhouette of a rocky ledge under shallow clear water. Tor's gaze remained fixed on those legs until the man spoke again.

"You're one of them football players, ain't you?"

"Tor North. First string offensive guard and second string outside linebacker."

"And one helluva special teams player. You're the one that threw that block sprung Jimmy Swift, ain't you?"

"I am."

"Helluva hit, young man. Ain't seen one like it for years."

"Probably since Herschel Ruggles played," commented Tor with what he hoped was delicate inducement.

"Oh, I ain't been here that long. Heard about him, though.

Hell, who ain't heard of that feller what lived even a short while round these parts. Legend, I guess you'd call him."

"Exactly how long has that been? Your living around here?"

The man leaned forward more on his broom handle, as though for additional support if the two were going to stand there jawing for a bit. Tor's gaze went once more to those muscular legs and he knew, without a doubt, that the old man needed no such artificial assistance. Herschel Ruggles would have been sixty-one years old this month. Tor was aware of this because he knew just about all there was to know about the man. This fellow here looked a good ten years older than that, and yet, who knew what the last forty years had been like for Ruggles. Disappearing down a tunnel carrying a football and the potentially debilitating aftermath suggested by such a mysterious exit from ordinary life might well have prematurely aged the man. For all Tor knew a desperate Ruggles had been on the run for all these years. The possibility, however farfetched, that he might be standing in the presence of the man he had thought so much about recently was as euphoric as it was paralyzing.

"Oh, 'bout a year now. Surprised you ain't seen me before. I do the cleaning round the stadium."

Tor pulled free from his mental stupefaction and looked around the large complex. "Just you?"

"No, not just me, young feller. You smarter'n that. But even though I ain't been here all that long, I know the ins and outs of this place better'n just about anybody."

"Really? Why's that?"

"Because I took the time to learn it, that's why." The man's eyes sparkled under the litter of oddly cut hair and Tor thought the old gent might actually start laughing. Tor glanced down the tunnel. "Find anything interesting while you were doing your learning?"

The man looked behind him, following Tor's gaze. "Depends on what you call interesting. Lights my fire, that's no lie. Hell, spend all my time here. Sleep here too."

"You live here?"

"Sure, why not? Warm and clean and a lot cheaper than the places they rent out 'round here. Pushing brooms don't pay all that good, and a body got to eat. Works out all fine, see?"

Tor said he could see that all right. "What's your name?"

"Benny, Benny James. Folks call me BJ. You g'on and do that too."

"Call me Tor, BJ. Look, what if I wanted a little tour through the stadium, would you take me?"

BJ cocked a fuzzy eyebrow at him. "You play football here every Saturday. Ain't you know the place by now?"

"No, I mean that part of the stadium." Tor pointed down the tunnel. "Past the locker room and the tape room and the laundry. Further on, into the bowels of the place, so to speak. I've never been there."

BJ moved his broom forward an inch or so before once more resting his chin on the handle. "Why you want to know about that?"

Tor tried to appear casual. "Like you said, it lights your fire. Maybe it'll light mine."

"Young feller like yourself, suppose to be getting your fire lit with the pretty young things running 'round here. Cheerleaders and such. They go for the fellers in the uniform on Saturday after-noon, now that ain't no lie."

"So you played football?"

"Nah, wanted to, but ain't got what it takes. Too light in the bones, can't run worth a spit and bleed too easy. I just watch, but I'm a good watcher. Over my time seen all the great ones play."

"So you've traveled quite a bit?"

BJ took a few moments to sweep up some paper shreds next to the tunnel entrance and scooped them into a dustpan and then into a trash can sitting next to the last row of seats on the lower level. "I get around. Big country, like to see what I can of it before I kick off."

"So will you show me the underground part of the stadium?"

BJ steadied himself on the broom handle before answering. "I tell you what, you come to see me tomorrow night right here around nine, I see what I can do."

"Why at night?"

"Got to work during the day. Don't worry, there's light in there." He added quietly, "At least in most of the places. We get to the others we use flashlights." He seemed to appraise Tor keenly. "You game?"

Tor stifled a chill deep inside of him before answering his new friend and now informal scout, BJ. "I'm game."

A slash of heat lightning, unusual for this time of year, greeted Tor as he made his way to meet BJ. The man was not there when Tor arrived at the entrance at which had begun, apparently, by far, the longest run of Herschel Ruggles' illustrious career. Tor took a cautious step forward into the concrete lair. Though he had been down that passageway many times before and after games and practices, something did not feel quite right. Perhaps it was as simple as there being no teammates around to lend comfort and the occasional well-intentioned jab to the kidneys. The fact was Tor had never before been down here alone. He took another step inside. This section was well lighted, the old light tubes hanging down from the vaulted ceiling of stone blinked and popped seemingly with incandescent glee. From somewhere in the distance, and darkness, there came the drip of water. Tor told himself there was nothing odd about that. Tunnels always leaked and made strange sounds as support beams and load-bearing walls held back the weight of the earth. He took several strides forward, past the locker room, and past the prep and treatment room. Here the players would sit immersed in the whirlpool in near-boiling water or lay on long tables for electro-massages, cortisone injections, complex taping, strapping and rigging of knees, ankles, shoulders and other susceptible spots, as well as additional treatments designed to help erase or at least diminish the physical punishment that inevitably came from throwing themselves against men of like weight, speed, strength, and determination week after bloody week. This was all familiar ground for Tor, nothing to be unduly nervous about. He had expected to see a few of his teammates in there getting some extra helpings of tape, heat or needle pricks, but the room was empty, the lights off. He continued on, wondering where his scout, BJ, might be. Perhaps the old fellow had forgotten. Maybe Tor should turn back. Yet he kept on going, placing his hand against the cold stone of the wall as he ventured to imagine what might have happened to Ruggles as he raced down this passageway.

No one that Tor could find had seen the man after he entered the tunnel. In those days everyone associated with the team was usually on the field during the game. When Ruggles had left the field of play, he had, almost certainly, been alone in the tunnel, at least for a few minutes. The very strange thing was that Ruggles apparently *had* gone into the locker room because his street clothes—according to what Tor could determine from the sketchy facts available—had not been in his locker. So had he come into the locker room, changed and left via the exit door that was locked and he wasn't supposed to have a key for? The problem was he wouldn't have really had time to do that. Tor well knew how long it took to get off football equipment. And the record showed that several people came into the tunnel about five minutes after Ruggles did. They would probably have been in there earlier, but absolute pandemonium had broken out on the field after Ruggles' run, and, the fact was, most people hadn't realized he had left the field at all. Most of them thought he was buried under a pile of his celebrating teammates in the end zone. It was only after the celebration died down that folks realized Ruggles wasn't there. Yet still, five minutes to change into street clothes and then leave undetected? And add to that the fact that Ruggles' uniform, shoulder pads, cleats, and all had never been found. Why would he take those items with him? How could the most famous football player in town leave undetected carrying his own football uniform? None of it made any sense.

The light was growing dimmer the farther in he went. Apparently, as BJ had indicated, the bulk of the underground guts of the place had never been lighted. What was the sense in that? Tor stopped and stood there for a couple of minutes, the erratic thuds of his heartbeat growing louder and even seeming to echo along the long tube of soggy stone and mortar. He had read Poe, and Tor half-expected to see a black, floppy raven sailing toward him, cawing its message of doom and spreading its utter terror over its poor earth-bound targets. The Fall of the House of Tor. It had no particular ring to it.

A flash of light behind him made Tor turn. He held up one hand to block the blinding strobe confronting him.

"That you?" called out a firm voice.

"BJ?" said Tor as he dropped his hand, but averted his gaze, as the light grew closer.

BJ walked up next to him, a powerful searchlight in hand. Tor noted that the man was not limping, and now needed no broom to steady him. Also, he did not seem so bent and physically wretched tonight. Maybe the night brought out the best in him, a side that was not allowed to show itself during daylight. Though the man was a complete stranger, and could have been a fugitive killer on the run for all Tor knew, the young man let out a breath of relief to at last have a companion to share the admittedly unsettling experience of this gloomy tunnel to who knew where. Maybe no ravens, but certainly bats could call this place home.

"Must've missed you. I was standing outside smoking a cig. Might've been late, too. Durn watch never keeps good time. Sorry."

"That's okay. Let's get going. I have an early lab tomorrow."

"You're the boss. But stick close, easy to lose your way down here. Done it more'n once."

"Well, don't do it tonight," muttered Tor.

They made a left at an intersection of two separate corridors, and then, after a short walk, hung a right and this new direction threw them into total darkness but for BJ's light. Also, at this point the floor of the tunnel angled downward at about ten degrees. Tor found himself having to slow his pace lest he tumble forward into BJ and wipe out the elderly man, and his all-important light, with an illegal block.

"What's down here?" asked Tor.

BJ looked back and grinned. In the arc of the light his features along the discomforting glint of nicotine-stained and uneven teeth seemed almost fiendish. It was the first time Tor had really seen the man's teeth, and the impression was vastly unnerving. The man seemed different somehow; Tor couldn't quite make out exactly in what way. Was he growing taller? Tor was almost six-feet-three and a very solid two hundred thirty-five pounds. It must be an optical illusion, thought Tor, for BJ seemed to be growing closer to him in weight and height.

"You'll see. Good shit."

They continued on, Tor creeping ever closer to BJ even as his dense muscles tensed for some possible action, Tor wasn't quite sure what. He also noticed that it was becoming harder to breathe down here. Tor obviously was aware that at ever increasing altitudes the thinning air made breathing very difficult at anything over roughly twelve thousand feet. After that, the higher you went the discomfort would increase by degrees until the oxygen-deprived mind and body would begin to hallucinate, weaken, experience seizures, and then commence to shut down with death following fairly quickly. Obviously going *down* into the earth presented similar dilemmas as dirt, rock, confined spaces and poor air flow combined to create comparable sorts of challenges as when one went trolling towards the heavens. In fact, it could produce the lethal atmosphere of carbon dioxide that had ended the life of John Milton Draven and company so long ago. And yet not really all that long ago. In fact, Draven's death had occurred fairly recently after Ruggles' disappearance, or so Tor suddenly recalled, when the coal baron had perished in the Gloria No. 3 from lack of air, but also with ligature marks around his neck.

The trip took quite a bit of time and more than once Tor glanced at his watch, which he could make out only because of its luminous fittings. The turns became so numerous that soon Tor was hopelessly lost, and thus totally dependent upon a man who was a complete stranger to him. Once they were even compelled to hop across a foot-long break in the path. When BJ had shone his light on it, the opening was revealed to be a drop of considerable distance, and Tor wondered how that could be. Where they were treading now, did it also have such precarious underpinnings? Were they walking upon the air or the earth? Were they one weakened stone from plunging to deaths that would remain forever concealed? Tor had no desire to be so entombed for eternity with a stranger named BJ who apparently underwent a metamorphosis into something bigger and stronger the farther underground he ventured.

He was just about to tell the fellow that they would turn back, when he saw it. A door! The light was shining upon a door. BJ glanced back at him, grinned another insufferable grin, and pointed to this dilapidated portal of warped oak planks and rusted iron.

"What is it?" Tor asked.

"Like I told you. The good shit. No, make that the great shit."

With astonishment, Tor watched as BJ pulled an ancient-looking key from his pocket and inserted it in the lock.

Tor gripped the man's arm, which he found to be surprisingly hard and muscled. "Where'd you get that key?"

"You spend a lot of time down here, you find stuff." The man let out a cackle that flew down the tunnel, bouncing off all sides as though aloft bats in rabid seizure.

Tor noted with equal surprise that BJ's bent torso appeared nearly straightened. They were almost eye-to-eye in fact. Had the laws of gravity been suspended down here, as they were in space? Should Newtonian scholars be alarmed?

BJ turned the key and pushed the door open. He held the light high as he entered. Tor hesitated for a moment. Something as naked and compelling as fear was close to routing his natural curiosity. He clenched his hands, silently recited the comforting theory of Occam's Razor, and followed BJ inside.

Tor first observed that his companion's light was not really needed here. There was light, natural light, of some unknown origin, though this far under the earth the possibility of such intrinsic illumination was problematic at best. The room was fairly large, perhaps twenty feet squared, with walls of quarried stone that appeared to be dry-stacked, for Tor could not make out any mortar lines. The large rocks were as uniformly placed as concrete block, and so tightly mitered at the corners that they matched the finest wood moldings Tor had ever seen. Skillful hands indeed had put together this place. Yet why waste such talent on a room that would never be used or even seen?

"Where's the light coming from?" asked Tor.

BJ merely shrugged his shoulders. "Ain't never been able to tell."

"So where's the 'great shit' as you put it?"

"Through there."

BJ pointed toward the far corner of the room that a compass would have shown to be the western side of the place. The light dimmed a bit there. Yet even Tor, whose eyesight was not the best without his glasses, which he had forgotten tonight, could make out an opening in the rock, once it had been pointed out to him.

"Where does that go?"

"Show you. Lot better'n telling. Come on."

BJ started forward, yet Tor did not move. BJ looked back.

"Come on, young feller."

"No," Tor said. "Now we go back."

"Ain't you want to see?"

"Not tonight. Another time. I need to think about all this."

"You sure? Great shit," BJ added, though his grin was less prominent now.

"I'm very sure," said Tor.

They retraced their steps, Tor a foot or so behind BJ. From his pocket, Tor drew out a piece of chalk. As they walked down the passageways, Tor held the chalk against the walls and marked the trail all the way back. When they reached the outside once more, Tor drew in a long breath. A lover of astronomy all his life, the stars had never been a more welcome sight. He glanced at BJ, and the man had returned to his stooped, decrepit appearance.

Of course it was all a hallucination, Tor concluded. The mind had a direct line to the autonomic nervous system and could cause physical symptoms of great severity, and also make the imagined seem perfectly real. Gravity was not suspended in the dimension humans dwelled, of that Tor was absolutely certain. Newton and his legions of followers could rest easy. BJ was stooped and in pain, and he would remain that way until he died. Tor thanked his guide, pressed a crisp twenty-dollar bill into the man's hand and walked off.

BJ stared after him for a bit, the expression on his features a mixture of curiosity and disappointment, and then the man headed back down the tunnel.

Tor returned to the tunnel two nights later, and again he was not alone. Jimmy Swift did not look pleased to be there, yet Tor had countered every one of Jimmy's sophistries for not coming with highly logical arguments of his own. When Jimmy had still refused, Tor had reminded him that Tor was the primary reason Jimmy Swift now dwelled in the record books of the university, and didn't that mean something? And didn't Mighty Johns football players have to stick together in this world of tribulation and strife? Didn't they? And Jimmy had finally answered that they did indeed, yet he did not look happy to be standing outside a tunnel that, as far as he knew, went straight to Hell without offering a return ticket.

Tor had done some more digging in the last couple of days. His findings, dutifully recorded in his notebook, had been interesting. The man calling himself BJ was not employed by Draven University as a janitor or for any other purpose. He had looked for BJ all over campus, without success. He had waited by the tunnel opening at the stadium, concealed, of course, the previous night, but the man had never shown. Tor had talked to legitimate members of the janitorial staff, and none of them had heard of or seen any man resembling BJ. After learning all this, Tor wondered how close he had come to shipwreck that night. It had been an impetuous, foolish act and Tor was neither impetuous nor foolish. Rational explanation for his irrational behavior was not read-ily available. However, the conclusion that BJ had cast a spell over Tor, though tempting, could not exactly pass muster in Tor's world of black and white.

Tor looked around to see if anyone was watching them. Yet it would have been difficult to make out anyone in the darkness unless he had been standing out in the open, jumping up and down and screaming out like a banshee. Tor took a deep breath, turned on his flashlight, as did Swift, and the two men headed inside the tunnel.

No one believed at the time that Ruggles disappeared that he would have kept jogging along with football in hand until he became hopelessly lost in the tunnels. Because his street clothes had been missing, the search efforts had focused instead on the door from the locker room that led to a stairway heading out the rear exit of the stadium. However, as Tor had found out previ-ously, this door was always kept locked, to prevent thieves and vandals from coming in and stealing equipment and the players' personal valuables. Ironically, Ruggles had been the cause of this new policy, because people had come in to take his jersey and other equipment as mementos. Yet unless Ruggles had had a key, he could not have escaped this way, and there was no indication in any of the accounts that Tor had discovered where he would have gotten such a key. The problem was the few police reports available were inconclusive as to whether this door had been found unlocked or not. While the case had never officially been solved, the "unofficial" verdict was that Ruggles, despite his out-ward appearance as a superior young man, had gotten himself in trouble somewhere, maybe with a girl, some in the town had whispered, though there was never proof of such, and he had taken the opportunity of his magical kickoff return to disappear.

"Maybe that's why he was so damn determined to score," observed one geezer Tor had spoken with. Tor's very strong impression was that this was far too simple an explanation for what had happened to the man. He had never found anyone who could corroborate Ruggles being in desperate circumstances over money, a woman or anything else. Indeed, he had a very promising professional football career ahead of him that, no doubt, would have ended in the Football Hall of Fame in Canton, Ohio.

Tor had visited his father and asked him about Ruggles' motivation to disappear. Peter North had been sitting in his leather chair in his walnut-paneled study, sipping a cognac from a special stock he kept on hand for occasions both grand and private. His father drank a little too much to make up for the bad back he had acquired from his playing days.

"It was a long time ago, so what do you hope to accomplish?" the father had asked his son.

"The truth," Tor had answered, a little apprehensively. The fact was his father made him nervous. He had never treated Tor badly, yet Peter North had not built his fortune on the basis of kind and generous qualities, but rather on discipline, patience, measured ruthlessness, and the ability to seize opportunity at the expense of all others without a jot of remorse or guilt. And yet wasn't that, generally, the codex of the magnate? "It's what scientists are always looking for," Tor had added, as confidently as he could.

Peter North had eased out of his chair and stood in front of his son. He was a big man, thought seriously running to dough with mutating wattles running along his neck and beginning to lay siege to his eyes. And yet Peter North's face still held vestiges of the rugged good looks that had won the heart of Tor's mother, and kept it until she had died four years ago.

"That's science," had said Peter North. "We're not dealing with chemical equations or mass times whatever. We're dealing with human beings, one of my good friends, in fact."

"I thought that would make you want to learn what really happened to him. I'm doing this for you."

Peter North had put a large hand on his son's shoulder. "You do what you have to, son, but this is not something you have to do for me. This is all behind me now. I made my peace a long time ago."

As he turned away, Tor asked one more question, one he had wanted to ask for many years, and yet the timing had never quite seemed right. "What did it feel like to play with Herschel Ruggles?"

His father turned back, swished the cognac in his glass for a few moments as he eyed the dying embers in the fireplace. It seemed to Tor that his father was recalling every detail of his long, wandering life, the residue of which was not locked inside walnut-paneled rooms and vats of cognac.

When his father spoke his voice carried, it seemed to Tor, distinct traces of a desperate, even painful core.

"It felt like one could never lose," said Peter North.

So now Tor was determined to do what had not yet been done even after forty years. He was going to search the tunnels for possible clues to Herschel Ruggles' disappearance.

"Do you know what you're doing, Tor?" asked Jimmy as they trudged along the dark passageway.

"I almost always know what I'm doing."

"Gee, that's almost comforting."

"Gee, that's almost funny, Jimmy."

"It smells awful down here."

"Mold usually does. Damp rock, wood, and dirt never have a particularly pleasant aroma. I can give you the exact chemical interactions, if you'd like."

"Do you know what you're looking for?"

Tor didn't answer immediately, for he was tracing the trail of chalk on the wall with his flashlight beam. He looked up ahead and stopped. "That," he said and pointed.

Tor didn't have a key to the room, as had BJ. He had brought a ring of old keys with him, however. As Jimmy held the light for him, Tor tried each one, and each of them failed. Tor sighed, but Jimmy patted the wood with his hand.

"Hell, the blocking sheds are harder than this. Come on."

They backed up as far as they could across the tunnel and then each took off running. They hit the door at the same time, and it went down easily, and both of them landed in the middle of the room. Tor quickly got up, suddenly worried that they might just have not only destroyed university property, but perhaps invaded BJ's sleeping chambers as well. However, there was no sight of the bent man who seemed to regain his youth and vitality at substrata levels.

Jimmy slowly rose and dusted off his hands. "An empty room, really cool. Can we go now?"

Tor pointed to the corner, at the opening. "Not yet. This is where I stopped the other night. The guy wanted me to follow him into that next space. That's when we turned back."

"Why didn't you go on?"

"I don't know, something didn't seem right to me."

Jimmy started over toward the opening that was revealed in the far corner. Tor grabbed him by the shoulder. "Wait a minute, Jimmy, don't be in such a hurry."

"Look, Tor, it's already eleven o'clock. I've got an early class tomorrow and I need some sleep. Are we going to check it out or not? Come on, I can bench three-twenty, and you almost can do four. I think we can handle the situation. You said the old guy looked ready to drop as it was."

"Yeah, but down here he looked different. Like he was getting younger the farther underground we went."

Jimmy stared at him, shaking his head. "What, are you sniffing some of the stuff in biology class?"

In response, Tor pulled out the pistol from his coat pocket. Jimmy stiffened when he saw it.

"What the hell is that for, Tor?"

"Just a precaution. It belongs to my dad. He brought it back from Vietnam. It's okay, I know how to fire it."

"Right! You'll shoot your damn foot off, or maybe mine."

"Guns and ammo are simple physics: matter and energy colliding to create another type of force. Push, pull, up and down, conversion of energy, depletion and repletion of matter, at atomic and subatomic levels it's happening all around you right now, Swift. So you better damn well get used to it."

"They'll kick your butt right off the team if they see you with that. And me too! And I can't afford this place without my scholarship, Tor. I don't have a rich dad like you."

"Look, there may be something in there we can't handle with just our brawn, Jimmy. The bottom line is that no one has ever searched down here for possible clues to Ruggles' disappearance. He may very well have run down here somewhere only never to be seen again. I don't plan on that happening to you or me. Now come on."

Tor edged toward the opening while he aimed the old pistol with one hand and held the flashlight with his other. Jimmy followed, crouched into a tight ball, as though ready to explode into whatever might be lurking around the corner, or maybe in preparation for sprinting away from it. Jimmy Swift looked like a young man who would indeed live up to his surname if anything remotely unusual came at them from underneath all this dirt, rock and football stadium birthed from the dirty coffers of a coal tycoon.

As they passed through the opening, Tor's fingers began to tingle and he had no idea why. And yet it took quite a bit of effort to hold onto the gun and flashlight. As he looked over at Swift to see if his friend was having the same reaction, it surprised him to see that Jimmy's image was blurry, almost holographic. Tor reached out to him, a part of him afraid that his fingers would reach right through Swift, but he touched flesh and Jimmy gave him a reassuring grin and soon the two were through the passageway and into the next space.

It was not as well lighted as the room they had just left, though there was an almost ethereal glow here. The space here seemed to be almost identical in size to the other. The walls were rough stone with clay between, and the drip of water and creak of earth was far more apparent, far more unsettling. Tor flashed his light up and down as he and Jimmy scanned the area.

"Nothing to see," said Jimmy. "Nothing to shoot," he added, looking anxiously at Tor's pistol.

Tor marched around the space, counting off. Twenty by twenty, he silently concluded. Then a determined look came upon his features. "Great shit," he said.

"What?"

"The guy BJ said there was great shit in here."

Jimmy looked around at the unfinished walls. "Maybe he has a lot lower expectation than we do. But then, to me great shit is a bottle of tequila and a night with Cindy Wilson in her itty-bitty cheerleader's outfit."

Tor seemed not to hear because his gaze had caught on the object and he wandered over to it, as though lost in a REM dream of lucid proportion.

"That's a dress, isn't it?" asked Jimmy who had come to stand next to his friend. They both stared at the cloth, which hung down from a projection of rock like a stalactite carved from fabric.

"Appears to be," answered Tor, who wondered why he hadn't seen it immediately. Jimmy was about to reach up and touch it when Tor stopped him. "It looks pretty old. It might fall apart."

"Look, it's not going to disintegrate. So what if it tears a bit? We need to check it out right. That's why we came all this way, right?"

"Right," said Tor. He reached out and nudged the dress. It did not fall apart under his probing. He carefully lifted it off. Revealed underneath was an even more curious object.

"A wig," said Jimmy.

"A blond, woman's wig," added Tor.

Jimmy picked up the hairpiece and examined it.

"Check to see if there's a manufacturer's label on it," said Tor. "I'll do the same with the dress."

The garment was knee length, of good quality and made of heavy wool dyed dark blue. It was in remarkable shape for having been in such a dank place. Tor looked for a label but found none. Jimmy was more fortunate.

He shone his light on the tag on the inside of the hairpiece. "Jenkins Wig Shop. They're over on Perkins Street near the courthouse," he said. "I've seen the place lots of times. Never been in, of course. How old do you think this stuff is?"

Tor looked around before taking the wig from Jimmy. "At least forty years old if it's connected with Ruggles' disappearance." He thought for a moment. "This must be the great shit."

"An old wig and a dress? It's not like its buried treasure or anything. That's what I'd call really great shit."

Tor lifted an eyebrow at his friend. "Treasure is in the eye of the beholder, Jimmy. Let's go."

When they reached the exit from the tunnel and breathed fresh air again, Jimmy looked at Tor. "What did you expect to find in there tonight?"

"I don't know, maybe a skeleton. An old football."

"Hey, do you think Ruggles disguised himself as a woman in order to disappear?"

"And then snuck back and left the dress and wig to let people know what he'd done? I don't think so. And besides," Tor held up the dress which was petite in size, "there is no way Herschel Ruggles could have fit in this. He was bigger than you, though not as big as me."

"Look, maybe it's not even connected to Ruggles. Maybe that guy you saw is a cross-dresser." Jimmy smiled and poked Tor in the shoulder.

"You're not taking this very seriously."

"Come on, Tor, it's been forty years. No one solved it all this time, what makes you think you can?"

"Because I'm smarter than most people," announced Tor boldly. "And maybe I care more than the people investigating it did. Maybe they were afraid if they discovered the truth, it would somehow hurt Ruggles' reputation."

"And you're not scared of that too? From all you've told me your old man was tight with the guy. What if you discover Ruggles did something really bad and had to go on the run for it? What do you think that will do to your father?"

Tor considered this for a few moments. "Sometimes the truth does hurt, Jimmy. But I'll take the truth over speculation and just plain wrong information any day. Once you accept anything less than that, the whole world goes to hell."

Jimmy shook his head and stretched his arms to the sky, working out the kinks induced by a cold, drafty tunnel. "You're a nut. But you're a Mighty Johns nut. So what do we do now?"

Tor held up the dress and wig. "We find out where these came from, if we can."

"It's been a long time."

"I'm a physicist, Jimmy. Time is just another part of the equation. Light traveling from the most distant quasar known takes almost fourteen billion years to reach Earth, so four decades is nothing to me."

As they trudged off the darkness was broken by the flash of a struck match near the tunnel entrance. The man lit his cigarette, his gaze on the departing two men. He glanced at the sky and then into the tunnel. The look on his face was not one of glee, yet it was also not one nuzzling on anger either. It was difficult to say what was running through the man's thoughts, other than perhaps the harsh and debilitating tug of melancholy. He smoked down his cigarette, stubbed it out with the toe of his scuffed shoe and disappeared into the tunnel as the eastward wind crowded in after his vanishing form.

Jenkins' Wig Shop had been in business for over fifty years. Tor suspected that its success was due to the abysmally cold winters here with the wigs giving possibly giving added warmth above and beyond that provided by hats and one's own hair. The shop smelled of mothballs and incense, an odd combination, Tor thought. There were no other customers, so he walked directly up to the counter, took the wig out of a paper sack, and motioned to the woman there.

"I was wondering if you could help me."

The woman slowly headed over. She was petite, though her build had run to stocky now as a body finished growing up had no choice but to swell to either side. She looked to be around sixty or so, and looked to be wearing a wig herself, one with short, ash blond locks that curled around her ears and etched a straight line across her wide forehead. Her makeup was carefully applied, assuaging away wrinkles and other blemishes. Her clothes were nicely organized and the colors flowed well together. A woman who cared about her appearance, Tor concluded. Then, as she drew nearer, he took a breath and almost gagged as the woman's perfume flowed out and engulfed him in its rancorous grip. The smell was blunt, stupefying. He wanted to let out an enormous sneeze, but felt that might do irreparable damage to both her self-esteem and his inquiry.

"I'll try, young man."

Tor swabbed away drops of moisture from his eyes and mentally threatened himself that if he sneezed or started to hyperventilate that he would have to volunteer to do Jimmy Swift's course work for the rest of the semester. Sufficiently mollified, he said, "This wig has your label inside, and I was wondering if you could tell me something about it."

"Like what?" The woman did not look much interested.

"Like who may have bought it. You see, I found it and I'd like to return it to the owner."

She picked up the wig. "I don't think they'd want it back. It's an old style."

"Right. Perhaps forty years or so."

"Forty years!" She looked up at him, stunned. "Where'd you find it?"

"In an old trunk in the attic of the house I'm staying at. The owner of the house didn't know anything about it. She said I could try and track it down. So that's what I'm trying to do."

The woman eyed him skeptically. "Lot of work for an old wig no one would want to wear anymore."

"Well, it's kind of a hobby of mine, a challenge so to speak. Do you think it could be about forty years old? I'm sure you're probably an expert in such things."

Obviously flattered, the woman examined the wig with a keener eye. "Been running this shop for over thirty years, my mother for over twenty before that. I know my wigs, that's for sure." She looked it over thoroughly, including the inside. "Well, it's at least forty years old, possibly older. That was the style back then, sort of a combo of Jackie Kennedy, Grace Kelly and Kim Novak, pretty popular back then."

"Any way to tell who might have purchased it? I mean does it have a hidden serial number or anything like that?"

Her small lips curved into a smile. "It's not a gun, son, it's a wig."

"So there's no way to tell."

The woman sighed, and then thought for a few moments. "Well, we've got all the old sales records in the back. Mother never threw anything away, and I guess I'm just as bad." She paused again. "You leave it with me, and I'll see what I can find. If it was just about forty years ago, it'll cut down the search quite a bit. I'll start there anyway and see if we hit something." She eyed him curiously. "Now are you going to tell me what's really going on?"

Tor assumed his most academic tone, which he found to be perfectly bewildering to most people, but one that adults readily accepted because they absolutely refused to acknowledge their ignorance.

"Well, the truth is, it's part of an experiment I'm conducting at the university. I'm getting my degree in science, and I'm trying to determine whether the energy levels released through the brain's neocortex are substantial enough to have left residue of the firing of the neural network connectors, think of them as latent byproducts of the synaptic impulses, on wigs and hats and such, anything that would have come in contact with that area of the brain. The hypothalamus, as I'm sure you know, is an extremely sensitive area lying within the ventral region of the diencephalon. It controls many of the interactions between the mental and physical, you know, metabolic functions, autonomic nervous system, that sort of thing. Since humans are really perfect communication transmitters what with our chemical, electrical, and water makeup, my theory is that an energy release from each of us—think even along the lines of telepathic communication—can be physically captured, and what better place to begin than on objects covering the head. It's my belief that physics and paranormal activity may actually be capable of extraordinary reconciliation. Of course, that's a very simplified explanation, and I don't mean to offend you in any way by telling you things you already know. So, as you can obviously see, that's why I'm so interested in this wig."

The woman stared at him, her lips moving slowly as though she were trying to repeat all he had just said and yet being utterly unable to replicate even a smidgen of Tor's convoluted albeit erudite-sounding rhetoric. Finally, she said, "You come back tomorrow afternoon, and I'll see what I have for you."

He thanked her and left, grateful for the rush of outside air to clear his sinuses and lungs of her potent fumes.

Inside the shop, the owner twirled the wig on her index finger as she watched Tor through the window as he headed down the street. Then she carried the decrepit bowl of hair to the back room.

While he waited for the answer on the wig, Tor decided to make another clandestine visit to the underground room. It was possible that he and Jimmy had missed something of importance, and Tor also wanted to test a theory of his. However, Swift had steadfastly refused to come this time, excusing himself on the grounds that he had a date with Cindy the cheerleader that included a fifth of Wild Turkey that no mystery, however enticing, could hope to compete with. Tor had accepted his declination with outward graciousness that concealed his bitter disappointment. Going down there alone held very little appeal, yet ever since he was a child, Tor's indefatigable curiosity always trumped his innate fear. However neither was he one to take undue risk, so he brought, among other equipment, two flashlights, a video camera, and his father's pistol, fully loaded.

The door was still lying on the floor. Tor entered the main chamber and studied the space for any changes. He saw none, and now he prepared himself to test his theory. He pulled the very small video camera from his backpack, turned it on and pointed it at himself.

"Tor North, Senior, Science Program, Draven University, November Nine, Twelve-thirty A.M. Herschel Ruggles Investigation, Report One. Underground Room." He strapped the video camera to a specially rigged helmet device that referees in professional football were now using to give a ground level, in-your-face view of the game to appease the more bloodthirsty fans, and pointed his head here and there to test its balance and range field. Satisfied, he stepped toward the opening that led to the other room. As he had on the last visit, he held the pistol in one hand, his flashlight in the other. He counted off his steps to the opening and then stopped right before he would've broken the invisible plane he had diagrammed in his mind.

"Testing theory one," he said for benefit of the camera and, ultimately, posterity. Tor had a very high opinion of what his future professional career would hold and he took great pains to dutifully record virtually everything he did. It would make his biographer's job that much easier, he felt. He took a deep, cleansing breath and made a very small measured step forward and then stopped. He swung his head and thus the camera around taking in a 180-degree sweep. He took another step and that's when he once again sensed the murkiness of the last trip through here, as though he were submerging himself in shallow, dirty water. Tor felt no sensation of panic, of drowning, for instance, or of being unable to escape his predicament. On the contrary, his mood was one of utter calm, of a serene peacefulness. He stepped forward again and once more did his camera sweep. It was then that the image caught his eye.

"Jimmy? Jimmy is that you?" Had Swift forsaken his planned rendezvous with Cindy, the cheerleader who, with a bit of whiskey inside her, had the reputation of being capable of satisfying a man in any way he so desired, regardless of the shame and physical spasm such risky lovemaking might cause her later.

The man flashed by Tor so fast he thought he had just stumbled into a real life quantum tunnel of his very own. And then Tor caught a tortured breath that started in his lungs and ended coming out his ears, because the man had carried a football in his right hand, and wore the old-style headgear of a gridiron player of four decades ago, and also Unitas-style high top black cleats and lumpy, antiquated shoulder pads that looked like the fake muscles used in bad movies of a by-gone time. Tor had seen photos of Herschel Ruggles and that man, that very man!—had been the one who had just raced by him. The iron chin, the fire of determined brown eyes, dead-set pupils that did not countenance even the possibility of defeat, had been right beside Tor North, almost touching him. And then he was gone. Tor almost dropped his light, even came close to firing off his damn gun. He staggered through the opening and into the "great shit" room and sank down against the wall, and rubbed his back against the abrasive surface, as though desperately seeking a firm footing in a reality after encountering possible madness in the last few seconds.

Hands quivering, he slipped off the camera, rewound it and looked at the little playback screen. The camera technology was digital and the images it captured were crystal clear. The images he was looking at were unusually sharp, yet they were just pictures of the wall. There was no man in uniform, no football, no spectral Ruggles galloping to his predestined destruction. Tor stared at the opening. He would have sworn to God he had seen twenty-one-year-old Herschel Ruggles carrying his football well past the goal line and into the spiraling, cavernous depths of the unknown. Damn it, he had seen the man right next to him. He had! The camera, though, did not share his view. According to this instrument, Tor had seen nothing even remotely out of the ordinary. Ever the believer in precise machine recordings of experiments, Tor was at a loss to explain how he could still cling, however precariously, to the notion in this case that he was right, and the equipment was somehow in error.

Although Tor was well aware of the theory known as the "observer effect." It said that an observer of some action could influence that action by the mere act of watching with a specific level of intent.

Had Tor intended with all his heart to see Ruggles tonight?

Had that same desire allowed Ruggles to be freed from whatever alternate dimensional state held him?

Maybe Tor simply had been hallucinating. It was an awfully tricky fence to straddle, between focused intent and imagination. He began to look at the situation rationally. He had been thinking of almost nothing except Herschel Ruggles for a long time now. He was in a dark, mysterious place, all alone, and his anxiety level, coupled with his very natural desire for something, anything, to happen, could easily have tricked his mind into seeing something that absolutely was not, and could not be there. Tor sighed when he realized that he indeed must have allowed himself to deceive himself. That's what it came down to. The atomic pot had boiled, just like it normally did, regardless of whether he wanted it to or not.

The mind was always playing these games. Tor knew that approximately five milliseconds were required for the sensory faculties, upon registering a sound or visual image, to communicate that fact up the nerve autobahn to the brain. However, since many human actions were performed within two or three milliseconds of the reception of a sensory impulse, for example, a starter's gun if one were in a race say, it could honestly be said that many things humans did were totally unconscious, without input from the mind because it took so long to receive the mental command to do so. And yet, if one were to ask the runner when he heard the starter's gun sound, he would say he heard it simultaneously with him leaving the runner's block, even though that was, neurologically speaking, an impossibility. And yet the brain tricked the mind into believing that it was actually so to cover up its own tardiness. A gap of two milliseconds may not seem like much to the uninformed, Tor knew, but in the arena of the mind-body equation, it was roughly equal to the duration of an earth year. And Tor's own brain had just undertaken a major jockeying effort on his weary mind, aided no doubt by his complete obsession with all things Ruggles. Tor sighed. His mind had just pulled the neuronal wool over him, and he had fallen for it like a freshman general studies lummox.

"Great shit, like I told you."

Tor freed himself from his musings and stared up at the man. BJ was grinning from cauliflower ear to cauliflower ear. "Great shit, you seen it too, ain't you. Seen *him*, I mean."

Tor slowly rose on weakened legs. BJ was dressed in the same clothes as before, looked the same, smiled the same quasi-insane smile, and he was standing as erect and straight as a sky-scraper, a brand new man at about forty feet underground, as the mole dug.

"Seen who?" asked Tor in a quavering voice.

BJ cocked his head a little to the side, and as Tor flashed his light that way, he was amazed at the muscles in the man's neck. They bulged out like a pair of swollen parentheses and had a sinister quality that Tor could not quite pin down. And yet how could a muscle be sinister, he asked himself? On the earth's surface, the man's Adam's apple had been encased in a scrawny tube of a vessel, not this maddeningly impressive thing Tor was staring at. Had the man's shoulders and arms also widened and thickened to rival Tor's own impressive, weight room-sculpted physique? Had Tor gone mad in the last minute or so? Was BJ even standing there, or was he also the holographic product of a wretched synaptic misfire?

"The man. The guy what had the football. That Ruggles fellow I'm betting. I seen the pictures. Ain't no lie. You think it's him, too, ain'tcha? That why you come down here asking all them questions. Am I right, or am I right?"

"I'm not sure what you're talking about. I didn't see anything." Tor held up his camera. "And there's nothing on here either."

BJ waved off that dilemma. "Why, you can't catch stuff like that on film. It's like a vampire. They ain't got no reflection in no mirror. Hell, everybody should know that, even college boys like yourself."

"Oh, you believe in vampires, do you?" Tor wondered if his pistol had silver bullets. Or was that for werewolves only? One needed a stake and a cross and a handy sun to handle a vampire, didn't one? And he had none of those things, particularly the sun. Not even at high noon would he have a sun down here to shrivel the son of Dracula to harmless confetti. He glanced around. Was there a coffin down here for his friend BJ? Was that where the man slept? Tor felt himself growing nauseous. Well, he hoped deep-throated, swivel-hipped, bouncy-breasted Cindy had been worth it for his no-account friend, Jimmy Swift. He hoped the lady really had been Miss All-World in the sack, for Tor did not see himself returning to the surface to find out the details of this vixen encounter for certain. Yet he vowed that he would haunt Swift for the rest of his life, particularly when he was about to bed another cheerleader. He would fix his feckless friend, if it took him all of eternity, which looked like it was staring him right in the face. The last time Tor had cried was when his mother had died. He felt the urge to do so again. *Damn you, Jimmy Swift and your ill-timed libido ways.*

"So you saw something?" Tor ventured weakly.

"Hell, I say I did. And from the white of your face, and you looking ready to puke, you saw the same thing. Don't try and lie, boy, I can see through any liar, and you ain't nearly as good as most I've come across in my life."

"I saw something," Tor finally admitted. "And it did look like Ruggles."

BJ slapped his thigh, which Tor noted was now about the same size as his own massive ones. Tor examined his body. Had he swelled too? No, he looked the same. All except for nerves that seemed forever wrecked and bare. And he did want to puke.

"Hell, I knew it. Runs by and then just disappears into nothing."

"Yes," Tor said. "How many times have you seen him, it? Him, I guess."

"Half-a-dozen or so. Wanted to show you the other night, 'cept you lost your nerve. Probably thought I was some wacko."

Something occurred to Tor. Why hadn't he and Jimmy seen the image when they had come through the passageway? Was there some principle Tor was unaware of that ruled out two people experiencing the dynamic that resulted from dimensional transference or whatever the hell it exactly was? Tor needed time to think, desperately so. This was all new territory.

BJ's gaze caught and then held on Tor's gun. "That's a pretty piece."

"My father's. He fought with it in Vietnam."

BJ looked puzzled and drew nearer. "Nam, huh? Mind if I take a look?"

Tor wasn't about to let the man have the weapon, but he held it our for examination. "It's loaded, so I don't want to let go of it, you understand."

"Sure, sure, can't never be too careful with a damn gun." He eyed the weapon closely. "You said your daddy brought this back from Nam?"

Tor nodded. "He fought in the Army, Second Lieutenant. He was wounded twice."

"Well, he didn't bring this gun back from Nam. This here's a German Mauser Parabellum nine-millimeter. Krauts used this make during WW Two. I ought'a know. I fought those bastards for three years. Had these damn pistols fired at my ass mor'n once. Do some hurtin' on you if it clipped you. Even took one off a dead Kraut right outside of Paris in Forty-four and then sold it to a Frenchie for nice bottle of US of A bourbon he'd gotten his hands on. Yep, definitely a World War Two piece. Ain't nothing like this ever used in Nam, son. Nosiree."

Tor looked down at the gun he held. "You don't look old enough to have fought in the Second World War." There was a small flicker of hope in his voice.

"Lied about my age. Got me a bunch'a medals," BJ said proudly. "Was there at VE and VJ days. Best time of my life. You ought'a check with your daddy about that gun, though. Something ain't right there."

"I will," said Tor, though he had no intention of doing so. "How come you left the dress and wig here?"

BJ looked puzzled. "Dress and wig? What, down here? You sick, son?"

Tor started to explain, but then stopped. He looked at the place where the dress had hung down. The small rock projection was there. BJ had been in this room before. How could he not have seen something so clearly out of place as a dress and wig in a secret room underneath a football stadium? And yet the man looked truly bewildered.

Tor said, "I guess I am feeling kind of woozy. I'm going to go now. Thanks for your help."

"Ain't done much. But I appreciate the twenty you gave me. To a feller like myself, difference between eating and not, so to speak." He let that statement just hang.

Tor pressed a couple of twenties into his thick hand. "Well, this'll make you twice as happy then. Good-night, BJ." He had thought about asking the man who he really was, now that Tor had determined he did not work for the university. Yet right now Tor didn't want to know the answer to that question. He had learned enough disturbing bits of information for one night. Tor very gingerly walked back through the space Ruggles had torpedoed through, and then he sprinted all the way back to winking stars and fresh air.

The next morning Tor made his way to the library to research World War II era pistols. Although BJ had seemed very authoritative on the subject of German weapons, Tor wanted to check it out himself. It didn't take him long to verify that what BJ had said was the utter truth. There was even a photo of a Mauser pistol in one of the books Tor had consulted. It was a perfect match. No Vietnam weapon at all. The Mauser was about sixty years old. His father had lied to him. Yet why?

He was debating possible answers when a hand touched his shoulder. He turned and found himself staring at Molly McIntyre. A senior Mass Com major, Molly was editor of the Draven school newspaper and also headed up the yearbook committee. Molly was smart, polished, and very comely in appearance with her shoulder-length auburn hair that she was forever flicking out of her dancing green eyes and her long, slim body that was topped by a substantial pair of breasts that were usually, as today, unrestrained by a bra. Tor liked her and yet her looks had nothing to do with it, he told himself. She was brainy and brainy was the biggest attraction there was for him. And yet he was a young man, albeit a scientist, and thus the bountiful bosom and dancing green eyes certainly didn't detract from the equation even for the Tor Norths of the world. Elements, after all, were relative.

"Hey, Tor, could you pull yourself away from your armament research and help me with something?" She had glanced at some of the books spread over his table before making this comment.

"Sure, Molly, what's up?"

"I want to talk to you about an idea I have for this project we're doing for the fiftieth anniversary of the university."

She led him over to a private room off the library and closed the door. The table she was working at was covered with books, press clippings, old photographs and the like.

"You're one of the few football players who actually have a brain, and part of the anniversary edition of the newspaper has to do with Herschel Ruggles, the football player. You know about him, of course?"

"A little," replied Tor warily.

"Well, he's still the school's greatest athlete, a Heisman Trophy finalist in his sophomore and junior years, and a favorite to win it as a senior. And his still unexplained disappearance is hands-down the school's greatest mystery. Did you know that people still talk about it?"

"Really? That's amazing," said Tor, accomplishing what he hoped was an authentic look of surprise. "Some people just can't help living in the past, I guess."

"Tell me about it," said Molly. "But it's not like I can ignore the man in the anniversary edition, particularly when he disappeared exactly forty years ago. Right?"

"Right, absolutely. And you needed me for...?"

She motioned him over to the table and picked up some old photographs lying there.

"These are photos of an event that took place about a year or so before Ruggles' disappearance. It was an awards banquet in his honor."

Tor studied the photos. In one of them, there was a group of people at the head table, including Ruggles and a tall elderly man with snow-white hair. A woman who looked to be in her thirties stood beside Ruggles and there seemed something very familiar about her to Tor.

"Who are those people with Ruggles?" he asked and pointed at the elderly man and the woman.

Molly looked surprised at his question. "Tor North, you of all people should recognize the founder of the school, John Milton Draven."

"Right, right. Draven. And the woman?"

"Wife number two, no, correction, number three. Her name was Gloria; you remember the old story. That's the name of the mine where Draven was buried alive."

"Right again. She's very beautiful."

"Most third wives are, Tor," replied Molly dryly.

He looked admiringly at all her work. "You've really researched this."

"So much so that I'm about to pop a brain wire. I mean I've got my own classes to attend to, and half my staff revolted on me complaining I'm some kind of ball buster. But if you're going to do something, you need to do it right. Here's my proposal to you. Could I do a story on you and Jimmy Swift for the part of the anniversary edition that deals with Ruggles? You two did collaborate to break the man's record. And it might give a nice modern day connection to the whole material. The last thing I want is for this to be boring. I'm not doing all this work to turn out a snore-inducer."

"I'll do it, if it'll help you out. In fact, I think it's a great idea."

"That's terrific, Tor, I really appreciate it." She paused and smiled shyly. "You know, we should go out for a beer sometime and talk. I've got some questions I want to pose to you. See, I was at the stadium when Jimmy broke the record. I saw the block you threw. Now, I'm no scientist, but it seems to me you used a little physics in your work that afternoon. Am I right?"

Tor couldn't help but smile at her wonderfully perceptive insight. "I'd love to have a beer with you. A woman who can appreciate good science is a woman I want to get to know better," he said enthusiastically. Suddenly embarrassed, he looked down. In doing so, Tor glanced at the photograph once more and it finally clicked. Why the woman looked so familiar. He thought he might pass out. Instead he picked up the photo, trying his best to keep his hands from shaking.

"Molly, do you mind if I borrow this photo? I'm sort of becoming interested in Ruggles and I can use this to maybe get Jimmy interested in doing the piece for you. He can be shy sometimes."

Molly nodded. "Sure, whatever you can do. Oh, but just so you know, the word on campus is that Swift and Cindy 'Prima-Donna' Wilson did a number last night that ended up right here on a table in the library, and shy was not a term that anyone would've applied to them. George and Jane of the Jungle were more like it. A real animal, Jimmy Swift."

"Well, I'm certainly not like that," said Tor gallantly.

"That's good to know," said Molly, in a very disappointed tone. "Although you could be quite a lady killer if you wanted to, what with your strong jaw, cute broken nose, and your 'brainy' glasses fronting those mischievous blue eyes. And being tall and having those broad shoulders of yours certainly doesn't hurt. Girls really fall for that combination of brains and brawn. It's very sexy, Tor."

"Thanks, Molly," said a traumatized Tor, who could think of absolutely nothing else to say.

"You know, from all I've found out with this project, Ruggles was quite the ladies' man."

Tor shook his head. "I've heard those rumors, but they're baseless. See, I've done a little digging into his life too."

"Really? Who did you talk to?"

"Well, people he played with. Or against. Fans, folks like that."

"Well, of course they aren't going to tell you the dirty linen things. God, men are so naïve about things like that. You all hold Ruggles up on this gigantic pedestal because of his athletic accomplishments. Men always do that with their sports stars. You forgive them their human frailties, their dark side. The most devoted fans won't even acknowledge that these guys have dark sides. I talked with a very different class of observer. And what I was told was that, in fact, Ruggles had quite an eye for the ladies. And not just from the student body, but faculty, faculty wives, and on up the ladder."

"On up the ladder, what do you mean by that?"

"Up the ladder, Tor, right to the very top. Now, I've got to get back to work." She put a hand on his forearm, her long fingers lightly squeezing the taut muscles there. "Now, don't forget about that beer." She let his arm go and he turned to the door.

Molly eyed the library table, and then glanced at Tor. When she next spoke, her voice carried quite a different tone, something between a purr and a deep, lung-depleting sigh, and it sent every single hair on the back of Tor's neck raging northward and liters of his blood galloping in the exact opposite direction. "FYI, Tor, the doors to these rooms lock. And I can be very quiet. When I want to be. And maybe I would, with the right man."

Tor did what any strong-willed, intelligent young scientist would have done when abruptly confronted by an aggressive woman over such a delicate subject as roaring, unadulterated carnal knowledge on a stout library table. He fled the room, almost accidentally cart-wheeling over said stout table in the process.

Tor carried the bag to the wig shop. Inside the bag was the dress from the underground room. Tor had painstakingly compared it with the dress that Gloria Draven had been wearing in the photograph he had taken from Molly. While Tor was no women's clothing expert, the dress was an identical match, from the color, to the intricate collar, to the buttons, to everything. And the wig was the second part of the equation. In the photograph, Gloria Draven had had longish blond hair, cut and styled in the manner of Grace Kelly and Kim Novak with a dash of Jackie Kennedy, as the owner of the wig shop had described Tor's forty-year-old hair-piece. The result was that if you put the wig and the dress together, you had Gloria Draven, or at least a reasonable facsimile thereof.

As for the image of Herschel Ruggles galloping through an underground room, Tor believed now that, instead of a hallucination, he was confronted with a time-space dimensional fissure. Not truly a step back in time, but a sort of fractured portal that offered glimpses of the past without one actually traveling back to that time period. Tor knew that it was theoretically possible, this sort of intermediate shared dimensional experience, but he had never thought he would see it firsthand, at least now while he was still in college. God, the magnitude of all that that discovery signified! He could devote his entire professional career to studying nothing else.

He had tried to explain all this to Jimmy, but his friend had still been recovering from his sexual smorgasbord with Cindy and his debilitating though no doubt superficially pleasing encounter with Wild Turkey. It was lucky there was no practice this week because of exams, and yet Jimmy Swift had not looked capable of much studying either. Tor didn't even want to think about the condition Cindy Wilson might be in. She probably couldn't even walk. And not just because of the Wild Turkey. George of the Jungle, my ass, fumed Tor.

He entered the wig shop and went directly to the counter. A young woman came out and greeted him.

"I was in yesterday and gave, I guess, the owner, a wig to look at for me."

"She's not in today."

"Oh, she said she'd have an answer back for me today. She was going to check the sales records to see if she could determine who had purchased the wig. I found it and was trying to return it to the owner."

"Oh well, I'll check in the back. What did it look like?"

Tor held up the photograph of Gloria Draven. "Like this

woman's hair."

The young woman looked puzzled but studied the photograph and went into the back to check. Tor rubbed his nose, for the same noxious scent of perfume was still heavy in the air. It was so thick that he looked around the shop for the woman, but found no one.

The young woman came out a few minutes later, empty-handed. "There's nothing back there like it."

"Was there a note? Maybe a message to give me? She told me to come back this afternoon."

"No, there was nothing like that."

"Is there away for me to contact her? Do you have her home phone?"

The young woman's manner changed, and she looked guarded, almost hostile. "We don't give out information like that. And you name is?"

Tor could easily read her thoughts. She had suddenly hit upon the possibility that he might be a sociopath, and was trying to wheedle information out of her in preparation for doing in his next victim.

"Tor North. I go to school at Draven."

The young woman's face instantly brightened. "That's right. I thought I recognized you. You're on the football team. I saw you when you helped that other player break the record."

Tor smiled, no longer the serial killer. "That's right. Whew, that perfume is really something."

"God, tell me about it. It's like cigarette smoke; it never goes away. Nobody has the heart to tell her though. Look, I'm sorry I can't help you. She didn't say why she wasn't coming in. She left the message last night. I can call her at home, if you want."

"Would you?"

She smiled again, picked up the phone and made the call. She listened for a bit and then replaced the receiver. "Just got the answering machine. I can try later."

"I'd appreciate it. Let me give you my number. If you or she can call me, I'd appreciate it. It's pretty important."

The young woman took the number and then shook Tor's hand. "Wow, to shake the hand of someone who helped break Herschel Ruggles' record. My grandfather would be so impressed."

"Who's your grandfather?"

"Herman Bowles. He was the trainer for the team during the Ruggles years. Believe me, I grew up listening to all those stories." She paused. "I wonder what really happened to him."

"Yeah, I wonder. Is your grandfather still around here? I'd like to go and shake his hand too."

The young woman's eyes lighted up. "Would you? He's right over in the next county. Just a half-hour away. He moved back from California about six months ago, after my grandmother died. I can give you directions. You can go anytime. He's retired. Lives alone. Never goes anywhere. I could call him and say you're going to drop by sometime. I won't say when, so you won't feel any pressure."

"What's your name?"

"Susan. Susan O'Riley."

"Well, Susan O'Riley, you can tell your grandfather I'll be by today," said Tor. "And I'm going to bring with me Jimmy Swift. Two legends for the price of one."

As Tor left with the directions to Herman Bowles' home he noted the name of the proprietor over the door: Linda Daughtry. He hoped she was in the phone book, because Tor intended on paying her a visit as well. Now he just needed to rescue Jimmy from his hangover hell and he was in business.

Herman Bowles lived at the end of a narrow road that one got to by driving through a cleft bored inside of a hill, like an extracted wedge of cheese. The steep walls that rose on either side caused sundown to occur inside the cleft at around three o'clock; thus it was dark when Tor and Jimmy arrived at the house. Tor had poured cup after cup of the most mind drilling java he could find down his friend's throat even as he had explained all that had happened. He had left out the part about seeing Ruggles, though, figuring that even stone cold sober, Swift would be unable, or at least unwilling, to grasp such a seemingly outlandish concept. Political science majors, Tor had found, were utterly bereft of moral courage, which, he concluded, probably boded well for their future endeavors.

Bowles was a short man with bandy legs, and a thickened torso with popped vein forearms revealed because he wore his shirtsleeves rolled up. He coughed hoarsely when he greeted the two young men, and explained that he was about halfway through his winter cold that was not helped by his pack-a-day Winston's habit. "I'm old," he confided in Tor with a wink and a smile. "And a man's got to pick his poison and then live and die with it, right?"

"Right," answered Tor, who suddenly wondered what his own poison in life would turn out to be.

They settled in the small living room of the little house that was decorated, as far as Tor could tell, in American sports memorabilia.

Bowles coughed up a chunk of phlegm into his handkerchief, cleared his nose and then slapped his withered thigh. "Can't believe you two are here sitting in my living room. Holy God."

"Nice place," said Jimmy as he glanced at a collection of vintage professional football cards that hung under glass next to the little bar set up in the far corner. On the bar's counter were arranged, pyramid style, whiskey tumblers from all the major college football conferences. The lamp tables and some of the chairs had college and professional football helmets melded ingeniously to the oak wood that was stained medium dark. The pattern of the furniture upholstery was a green football field covered with figures of famous football players frozen in action. Under their feet was a Philadelphia Eagles official rug. On the walls were posters of what appeared to be every major AFL-NFL quarterback of the last forty years with arms cocked, jaws set, eyes ablaze. Even the front door was festooned with a mural of none other than the craggy countenance of Raymond Nitschke, with a miniature shrine to Dick Butkus arranged on a nearby table. No young man remotely interested in the game of football could sit here and be unmoved.

"After my wife died, God rest her soul, and I mean no disrespect by saying this, I finally was able to pull out all my stuff and do the house the way I wanted."

"Nice place," Swift said again, and then rubbed his temples.

Bowles leaned forward. "So I got to know, what'd it feel like, breaking the record?"

Jimmy focused on him. "It felt good. It felt great. Couldn't have done it without Tor, you know."

Bowles looked over at Tor who said bluntly, "Matter of physics mostly." He paused, "I guess Jimmy never thought about continuing his run on into the tunnel, did you?"

Swift looked puzzled. "What?" Tor managed to surreptitiously plant a sharp kick against his friend's leg and Jimmy finally woke up to his role. "No, no way. Not like Ruggles. Herschel Ruggles, that is," added Jimmy, with all the adroitness and panache of the lamest actor ever to take up space on a celluloid roll. They had practiced this segue on the way over, and had performed it far better in the car.

Damn Cindy Wilson and the Wild Turkey, thought Tor. She deserved to be permanently impaired. Bow-legged, cane-bound Cindy for life she should be. "So you were the trainer on Ruggles' team?" he asked.

Bowles nodded. "Well, up until he disappeared, o'course."

"Boy that was something," volunteered Jimmy and then looked at Tor for approval and received none.

"Yes, it was," said Bowles thoughtfully. "Never could figure it out."

Tor said, "I guess there was always the question of Ruggles escaping through the locker room door, the one that led to the rear exit. Although he would have had to have had a key."

Bowles shook his head. "Nope. Don't think he went through the locker room. Of that, I'm certain."

Tor's jaw sagged. "How can you be so sure?" A possibility popped into his head. "Were you in the locker room when he came through? Maybe treating a player?"

"No, I was out on the field, working on some taping jobs."

"Do you know that Ruggles' street clothes weren't in his locker?"

"I heard that, but, hell, folks were always sneaking in there and stealing his stuff. And if he went and disappeared and all, think what that stuff would've been worth? And they never found his uniform either. Now, tell me, how do you pull off all that gear and then put on your street clothes and then walk off in your street clothes, *and* carrying all that gear and somebody not notice, tell me that, will ya? Hell, I wouldn't have put it past the police to have pinched that stuff and then written it up that those clothes and such weren't ever there at all. People are people and Herschel Ruggles was Herschel Ruggles."

Tor sat back. That made a lot of sense actually. "So, is that why you know he didn't go through the locker room?"

"No, I know he didn't go through the locker room because he would've seen him."

Tor almost fell out of his chair. "Who? Who would've seen him?"

"The feller who was in there soaking in the whirlpool. He didn't suit up that day. Only had the one on the injury list. Back then you played so long as nothing was broke too bad, not like today. He had bad back spasms if I remember right. Thought maybe a spinal contusion we'd call it today, so we kept him out. Put him in the tub and left him there. He was in the locker room the whole game."

Tor almost dug his fingers through the upholstery and the face of Joe Namath in his anxiety. "Who was the player?"

Bowles slumped into thought as he tried to recall. "Been a long time," he said apologetically. "Forty years about. Memory ain't that good no more." He added defensively, "And, Jesus, all the players come through there. And I'm a trainer. Remember bodies a lot better than names. Remembered spinal contusion, didn't I? That's something most wouldn't. And been out in California too long. In fact, left right after the season Ruggles disappeared. Worked at USC mostly, lots of fellers with weird names and nicknames come through there. Filled up the dang memory. If I'd stayed round these parts, probably know it off the top of my head. But I didn't and so I don't."

"What position did he play?" asked Jimmy. "That might help you narrow it down."

Bowles's eyes almost closed as he chewed on this. "Big feller. Lineman most likely," he finally ventured. Bowles thought about it some more, but he couldn't remember. "I'll think about it," he said, "most likely come to me."

Tor was confused. "Didn't the police question you? And the player?"

"Sure, they came around. Asked some stuff. Sure they talked to that player and all. I just assumed everybody told the truth. But you fellers have to understand something, back then, folks just thought it was an act of God, so to speak. I mean Ruggles wasn't like other people. That boy could run, jump, change direction, defied gravity like. Some of us, well, some of us just thought he decided to go back from where he really came from. You know, where he *really* came from," added Bowles nervously, and he shot a glance to the ceiling.

"What, like from another planet?" asked Jimmy, who looked like he might start laughing until Tor melted him with a grim stare.

"Well, maybe, another something, anyway. I know it sounds crazy. But then some other folks, they thought he might have wanted to disappear. You know, over some trouble or something. Nobody wanted to find the boy if he didn't want to be found, you know. I mean people come from all over to see him play. Even President Eisenhower one time. That boy put this place on the map. Nobody wanted to anything to hurt Herschel Ruggles."

"So, in other words, the police investigation wasn't all that thorough," said Tor.

"I guess you could say that. You heard the expression let sleeping dogs lie? Well, nobody wanted to mess up all that was good about Herschel Ruggles."

"And by that messed up all that was good about the town?

And the university?" said Tor a little testily.

"I guess you could say that."

Tor inwardly fumed. The investigation had been botched because people didn't want to sully their own reputation. A man had disappeared and the truth had never been allowed to come out simply to appease folks' vanity. It was yet another example of history written totally wrong. Was there *any* truth in our past? He looked Bowles. "But if you could remember that name, maybe we can do now what should have been done then."

Bowles looked deeply embarrassed. "It just ain't coming to me, son."

Tor just sat there, depressed right down to his hypothalamus, thinking that perhaps his entire destiny was to be forestalled by an ex-trainer with an excellent memory for physical ailments, but a faulty one for names. As he looked down at the chair he was sitting in, he noted, with some embarrassment that, in his heightened frustration, he had gouged out both eyes of Broadway Joe Namath. He discreetly covered this blasphemous defilation with his legs.

They talked some more about the greats of the past and present and then Tor and Jimmy took their leave. Tor left his cell phone number with Bowles in case he conjured up the critical name from his dubious memory bank.

Driving back through the shadows of the early dusk, Jimmy said, "Well, that wasn't that much help, but it will be if he remembers that name. Maybe that person, if he's still alive, could tell us what he saw."

"If anything," exclaimed Tor, who was obviously still very depressed. No wig, no name, how could it get worse? And was Bowles' memory really that bad, or did he have a reason to withhold the name from them? The possibilities were beginning to rival a thermodynamics problem. And for the first time he could ever recall, Tor's brain was beginning to tire.

He glanced at Swift and decided to change the subject to more pressing—if less important—modern matters. "Exams are coming up. I hope you're studying. The team can't afford for you to be put on academic probation like last year."

"I was in the library most of the night," Jimmy replied indignantly.

"So I heard," said Tor right back.

They drove to Linda Daughtry's home, the address of which Tor had managed to get from the phone book. The owner of the wig shop's residence was planted at the end of a cul-de-sac with mature trees ringing it that were shedding leaves at a rapid pace. It was a nice house, big, with lots of improvements to it, Tor noted. And there was a late model Lexus coupe in the driveway. The wig business must pay better than he thought. A dog barked from somewhere, perhaps from the woods next to the house. Tor and Jimmy walked up to the front door, and Tor knocked. They waited and he knocked again.

Jimmy eyed the car. "Looks like somebody's home. And I think I hear a TV going."

"Ms. Daughtry?" called out Tor. Most likely, he thought, she didn't want to face him. Perhaps she was hiding in the closet after making off with his forty-year-old wig for some inexplicable reason. With the way his luck was running, she was probably a wig kleptomaniac. "Ms. Daughtry?"

"Try the handle," advised Jimmy.

"That's breaking and entering."

"Not if it's not locked."

"That's a distinction the police do not make. Trust me."

Before Tor could stop him, Jimmy reached out, tried the knob and turned. The door swung almost silently open.

Tor looked at Jimmy in dismay. "Now you've done it. Step through there and it's a felony."

Jimmy promptly stepped through. "I'm a felon. Feels good. Come on, Tor, we can always say the wind blew it open."

Tor shook his head, yet quickly followed his friend inside.

They had not gone far when both men stopped and stared upward. Where the chandelier in the living room should have been was, instead, the unfortunate owner of the house. Linda

Daughtry was swinging slightly; perhaps the wind pouring in the opened front door had commenced her small body to moving back and forth from where it hung on the improvised gallows. The chandelier had been taken down and a strong rope had been run through the hook that had supported the light. Daughtry's eyes were open and seemed searching, her neck cocked at an angle and ligatured to such a degree that breathing and life were pretty much ruled out. And Tor noted that, ironically, her wig had fallen off, revealing that her real hair was composed of wilted fragments of gray surrounded by broad, peeling patches of scalp. A pathetic, forlorn figure in death was Linda Daughtry, yet when didn't death have such an effect? The stench from her putrid body was fierce and hit them both hard when the wind swung back and pushed the foul odor in their faces. The dead, Tor knew from his science labs, did not keep particularly well without ice or embalming.

This malodorous grenade propelled Jimmy Swift into giving up the last portions of the Wild Turkey still lingering in his gut, mixed with a half-dozen cups of coffee and a cheese Danish. The concoction did nothing to enhance the appearance of Daughtry's living room rug. And neither was Swift a particularly pleasant addition writhing around on it in a twister of physical crisis.

Tor, also shaken to his core, though without the accompanying nausea suffered by his friend, managed to dial 911. The police arrived shortly thereafter. Before they got there, Tor lectured Jimmy on what and what not to say, even as the fastest of the present day Mighty Johns cradled his head between his legs and fought hard to keep further Wild Turkey demons at bay.

The police were professional and appropriately suspicious of Tor and Jimmy's admittedly unusual story. Yet it helped matters immeasurably that one of the officers was a Mighty Johns booster. They soon found themselves free to go, but were told there would be follow-up questions. They went off with a slap on the back each and a big grin from the booster cop who couldn't stop talking about Jimmy's earth-shattering run. For his part, Tor was beginning to wish they never had broken the damn record.

He looked back once at Linda Daughtry dangling there and knew that no one, no matter what they had done, should have their lives snatched from them in that way.

As they drove away, Jimmy rolled down the window, leaned out and sucked in air. "I have never smelled anything that bad in my life," he said, when he pulled himself back in.

"Get over it," said Tor, who was in no mood for Jimmy's trivial complaints.

"Not since I fed my basset hound five cans of Vienna sausage and a quart of chocolate milk have I ever smelled anything so disgusting."

"Knock it off, Jimmy. A woman is dead. And maybe she's dead because of my questions about that stupid wig. Think how I feel." The guilt Tor was feeling was truly enormous. Scientists were supposed to be immune to such emotional assaults. Facts and accompanying results were wonderfully benign and uncomplicated that way. When an experiment failed, you simply recorded the result and moved on to another test. There was no grief, no shock, no feeling of personal loss. Tor the human being was ill prepared to deal with the death of a stranger over a mildewed wig.

"Gee, I didn't mean to offend you, Tor! But come on, I mean el primo stinko. I've never barfed like that in my life. My gut's still jumping."

Tor pulled the car over, grabbed Swift by the coat collar and jerked him so close they were almost nose-to-nose. "If you don't shut up right this minute, I will tell you in exacting detail precisely how the human body decomposes. And when I get to the subtopic of maggot infestation, I will be so incredibly graphic in my description that it will leave such an indelible impression on that pea-sized brain of yours, that I swear to God you will puke your guts out at least once a day for the rest of your entire life. Got it, Swift?"

Tor let him go, put the car in gear and drove off. For the record, Jimmy Swift didn't say a single word all the way back, although Tor did hear him whimper once or twice, the pathetic, record-breaking Mighty Johns son of a bitch.

After he dropped Swift off, Tor went back to his dorm room and lay on his bed, staring at a ceiling he had painted in galactic star clusters that represented his unique vision of what actually could be out there. He craved perfect knowledge, exact data. Tor wanted to see everything as precisely as it actually existed, free of error or speculation or gossip, free of the inane synthesis and the self-pitying psychosis of a collective, bleating world of fools steeped in nothing more than petty materialism while they remained ignorant of all that was truly worthwhile and valuable. The fact that there had been so much misinformation surrounding Herschel Ruggles, the man, and his disappearance, rankled Tor mightily. And yet there was a gnawing fear dwelling in some unexplored region of his magnificent brain that was actually nudging Tor into an acceptance of a lesser truth, a reductive conclusion of a half-ass proportion, a sorry compromise of sorts. And part of Tor almost acquiesced in such an uneasy truce. At the epicenter of his dilemma was this issue: When confronted with an unwelcome truth, what did one do? Did one let sleeping dogs lie? Most people would, and yet Tor never had. Here he was not so confident. And yet, as he lay there staring at his composition of the universe and beyond, the critical core of Tor North, the part that had made it his life's ambition to seek truth in its unspoiled form, regardless of the costs, both personal and otherwise, was finally able to throw off the bite and tug of this vicious, yet seductive force unleashed from the domicile of ignorance and quitters. He rose and went back to work. It was time to assemble real, hard facts, right from their source, just as any scientist would do. Ironically, the stars had pointed him in the correct direction. He had just discovered another quasar, right here on the planet earth of all places.

She hadn't attended a Mighty Johns game since the Ruggles era. Tor had checked. He couldn't determine if she had been at "the" game, yet he thought it likely that she had. She had been widowed for forty years now and had *never*—Tor had learned with the aid of Molly McIntyre and her valuable research—contemplated remarriage. The house on the hill created by fill dirt from one of her husband's vast tract projects had settled some as the combination of gravity and the sheer weight of millions of tons of displaced and compacted red clay sought lower ground. The house was built of stone. What else could it be considering the career and sensibilities of its creator? It had been quarried nearby, from another of the man's sedimentary trinkets. She reportedly lived there alone, but for the day servants, who cooked the meals, kept he dust and weeds at bay and laundered the clothes of the shrunken, elderly woman who was their long-time mistress. Yet at night she was completely alone, and preferred it that way, Tor had been told.

It had not been difficult to get into see her. He had called and she had called back, or a representative had at least. An appointment was arranged and Tor made the drive up the coiling black asphalt road, and waited for the iron gates with the initial JMD in heavy iron scroll to open and allow him in.

Tor knocked at the enormous wooden door that had been stained coal black in an apparent tip-of-the-hat to the long-dead man. A woman answered, obviously a maid judging from her garb. She led Tor down passageways of great length, with exquisite architectural detailing, and stylishly crowded with antiques, paintings and other objects of obvious taste and cost that did not impress Tor at all, for he had grown up in similar surroundings. The room he was led to was baronial. A fire belched and lurched in a cavernous opening that large enough to hold the Mighty Johns starting offensive eleven with room to spare. In the center of the room were two chairs arranged face-to-face. In one, she sat. Tor took the other, easing his bulk down as the fire cracked and popped across from him. The east wind pressed against the elongated windows where the last of the sun's jolly fingertips were sliding away to be replaced by the melancholic ink smudges of dusk. Faulkner the Giant would have been quite comfortable here, sipping his favorite and various libations in these depressingly Gothic confines, thought Tor, who was surprisingly well read in the literary sense for a scientist. Erskine Caldwell, on the other hand, would have fled for his scrawny life.

Tor set down the bag that he had brought with him and looked across at the woman.

Gloria Peyton Draven was now seventy-five years old and most people who knew her would say that time had not been kind to the woman from the age of forty on. That was often the case with earth angels possessed of an unassailable beauty during their youth. Rita Hayworth, Greta Garbo, Hedy Lamarr, they were goddesses all; what way was there to go but down. An odd wrinkle springing up here or there, the softening of the jaw line, the deepening, by millimeters, of the eye sockets, the thinning of lips and skin, the collapse of once proud cheekbones, though so subtle in individual touch, was, collectively all that was needed to rupture the ship, sending the bow to the waves' trough, and raising the screw to kiss the air, where neither was designed to survive for long. On the surface Gloria Draven was just that, a bitter shipwreck of vainglorious proportion, rare enough to be noticed, yet just common enough not to be pitied. Below the skin, though, Tor sensed something far more substantial than a former beauty disfigured and hollowed by time.

"I'm Tor North," he began quietly, yet firmly, deciding it was best to feel the woman out a bit, but not to be too timid about it. It was not time for timidity.

"I know." Her voice was not quite velvet and not quite suede, perhaps leather, Tor thought, not really understanding why he was using that type of textured comparison. And yet Gloria Draven did seem tactile somehow, tempting one to finger her arm, or pat her back.

"Probably from Jimmy Swift and me breaking Herschel Ruggles' record."

"I care nothing for football and never did. I know who you are because I know who you are," she said testily.

Tor looked at her strangely for a moment and then decided not to pursue this rather bizarre statement. He had other matters of importance to discuss with her and did not want to burn through his "political capital" over a possibly irrelevant matter. He thought best how to ask his next question. There was really no delicate way around it. "But you did care for Herschel Ruggles, didn't you?"

He watched her very intently, as though the woman was spread-eagled on a glass slide and he was doing a quick and dirty on her through an electron microscope. She trembled, only slightly, but Tor noticed it. When Molly McIntyre had said Ruggles had traveled up the ladder, all the way up the ladder, on his adulterous rounds with promiscuous wives, Tor figured Gloria Draven might reside right at the very top of that structure, in fact on the very step all the warning signs beseeched one never, ever to tread. When he had seen her in the blue dress standing there with Ruggles, he had become sure of it. And then there was the matter of the wig.

"I knew him."

"Many people knew him. Or knew of him. I think you probably knew him better than most."

Her thin lips of pale orange curled back revealing small, yellowed teeth. The image was that of a dog, fangs bared, protecting its home and hearth, ready to attack, or at least putting on a good show of so doing. The threat was often as effective as the act, wasn't it? Poli-sci major Jimmy Swift would surely know that technique.

"Oh you do, do you? You're a very young man, who has really experienced nothing of the world. I'm speaking of its vast generosity, and its depthless, aching cruelty. Do you really feel qualified to make judgments about someone who has seen far more of both than she ever wanted to in this life or any other?"

"What I'm trying to do is lay to rest, once and for all, exactly what happened to Herschel Ruggles when he ran into that tunnel. Some people think he disappeared on purpose, that he was in some kind of trouble. Maybe with a woman." He rested his chin on his fist and waited.

"And do you believe that?" asked the old woman.

"More to the point, do you?"

She dismissed him and his question with a quick stroke of her small hand. "I'm too old to play these silly games," she said.

"So am I."

This got her attention, however briefly. "Why are you really here?"

In answer he reached in his bag and pulled out the blue dress. As the material rose into the air, Gloria Draven's gaze and spirit seemed to rise with it. For a very long time all she did was stare at the cloth. To Tor it seemed that she had forgotten he was there, that it was just her and that old dress. He laid it over the arm of his chair and looked at her.

"You recognize it?"

She slowly nodded, her gaze still fixed upon it. "Where did you find it? You must tell me that."

"It's yours?" Again a nod, her lips moved erratically, yet no words came. "I found it in a very special room underneath the stadium. I also found a wig." He pulled another object from his bag. It was not the wig of course, but a reasonable facsimile that he had bought and which Molly McIntyre had helped him fashion in the style of forty years prior. He had finally decided to tell Molly everything that had happened. He had lost faith in Jimmy, and needed someone to share this burden, and the bewitching-eyed Molly with her first-rate brain had seemed the best candidate. They had sat up far into the night in her private sanctuary in the library. At first Tor could sense Molly was soaked in lascivious longing, as she eyed, again and again, that sturdy library table, and made suggestive remarks designed to inspire in him the same desperate desire that burned in her, and that would cause them to shed their clothes and repeatedly mount one another amid the stacks of Dewey Decimals until they lay numb from exhaustion. Yet once she focused on what he was saying, the lust in her features and voice slipped away and she began to listen intently and ask question after probing question. When Tor came to the part of the wig shop owner's murder, she cried out and gripped his arm.

"This is really getting dangerous, Tor. Someone obviously

doesn't want you to find out the truth. You have to tell the police. You can't do this by yourself."

"The police bungled it forty years ago, and there's no reason to believe that their modern counterparts are any less inept. But I have some ideas."

They had done more research, talked with some more people and come up with a new plan of attack, which included this meeting with Gloria Draven. Molly had wanted to attend, but Tor would not let her. She was back at the university right now, anxiously awaiting his return.

As Tor held up the wig, Gloria's features hinted at the tussle going on inside her.

"Do you recognize this?" asked Tor.

"No, I've never worn a wig."

"I understand that. I didn't mean do you recognize the wig, I meant do you recognize the hairstyle?" He pulled from the bag the last object he had brought with him. It was the newspaper clipping showing Ruggles, Gloria and her husband at the awards banquet. He passed the paper over to her. She looked at the paper and then the wig.

"I see your point," she said quietly.

"I'm sure you do." He paused, eyeing the dimension of the vast hall. "Do you have a basement corridor, stone, with low ceilings here?"

She looked surprised at this inquiry. "Yes, exactly so."

"I thought as much. They would have needed some safe place to study the effect. Would you help me engage in an experiment? I'm a scientist by training, you see, and I've found that the best way to really determine the truth is to, the best of one's ability, replicate the conditions and elements of whatever it is you're trying to prove."

Unlike the glazed look of the late Linda Daughtry when Tor had explained his need to locate the wig's provenance, Gloria Draven clearly understood what he was getting at. No, no empty former beauty here. This woman was intelligent and perceptive. "I'm afraid that I'm too shrunken and thickened to do the dress justice anymore."

She said this rather wistfully and Tor could see why that concession would have a distinct meaning to her. The years had gone by, and she was now very old. She *couldn't* do the dress justice any more.

"I was thinking about your maid, the woman who let me in. She seems to be the right size and height." He added quietly, "And age."

It took about an hour, for Tor had to get the lighting and other conditions in the lower passageway just the way he wanted, which included the removal of all furniture, paintings and other objects until the space was entirely bare. He smiled at the result. Yes, this would work out very nicely.

Gloria and Tor stood at the far end of the tunnel, for that was certainly what it was now, a tunnel, if not *the* tunnel.

In the spirit of a director about to commence his masterpiece, Tor called out, "Action."

At the far end of the tunnel, a door opened and a woman stepped out into the shadows. The maid, whose name was Diane, was wearing the dress and wig. When they saw her both Tor and Gloria Draven exchanged a startled glance. Tor had given the woman the photo from the newspaper and though Diane had no idea what any of this as about, an ignorance Tor had no intent of alleviating, she had gotten into the spirit of the exercise and, from a distance at least, thirty-five-year-old Gloria Draven once more stood in their midst.

"Thank you," said Tor, to Diane, who disappeared once more to transform herself from the mistress back to the maid. Tor turned and looked at Gloria.

"Remarkable," said the old woman. "Truly remarkable."

"From a distance, and under these conditions, anyone could be fooled into thinking you were there when you really weren't."

"Yes, but for what purpose?" Gloria looked a bit frightened now, which struck Tor as perfectly normal. It was all a bit frightening.

"If I were a young man, very much in love with a woman, and

I saw that woman, or what I thought was that woman, my first inclination would be to go to her. Of course, up close, I would realize the impersonation, but not until I was very close to her. And if she kept moving away from me, down a darkened tunnel, what would I do?"

"You would follow her," said Gloria Draven in a hushed tone, as a teardrop splashed onto her cheek.

"I would follow her," repeated Tor. "And when I realized the deception I would be confused, even angry, and then I would probably go back to what I was doing. Unless something prevented me from doing so."

"Prevented you from doing so." It was now Gloria's turn to do the mimicking.

"Were you aware that your husband knew about your affair with Herschel Ruggles?"

In response, the shrunken mistress of the house took Tor's hand and led him back upstairs to a small room that was not nearly so ornately lavish as the rest of the home's interior. A few odd jumble of chairs, a day bed, a plain writing table, no pictures on warm blue walls, a small, yet spirited fire fronted by a slender mantel of knotted pine, completed this tiny sanctuary, for that's what it seemed to be to Tor—a sanctuary.

"I spend most of my time here," she said in response to his look. "The rest of the house was not my doing, this was." She delicately displayed herself—displayed seemed to be the appropriate description to Tor—on the day bed and motioned for him to sit in a comfortable leather club chair, its seat worn away from years of bottoms rubbing on it.

"To answer your question, no I did not know, though that was awfully presumptuous, arrogant, silly even of me, for my husband was omniscient, at least in matters of importance to him. And I suppose, in a perverse way, I was such a matter of importance. Not in the sense that we had a good marriage, for we did not, but in the sense that I was a possession of his, and he was very jealous of his property."

"And not particularly pleased when others tampered with

such property," interjected Tor.

"Yes."

"Tell me about Ruggles."

"The photo you brought, that was the first time I had met him. It was a sports awards banquet, such silly nonsense. Grown men running around and hitting and hurting each other and then feted and rewarded and proclaimed great men for doing so. It made no sense to me at all."

"I could see that," said Tor. It had never made much sense to him either actually, other than an opportunity to experiment with the laws of nature, and, occasionally, to prove them wrong.

"At first I lumped Herschel in with all the other silly boys. I had of course heard about his reputation among the ladies, and I found that appalling, I really did. My marriage was not a source of happiness to me, and yet I had made my bed, and I slept in the damn thing every night, if you understand me." Tor said that he did. "Well, you can imagine my surprise when I found myself becoming attracted that very night to this young man. Yes of course he was handsome and tall and strong and everyone in the place was fawning all over him. He was an absolute magnet. He could have had any woman there, from the richest to the poorest, from the smartest and most sophisticated down to the dullest and dreariest among us."

"He could have had any one of them, anyone except you," Tor corrected her.

"Except me." She looked into the fire for a bit, and continued to do so even as she spoke again. "We talked, and the more we talked the more complex, troublesome and inspired I found him. He was a magnificent athlete, and the truly great ones, I've been told, so often stop right there. They possess great physical ability and nothing more, as thought God had wanted to spread the wealth a bit and so, upon creation, had never given all possible gifts to one person. Yet what I found most remarkable about Herschel Ruggles was his intense sadness, this quality of destructive melancholy I guess one would call it. I wasn't quite old enough to be his mother, yet I did have maternal instincts toward him." She stared into the fire. "He had also a curious ambivalence about his physical gifts that I discovered later he worked very hard to cover up. It seemed to me he spent his entire life trying to live up to the image that people had of him, and it made him terribly depressed." She looked at Tor. "This may be hard for you to believe, but I don't think Herschel Ruggles really even enjoyed playing football." An ironic smile graced her lips. "It was never him on that field, you know, not really. It was as though when the game started, he stepped out of his real self, left it on the sidelines, and became Herschel Ruggles the mightiest Mighty John there ever was or ever would be." She patted Tor's hand. "You could break his records, Tor, but you could never top the man. He was too talented, too good, you see. He wasn't like the rest of mankind. But with those great gifts come terrible burdens imposed by us, the less gifted. Do you know what it felt like to know that you that you were never supposed to lose? That you were never supposed to be stopped once your hands touched that ridiculous little ball. He carried that with him every day, just as he carried that ball, that ball and chain more like it. He needed to be the perfect student, the perfect athlete, and, despite those vicious rumors about his philandering, he was the perfect gentleman. I was his only indiscretion. You see the masses will suffer nothing less than flawlessness in our earth-bound gods. And, at least back then, ironically part of that faultless image was as a ladies man, a predator if you will, who took what he wanted of the fairer sex, and no one could begrudge him that, at least in those pre-feminist days. Yet he wasn't that way at all. Every day he carried those expectations, and they were crushing him. He could never be what he actually was, if he even knew who that person was. I truly felt sorry for him, though he never sought anyone's pity."

"And you helped him through? Intellectually? Emotionally?"

She smiled and a rapturous laugh came from somewhere deep inside her small body and whipsawed into the room with its urgency. "Tor North, we were lovers. Don't believe that we were not. I'm no saint. I'm probably not going to Heaven, though my penance has been long on this earth."

"I can see that."

"Yet I did bring some good to him. At least I think I did."

Now Tor reached across and took one of her hands in his. "Gloria, he followed you down that tunnel, or what he thought was you. Right in the middle of a football game, an important game to him because it would determine a bowl berth. In the midst of over twenty-four thousand fans screaming his name in triumph because he had just performed the most remarkable feat anyone had ever witnessed on a football field, he chose to follow you down a tunnel instead of returning to the game and basking in their idolatry. I'd say that you did more than just bring him some good. I'd say he loved you more than anything, far more than the game he played so brilliantly. If you believe nothing else, believe that. I don't need to conduct an experiment to verify the truth of the man's feelings for you. They are as obvious to me as the most indisputable principles of science, perhaps even more so."

Gloria Draven's eyes filled with plump tears that dribbled down her fallen cheeks and spattered onto the shawl she wore around her collapsed shoulders.

"I had always hoped it would be so," she said in a very small voice.

The crackle of the fire was the only sound in the room for the next five minutes. Tor averted his gaze as the woman continued to weep, with great dignity. He would do nothing to deny her that very personal moment.

She finally wiped her eyes and looked at him. "What can I tell you that will help?"

"Did you ever make an arrangement with Ruggles to see him during that game?"

"No. I wasn't even at that horrible event. My husband forbade me from going."

"Forbade you? Was that unusual?"

"Nothing my late husband did could be termed unusual, for his life was one long list of outrageous acts."

"Did it make you suspicious that on the very day he would not allow you to attend the game, that Ruggles disappeared? Did you ever envision a connection?"

"I am, by nature, a suspicious woman. I had my dalliance with Herschel, though we both saw it as much more than that. However, my husband's sexual indiscretions numbered in the dozens. The double standard was alive and well back then. I suppose I shouldn't have been surprised about my husband's continuing affairs even at his advanced age, what with my being wife number three and all. But to answer your question, no. I did not see such a connection. As I said I didn't know John knew about us, and my own belief, which you have just proved erroneous, was that Herschel himself had chosen to disappear. Chosen to disappear because of his depression, and chosen not to include me in that flight. In his new life, wherever it would take him."

Tor was puzzled by this response. It was an angle he had not considered. "Would you have gone with him?"

She said fiercely, "Would I have not!"

And with those words, the depths of her suffering finally reached Tor's brain, taking far longer than the customary five milliseconds, and yet it was so often the case with crisis of emotion, with its attendant calamitous battering of the heart and of the soul. "So all these years, you thought he had abandoned you?" He paused, though she made no move to respond. "That is great penance, Gloria." He paused and then added, "You might make it to Heaven after all."

"I would assume Herschel would be there waiting for me. It is nice to think that at least. I have had a long life, and though I am stronger than I look, I am also very tired. I never thought I would grow weary of living for who wants to die? But I am. I am tired of living, at least in this body. And in this world. I know it's hard for you to see that because you're young and vibrant, your whole life ahead of you. But it does happen, you know, that sense of 'this is enough. I'm finished.'"

Tor rose from his seat and her gaze rose with him. "I'll need the dress and wig back."

"You know what happened to him, don't you? My husband was involved."

"I have no hard evidence, but I believe so," said Tor, "though if he was he obviously had help."

Her eyes searched out his. They seemed to plumb the depths of his heart, soul, and mind, leaving nothing unexamined, like the able scientist always strove for and sometimes achieved. "Who? Who!"

"That's for me to find out. And I promise you that I will."

Tor had recruited Jimmy Swift once more for what he hoped was the final leg of this Odyssey-like journey. They had driven for eight hours, over both good and not-so-good roads. They could have flown, but Tor carried something that made traveling by plane problematic. As they neared their destination, Tor took in the very familiar scenery, each tree, hilltop and snaking-off crevice that always brought back distinct and mostly pleasant memories. How many times had he driven this route, turned at the same spot, advanced like a good hound toward home?

"Wow," was all Swift could say as the house—mansion rather—came into view.

"Casa North," said Tor with all the enthusiasm of a hopeless sinner near death. His father had built this place over three hundred and fifty miles from his alma mater in a ruggedly remote area that promised nothing to anyone. Peter North had made his fortune elsewhere, and then had retreated to this isolated location to erect his cathedral of glorious excess that few would ever see.

"If I had grown up in a place like this, I never would have left it."

"Yes you would, Jimmy. Trust me. There are only so many bathrooms one can use. And having to travel about a day to play with other kids got a little tedious."

Tor pulled into the parking area, and stopped his car in the same spot he always did, the one next to his father's big Mercedes. They went inside, were greeted by Peter North's valet of sorts, who was named William, and who had been with the family since before Tor was born. His father, Tor had learned, had always wanted an English born and bred butler, and William fit the bill.

"He's expecting you," said William. "He's playing billiards."

Tor was surprised. "This is Friday. He doesn't play pool on Fridays." Peter North was a man of exacting habits, and any deviation from this orbit, however trivial, was cause for speculation if not always concern.

"He knew you were coming. I think he thought you might like to play."

As the young men started off, William pulled Tor aside. "He's not quite all there, tonight, Tor. A little heavy in the cups, as they say where I'm from."

"I understand." And Tor did understand. He was not in the least bit surprised, in fact.

Peter North was indeed smacking billiard balls, sending them careening wildly along the velvet, a cigarette dangling from one corner of his broad mouth. Everything about his father was wide, thought Tor.

"Boys, come on in and see if you can give an old fart a good goddamn match."

He was indeed in his cups, as his words, while not exactly slurred, seemed extra heavily licked by his tongue before being expelled from his mouth.

Jimmy took up a pool cue. Tor did not. He put his bag down. "I'd like to show you something."

His father banked the seven-ball into the corner pocket. "Show away, buddy boy."

Tor reached in the bag and pulled out the Mauser. He set it on the edge of the billiard table. "Here's your pistol back. It's the one you said you brought back from Vietnam. It's a German make by the way, World War Two era, not Vietnam. Just so you know that I know."

Peter North straightened up and took a long drag on his cigarette. He blew the smoke out, and the wispy cloud almost obscured his entire face for a few seconds. Heavy lungs the man had. He picked up the pistol and Jimmy took a nervous step back, gripping the pool cue a little tighter.

Peter North checked the magazine and the balance of the weapon and then pointed the gun at the head of an eight-point buck hanging on the wall and fired an imaginary shot, killing the animal a second time.

"German, you say. I didn't know you had taken it. I guess I was mistaken about Vietnam. Or maybe you got it wrong, Tor."

"I don't get things like that wrong." He slipped his hand inside the bag once again. "I have something else to show you."

"You're just the show-and-tell boy today, aren't you?" Peter looked at Jimmy and smiled, slapped the young man on the shoulder, asked him how he was, if he wanted a drink. Didn't they all want a drink? No, they didn't, answered Tor for both of them.

Peter went over to the little bar in the corner and poured himself a martini and popped five olives, one after the other, into his mouth. The man had a large and voracious appetite about everything. When he did something, it was done! Tor had, until recently, admired that quality about his father.

He stopped chewing when Tor pulled the dress and the wig out of the bag.

"I don't know if you heard about Linda Daughtry. She's dead."

"Linda who?"

"Daughtry. Runs... ran the wig shop over near the university. She was found hanged in her home. Jimmy and I found her."

Peter did none of the things one was supposed to do when learning such awful news. He did not cry out, or hug his son, or ask if he was okay, before anxiously asking for all the terrible details. Instead, he swallowed his olive and his martini, picked up his cue stick and neatly smacked the four-ball home. He took a moment to chalk his stick and readied another shot.

"You know Linda Daughtry, Dad."

"If you say so, Tor. I know lots of people." He grinned at Jimmy. "It's not exactly page one news. Peter North knows folks."

"You both attended Draven. You dated a few times. I have a

photo of you both here." He lifted the paper our of the bag. "The college yearbook committee is putting together a fiftieth anniversary edition, and they've dug up lots of interesting things, including this photo of the two of you, with your names listed."

"Dated lots of women in college, son." Peter smacked Jimmy on the arm again. "Bet you do too, don't you, Jimmy? Bet you are one helluva skirt magnet. Probably teach my son some lessons, couldn't you? And after breaking that record, damn, I bet the gals are after you hook, line, and sinker, boy, don't lie and tell me they're not."

Before Tor could say anything else, his cell phone rang. He answered it, listened for a few moments, said thank you and clicked off.

His father had watched him carefully and then said, "Tor, if you've got some business, don't let me keep you son, I'm perfectly fine all by my lonesome."

"That was Herman Bowles, you remember Herman, don't you?"

"Can't say that I do."

"He was the trainer on the football team the years you played," volunteered Jimmy.

"Okay," said Peter evenly, "maybe I remember him. It's been a long time."

"He moved to California years ago, but then he moved back. Jimmy and I went to see him. He told us a little about the day that Ruggles disappeared. How there was no way he could have left through the exit from the locker room because there was a player in there all game long. He couldn't remember the name when we visited him. But it finally came to him. He just called me with it."

"Is that right?"

"Who was it, Tor?"

"How's your back, Dad? Those degenerating discs are painful. Started with your playing days if I remember right. You spent a lot of time in the trainer's room. Including the day Ruggles disappeared, although, that day, your back was just fine."

Jimmy looked from father to son with a deepening expression of disbelief.

"Bowles remembered it was you in the locker room that day. He felt like an idiot, because we had the same last name, but, like you said, it's been a very long time and peoples' memories aren't that good to begin with. But I already had found out from another source that it was you in the locker room."

"You always seem to have a pretty good memory, son." Peter had laid the cue stick aside, apparently no longer interested in playing.

"Did Draven pay you off first, and then you paid Linda Daughtry to impersonate Gloria Draven in the tunnel that day, or did Draven just pay the two of you separately?"

In response, Peter went over and made up another martini. "You sure you two don't want to join me?"

Jimmy shook his head while Tor just stared at his father.

"You were waiting in the locker room. Maybe you told Ruggles earlier that you had gotten a message from Gloria Draven, since Ruggles probably confided in you about the affair and perhaps you acted as a go-between for them. I spoke with Gloria Draven recently. She knew who I was, and not from playing football for Draven. She knew who I was because she knew who you were."

Peter North shook his head. "Gloria Draven. Didn't know she was still alive. Quite a beautiful woman."

"She's a lot more than beautiful, Dad. She's also very intelligent." Tor paused and then continued. "Or you could have forged a message from Gloria and left it for Ruggles. The note might have said that if he scored in the direction of the Mighty Johns locker room that he should just keep running into the tunnel, that she would be there to give him, what? A kiss? A hug. Maybe even the news that she was going to divorce her husband and marry him. Or perhaps it was as simple as Daughtry hanging out near the entrance. Ruggles scores, sees what he thinks is the love of his life and heads over. But she slinks inside and draws him in, ultimately to his death."

On this Peter put up a hand. "Hold on, son, just hold on. I want you two to come with me."

They followed him from the billiards room to his small office near the back of the house. He sat behind his desk and motioned for them to sit across from him in a pair of chairs. He lit up another cigarette and blew smoke at them. He smiled.

"So we were at the part where Daughtry gets Ruggles inside. And then what? I mean this is really getting good."

Tor was not listening. He was sniffing the air, and feeling his sinuses closing up in protest. It was the same smell as before. All lingering doubt had just been erased. Instead of triumphant, he felt crushed. This was still his father after all.

"You were in the locker room. They would have passed you. At some point, Ruggles is going to turn back to the game, especially if Daughtry keeps flitting away, which she has to do because she can't allow Ruggles to catch up to her and see that it's not Gloria. That's where you came in. You might have come out of the locker room, told Ruggles that Gloria was indeed waiting for him, farther down the tunnel, to keep him going after her. And yet, just in case he didn't you had a backup plan. Your German World War Two Mauser from Vietnam. I wonder, did old man Draven give it to you? I guess your guilt made you lie to me about the gun's origin. Hell, you could have said it was a collector's piece from World War Two and I wouldn't have known the difference. Yet perhaps you were trying to erase, in your own mind, what you had done."

"And what exactly was that, son? What had I done? Do you think I shot Ruggles in the tunnel in the middle of a football game and just happened to keep the gun I committed the deed with so the police could find it? And what exactly did I do with the body?" This was the first display of raw emotion Peter had shown and he tried to smile at Jimmy as soon as he was through. However, Swift was obviously having none of this game now, and Peter's expression showed that he too had wearied of it.

"You neither killed Ruggles yourself nor did you bury the body," said Tor. "You wouldn't have had time. You weren't the only one in that tunnel. There were others. Other men. At least three probably, counting Draven. Ruggles was a very strong man and they would have taken no chance. Now Draven was at the game that day, I checked. Only he left his seat shortly after the kickoff and never returned. I also checked that."

"That's my boy, a first-rate checker."

The words were now slurring from the old, big man, who looked older and smaller than ever, and Tor could not help feeling sorry as he stacked fact on top of fact. He had never competed against his father in anything. In all except science, Tor had never felt adequate to his old man. Not as good an athlete, surely not as dynamic a businessman. His father had charisma his son never would. Tor North, despite possessing brilliance in his chosen field, had always assumed himself an unequivocal failure in his father's eyes. Now it all seemed too easy, the great competitor vanquished long ago, perhaps by his own demons, and it was clear to Tor now that there must have been many of them for his father.

"There's a very curious room located very deep in the tunnel. It's the room where Daughtry kept the dress and wig, and also where she transformed herself into Gloria, something she obviously couldn't do beforehand, because someone might have seen her. Daughtry was the perfect accomplice because her mother ran the wig shop back then, and she could get a wig and fashion it properly without anyone knowing. And you and she had dated. You no doubt persuaded her to cooperate with your great charm and Draven's money as added inducement.

"You turned Ruggles over to Draven and his men, and then you went back to the locker room, since people would grow suspicious when he didn't return and would no doubt investigate. Here, your actions were critical. You were Ruggles' friend and teammate. If he came in here, you had to have seen him. I finally located all the old police reports. Ironically, one of the officers that came in response to the Daughtry murder is a Mighty Johns Booster. With his help I was able to get access to the records. They were buried in the basement of the courthouse and refuted much of the rumors swirling about this case. That's when I learned it was you in the locker room. You were very convincing with the police. You played the part very well, the loyal friend trying to cover for his teammate. Herman Bowles was convinced that Ruggles couldn't have come through the locker room because you would have seen him. Yet he didn't know what you had told the police, and he left for California soon thereafter anyway and was no longer a factor. And, as he told us, there wasn't much incentive for anyone to discover the truth about Ruggles, because that truth might reflect badly on their 'hero' and thus the town," Tor said bitterly.

Tor pulled out a piece of paper from his pocket. "You played it safe, though. You didn't come out and tell the police that Ruggles had slipped through the locker room, but you strongly intimated it."

Tor read from the paper: "While I was in the toilet, I believe I heard someone come in the trainer's area. I called out but received no answer. It sounded like the person was wearing cleats. Then, I think, but can't be sure, that I heard a door open and close." Tor put down the paper. "Vague enough to where they couldn't pin you down on exact details, but compelling enough to push them down the road you wanted. That's why the police investigation didn't proceed. They had no reason to search underneath the stadium because you had led them away from there. Possibly there were little tidbits of women trouble laid here and there from various sources, so they just stopped looking for him. No one possibly suspected foul play."

"Interesting story, son. You should be a writer of fiction, it's that good. No, really."

"Draven, no doubt being the sort of person he was—cold, manipulating, supremely competitive, ruthless, would have wanted to confront the man who was the object of his wife's peccadillo, if for no other reason than to let Ruggles, the greatest competitor of them all, know that Draven had trumped him. And right after his most memorable touchdown run ever. It couldn't be any more complete or triumphant. Snatching utter defeat from the jaws of victory. The old bastard must have cherished every moment of it."

Peter smiled and wagged a finger at him. "God, son, that imagination, and I thought scientists weren't supposed to even have one."

"I would hope that even if time had permitted, you would have refused to participate in the actual killing. Though very recent events make me doubt that conclusion." Jimmy looked at him, puzzled. "Linda Daughtry didn't hang herself, Jimmy," said Tor. "There was no chair underneath her body."

Jimmy shot a penetrating glance at Peter North, who looked only at his son.

"Go on," said Peter, "finish your tall tale."

"They took Ruggles to the room I've already spoken of, killed him there, and then buried him there. His grave and the rest of the room were then paved over with stone, the perfect hiding place."

"Interesting theory."

"It's more than that. At my direction, the police took up that stone floor and recovered Herschel Ruggles' body, or rather his skeleton. There were also remnants of his street clothes, shoulder pads, cleats, uniform—one could still see the famous number five on his jersey—and what was left of the football." Tor paused and then added, "Ruggles' arm was still curled around the football they tell me." Peter North sat up at this, yet said nothing. "Since there is no statute of limitations on murder, the case was never officially closed.

"And of course we have another far more recent murder to deal with." Tor took a long breath. "When did Linda Daughtry arrive here? A few hours after she spoke with me? It's a short flight." His father stared blankly at him. "She took a plane here; she didn't have time to drive it round trip. The police have already talked to the airline. As well as the cab company that drove her here." He took another sniff. "And the perfume smell here is the same that reeks at her shop. It's almost as good as a fingerprint, which, by the way, they found several of at her home.

Several that matched yours in fact after I told them to check. She told you about the wig I had found, which she recognized as being the one she wore to impersonate Gloria Draven forty years ago, and then she flew back. You flew back after her in your private plane. You went to her home sometime on the morning of the day that she was murdered and confronted her. Perhaps at the meeting here she told you she wanted money to keep silent. It's pretty clear that after Ruggles died you had been paying her to keep quiet about her role in all this. Whether she knew the plan was to murder Ruggles or not, and she probably didn't, she had a lot less to lose than you did. She was definitely the weak link in your chain. And from the little I saw of her and what I found out subsequently, she struck me as a woman shrewd and daring enough to take advantage of that opportunity, especially after you became wealthy. And you paid her, and continued to pay her. A very close examination of your financial records will show the trail, no doubt. And that will also solve the mystery of why the owner of a second-rate wig shop in a blue-collar town could afford such a nice house and luxury cars. Blackmail makes for nice, tax-free supplemental income. But then perhaps you were tired of paying. Perhaps you felt she wouldn't be able to keep her mouth shut if the case was stirred up again and she started to feel too much pressure. So down went the chandelier and up went Linda Daughtry."

Peter North leaned forward. "If you have so much evidence, why aren't the police here to arrest me?"

"Because I asked for and received permission to talk to you first. When I call them, they will come to take you." Tor's voice quavered as he said this, but he kept his gaze directly on his father. The man at least deserved that. No averting eyes from a disloyal boy. This was man-to-man.

Peter North absorbed this stunning information, to his credit, in a calm and dignified manner. "I see." He said the words with a lingering finality. He reached in his desk and pulled out a pistol, a large one.

"This is actually the gun I brought back from Vietnam, son.

Nasty thing. Take your head off if you're not careful."

"Jesus!" said Jimmy who paled at the sight of yet another weapon.

"Jesus, indeed," said Peter North, who aimed the gun at Jimmy and fired.

The shot tore into the young man's thigh and he dropped to the floor, screaming in pain, and pressing his hand against the large hole in his leg where the chalk white tip of his shattered femur poked through. A stunned Tor rushed to his friend's aid, ripped off a piece of his shirt and used a letter opener he grabbed off his father's desk as a tourniquet to stop the loss of blood. Tor was able to see that the bullet had fortunately missed the critical arteries located there, or else Jimmy would have bled to death in minutes. The bullet had gone through his leg and was imbedded in the floor. Tor tried to calm him down, but Jimmy was in terrible pain and kept shouting and thrashing.

Tor glared at his father, who just stood there, the gun still in hand. "Jesus Christ, Dad, why did you shoot him?"

Peter North looked surprised at the query. "Well, I couldn't very well shoot my own son, now could I? And I had to shoot somebody. I'm angry, Tor."

"Well, dammit, be angry at me. Not him. Not anybody else," screamed Tor. It was the first time he had ever raised his voice to the man.

"There are some clean cloths in that closet over there. And you might want to get him some water," advised Peter. "Or perhaps he could use that stiff drink now. After a particularly tough game Ruggles and me would knock back two six-packs to make the pain of a game go away. God, we had some great times together." He smiled even as Jimmy Swift bled.

It was then that Tor realized his father was insane.

Peter perched on the edge of his desk as he watched his son race to get the sheets and the water and apply them to the victim of his father's violence.

"He needs an ambulance. Call an ambulance," cried out Tor.

"Forget him, he'll be fine. Hell, you should have seen the hit

Ruggles took his sophomore year against Notre Dame. Four men plowed into him at the same time, I mean helmet to helmet. And what do you think happened?" Peter slapped his leg in glee. "The four went down and he didn't. I've never seen anything like it. Not in my entire life. He spun around and then catapulted backwards over them. Backwards! And scored. The guy was a cat, you couldn't knock him off his feet." He calmed down some as Tor finished with Jimmy and then used his cell phone to call an ambulance and the police. His father did not try to stop him.

The place was isolated and the help would take a while in coming, Tor knew, but he had stopped the bleeding and stabilized Jimmy, mostly by giving him a shot of whiskey, not water. He could have tried to take him to the distant hospital himself, but the bumpy roads might open the wound and it would be difficult to get him to the car without a gurney without doing more harm than good.

Peter finally broke his silence. "Why the hell did God make the bastard so perfect? So lucky?"

Tor turned and looked at his father, one of his hands still protectively on Jimmy's shoulder, his body between his friend and his father, just in case Peter decided, like the deer head, to take a second shot. Tor North, ever the blocker, ever the wall of safety.

"A friend wouldn't have betrayed a friend. Yet you did. And for what? All of this." He looked around the wonderfully and expensively decorated room. "A large sum of money was Draven's reward for your complicity. A stake you used to build an even greater fortune. I always thought you had made it all yourself. But you made it on the blood of your friend. You became rich and he became dead before he had even lived. Now tell me, who's the lucky bastard?"

"I named the goddamn stadium after him, didn't I? That cost me a million dollars! And I live with my guilt every day. You don't know the half of it, son."

"That means nothing to me because you created the source of your own guilt. Through your jealousy and your greed. So don't try the 'poor me' plea at the pearly gates. They'll laugh you out of the place."

"Ruggles had lived his entire life already. That was all he was good for, running with a football. Well, he had his great run and then it was time to move aside."

"Why, so you could take your rightful place as the anointed one? You were a mediocre lineman with marginal athleticism, just like me. You made a fortune using someone else's money that you obtained by helping to coax a man you called a friend to his death. And you murdered your accomplice because you were fearful your guilt would become known and you would lose all you had acquired so dishonestly, so horribly!" Tor hesitated as he watched his father's face go from lightheartedness powered by insanity to an ashen countenance governed if not exploited by returning reason. He didn't know which one scared him more, the insanity or the reason. "I always envied you. I aspired to be like you in a way though I thought I never could because you seemed so special. You were voted 'Most Honorable' of your college graduating class. Was there ever any greater irony? I wanted to make you proud of me, because I thought earning your respect and your acclaim was a good thing. God, I don't even like football but I played it because you did." Tor's shoulders dropped. "I feel like I've wasted my life, seeking approval from a man I should have loathed all these years instead of loved."

His father's expression had darkened to such a degree that Tor had no reason to believe that he would not break his uttered if informal rule and shoot Tor dead. And yet he stood his ground before the old man, because there was nowhere else to go, and it was finally time that this confrontation took place. Tor North, in all his athletic ineptitude, yet with all his intellectual preeminence, felt as though his greatest role now was as the proxy for Herschel Ruggles finally facing down his Judas.

Instead of raising the pistol on his son, Peter North went and sat back down at his desk. He lit a cigarette and picked a bit of flake off his tongue. "All you said was true, Tor, right down to the tiniest detail. I would expect nothing less from a genius." He said the last with not quite a sneer, yet not quite with love and kindness either. "I *was* a jealous man. Jealous of Ruggles down to the last fiber of my soul and my soul runs deep, boy. On a football field, there was none better than the great Ruggles. Off the field Herschel wasn't a ladies' man, like all the rumors said. And he wasn't a dumb jock, either, which actually would have made accepting his success a little easier for folks like me. That sort of perfection inevitably leads to mass revolt. We cannot accept people without flaws, Tor. Whenever we find them, we either stone them to death or *make* them flawed, one or the other. He was a good man, but with an abiding distress, a personal impotency that ran far deeper than I think even he realized. Do you know that, like you, he didn't particularly care for football either? After every game he kept telling, 'Pete, this is it for me. I don't like hurting people. I don't like performing for the crowds. I don't like having to be unconquerable on every play.' He would say this while we were drinking our beer and mending our wounds, and then come the next Saturday he would suit up and do it all again. Why, I don't know, other than he didn't have anything else in his life that rivaled what he could do on the field, although he didn't crave that level of success, not like most people would have. And yet it was like he had nothing to replace it with, so he kept doing it. But I'll tell you for a fact that Ruggles could have walked out of that locker room door after scoring that touchdown and never looked back. And he would've died a happy man."

"It's too bad you didn't let that happen."

Peter North stubbed out his cigarette on the top of his leather-tooled desk. "I almost did. That's the one part you couldn't find out, not with all your brains. Ruggles came into the tunnel after the touchdown run because I'd given him a note that said Gloria would be there waiting for him if he scored. You were right there; I acted as a go-between for them sometimes. Daughtry dressed up as Gloria and was waiting for him at first near the entrance, so he could see her, and then she slipped inside and went around the corner and a little way past the locker room. Draven and his goons were waiting farther down the tunnel."

"Why did Daughtry have to impersonate Gloria if you had already induced Ruggles into the tunnel with the note?"

"That was Draven's doing. He wanted Ruggles to believe that Gloria had betrayed him. That she really didn't love him at all. He was just that kind of a man. When he destroyed you, Draven destroyed you."

"And he has a university named after him. God, life is just so fair, isn't it?"

"I was the one who told Draven about Ruggles and Gloria. Draven was worth more than God. I thought, you see, I thought there might be something in it for me."

"Well, you were right about that, weren't you," Tor said as coldly as he could.

"I had the pistol in case I needed to persuade him even more. Ruggles came in, not even out of breath after that touchdown run, which, to this day I've never even seen. He passed the locker room, poked his head in and smiled. He said he'd seen Gloria. I told him she really wanted to see him, and had taken a great risk to come here. Those were my lines, my *paid* lines. I told him to go after her, that she was waiting for him on down the tunnel, I told him I'd cover for him." Here Peter paused and fingered his gun. "You know what he said to me? He said he wasn't going to do that. He loved Gloria, he said, but it would never work. She would never leave Draven for somebody like him. You have to understand that he didn't have a real high opinion of himself. Everybody talked about him playing professional ball. Back then those guys made jack-shit. But he never would've played after college. His heart wasn't in it. Hell, he would've won the Heisman that year, and probably never touched another football after that.

"And then I got the surprise of my life. It seems Ruggles wanted out right then and there. He knew I was banged up and in the locker room that day. The irony was, he was coming in there to see me, not Gloria. He made a proposition to me, in the middle of my little scheme with Draven, he made me a proposal, can you believe that?" Peter North laughed a deep, guttural laugh. "He said he wanted to disappear, hang it up, get on with his life somewhere else, somewhere else that didn't involve toting a ball along with all those impossible expectations. He could grab his street clothes, pop the locker room door, hell it would've been easy. He was going to hitchhike over to the bus depot in the next county and grab a ride out west, start over. I could make up a little cover story for him and that would be that. He wanted to go out on top he told me, because he said, 'Pete, you should've seen that run. My lord,' he said, 'Pete, even for me it was something to see. It was something really special.'" Here, Peter stopped to dab at his eyes, but the tears were coming too fast to be swiped away by his shaky fingers.

"And what did you do?" said Tor. He could barely breathe, looking at his father slowly dissolving in front of him like a photo that had just had acid poured on it.

"I smiled at my friend. Said I'd be glad to help. I walked over to his locker, grabbed up his clothes, then I pulled out my gun and pointed it at him." Peter shook his head violently presumably at the image this conjured at the image this conjured for him. "God, you should have seen his face. He had finally made his decision and the burden of the world had been lifted. And then here I came with my gun and my greed and my jealousy and blasted it all to hell and back." He stopped once more and looked squarely at his son. "I could have let him go, but I didn't. Instead, I took Herschel Ruggles, the mightiest of the Mighty Johns and a man whose feet I didn't deserve to lick, and I delivered him to the devil bastard of all devils. I presented him to a man whose heart was even blacker and colder than mine, if you can believe it."

"What did Ruggles say to you, if anything?" The tears were now streaming down Tor's face, matching his father drop for drop.

Peter took a breath. "He said... he said, 'You have a good life, Pete. And never forget your old friend, Herschel Ruggles.'" He looked up at Tor. "And damn if I ever have. He's been right here with me, all the way through my good life." He glanced at his son, his face heavy with anticipation. "Tell me something, where'd you find the wig and the dress?"

"A special friend led me to them," was all Tor would say. "The ambulance will be here soon, Dad. And the police."

Peter North stood, straightened his shirtsleeves and buttoned his collar button. He picked up the gun.

"Better let me have that, Dad." Tor reached out for the weapon.

"You'll have a good life, Tor. Because you deserve it. And if you'll do nothing else for me, do this. Forget your old man. Don't carry me around your neck all your life, because that's not your burden. That one, son, that one is all mine."

Tor reached out for the gun again even as his father placed it in his own mouth and pulled the trigger.

That foul east wind was blowing when, almost two years later, Tor came back to Draven University. He had graduated with the highest honors, and was now seeking further degrees in his beloved field of physics at a college in the west, the far west, away from this place, away from the troubling east wind and all the stench it carried. Jimmy Swift had recovered from his wound though he would never play football again, and needed a cane, in fact, to walk. He had gotten a good job with a senator on the Hill in Washington. No doubt he would've been a great success at parties, repeating his past glory as being the man who had topped the legendary Herschel Ruggles, speaking of the wound he had suffered and the sad history behind all that. Yet he had chosen not to do so. He had, with Tor's great appreciation and encouragement, made a decision not to live in the past, but to forge ahead with the future that could be his, bum leg and all. And he had done so with Molly McIntyre, now his wife. Tor had never bedded Molly atop the library table. They had remained friends, though, even as her love for the martyred Jimmy sparked and then flourished. He had just visited them on this trip east. They were expecting a child, they had told him. They were very happy and he was happy for them.

Now Tor had returned to the home of the Mighty Johns before heading back west. This would be the last time he would come here, he knew. He had no more ties to the area. After his father had died, Casa North had been sold, and Tor had given the proceeds away, along with the rest of the money his father had made. He didn't want it, for he knew it now to be blood money covered with filthy coal dust.

Tor kept his promise to Gloria Draven, and had told her the truth, or, at least his version of it. All Gloria found out from Tor was that Herschel Ruggles loved her, had run into that tunnel to be with her, and would have gone anywhere with her. He no doubt would be awaiting her in Heaven, Tor had said. With that knowledge, the woman quickly had left this life, on her terms. For Tor, there was absolutely nothing wrong with that, to hell with the pristine requirements of science. Perfection was not life; life was living with the flaws we all had.

The whole experience had been a painful one for him. Tor's dedication to the discovery of truth at all costs had been severely tested. And while his integrity had survived this tough squall intact, it had made him more fully respect not just the truth, but also the consequences of such truth. And yes, he had finally come to accept that sometimes the cold, harsh facts were better left unsaid.

That may have been one reason why he had felt compelled to make one final pilgrimage. To examine once and for all—and hopefully lay to rest as well for all time—the personal devastation that the solving of Herschel Ruggles' disappearance had caused him.

He examined the trophy case in the small stadium entry where photos of Herschel Ruggles and his gravity-defying ability dominated everything else. But in one corner there was a relatively new photo that Tor spent some time looking at. It was a picture of him snapped right as he hit that wedge of orange and black and allowed Jimmy Swift and he to have their moments of fame. It preserved for all time the image of the quantum tunneler who had exited before he had entered. It was a marvelous display of what brains and the art of physics could do on any given Saturday in the fall when the crowd wanted blood and pain, and young, reckless men would sacrifice all they had for a few precious seconds of glory on a field of dirt and grass, or neurons and cortical columns, if you still believed Tor North. If only these sedentary spectators understood the true cost of this "game," as they called it. They cheered on Saturday and then went home, secure in their patronage of such an outstanding sport. Would they so readily come on Sunday, or Monday, and help the player pee into a bottle because he was too sore and swollen to make it to the bathroom? Would they come and push him around in a wheelchair at age forty when his once splendid wheels were no longer capable of supporting him? Would they be there when at age fifty the player succumbed to the collective battering that had reduced his insides to that of an eighty-year-old? Tor thought not. Tor knew not.

In the tunnel, Tor needed no chalk line to find it. The fallen door had long since been removed. The floor, which had been dug up to remove Ruggles' body, had been repaired. Tor stepped through the opening and proceeded over to the entry into the "great shit" room that, of course, was no longer there, and in fact never had been, at least in mankind's puny one-dimensional existence. The second room had been alter ego of the first, albeit at a different and earlier point in time. It had been the room of Ruggles' execution and burial, before the stone had been laid over him. A time warp underneath Herschel Ruggles stadium had enabled Tor to step partially into the past and discover the clues he needed to solve the mystery of the man's disappearance, never realizing that it would also lead to the absolute destruction of his own father. Newton's Third Law of Motion still held true: When an object exerts a force on a second object, the second object exerts an equal and opposite force on the first. God, it had indeed. Tor would probably never fully recover from the blow.

And yet there was a distinct possibility that there had been another tear in the fabric of space and time here. Tor had come to believe that a crevice in the normally impenetrable walls of the dimensional universes that kept folks where they should be, had allowed a wronged man to rise, Phoenix-like, from his awful potter's grave, and go to a place of even greater depth under the earth and settle the score with the wretched, foul beast who had taken the wronged man's life away. And Tor tried to imagine what John Milton Draven's face must have looked like when he saw the spectral image of Herschel Ruggles enter that small pocket of life at the Gloria No. 3 mine. What he must have been thinking even as he felt those iron fingers close around his scrawny throat, inexorably tightening until the John of the Mighty Johns had been defeated by a force he could never come close to equaling, in life or in death. Tor could not prove if Ruggles, utilizing some dimensional gash, had actually been able to take out his revenge on Draven, yet a big part of Tor hoped he had. There were many things Tor had unearthed that could not be explained by conventional means. Yet even if the football star had been unable to have a final confrontation with his killer, Herschel Ruggles had lived on, in part because of the disappearance orchestrated by Draven, a bleak, insufferable man, who history had totally forgotten. Now that was the greatest of ironies, the most magnanimously satisfying of justice. No scientific formula could have done it any better justice.

"I told you, great shit."

Tor whirled around and stared at the doorway, where a figure, tall and strong, looked back at him. In the poor light it was impossible to see who it was, yet Tor had no doubt as to the man's identity.

"BJ?" The man did not step forward, and Tor did not shine the light he carried with him at the man. "Who are you really?" asked Tor as he stared at the young, vibrant physique that had supplanted the bent and decrepit man nearing his very last mile. In a neat reversal of the pull of time, this man calling himself BJ had grown far younger since Tor had last seen him, and Tor could not begrudge him that. This man looked like he could now play football at a level that ranked right up there with the greatest, with those legends seemingly not bound by the laws of physics that kept the rest of mankind grounded and mostly floundering. He looked unconquerable. He looked... perfect.

"Just a man who moseys around, helping folks who some-times need it."

"You helped me," said Tor. "You made a lot of things clearer to me."

"You helped yourself."

"I want to thank you."

"You already have."

And though he never remembered how it came to be, Tor somehow found himself out of that room and free of that tunnel and standing under the bluest sky and under the most brilliant sun he could ever recall in this stark manmade valley of perpetu-ally darkened hues. And even that stubborn east wind had sub-sided, bothering him no longer, as Tor North walked out of Herschel Ruggles Stadium for the last time.

THE BEST OF THE REST

BY OTTO PENZLER

America's game, for such a long time, was baseball. Now, it is football. What does this say about us as a country? Is the image of baseball as a soft summer game, played in the sunshine in idyllic cornfields, accurate? And is it the diametric opposite of football, the violent cold-weather game played under steel gray skies on chewed up, muddy, or half-frozen tundra?

Well, yes. Baseball is pick-up games, and high school ball, Pee Wee Leagues and Little Leagues, and minor leagues as well as the majors. If you have enough kids, a ball and a bat, some gloves and some grass, you can get up a game. Dads play catch with their sons (and, nowadays, with their daughters), moms go to games, and a rain storm sends everyone home.

Football needs a lot of very large guys, helmets, cleats, pads and drugs to build up muscles or to ease the pain, since the big guys are hitting each other as hard and as often as possible. Moms shudder to hear that their sons are going out to play football, and daughters need not apply. Except in the South, games are played in driving snowstorms, sub-freezing weather, rain and sleet, and no one goes home unless there's an earthquake.

The perception, accurate or not, is that football is an urban sport, while baseball has the feel of a small town game. Cities are tougher, more violent, than villages, and football is tougher, more violent, than baseball.

If a baseball player is hit by the ball, or another player, it is almost always an accident, a mistake. If a football player isn't hit by another player, it's a mistake. The tempo of the game is faster, the action on the field louder and rougher, which may be a microcosm of today's music, films, books, television shows—of life in the 21st century in general.

Baseball has the joyous Sammy Sosa, the gentlemanly Cal

Ripken, the reserved Greg Maddux, the modest Derek Jeter, the inspirational Tony Gwynn. Granted, it also has the thuggish Albert Belle, the boorish Bobby Bonds, the selfish Ruben Sierra and the whining Carl Everett, but they are amateurs compared to the rap sheets that pass for the biographies of National Football League stars.

When contemplating the relationship of crime and football, where does one begin? Is it with Jim Brown, arguably the greatest running back in the history of professional football? Brown was repeatedly arrested for violence against the women in his life, including the beating of his wife, sexually molesting two teenaged girls, and inevitably, rape. Largely because of his fame, he was never convicted of a single crime.

Neither was O.J. Simpson, acquitted in a mockery of a criminal trial of killing his wife and a male friend. When found guilty in a civil suit, he fled his state's jurisdiction and lives happily today, relentlessly searching for his wife's murderer (as he vowed to do after the trial) on the golf courses of Florida.

Rae Carruth, the first-round pick of the Carolina Panthers, wasn't quite as lucky as his predecessors. He got 25 years in a North Carolina prison for arranging the heinous murder of his pregnant girl friend, and might have gotten away with it if he and his co-conspirators hadn't had a collective IQ that measured a single digit.

But we also shouldn't forget Ray Lewis, the 2001 Super Bowl MVP who wore a Baltimore Ravens uniform instead of prison stripes, having beat charges of murder and battering a woman (twice on the latter count). The brawny linebacker clearly subscribes to the tasteless old joke: "What do you say to a woman with two black eyes?" "Nothing. You've told her twice already."

These men, the biggest and strongest athletes in the nation, seem to find their manhood in assaulting women. Mario Bates of Detroit was convicted of beating his wife. Denard Walker, now a multi-millionaire with the Denver Broncos, was convicted of hitting his girlfriend, the mother of his son. Corey Dillon, in the same year that he set a single game rushing record of 278 yards for the

Cincinnati Bengals, beat his wife but pled guilty to a lesser charge to avoid trial. Mustafah Muhammad of the Indianapolis Colts was convicted of hitting his wife but still suits up every Sunday.

There are more, many more, but you get the idea. Crime is no stranger to the world of football and those who inhabit that world. The stories in this book illuminate a wide range of crimes —some nearly as heinous as those committed in real life by people who continue to be idolized—some on Sundays, some every day of their lives.

So here is a killer line-up of authors, a virtual Pro-Bowl of some of the finest practitioners of the mystery genre at work today. While many of these adventures seem chillingly realistic, almost journalistic, they are all fictional stories about fictional characters (I think).

David Baldacci is one of the best-selling writers in the world. His thrillers have broken sales records in the United States and abroad, beginning with *Absolute Power*, which was quickly filmed with Clint Eastwood and became a box-office smash.

Lawrence Block remains one of the most popular and versatile writers in the mystery world, creating such significant characters as Bernie Rhodenbarr, the bookselling burglar; Keller, his amoral hit man: and Matthew Scudder, the recovering alcoholic private detective.

Arguably the greatest private eye writer of the past quarter-century, James Crumley has created protagonists who are alcoholic, drug abusing, borderline criminals but nonetheless have a powerful moral code. His *The Last Good Kiss* is a genuine classic of detective fiction.

Few mystery writers of the past decade have been more honored for their short fiction than Brendan DuBois, whose work has appeared in numerous periodicals, including *Playboy* and *Ellery Queen's Mystery Magazine*. "The Dark Snow" was picked for the *Best American Mystery Stories of the Century*, edited by Tony Hillerman.

Tim Green played as a linebacker in the National Football League for many years before his charm and intelligence brought him into the broadcast booth as a color commentator for NFL games. His most recent novels have moved off the gridiron into the courtroom to outstanding critical acclaim.

Colin Harrison, former Deputy Editor of *Harper's* magazine, has written some of the most violent, yet critically lauded, thrillers of the past decade, including *Manhattan Nocturne,* which is so dark that "the only comfort comes from the neon flashes of his prose," according to *People* magazine.

Dennis Lehane, creator of the dazzling Patrick Kenzie and Angela Gennaro series of Boston private eye novels that are as good as it gets, moved out of the series last year with *Mystic River*, which made the *New York Times* bestseller list for nine weeks.

The colorful Mike Lupica, America's best-known sports-writer, appears on the weekly television series, "The Sports Reporters," as well as having a regular column in the *New York Daily News*. His first novel, *Dead Air*, was nominated for an Edgar Allan Poe Award in 1987.

Although Brad Meltzer has written only three books (*The Tenth Justice, Dead Even* and *The First Counsel*) all three have made the *New York Times* best-seller list and caused *People* magazine to rank him with John Grisham, Scott Turow and David Baldacci.

The best-selling Carol O'Connell has been compared with Ruth Rendell and Minette Walters (*Minneapolis Star-Tribune*) and William Faulkner (*People* magazine), among others, but she remains a totally original author. "The Arcane Receiver" is her first short story.

Anne Perry, the wildly popular author of Victorian detective stories, cheated and wrote about rugby, saying it qualifies as foot-ball and, when you read this powerful story, you'll see that American football could be substituted without changing the criminal aspects. She won an Edgar for her short story, "Heroes."

Gary Phillips writes tough, hard-boiled detective fiction set in Los Angeles. His private eye hero, Ivan Monk, made his first appearances in *Violent Spring* (1994), which was optioned for an original TV movie by HBO.

Few writers in the past dozen years or so have been nominated or won more awards than Peter Robinson, whose Yorkshire Detective Chief Inspector Alan Banks made his debut in *Gallows View*. His short story, "Missing in Action" won the Edgar in 2001, the year after *In A Dry Season* was nominated for Best Novel, as had *Wednesday's Child* in 1992.

Orin Boyd is a tough Long Island street cop, as was author John Westermann for twenty years. Boyd first appeared in *Exit Wounds* (1990) and then in *The Honor Farm* (1996), which was a recent big-budget movie starring Steven Segal.

Now, enough of the pre-game stuff. Turn the page for the kickoff.

THE EHRENGRAF REVERSE

BY LAWRENCE BLOCK

"I didn't do it," Blaine Starkey said.

"Of course you didn't."

"Everyone thinks I did it," Starkey went on, "and I guess I can understand why. But I'm innocent."

"Of course you are."

"I'm not a murderer."

"Of course you're not."

"Not this time," the man said. "Mr. Ehrengraf, it's not supposed to matter whether a lawyer thinks his client is guilty or innocent. But it matters to me. I really am innocent, and it's important that you believe me."

"I do."

"I don't know why it's so important," Starkey said, "but it just is, and—" He paused, and seemed to register for the first time what Ehrengraf had been saying all along. His big open face showed puzzlement. "You do?"

"Yes."

"You believe I'm innocent."

"Absolutely."

"That's pretty amazing, Mr. Ehrengraf. Nobody else believes me."

Ehrengraf regarded his client. Indeed, if you looked at the man's record you could hardly avoid presuming him guilty. But once you turned your gaze into his cornflower blue eyes, how could you fail to recognize the innocence gleaming there?

Even if you didn't believe the man, how would you have the nerve to tell him so? Blaine Starkey's was, to say the least, an imposing presence. When you saw him on the television screen, catching a pass and racing downfield, breaking tackles as effortlessly as a politician breaks his word, you didn't appreciate the sheer size of him. All the men on the field were huge, and your eye learned to see them as normal.

In a jail cell, across a little pine table, you began to realize just how massive a man Blaine Starkey was. He stood as many inches over six feet as Ehrengraf stood under it, and was big in the shoulders and narrow in the waist, with thighs like tree trunks and arms like—well, words failed Ehrengraf. The man was enormous.

"The whole world thinks I killed Claureen," Starkey said, "and it's not hard to see why. I mean, look at my stats."

His stats? Thousands of yards gained rushing. Hundreds of passes caught. No end of touchdowns scored. Ehrengraf, who was more interested in watching the action on the field than in crunching the numbers, knew nevertheless that the big man's statistics were impressive.

He also knew Starkey meant another set of stats.

"I mean," the man said, "it's not like this never happened before. Three women, three coffins. Hell, Mr. Ehrengraf, if I was a hockey player they'd call it the hat trick."

"But it's not hockey," Ehrengraf assured him, "and it's not football, either. You're an innocent man, and there's no reason you should have to pay for a crime you didn't commit."

"You really think I'm innocent," Starkey said.

"Absolutely."

"That's what everybody's supposed to presume, until it's proved otherwise. Is that what you mean? That I'm innocent for the time being, far as the law's concerned?"

Ehrengraf shook his head. "That's not what I mean."

"You mean innocent no matter what the jury says."

"I mean exactly what you meant earlier," the little lawyer said. "You didn't kill your wife. You're entirely innocent of her death, and the jury should never be in a position to say anything on the subject, because you should never be brought to trial. You're an innocent man, Mr. Starkey."

The football player took a deep breath, and Ehrengraf was surprised that there was any air left in the cell. "That's just so hard for me to believe."

"That you're innocent?"

"Hell, I *know* I'm innocent," Starkey said. "What's hard to believe is that *you* believe it."

But how could Ehrengraf believe otherwise? He fingered the knot in his deep blue necktie and reflected on the presumption of innocence—not the one which had long served as a cardinal precept of Anglo-American jurisprudence, but a higher, more personal principle. The Ehrengraf presumption. Any client of Martin H. Ehrengraf's was innocent. Not until proven guilty, but until the end of time.

But he didn't want to get into a philosophical discussion with Blaine Starkey. He kept it simple, explaining that he only represented the innocent.

The football player took this in. His face fell. "Then if you change your mind," he said, "you'll drop me like a hot rock. Is that about right?"

"I won't change my mind."

"If you get to thinking I'm guilty—"

"I'll never think that."

"But—"

"We're wasting time," Ehrengraf told him. "We both know you're innocent. Why dispute a point on which we're already in agreement?"

"I guess I really found the one man who believes me," Starkey said. "Now where are we gonna find twelve more?"

"It's my earnest hope we won't have to," Ehrengraf said. "I rarely see the inside of a courtroom, Mr. Starkey. My fees are very high, but I have to earn them in order to receive them."

Starkey scratched his head "That's what I'm not too clear on."

"It's simple enough. I take cases on a contingency basis. I don't get paid unless and until you walk free."

"I've heard of that in civil cases," Starkey said, "but I didn't know there were any criminal lawyers who operated that way."

"As far as I know," Ehrengraf said, "I am the only one. And I don't depend on courtroom pyrotechnics. I represent the innocent, and through my efforts their innocence becomes undeniably clear to all concerned. Then and only then do I collect my fee."

And what would that be? Ehrengraf named a number.

"Whole lot of zeroes at the end of it," the football player said, "but it's nothing to the check I wrote out for the Proud Crowd. Five of them, and they spent close to a year on the case, hiring experts and doing studies and surveys and I don't know what else. A man can make a lot of money if he can run the ball and catch a pass now and then. I guess I can afford your fee, plus whatever the costs and expenses come to."

"The fee is all-inclusive," Ehrengraf said.

"If that's so," Starkey said, "I'd say it's a bargain. And I only pay if I get off?"

"And you will, sir."

"If I do, I don't guess I'll begrudge you your fee. And if I don't, do I get my retainer back? Not that I'd have a great use for it, but—"

"There'll be no retainer," Ehrengraf said smoothly. "I like to earn my money before I receive it."

"I never heard of anybody like you, Mr. Ehrengraf."

"There isn't anyone like me," Ehrengraf said. "I've thrilled to watch you play, and I don't believe there's anyone like you, either. We're both unique."

"Well," Starkey said.

"And yet you're charged with killing your wife," Ehrengraf said smoothly. "Hard to believe, but there it is."

"Not so hard to believe. I've been tried twice for murder and got off both times. How many times can a man kill his wife and get away with it?"

It was a good question, but Ehrengraf chose not to address it. "The first woman wasn't your wife," he said.

"My girlfriend. Kate Waldecker. I was in my junior year at Texas State." He looked at his hands. "We were in bed together, and one way or another my hands got around her neck."

"You engaged Joel Daggett as your attorney, if I remember correctly."

"The Bulldog," Starkey said fondly. "He came up with this rough sex defense. Brought in witnesses to testify that Kate liked to be hurt while she was making love, liked to be choked half to death. Made her out to be real kinky, and a tramp in the bargain. I have to say I felt sorry for her folks. They were in tears through the trial." He sighed. "But what else could he do? I mean, I got out of bed and called the cops, told everybody I did it. Daggett got the confession suppressed, but there was still plenty of evidence that I did it. He had to find a way to keep it from being murder."

"And he was successful. You were found not guilty."

"Yeah, but that was bullshit. Kate didn't like it rough. Fact, she was always telling me to slow down, to be gentler with her." He frowned. "Hard to say what happened that night. We'd been arguing earlier, but I thought I was over being mad about that. Next thing I knew she was dead and I was unhooking my hands from around her throat. I always figured the steroids I was taking might have had something to do with it, but maybe not. Maybe I just got carried away and killed her. Anyway, Daggett saw to it that I got away with it."

"You didn't go back for your senior year."

"No, I turned pro right after the trial. I would have liked to get my degree, but I didn't figure they'd cheer as hard for me after I'd killed a fellow student. Besides, I had a big legal bill to pay, and that's where the signing bonus went."

"You went with the Wranglers."

"I was their first-round draft choice and I was with them for four seasons. Born in Texas, went to school in Texas, and I thought I'd play my whole career in Texas. Married a Texas girl, too. Jacey was beautiful, even if she was hell on wheels. High-strung, you know? Threw a glass ashtray at me once, hit me right here on the cheekbone. Another inch and I might have lost an eye." He shook his head. "I figured we'd get divorced sooner or later. I just wanted to stay married to her until I got tired of, you know, goin' to bed with her. But I never did get tired of her that way, or divorced from her, either, and then the next thing I knew she was dead."

"She killed herself."

"They found her in bed, with bruises on her neck. And they picked me up at the country club, where I was sitting by myself in the bar, hitting the bourbon pretty good. They hauled me downtown and charged me with murder."

"You didn't give a statement."

"Didn't say a word. I knew that much from my first trial. Of course I couldn't get the Bulldog this time, on account of he was dead. Lee Waldecker walked up to him in a restaurant in Austin about a year after my acquittal, shot him in front of a whole roomful of people. I guess he never got over the job Daggett did on his sister's reputation. He said he could almost forgive me, because all I did was kill Kate, but what Daggett did to her was worse than murder."

"He's still serving his sentence, isn't he?"

"Life without parole. A jury might have cut him loose, or slapped him on the wrist with a short sentence, but he went and pleaded guilty. Said he did it in front of witnesses on purpose, so he wouldn't have some lawyer twisting the truth."

"So you got a whole team of lawyers," Ehrengraf said. "The press made up a name for them."

"The Proud Crowd. Each one thought he was the hottest thing going, and they spent a lot of time just cutting each other apart. And they sure weren't shy about charging for their services. But I'd made a lot of money all those years, and I figured to make a lot more if I kept on playing, and the Wranglers wanted to make sure I had the best possible defense."

"Not rough sex this time."

"No, I don't guess you can get by with that more than once. What's funny is that Jacey *did* like it rough. Matter of fact, there weren't too many ways she didn't like it. If the Bulldog was around, and if I hadn't already used that defense once already, rough sex would have had me home free. Jacey was everything Daggett tried to make Kate look like, and there would have been dozens of people willing to swear to it."

"As it turned out," Ehrengraf said, "it was suicide, wasn't it? And the police tampered with the evidence?"

"That was the line the Proud Crowd took. There were impressions on her neck from a large pair of hands, but they dug up a forensics expert who testified that they'd been inflicted after death, like somebody'd strangled her after she's already been dead for some time. And they had another expert testify that there were rope marks on her neck, underneath the hand prints, suggesting she'd hanged herself and been cut down. There were fibers found on and near the corpse, and another defense expert matched them to a rope that had been retrieved from a Dumpster. And they found residue of talcum powder on the rope, and another expert testified that it was the same kind of talcum powder Jacey used, and had used the day of her death."

"So many experts," Ehrengraf murmured.

"And every damn one of 'em sent in a bill," Starkey said, "but I can't complain, because they earned their money. According to the Proud Crowd, Jacey hanged herself. I came home, saw her like that, and just couldn't deal with it. I cut her down and tried to revive her, then lost it and went to the club to brace myself with a few drinks while I figured out what to do next. Meantime, a neighbor called the cops, and as far as they were concerned I was this old boy who made a couple million dollars a year playing a kid's game, and already put one wife in the ground and got away with it. So they made sure I wouldn't get away with it a second time by taking the rope and losing it in a Dumpster, and pressing their hands into her neck to make it look like manual strangulation."

"And is that how it happened?"

Starkey rolled his eyes. "How it happened," he said, "is we were having an argument, and I took this hunk of rope and put it around her neck and strangled the life out of her."

Ehrengraf winced.

"Don't worry," his client went on. "Nobody can hear us, and what I tell you's privileged anyway, and besides it'd be double jeopardy, because twelve people already decided they believed the Proud Crowd's version. But they must have been the only twelve people in the country who bought it, because the rest of the world figured out that I did it. And got away with it again."

"You were acquitted."

"I was and I wasn't," he said. "Legally I was off the hook, but that didn't mean I got my old life back. The Wranglers put out this press release about how glad they were that justice was served and an innocent man exonerated, but nobody would look me in the eye. First chance they got, they traded me."

"And you've been with the Mastodons ever since."

"And I love it here," he said. "I don't even mind the winters.

Back when I played for the Wranglers I hated coming up here for late-season games, but I got so I liked the cold weather. You get used to it."

Ehrengraf, a native, had never had to get used to the climate. But he nodded anyway.

"At first," Starkey said, "I thought about quitting. But I owed all this money to the Proud Crowd, and how was I going to earn big money off a football field? I lost my endorsements, you know. I had this one commercial, I don't know if you remember it, where Minnie Mouse is sitting on my lap and sort of flirting with me."

"You were selling a toilet-bowl cleaner," Ehrengraf recalled.

"Yeah, and when they dropped me I figured that meant I wasn't good enough to clean toilets. But what choice did they have? People were saying things like you could just about see the marks on Minnie's neck. Long story short, no more commercials. So what was I gonna do but play?"

"Of course."

"Besides, I was in my mid-twenties and I loved the game. Now it's ten years later and I still love it. I got Cletis Braden breathing down my neck, trying to take my job away, but I figure it's gonna be a few more years before he can do it. Love the city, live here year round, wouldn't want to live anywhere else. Love the house I bought. Love the people, even love the winters. Snow? What's so bad about snow?"

"It's pretty," Ehrengraf said.

"Damn pretty. It's around for a while and then it melts. And then it's gone." He made a fist, opened it, looked at his palm. "Gone, like everything else. Like my career. Like my damn life."

For a moment Ehrengraf thought the big man might burst into tears, and rather hoped he would not. The moment passed, and the little lawyer suggested they talk about the late Mrs. Starkey.

"Which one? No, I know you mean Claureen. Local girl, born and bred here. Went away to college and got on the cheerleading squad. I guess she got to know the players pretty good." He rolled his eyes. "Came back home, went to work teaching school, but she found a way to hang around football players. I'd been here a couple of years by then, and the Mastodons don't lack for feminine companionship, so I was doing okay in that department. But it was time to get married, and I figured she was the one."

Romeo and Juliet, Ehrengraf thought. Tristan and Isolde. Blaine and Claureen.

"And it was okay," Starkey said. "No kids, and that was disappointing, but we had a good life and we got along okay. I never ran around on her here in town, and what you do on the road don't count. Everybody knows that."

"And the day she died?"

"We had a home game coming up with the Leopards. I went out for a couple of beers after practice, but I left early because Clete Braden showed up and joined us and I can tire of his company pretty quick. I drove around for an hour or two. Went over to Boulevard Mall to see what playing at the multiplex. They had twelve movies, but nothing I wanted to see. I thought I'd walk around the mall, maybe buy something, but I can't go anywhere without people recognizing me, and sometimes I just don't want to deal with that. I drove around some more and went home."

"And discovered her body."

"In the living room, crumpled up on the rug next to the fireplace, bareass naked and stone cold dead. First thing I thought was she had a fainting spell. She'd get lightheaded if she went too long between meals, and she'd been trying to drop a few pounds. Don't ask me why, she looked fine to me, but you know women."

"Nobody does," Ehrengraf said.

"Well, that's the damn truth, but you know what I mean. Anyway, I knelt down and touched her, and right away I knew she was dead. And then I saw her head was all bloody, and I thought, well, here we go again."

"You called the police."

"Last thing I wanted to do. Wanted to get in the car and just drive, but I knew not to do that. And I wanted to pour a stiff drink and I didn't let myself do that, either. I called 911 and I sat in a chair, and when the cops came I let 'em in. I didn't answer any of their questions. I barely heard them. I just kept my mouth shut, and they brought me here, and I wound up calling you."

"And it's good you did," Ehrengraf told him. "You're innocent, and soon the whole world will know it."

Three days later the two men faced one another in the same cell across the same little table. Blaine Starkey looked weary. Part of it was the listless sallowness one saw in imprisoned men, but Ehrengraf noted as well the sag of the shoulders, the lines around the mouth. He was wearing the same clothes he'd worn at their previous meeting. Ehrengraf, in a three piece suit with a banker's stripe and a tie striped like a coral snake, wondered not for the first time if he ought to dress down on such occasions, to put his client at ease. As always, he decided that dressing down was not his sort of thing.

"I've done some investigation," he reported. "Your wife's blood sugar was low."

"Well, she wasn't eating. I told you that."

"The Medical Examiner estimated the time of death at two to four hours before you reported discovering her body."

"I said she felt cold to the touch."

"She died," Ehrengraf said, "sometime after football practice was over for the day. The prosecution is going to contend that you had time before you met your teammates for drinks—"

"To race home, hit Claureen upside the head, and then rush out to grab a beer?"

"—or afterward, during the time you were driving around and trying to decide on a movie."

"I had the time then," Starkey allowed, "but that's not how I spent it."

"I know that. When you got home, was the door locked?"

"Sure. We keep it so it locks when you pull it shut."

"Did you use your key?"

"Easier than ringing the bell and waiting. Her car was there, so I knew she was home. I let myself in and keyed in the code so the burglar alarm wouldn't go off, and then I walked into the living room, and you know the rest."

"She died," Ehrengraf said, "as a result of massive trauma to the skull. There were two blows, one to the temple, the other to the back of the head. The first may have resulted from her fall, when she struck herself upon the sharp corner of the fireplace surround. The second blow was almost certainly inflicted by a massive bronze statue of a horse."

"She picked it out," Starkey said. "It was French, about a hundred and fifty years old. I didn't think it looked like any horse a reasonable man would want to place a bet on, but she fell in love with it and said it'd be perfect on the mantel."

Ehrengraf fingered the knot of his tie. "Your wife was nude," he said.

"Maybe she just got out of the shower," the big man said. "Or you know what I bet it was? She was on her way to the shower."

"By way of the living room?"

"If she was on the stair machine, which was what she would do when she decided she was getting fat. An apple for breakfast and an enema for lunch, and hopping on and off the stair machine all day long. She'd exercise naked if she was warm, or if she wore a sweat suit she'd leave it there in the exercise room and parade through the house naked."

"Then it all falls into place," Ehrengraf said. "She wasn't eating enough and was exercising excessively. She completed an ill-advised session on the stair climber, shed her exercise clothes if in fact she'd been wearing any in the first place, and walked through the living room on her way to the shower."

"She'd do that, all right."

"Her blood sugar was dangerously low. She got dizzy, and felt faint. She started to fall, and reached out to steady herself, grabbing the bronze horse. Then she lost consciousness and fell, dragging the horse from its perch on the mantelpiece as she did so. She went down hard, hitting her forehead on the bricks, and the horse came down hard as well, striking her on the head. And, alone in the house, the unfortunate woman died an accidental death."

"That's got to be it," Starkey said. "I couldn't put it together. All I knew was I didn't kill her. You can push that argument, right? You can get me off?"

But Ehrengraf was shaking his head. "If you had spent the twelve hours preceding her death in the company of an archbishop and a Supreme Court justice," he said, "and if both of those worthies were at your side when you discovered your wife's body, then it might be possible to advance that theory successfully in court."

"But—"

"The whole world thinks of you as a man who got away with murder twice already. Do you think a jury is going to let you get away with it a third time?"

"The prosecution can't introduce either of those earlier cases as evidence, can they?"

"They can't even mention them," Ehrengraf said, "or it's immediate grounds for a mistrial. But why mention them when everyone already knows all about them? If they didn't know to begin with, they're reading the full story every day in the newspaper and watching clips of your two trials on television."

"Then it's hopeless."

"Only if you go to trial."

"What else can I do? I could try fleeing the country, but where would I hide? What would I do, play professional football in Iraq or North Korea? And I can't even try, because they won't let me out on bail."

Ehrengraf put the tips of his fingers together. "I've no intention of letting this case go to trial," he said. "I don't much care for the whole idea of leaving a man's fate in the hands of twelve people, not one of them clever enough to get out of jury duty."

Puzzlement showed in Starkey's face.

"I remember a run you made against the Jackals," Ehrengraf said. "The quarterback gave the ball to that other fellow—"

"Clete Braden," Starkey said heavily.

"—and he began running to his right, and you were running toward him, and he handed the ball to you, and you swept around to the left, after all the Jackals had shifted over to stop Braden's run to the right."

Starkey brightened. "I remember the play," he said. "The reverse. When it works, it's one of the prettiest plays in football."

"It worked against the Jackals."

"I ran it in. Better than sixty yards from scrimmage, and once I was past midfield no one had a shot at me."

Ehrengraf beamed. "Ah, yes. The reverse. It is something to see, the reverse."

It was a new Blaine Starkey that walked into Martin Ehrengraf's office. He was dressed differently, for one thing, his double-breasted tan suit clearly the work of an accomplished tailor, his maroon silk shirt open at its flowing collar, his cordovan wing tips buffed to a high sheen. His skin had thrown off the jailhouse pallor and glowed with the ruddy health of a life lived outdoors. There was a sparkle in his eyes, spring in his step, a set to his shoulders. It did the little lawyer's heart good to see him.

He was holding a football, passing it from hand to hand as he approached Ehrengraf's desk. How small it looked, Ehrengraf thought, in those big hands. And with what ease could those hands encircle a throat. . .

Ehrengraf pushed the thought aside, and his hand went to his necktie. It was his Caedmon Society tie, his inevitable choice on triumphant occasions, and a nice complement to his cocoa brown blazer and fawn slacks.

"The game ball," Starkey announced, reaching to place it on the one clear spot on the little lawyer's cluttered desk. "They gave it to me after Sunday's game with the Ocelots. See, all the players signed it. All but Cletis Braden, but I don't guess he'll be signing too many game balls from here on."

"I shouldn't think so."

"And here's where I wrote something myself," he said, pointing.

Ehrengraf read: *To Marty Ehrengraf, who made it all possible. From your buddy, Blaine Starkey.*

"Marty," Ehrengraf said.

Starkey lowered his eyes. "I didn't know about that," he admitted. "If people called you Marty or Martin or what. I mean, all I ever called you was 'Mr. Ehrengraf.' But with sports memorabilia, people generally like it to look like, you know, like them and the athlete are good buddies. Do they call you Marty?"

They never had, but Ehrengraf merely smiled at the question and took the ball in his hands. "I shall treasure this," he said simply.

"Here's something else to treasure," Starkey said. "It's auto-graphed, too."

"Ah," Ehrengraf said, and took the check, and raised his eye-brows at the amount. It was not the sum he had mentioned at their initial meeting. This had happened before, when a client's gratitude gave way to innate penuriousness, and Ehrengraf routinely made short work of such attempts to reduce his fee. But this check was for more than he had demanded, and that had not happened before.

"It's a bonus," Starkey said, anticipating the question. "I don't know if there's such a thing in your profession. We get them all the time in the NFL. It's not insulting, is it? Like tipping the owner of the restaurant? Because I surely didn't intend it that way."

Ehrengraf, nonplussed, shook his head. "Money is only insulting," he managed, "when there's too little of it." He beamed, and stowed the check in his wallet.

"I'll tell you," Starkey said, "writing checks isn't generally my favorite thing in the whole world, but I couldn't have been happi-er when I was writing out that one. Couple of weeks ago I was the worst thing since Jack the Ripper, and now I'm everybody's hero. Who was it said there's no second half in the game of life?"

"Scott Fitzgerald wrote something along those lines," Ehrengraf said, "but I believe he phrased it a little differently."

"Well, he was wrong," Starkey said, "and you proved it. And who would have dreamed it would turn out this way?"

Ehrengraf smiled.

"Clete Braden," Starkey said. "I knew the sonofabitch was after my job, but who'd have guessed he was after my wife, too? I swear I never had a clue those two were slipping around behind my back. It's still hard to believe Claureen was cheating on me when I wasn't even on a road trip."

"They must have been very clever in their deceit."

"But stupid at the same time," Starkey said. "Taking her to a motel and signing in as Mr. and Mrs. Cleveland Brassman. Same initials, plus he used his own handwriting on the registration card. Made up a fake address but used his real license plate number, just switching two digits around." He rolled his eyes. "And then leaving a pair of her panties in the room. Where was it they found them? Wedged under the chair cushion or some such?"

"I believe so."

"All that time and the maids never found them. I guess they don't knock themselves out cleaning the rooms in a place like that, but I'd still have to call it a piece of luck the panties were still there."

"Luck," Ehrengraf agreed.

"And no question they were hers, either. Matched the ones in her dresser drawer, and had her DNA all over 'em. It's a wonderful thing, DNA."

"A miracle of modern forensic science."

"Why'd they even go to a motel in the first place? Why not take her to his place? He wasn't married, he had women in and out of his apartment all the time."

"Perhaps he didn't want to be seen with her."

"Long as I wasn't the one doing the seeing, what difference could it make?"

"None," Ehrengraf said, "unless he was afraid of what people might remember afterward."

Starkey thought about that. Then his eyes widened. "He planned it all along," he said.

"It certainly seems that way."

"Wanted to make damn sure he got my job, by seeing to it that I wasn't around to compete for it. He didn't just lose his temper when he smashed her head with that horse. It was all part of the plan—kill her and frame me for it."

"Diabolical," Ehrengraf said.

"That explains what he wrote on that note," Starkey said. "The one they found at the very back of her underwear drawer, arranging to meet that last day after practice. 'Make sure you burn this,' he wrote. And he didn't even sign it. But it was in his handwriting."

"So the experts say."

"And on a piece of his stationery. The top part was torn off, with his name and address on it, but it was the same brand of bond paper. It would have been nice if they could have found the piece he tore off and matched them up, but I guess you can't have everything."

"Perhaps they haven't looked hard enough," Ehrengraf murmured. "There was another note as well, as I recall. One that she wrote."

"On one of the printed memo slips with her name on it. A little love note from her to him, and he didn't have the sense to throw it out. Carried it around in his wallet."

"It was probably from early in their relationship," Ehrengraf said, "and very likely he'd forgotten it was there."

"He must have. It surprised the hell out of him when the cops went through his wallet and there it was."

"I imagine it did."

"He must have gone to my house straight from practice. Wouldn't have been a trick to get her out of her clothes, seeing as he'd been managing that all along. 'My, Claureen, isn't that a cute little horse.' 'Yes, it's French, it's over a hundred years old.' 'Is that right? Let me just get the feel of it.' And that's the end of Claureen. A shame he didn't leave a fingerprint or two on the horse just for good measure."

"You can't have everything," Ehrengraf said. "Wiping his prints off the horse would seem to be one of the few intelligent things Mr. Braden managed. But they can make a good case against him without it. Of course much depends on his choice of an attorney."

"Maybe he'll call you," Starkey said with a wink. "But I guess that wouldn't do him any good, seeing as you only represent the innocent. What I hear, he's fixing to put together a Proud Crowd of his own. Figure they'll get him off?"

"It may be difficult to convict him," Ehrengraf allowed, "but he's already been tried and found guilty in the court of public opinion."

"The league suspended him, and of course he's off the Mastodons' roster. But what's really amazing is the way everybody's turned around as far as I'm concerned. Before, I was a man who got away with killing two women, but they could live with that as long as I could put it all together on the field. Then I killed a third woman, and they flat out hated me, and then it turns out I didn't kill Claureen, I was an innocent man framed for it, and they did a full-scale turnaround, and the talk is maybe I really was innocent those other two times, just the way the two juries decided I was. All of a sudden there's a whole lot of people telling each other the system works and feeling real good about it."

"As well they might," said Ehrengraf.

"They cheer you when you catch a pass," Starkey said philosophically, "and they boo you when you drop one. Except for you, Mr. Ehrengraf, there wasn't a person around who believed I didn't do it. But you did, and you figured out how the evidence showed Claureen's death was accidental. Low blood sugar, too much exercise, and she got dizzy and fell and pulled the horse down on top of her."

"Yes."

"And then you figured out they'd never buy that, true or false. So you dug deeper."

"It was the only chance," Ehrengraf said modestly.

"And they might not buy that Claureen killed herself by accident, but they loved the idea that she was cheating on me and Clete killed her so I'd be nailed for it."

"The Ehrengraf reverse."

"How's that?"

"The Ehrengraf reverse. When the evidence is all running one way, you hand off the ball and sweep around the other end." He spread his hands. "And streak down the sideline and into the end zone."

"Touchdown," Starkey said. "We win, and Braden's the goat and I'm the hero."

"As you clearly were on Sunday."

"I guess I had a pretty decent game."

"Eight pass receptions, almost two hundred yards rushing—yes, I'd say you had a good game."

"Say, were those seats okay?"

"Row M on the fifty-yard line? They were the best seats in the stadium."

"It was a beautiful day for it, too, wasn't it? And I couldn't do a thing wrong. Oh, next week I'll probably fumble three times and run into my own blockers a lot, but I'll have this one to remember."

Ehrengraf took the game ball in his hands. "And so will I," he said.

"Well, I wanted you to have a souvenir. And the bonus, well, I got more money coming in these days than I ever figured to see. Every time the phone rings it's another product endorsement coming my way, and I don't have to wait too long between rings, either. Hey, speaking of the reverse, how'd you like the one we ran Sunday?"

"Beautiful," Ehrengraf said fervently. "A work of art."

"You know, I was thinking of you when they called it in the huddle. Fact, when the defense was on the field I asked the coach if we couldn't run that play. Would have served me right if I'd been dumped for a loss, but that's not what happened."

"You gained forty yards," Ehrengraf said, "and if that one man hadn't missed a downfield block, you'd have had another touchdown."

"Well, it's a pretty play," Blaine Starkey said. "There's really nothing like the reverse."

SEMI-PRO

BY JAMES CRUMLEY

Riley swore to himself that the first time was a fluke, almost a freak accident. Hell, he'd swear on his daughter Tricia's ailing heart that he hadn't meant to go into the bank. After his unsuccessful negotiations with the district purchasing officer, a lean brown man who looked as if he didn't have any funding problems, Riley decided to park in a downtown lot near the river, a lot in the center of the last decent bit of the old city, where he could have a quiet drink when he finished his customer calls. He would stash his old Honda, and make his calls on foot as he had many times.

His customers survived on the outskirts of the potholed streets and ranks of abandoned buildings filled with broken windows. Most of the dull faces that stared at his passage from the gutters and corner bars were black, a black gone gray as if all the anger had been washed from them. His customers were all white, aging dentists who yanked rotten teeth from winos and welfare bums for cash on the barrelhead. He had just finished with his last dentist, a blue-faced old man, his skin marbled by years of morphine abuse, when Riley stepped out into the street, the sky opened and dumped a steady burst of rain straight down. Riley knew he was at least a dozen blocks from his car, so he ducked into a nearby doorway, a secondhand military surplus store. When it seemed that the rain wasn't just a summer squall but a serious downpour, Riley bought a used camouflage poncho and bush hat, then hiked through the damp, derelict neighborhood of abandoned storefronts and moldering buildings that marked the decaying center of the dying city, an area of town so blighted and poor that even crack whores avoided it.

Riley turned down an alley, thinking it a shortcut. The rain halted as if somebody had turned off the faucet, and a sudden burst of sunlight swept like a sheet of white fire off the wet bricks. Disoriented by this sudden turn of events, Riley slipped on his sunglasses, then turned a corner to find himself facing a large heavily tinted plate glass window framed by two concrete pillars. Large gilt letters announced the Downtown Branch of First Farmer's Bank in an arch over a dark figure. He was as stunned to find a bank in this neighborhood as he was to realize that the dark caped figure was his. The dropping brim of the cloth had hid his bald head and with the dark glasses, almost obscured his face. In the poncho his long, lanky body looked much more stocky and somehow shorter, not himself at all.

Everything became immediately clear. Riley was in and out of the bank within three minutes. The pen, the note, and forty-five hundred in cash stashed in his nondescript briefcase. A moment later, he stopped in the alley to stuff the poncho and hat inside, too. Now he was home free.

Mildred and Tricia were sitting in the front porch swing, sipping sun tea and basking in the late afternoon sunlight like a pair of permanent invalids, when Riley pulled into the driveway of the rundown split level ranch. He had stayed out on the road for ten days straight, trying to get ahead before the start of football season. But for all the fuss Mildred and Tricia made, he might have been gone ten minutes. They didn't even look over when he climbed out of the car, just kept their pale faces turned into the sun creeping toward the northwestern horizon.

"How are my girls?" he said with a heartiness that rang as false as a con man's laughter. Mother and daughter raised their faces and dipped their heads in unison like a pair of strange birds. "UPS show up?" he asked. Mildred inclined her head toward the garage. Riley gathered his jacket and briefcase, shut the car door quietly, then walked slowly toward the front porch.

"Is your hip bothering you?" Mildred asked as he mounted the steps. "Your hip always bothers you after the long trips."

"I missed a few days running," he said as he leaned into the medicinal miasma that always seemed to surround his wife and daughter. "You ready for school to start?" he asked Tricia, who smiled briefly at him, a flash of pure love, then she turned her face into her mother's shoulder. He felt his heart fake left, then go deep.

"We'll talk about it after dinner," his wife said in her calmest nurse's voice, a voice that chilled him to the bone.

"I think I'll get in a quick run before dinner," Riley said, then slipped nimbly around the swing and through the front door like a man escaping his fates.

After a short run through the almost empty subdivision, a shower, and a typically bland dinner, Riley allowed himself a visit to the garage. A dozen brown boxes were stacked in the space where he usually parked his Honda. He felt like a child at Christmas and made himself grab a beer from the garage refrigerator before he picked up the utility knife, then started checking his boxes. He was halfway through the six pack before he had finished the inventory of the boxes. It was all there, the debris of an inner city high school that could no longer afford its sports teams: piles of football jerseys and pants in bright blue and yellow; helmets slick with the sweat of tough kids, tough kids kicked out on the streets with lots of energy and no football to play; and a jumble box of cleated shoes. Everything might be a bit small for the adult men of his team, the Bonnerville Rangers, but luckily kids were large these days, and Riley was sure that he could at least outfit his usual traveling squad of fifteen to twenty. The Rangers played eight or nine Saturday afternoon games on rented high school fields all over the northern plains. The players, mostly ex-small college players, all chipped in for uniforms, gas, and motel rooms, rode in borrowed vans, sometimes covering five or six hundred miles on a weekend. They played without insurance or pay, played for the pure love of the game. Riley absolutely lived for those weekends. It was the only fun he had in life. But the team's uniforms were ragged, the morale sagging like the linemen's beer-bellies. This was going to change everything. He saw that the moment he saw the stranger reflected in the bank's window.

He was happily repacking the boxes when Mildred stepped through the door from the kitchen.

"Where'd you get the money?" she asked.

He couldn't believe he hadn't even thought about what sort of lie he had to tell his wife. The bank job had been such a sudden chance, that a lie hadn't even crossed his mind. After he had robbed the bank, which he knew he hadn't meant to do, he had gone back to his cheap motel, changed, then run for a full hour through the damp twilight. The next morning he had gone back to the school board's purchasing officer and, much to the arrogant black man's amazement, arranged the sale and shipment, then gone about his road-trip business without another thought.

"I went to the races," he answered her without looking up or thinking. The same way he had gone into the bank.

"The races?"

"Yeah, the horse races," he said. "You know that place in Nebraska with the funny name."

"The funny name?" she said. Not in interrogation, but in amazement.

"Ak-sar-ben," he said. "One of my customers took me."

"You don't know anything about horse racing," she said.

"No. But he did," he said. "We picked a couple of early winners, then went in on a quinella. We hit it. Big. Then I saw this equipment on sale. Cheap."

"Well, I hope you saved some money," she said, no longer amazed. Riley had never lied to her, never lied to anybody in his life as far as she knew. "Tricia has to go to St. Catherine's this fall even if I have to work two shifts. She needs the extra care and attention. Desperately. It's eight thousand with the scholarship."

"No problem," he said. "It won't be a problem."

As he stood over his sleeping daughter hours later, the smell of her warm breath thick in his throat, stood over her as he had so many times in so many hospitals. Riley repeated himself, "It won't be a problem."

Tricia had been born with a hole in her heart, a hole the size of a dime in a heart no larger than a walnut. They fixed that, then found something else wrong, then another complication. Operation after operation. Hospital after hospital. Then when it all seemed over, the allergies started. The poor kid was allergic to everything in the world: grains, lactic acid, Asian lady bugs, her own dandruff, stress. But she endured. She didn't prosper, but she endured. Like a weed struggling through the wet cardboard and shadowed bricks of an alley, Tricia hung onto life, her smiles as rare as sunshine in a dark corner. And Riley would do anything for that smile.

The next afternoon as he ran through the deserted subdivision his father-in-law had left them, Riley felt his hip ease. He hadn't found it out until he tore his ACL playing football in the Army, but he had been born with his right leg slightly shorter than his left. The deformity interfered with his down field speed but gave him a very deceptive gait. He wasn't fast but he was very hard to cover. All through his football career—high school, and four years as a starter at a small Christian college in North Dakota, three years of Army ball, and six years playing semi-pro— he had left a crumpled trail of linebackers and defensive backs behind him. He had large, sure hands, but no speed, no future, just the occasional release of the semi-pro games. Without them, Riley knew he would go mad.

He pulled the next job to cover the rest of Tricia's tuition the Saturday morning before their first game. He had combed the Salvation Army, St. Vincent de Paul's, and all the second-hand stores until he found a pair of wingtips with two inch lifts, a cashmere top coat that fit over his small shoulder pads, and a large black fedora. He also bought two road flares to stick in his belt. At the first bank he had written on his note pad *$4200 or the bomb goes off. I'm a desperate man. Please.* So this time he thought he might as well carry something that resembled dynamite.

This time he wrote the note—*$4600 or I light the fuse. I'm crazy. Please believe me.*—before he left the motel. Then he drove six blocks to the small branch bank that advertised mightily that it was open Saturday mornings. Once again he was in and out less than three minutes. And the surveillance tapes he watched on the evening news at the motel bar with a post-game beer looked nothing like him.

At the game that afternoon after the robbery, Riley had to admit that he was jacked. He caught six passes, two for touchdowns, and played outside linebacker like a white Lawrence Taylor. When the quarterback, his only buddy on the team, B. J. Moffett, told him that he had played a great game, Riley responded, "Maybe I should go pro." But he didn't think he was talking about football.

It was a great season. Tricia blossomed at the new school, radiant in her green and black tartan kilts and green sweaters. Her hair seemed blonde now, a color rather than colorless, her face tan, and her smile bright as sunshine reflected off the Bonner River. Even Mildred began to glow, and occasionally they made love like newlyweds again. This team warmed to its new uniforms and won the first seven games. Riley hit two more banks, without pattern or trouble, thought about growing a mustache but decided against it, traded up for a slightly newer Honda, and bought two real sticks of dynamite, capped and fused, and an S & W .38 snub-nose, so old the bluing had worn off the short barrel, from a retired railroad brakeman in a bar in Williston, North Dakota. If he was going to be a bank robber, Riley thought, he damn well wanted to look like one.

The last game of the season was in a small city just south of the Canadian border, but given the blizzard that blew in the night before, they might as well have been playing inside the Arctic Circle. Riley hadn't noticed that the football shoes he had bought from the first bank job were fitted with long cleats for the mid-western mud. The cleats acted like the blades on ice skates on the frozen turf, and the Rangers were ten points down before one of the wives managed to find an open sporting goods store with a supply of shorter cleats. On the next to the last play of the game, the usually sure-handed Riley was ten steps past the cornerback when he dropped a certain touchdown pass, so they were still down on the last play. B. J. called a hook and ladder, then gave Riley the sort of look that says "The rest of your life hangs on this play, sucker."

When Riley hooked, the corner played him to hook and go, as he had all afternoon, so the defensive back was seven yards away when B. J. slammed the pass perfectly into Riley's gut, put it into the spot where it couldn't be missed. Then B. J. cut for the end of the line like a scatback. The corner came up just in time to touch Riley's hips as he pitched out to the sweeping B. J., who raced unimpeded to the goal line for the winning touchdown.

It was an absolutely perfect moment. Nearly as effortless as the last bank had been. The bank Riley swore would be his absolute last one.

And it would have been. But some wealthy meat packer from Minnesota, one of those fat guys who always thought he could have played football if he wanted to, had a bright idea. He decided to gather up three of the best semi-pro teams in the mid-west and northern plains states to take on his Meatgrinders, a collection of major college and ex-pro players who hadn't been beaten in recent memory. The meat packer was willing to cover the food and the motels, but Riley's team had to cover travel expenses and time off the job to make the long trip to the two-day tournament. In addition, they were tired. The excitement of win-ning the game in the blizzard had worn off. All they could feel now was the cold, hard playing fields of middle age facing them, the knives of endless arthritis pains, hip and knee replacements, ribs and fingers that ached for no good reason. None of the players wanted to go, not even B. J., but Riley nagged and nagged until he promised to cover everybody's expenses out of his own pocket.

So to speak.

He drove through the snow to Minnesota to hit the meat packer's own bank. His biggest job. *$11,500 please* was all the note said. The lighter next to the short fuses said it all. Riley would have to admit that some of the other jobs had excited him enough so that it took a porno film, a cheap hooker, or a pint of bourbon to get him to sleep. But this one gave him such a great pleasure that he had to drive to Minneapolis, check into an expensive hotel, and cavort with a five hundred-dollar call girl. They shared a bot-tle of French champagne. She was as beautiful as any woman he had ever seen on television, smart and funny, and as natural about the professional act as Riley was on a football field. If it hadn't been for Tricia, Riley might have thought more seriously about this bank robbery thing as a permanent way of life. He seemed to have a hidden talent for it. Just as his short leg gave him an oddly deceptive quickness on the playing field.

Three days later he was back in the meat packer's city on a perfect late fall day for football. A cloudless blue sky, balmy air rustling the changing leaves, and a lush green playing field that sparkled like an emerald. The Meatgrinders beat the Rangers 49-0. Riley's team only crossed the fifty-yard line once, and only then because of a muffed punt. Riley dropped seven straight passes before he left the game with a concussion in the third quarter. He spent the rest of the game on the bench, his head in his hands, trying, unsuccessfully, to remember the call girl's number in Minneapolis. His head hurt so badly he couldn't even visualize her face. The only thing he was damn certain sure of was that he was going to hit another bank on the way home. Maybe even two. Or three.

After the game, the team sat glumly in the motel bar, drinking steadily through Riley's money. They had been beaten as soundly as if they had gone up naked against a hockey team. Nobody would talk to him. B. J. wouldn't even look him in the eye. By the time they closed the bar, Riley wasn't just the last team member in the bar, he was the last customer. The bartender had to shoo him away like a pariah dog.

Riley stayed in the motel an extra day, telling Mildred on the telephone that the concussion was bothering him. In fact, he couldn't tell the concussion from the hangover, the physical pain from the personal loss. His season of glory had ended on a sourball note that seemed lodged in his throat.

The next day he woke with a terrible tremble in his hands and thought about a drink, thought about Minneapolis but instead headed west toward home. He bought two parkas and two ski masks in the first town he came to and hit the first bank he saw in the next one. *$15,000, please*, and another just down the street for *$20,000, pretty please*. This time, for the first and second times, he lit the lighter. His hands were shaking so badly that the flame wavered wildly, and both the tellers burst into tears as they stuffed the cash into trash sacks, their faces stiff with terrified grins.

Outside of town he finally got control of himself, and turned north on a secondary road, driving the speed limit until he found a county park at a crossroad, where he parked. He climbed out of the Honda, dumped half the garbage out of the trash barrels, then stuffed the parkas and ski masks into the barrels and replaced the garbage on top of them. In the slush of the second barrel, he found a small doll with a short blue dress and ratty blonde hair. Like something a child might win at a cheap carnival, then discard without thought.

He sat down for a moment at one of the picnic tables, then looked around. Gray fallow fields stretched toward the horizon in all directions, a gray as dismal as the faces of the junkie dentists who were his customers, a gray he could see deep beneath the cheap porcelain of the false teeth he sold. The branches in the windows looked as if they had never held a leaf. A flat ashen cloud covered the sky. Even the thick grass along the small creeks that wound through the fields looked as if it had been burned. Winter seemed to have arrived without the benefit of fall. He knew he had never been in this spot before, but it seemed as familiar as his face in the shaving mirror.

Riley stood up, opened the trunk of the Honda, and took out his Ranger warm-up jacket. He put his .38 in the right-hand pocket, then stuffed the two sticks of dynamite in his belts, and went looking for his life's work.

Of course, they were waiting for him like a bad-tempered linebacker with a forearm shiver cocked in his beefy shoulder. He found a small empty bank in a farming community. *All of it, please,* the note said this time. A young FBI agent came up behind him and tapped him on the shoulder with his Glock as the teller shoved the stacks of bills into a trash sack, her eyes locked on the wavering flame of the lighter.

"Mr. Please, I believe," the young man whispered with a chuckle in his throat. "This is the FBI ..."

Riley lit the fuses before the kid could finish, turned and put a .38 round at close range into his thigh before he could move his Glock. The kid hit the ground like a quarterback sacked by a Brahma bull, the pants of his suit on fire. Riley tossed the dynamite sticks toward the side of the bank, then grabbed the sack of money, and ran for the emergency exit. The other two agents fired at him but missed—because of his confusing gait, he assumed—before they dove over the tellers' counter to escape the blast.

Riley heard the dynamite go just as he slammed the exit door, then he was down the alley in a rocking burst of speed, his legs pumping like wings. He was going to score one more time.

The Honda was just around the corner, running, but just at the end of the alley, an old gray-haired man in rumpled khakis, the bank guard discounted by the FBI, stepped around the corner, and fired a single round from a model 70 Winchester .30-06 dead center into Riley's heart. Riley didn't even have time to consider the irony before he died. He probably wouldn't have enjoyed it, anyway.

A SUNDAY IN JANUARY

BY BRENDAN DUBOIS

Every time, the dream is the same.

He's on Nickerson Field at Boston Tech running downfield. There's less than thirty seconds to go in the first half and the score is tied, 7-7, and his knees hurt and the small of his back is aching, but by God, he is racing, he is running towards daylight. In his mind he counts off the number of paces, breaks left and beyond the clutter or the other players, Boston Tech Eagles and Stanford Cardinals, here it comes, like a friggin' airmail package itself, coming from the powerful hands of the team's quarterback, Jimmy Eaton, and the ball is arcing over perfectly. In the distance he knows the crowd is on its feet, screaming, yelling, chanting, and strangely enough, all he can hear is his own puffing, his own exertions, as his hands come up and he keeps on moving, the ball comes down like before, like hundreds of times before, a piece of friggin' cake.

Caught. In his hands. And he swivels back and snaps the ball tight against his side, and right ahead of him, nobody in front of him at all, except one zebra-clad official, waiting for him at the end zone, he's racing for a touchdown, he's going to make it, he's going to make it fine...

That's usually when the dream ends. Which was fine. For as Brian Flynn woke up and stared at the cracked plaster ceiling of his third-floor apartment, he didn't care to relive that moment anymore. Not today, at least. Not today. He rubbed at the sleep-crust in his eyes, tasted cigarette smoke and stale beer on his tongue. Ugh. Another rugged night at the Iron Pike Lounge. He stretched for a moment and then swiveled out of bed, bare feet slapping on the hardwood floor. Almost noon time. Jesus. He scratched at his ribs, and then frowned as he pinched some of the flab that was starting to form around his gut. So soon? Damn, he had been out of college less than five years, and already, already, he was going to pot.

There was a rumbling noise as a jet came overhead, heading into Logan Airport, just a few hundred yards away. The rent in this triple-decker was reasonable, and Brian knew why, right from the start: having big jets blasting in every five or six minutes overhead could scramble your mind, if you'd let it. But he had gotten used to it, these past couple of years, and before he got up, another jet rumbled overhead, making the windows shake, and he had a quick fantasy. Maybe today. Maybe this special Sunday, Jimmy would come through. It wouldn't take much. A special delivery package coming to the door with the necessary tickets and paperwork, and in thirty minutes, hell, make that twenty minutes, he could be over at Logan Airport. Don't even bother packing. Just get on the jet and in a few hours, be there in New Orleans, with about a hundred thousand or so other crazed fans, and he would have a good seat, the best, 'cause Jimmy Eaton had promised him, all those years ago—

When the phone rang he actually jumped, almost jumped out of his skin. He leaned over, knocked over the previous week's issue of *Sports Illustrated*, his heart thumping, wondering, could it be true? Could it?

"Yeah?" he said.

"Brian?" came the familiar voice, but not the one he was hoping to hear. The connection was bad, for he knew the call was coming from a payphone.

"Yeah, Mister Spinelli," he said, feeling the racing of his heart slow down some. "It's me."

"Good, good," came that smooth voice, the one he had never trusted, all the years he worked for him. "I was wonderin' what you got goin' today, 'cause I need some work done."

"Today?"

"Yeah, today. Why not today?"

Brian coughed, wished he hadn't drunk so much last night, after work was done. "Well, you know. The game's today. The Super Bowl. The Giants versus the Ravens. The great re-match. The Grudge Bowl."

Mister Spinelli came back with a snap comment about what

Brian could do with the Super Bowl, and said, "Look. I don't care what's going on today. I need something done. You meet up with my nephew Frank in three hours. In front of the Sporting Club. Okay? You do exactly what he tells you to do, just like you were working for me. Okay?"

"Sure, Mister Spinelli, I'll take care of it...but..."

"Yeah, what?

He paused, knowing how silly it was going to sound, but he couldn't think of anything else to say. "I mean, well, do you know how long it's gonna take? I mean, kickoff is at six o'clock, and—"

"Kid," he said, the smooth voice now tinged with iron. "Listen up, all right? You go see my nephew Frank, you do what he tells you to do, and if it takes you until February, you do it. Understand?"

"Yeah, I understand, but—"

And he was now talking into a dead phone. His boss had just hung up. He coughed and his head started throbbing, the usual late morning headache that came from too little sleep and too many beers. He lowered his head into his hands, looked down at the floor, noted two things. The first was the *Sports Illustrated*. looking up at him, and there, in the uniform of the New York Giants, was Jimmy Eaton, his teammate back at Boston Tech. The headline on the cover said, CAN GENTLEMAN JIMMY PULL IT OFF? It was a great photo of him in action, back in the semi finals, where they had crushed the Vikings and Jimmy had connected, over and over again with his receivers. Even with the helmet and facemask, Brian could make out the slightly arrogant look about his team-mate's eyes, as he was there, doing the one thing he loved, most of all.

And for a while, he had shared that love, until one day just a handful of years ago, at Nickerson Field, and Brian again noted the other thing: the long, pink and twisting scar on his right knee. He got up and his knee clicked on him, and then he stumbled into the bathroom to take a shower.

And if the dream had gone any longer, this is what would have happened:

About twenty yards from glory and the end zone, something

strikes his right knee, hard and sharp, and he tumbles to the ground, feeling his knee hyperextend and then something go pop! with a horrible vibration that shoots up from his knee and right to his chest. He rolls and gasps in agony, the ball flying from his hands, the sky and turf and grandstands spinning about in his view. He finds himself on the turf, staring up at the sky, breathing hard, hoping against hope as he moves his right leg, and then almost screams as the burning pain shoots up and down his leg. Soon, one of his teammates and another and an official and a trainer all show up, and he's panting, and he tries hard not to gasp as he's helped up to his feet, and starts limping to the side-lines. His helmet is now off, his sweaty head cold and open to the air, and he searches the loose collection of the Stanford team, try-ing to see who had nailed him like that, clipping him from behind, and he just grimaces as he makes his way off the field.

In the North End of Boston, Brian walked up to the Messina Social Club, hands in the pockets of his leather coat, trying to avoid the puddles of frozen slush and snow. The Social Club was in the bottom floor of a brick building that had its windows paint-ed black. The streets were nearly deserted in this popular section of Boston, and he glumly knew why: it was Super Bowl Sunday, and anybody with half a brain and a body just above room tem-perature would be someplace warm and comfortable, watching the upcoming game. Not walking along this frigid sidewalk, going to meet that shrimp of a guy, standing up ahead of him.

The shrimp of a guy turned around, his face red, wearing a tan cashmere-type coat with a fur collar and dark gray slacks. His hair was thick and black, and slicked back in some sort of pom-padour. He frowned as Brian approached.

"You're late," he said.

And he was going to snap back, yeah, well, frig you too, except he remembered who this shrimp was: the nephew of his boss. "Sorry," he grumbled. "Got here as fast as I could, Mister Spinelli."

The young guy looked like someone had just peed on his shiny shoes. "Man, forget that crap. Not yet at least. My uncle, he's the only who gets that kind of respect, okay? He's Mister

Spinelli. You call me Frank."

He nodded. "All right, Frank it is."

"Good," he said, little puff clouds of steam coming from his mouth. "Let's get driving, okay? We've gotta go see somebody this afternoon."

"Who's that?" Brian asked.

"You'll find out," he said. "Your car, what is it?"

"A Lexus," he said.

"Hey, not too bad," Frank said. "That'll be good. C'mon let's go."

Brian led the nephew back to his Lexus, which was illegally parked in a section of the North End that demanded a residential sticker for each vehicle, but in his visits to this clannish neighborhood, not once had he ever gotten a parking ticket. Go figure. And he knew this kind of car was crazy, considering the dump he lived in, but he needed something nice in his life, and this black Lexus was it. As he unlocked the driver's door, he said, "Hey, Frank."

"Yeah?"

"Any idea how long this is gonna take?"

The young guy smirked. "As long as it has to. Why, you got some broad you gotta roll around on later?"

Again, that little sense of embarrassment, from having talked to this guy's uncle a little while ago on the same subject. "No, it's just this afternoon, well, you know."

Frank's eyes narrowed. "No, I don't know. Let me in on it, why don't you."

Shit. "Well, it's the Super Bowl, and kickoff is at six and—"

Frank opened the passenger's side door. "Frig that. It's just a football game. A game for us to make money on from nitwit gamblers. That's all. C'mon, we got work to do. And there's no time to waste."

Sure. No time to waste. And that's what's being said, back in the trainer's room, in the locker room during halftime. He's in a plastic chair, his right leg extended out onto a padded bench, the team doctor and the coach both staring at him, like they were saying, c'mon, Brian, enough of the joke. The score is still tied, seven to seven, and there's a whole 'nother half coming up. Stop telling us your knee hurts.

The coach, a heavyset man whose hunger for a winning season caused his marriage to fail last summer, says, "Brian, there's not much time. Are you sure it's not feeling any better?"

He moves, tries to hide the grimace. "Hard to say, coach."

The doctor, a retired guy who's an alumni of the school, and who shares the same hunger for a winning season as the coach, says, "Without a visit to Mass General, it's hard to see what's going on in there, Sam. Could be something minor, could be something major."

Coach mutters some profanities and rubs his large hands across the top of his crewcut. "Isn't there anything you can do?"

The doctor blinks behind his black-rimmed glasses, and says, "That's a pretty tall order."

"What do you mean, a tall order?"

"It depends," the doctor says. "Depends on what's wrong inside the knee."

"But we just need him for another half!"

Brian watches the debate going on, conscious of the throbbing in his knee, also conscious that these two older men are debating his future. He knew he should be paying more attention, but damn it, he wants to go out and kick some Stanford butt.

The doctor says, "I've got something experimental. A cortisone extract. A shot of that and..."

"And what?" coach demands.

"Then he'll be good to go for the rest of the game. Won't feel a thing. But Jack, right after the game, he's got to get that knee looked at. I mean, well, the shot isn't going to fix what's wrong. It's just going to let him play."

Coach looks at the doctor and looks at Brian, and says to the doctor. "Give me a sec, will you?"

The doctor leaves and coach comes over and actually kneels down on the dirty concrete floor, actually gets down on his knees and says, "Brian, this day...this is the day I've worked for, prayed for, sweated for. We win this and we're on a fast track to a bowl championship, the first one in my life, the first one in over a decade for this school. The other guys on the team...they're good but you and Jimmy, you've got magic. I know...Lord, how I know, if I can get you out for another half, you and Jimmy, you'll give me that bowl game. You'll give us that bowl game. I know you'll do it."

Brian moves his knee again, almost moans at the agony. "Coach, it still hurts like hell..."

The coach pats him on the thigh. "Remember this, Brian. Remember what I've always said. There's no 'I' in team. Your teammates, your college, everybody's relying on you, Brian. I know you can do it, if you really want to, because I know you don't want to let down the team. Right?"

Brian coughs and says, "Yeah, you're right."

"So what do I tell the doc? It's up to you, Brian. We've got less than ten minutes. The team's waiting for you."

Another move of the knee, and maybe Brian is fooling himself, but it doesn't quite hurt as much as it did a couple of minutes ago. The doc, well, he must know what he's talking about. Jesus, he's a doctor and knows these things.

"Coach," he says.

"Yeah?"

"Give me the shot," he says.

The coach grins, bounces up to his feet. "I knew I could count on you, Brian. You're the best team player I've ever seen."

In his Lexus, he headed out and Frank said, "Get on the Interstate, hook up with 1-95, and start heading north."

"Okay."

Traffic was light and again, that little pang in his heart that told him why. He looked at the dashboard clock. It was just past 2P.M. He had already missed nearly two hours of the pre-game show, and he knew that sounded silly, but what the hell. Before this morning's phone call, he had the day planned already, to get down to the Eastie Sports Bar, where some of the patrons knew of him and his winning seasons at Boston Tech. The large screen televisions would be on and he'd have a great seat up front, appetizers and food and drinks all coming to him, and he wouldn't have to pay a thing. He'd sit there and eat and drink and get a good buzz on, and he'd watch all the talking, the interviews, the background pieces on the television, smiling in spite of himself each time he saw a bit on his old teammate, Jimmy Eaton, now the star quarterback for the New York Giants. And if he was lucky, maybe the network guys would show some Boston Tech footage, and there he'd be, catching those long bombs coming from Gentleman Jimmy's graceful hands. Then there would be hoots and cheers in the bar, and if he was real lucky, maybe some pretty young thing would like to see the scar on his knee that put him down forever. Most pretty young things liked seeing a scar like that, fired up their maternal instincts or something, and maybe after the game, he could have some playtime back home.

Sure.

But right now, he was in his Lexus with Frank Spinelli, the nephew of his boss, and he wished he hadn't answered that damn phone.

Damn it.

Brian reached down, flipped on the radio, and got the station on AM-850, the local sports radio station, WEEI. At least he could hear some—

Frank said, "The frig is that?"

"Radio," he said. "Just want to hear some pre-game stuff for the Super Bowl."

"Christ, shut it off or find some music," Frank said. "I'm not going to listen to this sports crap, all the way north. Football...a game for dummies. Give me baseball any day of the week. That's a thinking man's game."

Brian cleared his throat. "The thing is, I know the quarterback for the Giants. He and I used to play together, on the Boston Tech team."

Frank snorted. "Yeah? And when I was kid, John Gotti gave me a slice of birthday cake, when I was ten years old, before the Feds snapped him up. Big deal."

He felt his fingers tighten on the steering wheel, and then he tried to lighten up. Any other guy, Brian would have slowed down and tossed him out. But this was the boss's nephew. Allowances had to be made.

So instead of whacking the guy in the face, Brian reached down and turned off the radio.

Frank said, "All right. Take the Topsfield, exit. Okay?"

Brian nodded, and a bit later, Frank said, "Hey, dummy. I asked you a question."

Brian said carefully, "Sorry, Frank. I nodded my head. I thought you saw. Topsfield exit, got it."

"Good," Frank said, settling down some in his seat, folding his arms. "Football. Jesus."

He kept on driving, looking at the minutes slip away on the dashboard clock.

So the second half goes on, and he's so full of himself and Jimmy is so happy to have him back on the field, that he completes a whole crapload of passes and scores three more touchdowns, and the rest of his teammates, emboldened or happy or whatever at his unexpected return, manage to close down the Stanford offense. And through the whole second half, Brian cannot believe how good his knee feels. The doc had come in with a needle that looked like it could be used on a rhino, but sweet Mary, after that initial sting, his knee feels wonderful. He moves it back and forth, back and forth, not even a twinge, and in one of the huddles, Jimmy says, "Brian, baby, I knew you could do it."

And so now the game is over, they won, hell, they crushed those Stanford yahoos, and there's cheering and Gatorade being tossed around, and backslaps and handslaps and headbutts, and coach, maybe just drunk on the victory or whatever, and he's up on a folding chair, actually weeping, saying how proud he was of his team, and especially Brian, because he proved what a team player he could be, and there's more chants and coach says, "Brian, come on up here and take a bow!"

So he moves through the crowd, his right knee now feeling a bit warm, and as he steps up to stand on a chair, right next to the coach and bask in this special moment, his knee turns to thick, liquid soap, and he falls right on his ass, right there.

Traffic was incredibly thin on 1-95, heading north, and just a half hour or so out of the city, the landscape changed, to long expanses of fields and marshland and woodland. Frank murmured, "Okay, here's the exit. You get to the exit, top of the hill, take a left."

"Sure," he said.

Even with little or no traffic, Brian used the directional.

Always nice to be law abiding, especially considering what was going on with Frank and whatever was on the agenda for Topsfield. Brian had no illusions, knew why he was here, and again, that sour taste in his mouth and soul of how and where he had ended up. There was going to be some kind of physical activity this afternoon, and Frank looked so typical: a weak little squirt who only got things done through other people's muscle, and that's what he was now.

Other people's muscle. Part of the Spinelli team. Rah, rah, friggin' rah.

At the top of the hill again he came to a full stop. He looked left and then he looked right, and then he made a left.

Frank grunted. "Just keep on going."

"Yeah."

Just keep on going.

So in a space of time so quick that it actually makes him nauseous, Brian becomes intimately familiar with the inside of hospital rooms, as a series of orthopedic surgeons work on his increasingly shattered knee. He remembers a time as a kid, playing on Revere Beach, building a sand castle near the water's edge. It wasn't special or huge or anything, but the damn thing was just his. Okay? So the tide comes in and the water starts crumbling away the castle walls, and he starts making repairs, one right after another, and more water comes in, and the sand becomes slick mud, and no matter how hard he works, how hard he tries, the tide is relentless, chewing up everything.

Just like his knee. First one little procedure and then another little procedure and another. And instead of things getting better, things are getting worse. Mom and Dad, workers at the Edison Plant in Southie, they just nod at all the right places as the doctors tell them how wrong things are inside his shattered knee, and Brian doesn't hear them, not at all, because he already knows one thing: he will never play football again.

Never. Ever. Until he is dead and buried and what's left of the *Boston Globe* and the *Boston Herald* run his little obituary, mentioning that for a while, he was a god on the football field at Boston Tech.

Once upon a time.

In Topsfield, the road cut through old farmland and woods, and Brian saw the long driveways and gates in front of the homes that were out there on the quiet lots, blanketed by fields of snow. Half million, million and two million dollar homes, easy. He looked over at Frank.

"Still going the right way?" he asked.

"Yep."

Brian paused, looked again at the clock. Well past 3P.M. He took a breath. "You going to tell me what's going on?"

Frank moved in his seat, rearranged his coat. Brian glanced over and then quickly glanced away, having seen the butt of a pistol, holstered at the nephew's side. But if Frank had given any indication of being spotted with a weapon, he didn't say a thing.

Instead, he said, "You'll find out. Soon enough."

One of those times, in a hospital room, his leg strung up and not moving, his ass hurting because some sores are starting to develop back there, he gets a visit from Gentleman Jimmy himself, strolling in on two fine legs and knees, tall and lanky, even for a quarterback.

"Hey," Jimmy says.

"Hey yourself," Brian says back, glad in a way to see the lunk come by, but a little pissed 'cause he was just about to ring a nurse for a pain pill, but he doesn't want Brian to see him beg for a little medication, so he'll have to put up with that throbbing for a while.

Jimmy wanders around the tiny room for a bit, and they talk about classes and upcoming graduation and a couple of girls they've met, back at the Iron Pike Lounge, off-limits to the team but everybody goes and so what, it's been a great season. A wonderful season, except for Brian, of course.

Brian can tell Jimmy is getting bored—hell, being his best receiver, sometimes he knows what's going on inside of that thick skull before he does—and Brian lies and says, "Hey, Jimmy, I'm about ready for a sponge bath. Unless you want to see some grandmother in a nurse's uniform scrub me down, maybe you might want to head out."

Jimmy looks grateful at that and he heads for the door, but turns and says, "Hey, Brian."

"Yeah."

"Um...I just want to let you know, my family and me, well, we think it's gonna look pretty good for me, with the pro draft and all that."

Now Brian is filled with such hate and jealousy, it actually drives out the pain in his knee. One lousy clip from a Stanford player. One overbearing coach. One slimy doctor. All three conspiracies, keeping him in the hospital, when he should have had that bowl victory, he should be getting drafted, just like Jimmy.

"Great," he lies. "Good for you."

"But...hey, I want to let you know. If I get in, you'll get to see some games, for real."

"Sure," Brian says. "Thanks. And what about the Super Bowl?"

Jimmy laughs. "M'man, if I ever get there, you'll be my special guest. Fifty yardline seats and the whole shebang."

"Guaranteed?"

"Guaranteed."

Frank said, "Okay, right there. See the driveway on the left?"

On the left was a driveway, disappearing into a stretch of trees.

"Yeah. You want me to take it?"

"No dummy," Frank said. "Just drive by, pull over to the side of the road. We're gonna keep watch on something."

Brian felt that burn of anger flash up again. Any other guy... He slowed down, noted the driveway and saw up ahead, a wide spot to the right, near a snowbank. He pulled over and switched off the engine and Frank moved about in his seat, so he could look out the sideview mirror. Brian felt his knee ache. It usually ached when bad weather was approaching. Or if he had been driving for a while. Or if he had been sitting in one spot for a while. Or standing in one spot for a while. Or just breathing. Yeah, usually the damn thing ached from just being alive, but there you go. Gentleman Jimmy is at the Super Bowl, and he's in Topsfield, Massachusetts, with a low-rent gangster.

Guaranteed.

So the summer after graduation, he finally can toss the crutches away and he's burning some time, burning off some laughs and good times and drink and eager young things, 'cause he knows, when the news starts up in late summer about the NFL training camps and the promising rookie, Jimmy Eaton from Boston Tech, he knows he will be in one pissy mood. But not now. The summer is warm and the girls are tanned and those who come to the Iron Pike Lounge, most of them at least pretend to know sports, and it's so friggin' easy to take one back home that sometimes, bored with it all, he'll even string one along and dump her when she heads to the ladies room for a whiz, just to do something different.

The Iron Pike Lounge is in a redeveloped section of Boston Harbor, and attracts a mix from all over the city: foreign students from the colleges (Eurotrash, they're called), regular students with bucks, some dot-commers who haven't gone bankrupt yet, and some wiseguys, tossed in like the spice in some big stew.

One night, a Saturday night—what else?—he comes out of the bathroom, a couple of beers under his belt, and there's a ruckus at the front. The bouncer is getting popped around by a couple of construction guys, it looks like, who're dressed in torn tanktop shirts, dirty jeans, and those big yellow workboots. Right away he knows what's going on: the Iron Pike Lounge has a strict dress code, and part of that code is trying to keep out the muddy and dirty construction workers from the Big Dig. Brian's come to see this place as a second home and he doesn't like what's going on, so he goes over to help, and a barstool on the back of one guy's neck and a swift kick to another guy's balls later, the situation is clear.

Or so it seems.

An older guy comes up to him, dressed pretty fine, hair silver and white, and he presses a little roll of cash into his palm. "The name's Spinelli," he says. "This is my place and I like what I saw. You working or anything?"

Like most guys growing up in Southie and other parts of Boston, he knows right away who Spinelli is. Suspected of lots of things, but never convicted. Brian takes the little roll and says, "No, Mister Spinelli. I'm out of school and I'm just looking to have some fun this summer, that's all."

Which isn't part of the whole story, no sir, 'cause he knows that in his heart of hearts, he's scared to death of what's going to happen after Labor Day, when the warm days and good times go away, and he has to face up to facts that his degree in communications from Boston Tech—gotten only through the judicious use of tutors and sympathetic professors—ain't going to be paying the rent anytime soon.

Spinelli laughs, punches him on the arm. "I know you. The football kid, right?"

"That's right."

Spinelli nods, taps his fingers on the roll of money in Brian's hand. "Things work out, you can work on my team. Okay?"

Brian sneaks a quick look at the bills, sees Ben Franklin's face on all of them.

"That'd be fine, Mister Spinelli," he says, and that's it, right there. He's on a new team, making some serious money for the first time in his life.

So in the car they sat, and Frank was motionless, just staring at the sideview mirror. Brian wanted to say something, anything, but sure as hell didn't want to be the first to say a word. So he sat as well, stewing over the long minutes slipping away, the sun starting to set beyond the trees. Super Bowl Sunday. A day in January, once a year. A billion people on this planet watch television on this day, except for him. A once-a-year event, gone, and he knows the damn quarterback personally, used to play ball with him.

Jesus, the odds of that happening to him...

Frank finally moved. "There. Okay, that's good."

Brian looked in the sideview mirror. A silver Mercedes SUV came out, with a woman driving. It looked like a couple of kids were in the rear seat. Frank laughed, slapped his knee. "Perfect, damn it, perfect."

"What's going on?" he asked.

Frank laughed again. "What's going on is a beautiful plan, that's what. That guy's house up there, that belongs to Tony Pournelle. Used to run with some of Mister Spinelli's relatives down in Providence. Now that his wife and kids are gone, we can pay him a visit. Let's get up there."

Brian started the car, made a careful U-turn on the narrow road. "How did you know the wife and kids were leaving?"

"Because we had someone make a call, about a friend of hers who needs some help. All crap, of course, but by the time she finds out, it'll be too late." And that brought another bout of laughter.

He slowed the car down, made a right hand turn up the driveway. "I don't understand," Brian said. "All this, just for a meeting?"

Frank looked eagerly through the windshield. "Christ, no, it's more than that. Tony got into one of those Internet start-up companies, made a ton of money, a lot of money, and he was working with Mister Spinelli on some laundry deals, you understand? But Tony got greedy, Tony started skimming, and if word gets out that someone can do that to Mister Spinelli and get away with it, then...well, things aren't so good for my uncle. So we're here to bring a message."

After saying that, Frank pulls the pistol out, works the action, the snick-slack sounding very loud in the car. Brian's feet and lower legs felt chilled, as the house came into view. Made of brick and wood and exposed beam, it had an attached four-car garage. There was a circular driveway and Brian said, his voice choking, "Hey, Frank. Tell me what's going on. Are you going to shoot him?"

Frank looked over, amazed. "Of course not, dummy."

"Oh," Brian said, feeling his body almost sag with relief, even his knee feeling better.

All for about one second.

Frank passed the pistol over, so it now rested on his lap.

"You're going to shoot him," Frank said.

So he starts off at the Iron Pike Lounge as a bouncer, dressed nice, making okay bucks, feeling pretty good about checking ID's and preventing idiots and other trash from coming in. A nice little power trip, after knowing he'll never be on the football field again. Mister Spinelli takes a shine to him and soon, he's paying some visits over at the Messina Social Club, a shadowy place with lots of cigar and cigarette smoke and Italian music and dark conversations in the corner. Sometimes Mister Spinelli just likes to show him around, say, "Hey, how do you like the size of this kid, hunh? Newest member of the team. You oughta see what he can do for me."

And after a while, other things get done as well, like knocking around guys every now and then who owe Mister Spinelli or one of his buddies some money. Nothing serious, just like some of the bouncer work. And one year blends into another and blends into another, and for a while, he even stops looking for Jimmy Eaton's name in the sports pages, 'cause he's on a new team now, a new team that would make the members of his old Boston Tech team run away in terror.

But then Jimmy Eaton catches a few breaks, gets to be starting quarterback for the Giants, and Lord, it's going to be a New York-Baltimore re-match at the Super Bowl, and New York is thirsting for vengeance after the defeat at Super Bowl XXXV, and leading the troops, leading the team, is one Jimmy Eaton.

And Brian is on another team, one that does most of its work in the shadows.

And he wonders again, about that day on Nickerson Field, if that Stanford player had just missed him.

What if.

Brian was conscious of the weight on his lap, the heaviness almost making him feel sick. He said, "What the hell are you talking about? I'm not going to shoot anybody, not at all."

Frank reached over and slapped his face, and Brian was so shocked, he just shut up. Frank said, "Look, moron, what did my uncle say this morning? Hunh?"

"He said to meet up with you, to do what you wanted."

"Right," Frank said. "And I know what he said 'cause he repeated it to me, just before I left this morning. He told you that you were to do everything I said, just like you were working for me. Right? That you were going to do anything and everything."

Brian just nodded. He knew what was going on. He was trapped.

"So that's it," Frank said. "You put that pistol at the small of your back. It's ready to go. We go inside and talk a bit to Tony, and then I'm going to look at you, and I'm going to say, 'Now would be fine.' All right? 'Now would be fine.' And then you take that pistol out, put it right up to the back of his head, and you pull the trigger. Got it?"

"Yeah," he whispered.

"No, say it louder," Frank said. "I want to hear it, because if it doesn't go right, doesn't go right at all, then my uncle is going to be very upset with you. And knowing my uncle, that means today's Sunday, and you're not ever going to be around to greet Monday. Got it?"

"Yeah," he said, his voice now louder.

"Good," Frank said. "Let's get a move on."

So when the Giants win their spot to the Super Bowl, to face again the Ravens who had humiliated them, Brian begins the long wait, the long wait for the phone call or letter or FedEx package, or something from Jimmy Eaton, because he had promised, all those years ago in the hospital room, to take care of him. Feeling like a six-year-old, he even writes a small congratulatory note to Brian, gently reminding him of the promise, made all those years ago.

And there's nothing. Not a thing.

Hell, Brian even sees a story in the *Globe* about the coach from Boston Tech—now retired—who is going to be at the game, courtesy of his star player from years ago, Gentleman Jimmy, and in the entire length of the story, not once does the coach mention the other half of his winning team, one Brian Flynn.

Not once.

Not a mention of that special team, that special bond, the team that had no 'I' in it, the team that accomplished so much, over Brian Flynn's shattered knee and equally shattered dreams.

Up at the door, Frank pushed the doorbell, and in a few seconds, a man opened the door. He was in his mid to late-forties, nervous looking, wearing pressed jeans and an MIT sweatshirt. Seeing Frank, it looked like his whole face and shoulders just sagged.

"Frank," he said.

"Tony," Frank said. "Look, we've got to talk, all right?"

Tony said, "It can all be fixed, I know why you're here, and—

Frank gingerly pushed his way past him, and Brian followed.

Frank was using a tone of voice Brian had never heard, very soothing. "Tony, look, you're in a bit of trouble. All right? But nothing that can't be fixed. That's why I'm here. That's why my uncle's back home. He wants me to fix it, that's all. You've got nothing to worry about."

Tony smiled, nodded. "Good. Okay, that's good. C'mon, let's have a seat. I'll get you a beer or something."

Brian walked in, the weight of the pistol against his back feeling like it was an anvil, ready to tear his pants and fall on the polished wood floor. Tony was talking and Frank was talking back, and he was ignoring everything. His mind was a jumble of everything, everything from that day he busted his knee to the day he started working for Spinelli, going from a college team to an organized crime team, and all because that illegal clip, that clip that broke his knee.

Now they were in a living room, overstuffed couches and chairs, and the turmoil in his mind stopped, for at least a moment or two, for before him was a magnificent sight. There was a big-screen television on the near wall, the biggest screen he had ever seen. It was the Super Bowl, of course, and just a few minutes before kick-off. The Giants were coming out onto the field, named right after another, and the sound...He looked around the living room again, saw the speakers in the corners of the room, near the bookshelves and cabinets. Christ, it was like he was down there in New Orleans, right on the sideline, for he could make out the cheers and the music and even the breathing, for God's sake, of the players coming out. And that screen...it was like he could reach out and pull up a handful of turf

Tony and Frank were on the nearest couch, talking again about respect and loyalty and debts and all that, and Brian saw the spread out in front of them on a large coffee table, coldcuts and cheese and shrimp and lobster tails and beers on ice, and he looked back and there was Gentleman Jimmy Eaton Himself, trotting out, helmet in his confident and strong hands, his eyes bright and smiling, and God, the kid does look good, doesn't he?

"Brian!" Frank said, his voice loud. "Didn't you hear me?"

Brian turned. "What?"

"Now would be fine, Brian," Frank said, his face getting red.

"I'm sorry, what?" Brian said, looking back again at the

screen, at Jimmy Eaton, taking his spot in the line of other Giants players.

"You idiot, I said, now would be fine!"

He turned. Tony looked confused. Frank looked mighty pissed.

"Oh," Brian said. "Now I hear you."

And like he had been told, he pulled out the pistol and shot once.

Just five minutes, he thought, sipping a beer. That's all. I just missed five minutes of the game and nothing much happened, just the Ravens got possession and their drive to a touchdown got ground down in mid-field. A punt just took place, and in a few seconds, he'll get to see what he's been waiting for, all day: his old college teammate, playing in the Super Bowl.

A man's voice from the kitchen. "It's all set."

"Good," he said, still amazed at the quality of that picture.

He looked up and Tony came in, his face white, wearing a new pair of jeans, his old pair having been soiled a few minutes earlier. "The wife and kids won't be back for a couple of hours. She's angry but...man, I'll live with that."

"Good," Brian said. "Hurry up, it's the Giants' ball."

"All right," Tony said, sitting down on the couch, which now smelled of upholstery cleaner. A window to the side was also open, to clear out the stench of burnt gunpowder. The pistol, with one round expelled, was on the coffee table, next to the shrimp platter.

Jimmy came out and four downs later, they'd gained fifty yards.

"Good for you, Jimmy," Brian said, the beer tasting mighty fine. Then the Ravens called a time-out, and the big screen shifted to a commercial.

"Uh, Brian," Tony said.

"Yeah," he said.

"I mean, saying thanks and all, well, that just sounds so pitiful," Tony said. "I can't believe you saved my life like that."

"Well, it happened, so let's just watch the game, okay?"

"But why? I still don't understand why."

The beer bottle felt cold and crisp in his hand. "Let's just say I got tired of being a good team player."

Tony shook his head. "You're going to be in a lot of trouble later."

"Let later take care of itself," Brian said, remembering with joy the shocked look on that idiot nephew's face when he realized the pistol was pointed at him. One shot and a few trash bags later, the cooling body of Frank Spinelli now rested in the trunk of Brian's Lexus. For later, everything was later, after the Super Bowl.

"Look," Tony said. "I owe you. I owe you everything. I've got friends on the West Coast, you can catch a red-eye, be in Los Angeles by tomorrow morning. We can set you up."

Brian looked away from the television. "Set me up how?"

Tony looked confused. "Set you up. Take care of you. That's what I mean."

Brian glanced down at the pistol, then back at Tony, remembered the day in the locker room, submitting to that injection, remembered the day he agreed to work for Spinelli. "Take care of me how? Have me working for you? Working for your friends? Being part of your team, doing whatever you tell me to do? Is that it?"

Tony bit his lower lip. "No, not at all. Just rewarding you, that's all. You can be on your own. You don't have to be a member of any team. That's all."

Brian took another swallow of the beer, felt himself relax a bit more. No more team. No more working for anybody or anything. Just working for himself. He liked the sound of it.

No more team.

"Sure," he said, picking up the pistol and putting it on the floor, under the couch. "That sounds fine. But Tony?"

"Yeah? "

"Let's just watch the game, okay?"

"Sure," he said.

And on the big screen, Jimmy Eaton was back on, and the ball was snapped. Brian watched, knowing the kind of movements Jimmy had, and he was surprised, really surprised, at how good he felt, when Jimmy connected and the Giants were the first on the scoreboard, and Brian held up his beer bottle in a toast.

"Good job, Jimmy," he said. "I always knew you could do it."

WHATEVER IT TAKES TO WIN

BY TIM GREEN

I suspected I knew why Alexander Moss had been murdered as soon as they told me what he did. Not what he did as in being a lawyer for a prominent firm in New York City, although that seemed worthy of an early death to me, but as in what he did for the NFL. I know how things like this work because I used to play in the NFL. Don't get excited. That was back before you could retire for the rest of your life on your first year's salary. Anyway, I played for a coach who used to say the NFL stood for "Not For Long." That was Moss's experience, not for long. He hadn't been an inspector for the league's office for more than a year before he found himself at the wrong end of a blunt object.

As for me, after a lackluster career in New York as a second string offensive lineman and a handful of years after that kicking around in the Canadian League, I turned into a dick. That's what my dad said to me when I told him I got my Private Investigator license. "You're a private dick," he said, then he belched into the phone and laughed. My old man is what you'd call a four-hundred-pound pisser."

So, I went back to New York and got lucky in my first year as a dick when the owner of my old team, Bud Kruetz, got the feeling his wife was doing the two-step with one of his players. He knew me because when I was a player on his team I was basically a suck up. You know, the big guy with the happy grin who's always slapping the owner high five on the sideline when the team scores and everyone else is avoiding him like a leper. I was good at it though. Kruetz, he knew me by name and he personally told me how sorry he was when I got cut. I even got invited out to his place in the Hamptons one time with the quarterback and our star running back to meet some of his friends at a pool party that was silly with hookers.

Anyway, I was the kind of guy who saw things and kept my mouth shut, and he wanted to keep the whole thing with his wife quiet. Well, Mrs. Kruetz, a twenty-eight-year-old blonde looker, really was doing the two-step, and just about every other move you can imagine with Bo Riddle, the team's backup middle line-backer, a rookie from Tennessee. I got a shot of them in the act. Well, Bo was arrested the next week and a funny thing happened. They found a bag of cocaine in his car. The team cut him and he was blackballed from the League. Surprise. He wasn't a good enough player to overcome a habit like that.

The wife got her walking papers too. I, on the other hand, had established my reputation as a slippery guy who could get in and get out, quietly. I wasn't out of football for a year before I was making more money, if you figure in the exchange rate, than I did beating my brains out up in Saskatchewan. You can't even imagine how many rich guy's wives are doing the two step on the side and it was pretty much keeping me in Heineken and Montecristo No. 2s when I got called into the League office on Park Avenue.

Being was murdered at night in Atlanta wasn't that unusual, but the six fresh hundreds tucked inside the wallet in Moss's coat left the boys on Park Avenue thinking the same thing I did about their inspector. What they didn't know was the depth of this particular pool of shit. When the Atlanta Falcons turned into a Super Bowl team over night, it wasn't too unusual either. Free agency left teams in the NFL bouncing up and down like a concrete room full of super balls. What was unusual was the number of teams that complained about a peculiar clicking noise in their coach-to-quarterback communications whenever they played the Falcons.

So, going by the book, the League sent Moss down to Atlanta to poke around the locker room. Being a big mouth Manhattan lawyer, Moss, true to form, didn't exactly tiptoe around. He wasn't there more than forty-eight hours before some-one scrambled his brains in the parking garage at the Marriott Marquee. The Atlanta Police didn't have a clue as to who killed him or why, and the League preferred it that way. They were keep-ing the whole thing quiet on account of their reputation. One of their worst fears is some kind of conspiracy between a player or a coach and the mob to fiddle with the outcome of the games. It had happened before and been kept quiet before. If that was the case now, then this particular pool of shit was about twelve feet deep.

Well, the League commissioner, a golfing buddy of Mr. Kruetz's was understandably off his game. After a bad day at the Montclair Country club, he unfolded his little problem over a couple or four scotch and sodas in the clubhouse. What the League needed to do, they decided, was find someone who could get inside this team and find out exactly who is involved. Then the League could take care of it in their own quiet way, without exciting the scum-sucking scavengers in the media.

That's where I came in. At six foot three and three hundred pounds after a sauna, I wasn't exactly inconspicuous, but I was only a year and a half away from the game and still in halfway decent shape for a big fat offensive lineman. They figured they could put me into the locker room and find out the real deal.

"I think it could work," I said intelligently. On its own, my hand crept down my pants leg to caress my knee, the one with the purple train tracks running up one side and down the other and no cartilage on the inside. "The only problem is getting me on the roster..."

The commissioner considered the polish on his thumbnail, slowly revealing the Ivy League smile he used whenever he was talking to a lower life form. Quietly he said, "I've got that all taken care of."

Now I can tell you that bothered me because I always like knowing what it is that's making things happen behind the scenes. Call me the curious kind. And now I wanted to know who it was the commissioner was going to get to put me on that team. If it was Clem Samuels, the Falcons head coach, well, he was already near the top of my list of suspects. If it was the owner, I didn't trust him either. The last thing I wanted was to be snooping around for a killer when the killer knew I was snooping around.

But before I could get to that, they started talking dollars. If

I was going to act like a player for few weeks, they were going to pay me like a player for few weeks, so I just kept listening. Also, I'll be honest, I couldn't help getting that giddy tingling feeling sitting there in that office on Park Avenue with a couple of important men who needed me to help them. They even hinted that if this worked out, there might be a retainer in it for me for future services of this kind. I could see myself back in and around the game, the players, the agents, the TV jockeys, the owners and of course the women, and me wearing custom made suits and eating on an expense account, a kind of secret agent of sports.

Atlanta was bringing me in as a backup offensive guard. Since I was never a starter in New York and the last four years of my career were up in Canada, no one knew who in hell I was, but that was the idea. I was big enough to look the part and I knew enough about the game to bluff my way through a couple weeks of mid-season practices. As long as no one lost his head and I didn't somehow get thrown into the mix of a real game, I could coast through the football part without getting myself killed.

Getting killed off the field was another problem. Whoever took out Moss wasn't going to spare me because of my good looks. I couldn't really hope for a confidant on the team either. If someone was intercepting the signals between the other team's coaches and their quarterback, every player on Atlanta's team was benefiting from it. When you went to the Super Bowl, you not only got a big cash bonus you also ended up increasing your value around the league. Every year, the teams that didn't go to the Super Bowl raided the rosters of the teams that did by offering players ridiculous amounts of money in hopes they carried with them the secrets of success.

When it comes to winning, players aren't fussy about how they get there. If someone on the team had figured out a way to get an edge, there wasn't a football player I ever knew who'd have a problem with benefiting from it. Still, I needed to make a friend, someone who could introduce me around to the other players, preferably someone respected, but a lineman who wouldn't be directly involved in a scam like this. The way I had it figured, the killer was someone on the defense who had something to do with the play calling, most likely either the middle linebacker or one of the safeties.

To truly capitalize on knowing the plays the other team was going to run, you had to be able to adjust your own defense. If you knew it was a pass, you could call a blitz. If you knew it was a run, you could crowd the line of scrimmage. Either one would give you the edge that could win a championship. The middle linebacker usually called the defensive plays, and therefore was the most likely man to making adjustments just seconds before the ball is snapped. But then there was also the free or strong safety. One of them would call the coverage for the secondary and could benefit from knowing the upcoming play as well. Also, it was possible that none of the players was smart enough to figure the whole thing out and a coach was involved.

The first day I arrived was a Wednesday, the hardest workday of the week for an NFL player. Still sore from Sunday's game, most players were surly about the long meetings and even longer practice that were inevitable. Because of that, it didn't surprise me that no one really bothered with me much during the morning of meetings. The rest of my fellow offensive linemen greeted me in their meeting room with the congenial grunts and few wry smiles. No one offered anything in the way of friendship, but that was okay. I needed to get close to someone on the defense.

That wasn't as easy as it might sound. Even though they're part of the same team, offensive and defensive players don't spend much time together. When they do, it's usually contentious. Case in point: Byron Hamer, the Falcon's All Pro defensive tackle. My locker was right next to Hamer's. But because we didn't have the same meeting schedule as the defensive guys, the first time I really met Hamer was on the field.

One-on-one pass rush drills were held on a small patch of grass in the end zone of the practice field. It was just me and Hamer. Ten feet behind me was a foam dummy representing the quarterback. I was supposed to protect it at all costs. Hamer was a gigantic Tasmanian Devil with a reputation for whirling and

TIM GREEN

darting and pummeling and punishing everyone in his way.

Hamer's face was screwed up behind his iron mask. Drool leaked from the corner of his snarl. I got down in my stance without a concern in the world for the foam quarterback. All I cared about was not getting hurt. I hoped Hamer would choose to go around me. Off to the side, the ball was snapped. I stepped back and braced myself with my eyes closed. Instead of going around me, which would have been an easy thing to do, Hamer jacked his hands up under my pads and drove me up into the air and backward. I lurched sideways and began to topple. In my panic, I grabbed hold of Hamer's shoulder pad with a force that was twofold because it was born of fear.

I went down, and so did Hamer. He spun and twisted. His cleated feet dug up the grass and they tore into my calf. My flesh gave way and he slipped in a streak of blood and went down again. The whistle blew. The dummy quarterback was safe. Hamer glared at me. He took a vicious swat at the side of my helmet with his hand filling my head with stars and bells.

"Fucking holding!" he bellowed, waiting for me to retaliate.

I gasped for air and nodded my head that it was indeed holding.

"Get off it Hamer!" the offensive line coach barked. "He beat your ass clean!"

The drill continued and I was grateful when the whistle blew ending the session before Hamer could get another shot at me. The trainers had meandered over and stemmed the flow of my blood, but it left me hobbling for the rest of the day. I had a clear picture now of why I had quit the game to begin with.

I didn't have to face Hamer again until team drills. There were eleven on eleven man sessions with the scrubs pretending to be the upcoming opponent. They weren't supposed to be live drills, but you wouldn't know that from the way Hamer banged me around without mercy. Finally, the day ended with a lively set of wind sprints that left me flopped over in the grass packed in a mound of ice.

By the time the trainers were sure I wasn't going to die,

152

most of the team had showered and gone home, but Hamer was still there. He'd been in the weight room, and his combination of viciousness and dedication impressed me. I dragged myself to my stool and sat there in front of my locker, stripped down, the fat hanging forlornly from my torso. Despite the half an hour packed in ice, I was still covered with a rash of sweat beads.

"Wanna go get a cold beer?"

I looked up and around behind me. It was just me and Hamer and after an uncomfortable minute I figured the invitation was directed at me.

"I...yes," I blurted out. I didn't hold his ferocity on the field against him. I knew how the game was played. To be the best, you have to do whatever it takes to win.

"I like the way you scrap," he grunted.

I scanned his face for signs of sarcasm. He stood there in nothing but a towel. His torso was pale fortress of muscle, superficially scarred and torn from the futile attempts of lesser men to assail him. He reminded me of an unfinished Michelangelo, rough cut from a block of unpolished marble. He was as wide as a doorway and taller than I.

His face was more delicate than his figure. Planted above a massive square jaw was a small almost cherubic mouth. His nose was smooth and round like the bulb on the end of a horn. He wore his sandy blond hair cut short like a boy's but with bangs that nearly infringed on the long lashes of his pale blue eyes. For all that, Hamer was no more handsome than I. The difference was, Hamer was an All Pro who had just signed a five-year forty million dollar contract that I would soon see left him in no short supply of bimbos.

A cold beer between two football players after a long hot practice is a bond of brotherhood. You can feel the first swallow careening down into your gullet like a train. Then you savor the mist of the alcohol as it rises up through your dehydrated body clouding pleasantly in your brain. After a steak dinner at a restaurant with waiters who wore black ties, Hamer took me to his favorite strip club. The women poured themselves over us like cream. Twelve Heinekens later, I found myself back at Hamer's mansion in a hot tub between a redhead and a blonde.

The next morning, Hamer kicked the bottom of my bed without regard for the sleeping tousle-headed girls. In the kitchen, there was a guy at the table dressed in a pink oxford button down and charcoal slacks. The guy looked harmless enough with his pock marked face, a thin head of straw blonde hair and a frame that looked like it was built on bird bones. Jim Bench was his name, and when Hamer moved past him as if he were nothing more than an appliance, Bench offered up a gaggle of obsequious smiles. Nevertheless, Hamer introduced me to Bench as his business manager. I thought it was strange that a business manager would be sitting at the breakfast table eating jam and toast in his socks, but maybe that's because I never had a $40 million contract to manage.

Hamer gave me a big travel cup full of hot murky coffee and we rode quietly into the team complex in his midnight blue Mercedes sedan. I know you might think I was in for an easy day, but you're wrong. If anything, Hamer seemed more determined to hurt me on the practice field. But after practice the same quiet invitation awaited me in the locker room.

Running with Hamer gained me acceptance faster than if I'd broken into the starting lineup. When we played a game in Chicago that weekend, I knew why. The defense, and even the entire team, seemed to draw strength from Hamer's efforts. He was maniacal. He thrashed opposing linemen and knifed through the line of scrimmage making plays in the backfield at the most critical moments. When the team needed a big play, somehow, everyone knew Hamer would make one.

During the game, I sensed what Hamer was doing. You couldn't be on the sideline and not sense it. My attention, however, was focused on Grimly, the middle linebacker and Johnson, the free safety. Surreptitiously, I listened to the defensive coordinator as he conferred with his assistants and hand-signaled in the plays to Grimly. I watched carefully and listened as both Grimly and Johnson roared out a series of instructions that changed whenever the offense shifted.

I soon realized that I wasn't smart enough to figure out what was going on even if I knew what the defensive plays being called really meant. From what I could see, it was possible that either Grimly or Johnson was being fed information into their ear right before the offense came to the line to run the next play. It was also possible that they weren't. I scanned the mob of Bears fans and considered that quite likely among them was a person with a case full of electronic equipment sophisticated enough to intercept the Bear's offensive signals and then transmit them down on the field into someone's ear.

I frowned to myself. I should have thought about that before now. Whoever was getting the signals either had an earpiece like the kind old people wear or a tiny speaker in their helmet. After the game, I shed my clean white uniform slowly in order to keep an eye on Grimly. Unfortunately, the linebacker's dark hair hung in long sweaty ropes down over his ears. I watched carefully and followed him into the shower hoping for a glimpse of his naked ear.

Grimly caught me staring at him through the steam and the spray and his scowl left my round cheeks burning with embarrassment. I couldn't very well follow him back out into the locker room after that, so I directed my attention toward Johnson. He had come from the other end of the locker room, so watching him didn't do me much good. He could easily have taken an earpiece out without my seeing it.

To date, my detective work was about as neat as a bowl full of barbecue and I knew it. I had to stop flopping around and watch both men closely without being noticed. I also had to find a way to search their helmets. I needed physical evidence. Whoever was intercepting the other team's signals wasn't going to just spill their guts to me over a cold beer.

While I would have to wait for the next game to watch for an earpiece, examining the helmets was something I could do almost immediately.

Monday is the day most NFL teams use to watch film from Sunday's game, lift weights, and do some running. I made sure I was the last player to leave the facility. On my way out, I wedged a piece of cardboard into the door latch that led from the locker room to the players' parking lot. I watched most of the Monday night game at a Buckhead bar with Hamer and left him on the dance floor, drunk with a long tall brunette. It was midnight when I arrived back at the facility.

The locker room was dark, but a single light from the equipment room shed enough gloom for me to find Grimly's locker. The helmet was hung deep in the cavernous locker and I reached warily into the black space, illogically fearful of having my hand caught in some kind of a trap.

"Hey!"

My stomach jumped into my neck at the sound and my heart unloaded every ounce of adrenaline it had into my blood stream. I cried out in panic and jumped away from the locker. The fog from eight or ten beers was blasted clean out of my brain. A sharp beam of light cut at my eyes and I squinted into its glare.

"What are you doing, Wiggins?" came the surly voice of Clem Samuels. Samuels was one of those military types with a silver flat top, dark piercing eyes, and the voice of a jackhammer.

"I was, I w-was..." I stuttered.

"Oh I know what you're doing," Samuels said in an evil whisper that was hoarse from a lifetime of screaming. "I just want to know what you think you're doing here. You aren't supposed to be here, now. This facility is closed."

Samuels wore the wicked smile of a teacher catching the student he hates most in the act of cheating on an exam. His words made my guts feel loose.

"I knew signing you was fucked," he continued. After a painful silence, he said, "Let's say for the hell of it someone was getting the other teams' signals. Okay, don't you think that's all over now that people are poking around this team?"

I finally recovered what was left of my dignity and said as forcefully as I could, "From what I've seen, this team keeps doing pretty well."

"Of course we do well!" he barked. "This is my team!"

"I'll tell you what I'll do," he said, dropping his voice back down into an uncharacteristic whisper. "I won't let out what a fat, bumbling buffoon you are, Wiggins, but you just keep your mouth shut and stop poking around. You do that, and you can just coast through what otherwise could prove to be a very ...difficult time of your life..."

Samuels let his smoky threat linger between us for a moment before blowing out the words: "Don't you get it? You're a nobody! They put you on this case because they don't want to find out what really happened. If they did, you don't think it would be you I'm standing here talking to, do you?"

I glared right back at him, but I've never been one to think of anything particularly witty or bold to say until after a crisis has long passed.

"Well, now we know where each other is coming from," Samuels said contemptuously, "you can get the hell out of here. And don't ever let me catch you snooping around this locker room again."

I personally don't think there's anything as dangerous as an indignant fat man, and by the time I reached my room at the Residence Inn, I was ready to pull out all the stops. I didn't know if what Samuels said was true, but if it was, I had been duped. If it wasn't, then I had been challenged. Either way, I was resolved to find out who was getting those signals. If the commissioner chose to do nothing with the information, that was his business, but I was going to let him know that if he wanted an incompetent sand-bag, he had the wrong guy.

I took out a couple bottles of beer from the icebox to settle my nerves. Even so, I lay awake in bed for along time twisting myself up in the covers and planning my next move.

Tuesday was our day off. I waited until eleven, then drove straight to Hamer's mansion. This was clearly a case of not what I knew, but who. Hamer could do anything and go anywhere inside the Falcons organization. No one would question him if he went into the locker room on a Tuesday and came out with a dozen helmets under his arm. When I found him, he was driving golf balls off his back patio into the pond that separated his back yard from the Jack Nicklaus golf course that was the centerpiece of his development.

He was dressed in nothing but a pair of gym shorts and there were already two empty beer cans beside a bucket of balls. He was wedging the tees between the redwood planks in his deck. His feet were bare.

"Have a beer," he grunted after hooking a ball somewhere off into his neighbor's trees.

I took a cold can from the cooler, cracked it open with a hiss, and sat down in a deck chair.

"I need a favor," I said.

Hamer narrowed his eyes and teed up another ball. He smacked it good, right out into the middle of the pond.

"What's that?" he asked.

In a rush of words, I explained to him who I really was and why I was there. I told him my theory on what was happening and how.

"I need those helmets and I want you to get them for me...today," I added boldly.

Hamer's smile bore a curious twist and to my surprise, he agreed.

"But if something's going on," he continued, "I don't want any trouble. I don't want to get mixed up in anything. I'll get you the helmets, but then I'm out of it."

"Hamer," I said offering up my hand to his iron grip, "I appreciate this...I really do."

Hamer was going to finish his bucket of balls and then attend to some personal business. I agreed to stand by on my cell phone at my apartment. I spent the long day checking to make sure my phone was working and trying to piece together who was who on the soap operas I used to watch when I was a real player. At six, I began calling Hamer's house and his cell phone, but got no answer. My mind got loose on me and I started to think up some crazy things. I had a beer. That and the thought of Hamer's ferocity alleviated my fears of him running into trouble.

A little after nine my phone went off. Hamer had what I needed. He said he'd meet me at the Buford Dam. I just said yes.

Night had already come on, but as I got into my car the rumble of thunder made me look up and I saw a thick set of inky clouds rolling in from the west. Halfway to the dam, heavy rain began to blister the hood of my car. When I got there, a stuttering cluster of lightning flashes illuminated the long curve of the dam that buttoned up the Chattahoochee River creating Lake Lenier.

At the halfway point on the lake side of the road were two vehicles. One I knew was Hamer's Mercedes. The other was a big crimson Ford Excursion that loomed ominously over the sedan. I stopped my car and watched for a moment before proceeding out onto the dam. There was no other traffic in sight. I had pulled up nose to nose with Hamer's Mercedes and could clearly see that it was empty. I turned off my lights and saw the two dark figures down the bank at the water's edge. The big one was Hamer.

Without thinking, I took the 9mm Glock from my glove box and stuck it into the pocket of my windbreaker. With my hood up, I got out and stumbled down the rocky slope to the flat concrete rim of the dam. Water ran in slick black sheets off the concrete and spilled into the turgid water. I was thankful at least that Hamer was on this side of the dam. The other side boasted a two hundred foot sheer drop to the neutered river.

During the next flash of lightning, I recognized the small thin figure next to Hamer to be Jim, his business manager. His thin blonde hair was plastered to his head in dark strips and he wore a crooked sneering smile. His eyes were lit with rage. I reached into the pocket of my coat and gripped the pistol without removing it. I got close to the two of them, but not too close.

"You have the helmets?" I said, licking rain from my lips and squinting at the two of them.

"We've got to talk, Wiggins," Hamer said. His voice was conciliatory. He too was wearing a hooded jacket and when the next bolt of lightning hammered the air, I could see that the moon of his face was impressed with the peaks and valleys of anxiety.

"About what?" I said steadily.

"About this," Jim suddenly shrieked. He stepped forward and leveled a pistol at my head at nearly point blank range. Lightning flashed.

"Jim!" Hamer shouted.

The gunshots were gobbled up by an impressive thunderclap but each one hit its mark.

Jim staggered back and crumpled into a heap.

Hamer threw himself at me and before I could get off another shot, he pummeled me to the concrete. My hand was out of its pocket now and still locked onto the gun. Hamer grabbed for it and in the struggle I shot off another round. His body went limp and I scrambled to my feet, sucking wind from the battle.

Rain poured down on the two dark figures. I bent over with my hands on my knees. I was nauseous as well as breathless. But when I dipped my head, Hamer came instantly to life and shot at me from the ground like a wolverine. I went down fast and the gun spilled from my hand. His lifelessness was a feint, as if he were pass rushing me, pretending to run around me, then coming straight in.

In seconds, he had a knee planted in my chest, one hand around my throat and the other directing my own gun at my face.

"Jesus!" he shrieked. "You killed him! You killed Jim!"

His hand throttled my neck and my head bumped up and down against the concrete. I felt the gun pressing against my temple and I shut my eyes against its blast. After a few moments, I became acutely aware of the heavy sound of Hamer's breathing mixed with the spattering rain.

"Are you going to...kill me?" someone asked. I realized the words came from me and I opened my eyes to see.

"Wiggins, damn it," Hamer moaned, "we could have all worked together."

"He was going to kill me," I squeaked.

Hamer nodded his head.

"That's right," he said sadly. "You're right."

Then he got up and stuck my gun in the waist of his pants. Without a word, he walked over to Jim's body and stood there, as if contemplating a puzzle. I got up and walked over next to him. The two holes in Jim's chest were remarkably close to his heart and still pumping a steady flow of blood. His white dress shirt was horribly stained.

"Ten percent," Hamer said.

Lightning flashed and I looked into his face.

"What?" I asked incredulously in the ensuing darkness.

Instead of answering, Hamer began mumbling to himself and searching for something at Jim's feet. There was a dark green backpack there and from it, Hamer unfolded a large nylon duffel bag. After rolling Jim's lifeless body into the bag, Hamer removed a twenty-five pound plate that he'd taken from the Falcons weight room. He slipped the plate into the bag at Jim's feet, zipped it up, and rolled it over the lip of the concrete into the lake. The bag gurgled and burped for a few moments, then slipped neatly beneath the water's surface.

I stood there with my mouth hanging open. I knew that water was two hundred feet deep. The word was, the deep murk surrounding the intake valves was populated with catfish the size of cows. I imagined Jim's body decomposing down there in the warm water and the bag turning into a kind of biological lollipop for those big cats. A small shudder scampered down my spine.

"Ten percent," Hamer said, turning to me. "That's the deal ...that's about half a million a year."

I just looked at him.

The commissioner was obviously pleased with me when I made my full report in his office on Park Avenue three weeks later. I told them exactly what they wanted to hear. I found nothing. There was nothing to find. The NFL's integrity was completely intact. Mr. Kruetz beamed proudly in my direction and nodded his head at every last detail of the fiction.

They told me the NFL appreciated the thoroughness of my efforts. They'd even gotten a complaint, indirectly from Coach Samuels, and both Mr. Kruetz and the commissioner remarked on my fortitude for standing tall in front of the venerable man. I politely listened to their vague suggestions that a more formal agreement with me for investigative services was forthcoming. The timing had to be right, but they had no doubt that the proper opportunity would soon arise.

I smiled stupidly and fondled the handle of the black leather carry on bag that rested on the floor beside my chair. I was probably pushing my luck by bringing the same electronic device that was undermining them into the commissioner's office, but life is all about timing. The commissioner had requested a wrap-up meeting with me on Monday morning and I had to catch a plane to Denver in order to be there in time for the Monday night game. The Falcons were playing the Broncos and it was imperative for Hamer to get a couple of quarterback sacks on national television. A performance like that could lead to some national endorsements and with ten percent of the action, I certainly didn't intend to let my new partner down.

GOOD SEATS

BY COLIN HARRISON

I never thought any of this'd happen; I just expected I'd drive home to Miami after my twin brother Jimmy's funeral. There was his face, looking up at me from the satin, just like mine, smack-dab perfect, except I had a beard and long hair and he kept everything mowed down, just a little goatee. But we have the same face, mostly. His teeth were not as good, a couple broken. At least the funeral parlor guys shut his eyes. I knew it'd be an awful thing to see, and it was, his widow Sharla crying uncontrollably, along with their two kids, and it put me in a mood, a bad mood. I don't usually get like this, only every few years, really, but this time my brother, my *dead* brother, was involved. Jimmy wasn't the best guy in the world, I mean,he was never going to turn around his life and become President of the United States, like someone else we didn't vote for, but his kids loved him. I know it. I saw them cry. The only good thing, I guess, is that Dad was long dead and Mom is so far gone she thinks her hairdresser is Liberace. Anyway, everybody went back to Sharla's mother's place after the funeral, just to talk and cry and remember Jimmy and to say wasn't it terrible how he died, but I didn't feel like doing that, no way, I just slipped out of there with the keys to Jimmy's house in my pocket. I haven't been back up north to the old neighborhood much but I still remember my way around, so it didn't take me long. His house is a two bedroom ranchburger out in Riverhead, Long Island, which isn't exactly the town we grew up in any more.

So I have the keys and figure hell, I'll just look around the place one more time, see if there's anything that tells me something. The first time I was there was right after the murder and I was still shocked, which is natural, even though I've seen a few things. Done them, too. But no matter what, it's a shocking thing to get the call and be told some dudes somehow got into your brother's house, waited for him to come home, and then practically cut him in half and left him propped up watching television with a baseball cap on his head.

But this time through I'm in a different mood, a bad one sure, but also a thoughtful mood. So I just slip in the back door. Sharla's left the alarm off, which is good because I didn't know the punch code. Jimmy was careful with stuff like that. Inside, there's cereal on the floor, one of the kids' tricycles. Except for the crime scene trash that the police left, the place is just the same as when Sharla found Jimmy. Just the same, poor mutt. Downstairs they took the sofa away that he was on but there's still a big stain of blood on the carpet, the lamps knocked over, the Ping-Pong table collapsed where they fell on it. Jimmy was just a little smaller than I am, but he still went about 255 pounds, so it must have been two guys at least. The coroner said he had contusions and abrasions on his head, which meant they beat on him pretty good. Usually a guy who owes you money is shot in the head, so why these guys had to go and leave my brother there looking like an open cooler in a bait shop is beyond me. It's cruel, if you think about it.

So I was looking around the house, picking things up, putting them down, nosing through all the junk. Jimmy was messy as hell. It's true that he had a pretty good meth lab going in the basement, and the police had been all over that, looking for phone numbers, records, anything they could find. So I didn't bother with that, and I figured it was better to keep my fingerprints to a minimum, anyway. They've got them anyway, down in Florida. And my blood. You have to be careful in New York State. They passed a new law a couple of years ago in Albany and the state keeps a DNA registry; there's a backlog of 40,000 blood samples, but the state lab will catch up eventually. So I kept my gloves on, just to avoid any problem, and sort of drifted around the house. He kept his business and his family stuff pretty well separated. Sharla hadn't been back since the murder and it was going to be a shock all over for her. I'm really sorry for her and for the kids. She was never a great wife, but then again Jimmy was not so true-blue, either. It's a known fact that Jimmy married her because she had the best rack in Eastern Long Island. When she was twenty-two, at least. I mean stacked and racked. Guys used to come up to her at the stock car races in Riverhead, when she was sitting between me and Jimmy, and say stuff to her. Which, if you knew us, was pretty dangerous, okay? They were willing to take the risk. She was that hot. One time this black guy from Harlem who everybody said might make the NBA as a center says something to her in the city and Sharla kind of likes it, I could tell, wants to push her luck a bit, puffed her chest out and so on, and Jimmy very quietly pulled out his gun and asked the black guy where did he want the hole. Real low, like this: *Tell me where the hole should be, I want to get it right.* The guy left. Sharla did something to guys, looking at her, it was her mouth, too, kind of ugly and twisty in a good way. I always wanted to fuck her, I admit it. I even told Jimmy, but he knew anyway. Being twins, we basically could read each other's minds. I know you want her, too, he said once. Yeah, I did. But the fact that I admitted it made it okay. And I told Jimmy that if he wanted to keep Sharla then he was going to have to marry her and get her knocked up and make some money. That's the secret. If you love her, I said. If it's just jealousy, let her go. I don't think he knew the answer. They got married and then suddenly ten or twelve years go by, she's had four kids, nobody's looking at her tits anymore, and probably Jimmy's looking at someone else's. Now Sharla has no source of income and four kids who eat seven boxes of cereal a week. I'm not exactly flush but I asked her how much the funeral would cost and she said eight thousand. I told her I'd cover it.

So anyway I'm thinking about all this as I'm looking in the drawers, finding all the stuff you usually find, and I look in the refrigerator, which was full, and in the freezer, and the garage and I keep thinking, Come on, the guys were in the house a couple of hours waiting for Jimmy to come home, the police figured that out at least because somebody made a call from the house to a payphone in Riverhead and it wasn't Sharla. So they had a couple of hours to snoop around. Sharla said she thought that the cash jar she kept on top of the refrigerator had been emptied, so that's a clue. Anyway, I poked around Jimmy's desk, pretty amazed at all the unpaid bills he had going, considering what the police said he was making with the meth lab, when I notice his calendar above his desk with Sunday, December 10 circled, Jets against the Lions.

I remembered that he'd said he'd bought two tickets to the game. From a scalper. Good seats.

Well, a guy like Jimmy, he doesn't leave Jets tickets around. He put them somewhere he won't lose them. Like his underwear drawer. I look there, no luck. I looked in the hutch in the dining room, which was the place our father used to keep *his* Jets tickets. (I mean before he walked too close to one of those big General Electric engines they have on 747s, back in 1986. He'd worked at JFK for eighteen years. Things got bad for us after that.) Then I went back to Jimmy's desk with all the paper on it and methodically went through every piece. I counted twenty-eight unpaid bills, poor mutt. The gas, the water, the real estate taxes, everything. Maybe he sold the tickets, I thought. He definitely needed the money. But then I looked under the phone, which is where he might have kept them, and I found one of them. Just one long green Jets ticket, with the date, seat number, and everything. Why just one? Did he give away one? I don't think so, that wasn't Jimmy. He cared about the Jets, unlike me. I'd given up reading the sports page. But Jimmie was a fan. Vinnie Testeverde made him crazy—sometimes great, sometimes terrible. He loved Wayne Chrebet though. Imagine, a short slow white guy who catches touchdowns in the NFL. Amazing. So I don't think Jimmy just gave away the ticket. And I'm thinking that if you're going to sell the tickets for money, you sell them *both*. Much more value that way. If you're going to take a buddy to the game, you take both tickets with you. It didn't make sense.

Then I remembered that the killers had been in the house a while. Maybe one of the them had noticed one of the tickets and put it in his pocket. Sharla hadn't been through the house yet because of the shock. She wouldn't know it was missing. She might not have noticed anyway, since the kids were always screaming and hanging off of her, and Jimmy more or less came and went. She might not even have known he bought two tickets, things being what they were between them. He could have put the two tickets under the phone on his desk and what with the papers and the lifting of the phone and general messing around, one of them could have started to float around in that mess. Then along comes one of the killers, sees it, and thinks, the guy is going to be dead anyway, I might as well not let the ticket go to waste. That was my analysis, anyway. I always try to tell myself not to jump to conclusions, but that was the best analysis I had. I was sure he'd said two tickets. He might have said don't mention it to Sharla. I can't remember, though.

So I have the other ticket there in my hand. The game is two days away, in the stadium in the Meadowlands, in Jersey. I'm supposed to drive back to Florida. But then I keep thinking, the killer has the other ticket. If I go to the game, then I might be sitting next to my twin brother Jimmy's killer.

On the other hand, I could drive home and just forget the whole thing. But who can do that? Not me.

I could give the ticket to the police, of course, and see if they would follow up, maybe send someone to the game, but this option doesn't appeal. This option leaves me out, removes my own opportunity to see what's what. Generally I try to avoid cops; we usually have differences of opinion, you could say.

And anyway, the Police had their chance already.

When I get to the game two days later, the weather is cold and rainy, really blowing across the parking lot. It's mostly campers, vans, big SUVs. People are kind of excited and scared. If the Jets win they can sneak into the playoffs, and if they lose they're out of it. Another season blown. Everybody has on ponchos, many with the Jets logo. The parking lot is filled early, of course, with guys cooking out, throwing balls around. Basically it's a temporary village with everybody wearing green. Naturally, I'm looking at every guy, thinking Jimmy's killer is here.

I spent the last couple of days preparing, I admit. The first thing I did was I called home and told the guys I wouldn't be at work on Monday. Still broken up over my brother and all that. Which is true, but just not in that way. I was staying in one of those shit hotels off Ninth Avenue, paid in cash, said my name was Wayne Testeverde. The guy at the window, some Pakistani, didn't get it. Then I bought a few items that I thought I might need. What those are will become clear soon enough, okay? Then I drove over a day early and memorized the parking lot at the Meadowlands. It can be confusing as hell, especially after a game late in the season when it's dark. All trucks find little camp fires and it's hard to tell which side of the stadium you're on. Our dad used to write down the section number and stick it in his pocket, even though he'd been there a million times. I myself have gotten lost more than once looking for my car. So there was that preparation.

At the Meadowlands, they check your backpack for glass bottles or video cameras, both of which you can't bring in. But they don't pat you down, not yet anyway. I know they used face recognition technology at the last Super Bowl, for terrorists and snipers and stuff, a hundred cameras scanning the people coming in hooked up to big computers, but they don't have that yet at the Meadowlands stadium. And they don't make you go through a metal detector. So I had options under my poncho. I mean everybody looks like everybody else. You got about five basic poncho patterns and under that people have all kinds of different Jets hats and jackets. I myself am in a poncho over a green Jets windbreaker over a Jets cotton and leather jacket. I've got three different Jets hats in my pocket, too. I figure that I can keep changing my appearance if necessary.

So I get to my seat pretty early. Detroit is closer to my side, the Jets down the other end. The punters are practicing their high kicks, the receivers taking long throws. The ball is going to be wet, that's for sure. They're warmed up. I won't say too much about the game. If you saw it on television, you know it was stupid and forgettable. Sure, the weather destroyed their passing game. But the Jets suck, and that's all there is to it. You don't love football because of games like that one. I myself barely paid attention. What I was watching for was who was going to sit next to me. They won't know it's me, though. I'm way under the poncho, hat low, sunglasses. Nobody's going to recognize me, the Jimmy-likeness, I mean, not with the heavy beard and long hair.

Then I realized I didn't know if it was the seat to my left or the one to my right that Jimmy had bought. I'm in the middle of the row. Eventually along comes this old guy, I call guys like him bleacher birds. He's got the cooler, the radio, the little television. A poncho as big as an igloo. He's a regular, I think. But maybe he looks like a mob guy, a regular old mob guy. Maybe a little too old.

Hard to say who's a killer, who isn't. You can get fooled. You can't jump to conclusions. So I'm watching. Everything is ritualized with him. I watch him closely. He gives me a nod, sits down. Then he takes out a cigar and lights it and plugs it into the back of his mouth. No problem. Nothing big going on.

I try a little conversation. "I guess they better do it today, huh?"

He nods. "Yeah. I didn't like the spread, either."

"Testeverde's arm's been looking pretty floppy lately."

"Yeah," he says. "He's getting old."

"Season's a bust."

"Yep."

"I mean the whole thing got sort of cut in half," I say.

Old guys looks at me funny, maybe because I have on my sunglasses. "What do you mean?"

"First half we had all this hope, second half nothing but bad news."

"I been out here so long my heart's been busted a million times," he says.

This is my opening. "Season ticket?" I say.

"Yeah, since '83."

He's not the killer then. "You've seen some bad seasons."

"Tell me about it." Then he plugs in his cigar again and is lost under his poncho looking at the scores from the other games. The wind is blowing badly.

I'm looking around now for who else is going to be sitting down and then I see this blonde babe coming down the steps. She's not going to be sitting next to me but I look anyway. She's got a rack on her, the kind when you see it, it sort of hurts you. You can tell, even though she's wearing a poncho. I forget even why I came to the game. But then she stops and looks at her ticket and then turns up my row and comes over and sits down next to me, doesn't look at me once. I've got my binos up against my eyes, a whole hot-dog in my mouth, mustard in my beard, hat low, the whole thing. I look like nobody she knows.

And I don't see how it could be her. It's not right. She doesn't look like a killer. She's all girl. I watch her carefully. She wipes off the seat with a hot-dog napkin and sits down carefully and adjusts her poncho and everything. She looks a little out of place, too. A girl like that never goes to a football game alone, let me tell you. Either it's with a guy or with another girl. You see that at the game, football chicks, either looking for the pick-up or just into the game, all those tight little uniforms, big ass muscles. But she doesn't look like either case. She's good looking thought, in that sort of scanky Jersey way, too much hair, nails too perfect. Bitchy beautiful, Jimmy would have said.

But I got figure her out. I watch her as carefully as I can but I'm not getting anything. The game is ridiculous. All rain. Testeverde's a bum. Bleacher-bird is basically a green tent with binoculars sticking out. I'm feeling pretty stupid. Me and my big plans. Maybe I had it all wrong. Then the girl takes out her purse to look for something. She holds a set of keys in her hand and the keychain says Riverhead Honda. I know that place. It's on Route 58 as you're going through. So she's from Riverhead, that's something. That's a lot, actually, since Riverhead is about 95 miles to the east. You have to go all the way around New York City to get here from there. So that's something, I tell myself.

Then she takes out her cell phone and calls. "I'm ready," she says, "if you want to." She's not really watching the game. "Just bring me some hot chocolate, okay?" Then she says, "D102, Row 8, Seat 16. You can remember that, also the hot chocolate."

A few minutes later, a big guy comes down the aisle. Big arms, neck, the whole thing. She stands up. Even under the poncho, I can see she's got a peach on the back end there. She walks down the row—everything stops for a big play—then takes her hot chocolate and says something to the guy and then he comes along the row. She's given him the ticket stub. Also the cell phone. He steps along the row, pretty polite, and sits down next to me. Doesn't even look at me. Now my heart is starting to get going, second gear, anyway. This might be the guy.

I'm going to unpack this mother-fucker, I think. I'm going to stay cool, and figure it out.

"Were you up top?" I asked.

"Yeah, wet as hell up there."

"Jets are killing me here," I say.

"Me, too," he says

"They started so well. You see the Miami game?"

"That was beautiful." It was, too. One of the greatest comebacks in NFL history. "I don't think Testeverde's got much left."

He sits on this a while. Then he says, "And they let Keyshawn Johnson go." He shakes his head like this is the saddest thing he knows. But the saddest thing is that somebody, probably him, cut my brother in half and left him on the sofa for his kids to find him when they came home from soccer practice. That's the saddest thing I ever heard. Sharla is going to need years to work her way out of this one, even if the kids aren't permanently screwed up, which they will be.

"You from Riverhead by any chance," I say.

"Why you ask that?"

I've been too direct. A mistake.

"The girl that was here's from Riverhead."

He looks at me funny.

"No, I'm from somewhere else."

I nod, like I'm stupid and this is a good answer.

"Where you from?" he says.

"Way down Miami."

This seems to make him relax."You up for the game?"

"Yeah," I say. "Visiting family, whatnot."

"That's cool," he mumbles, watching the game now.

I have a ten inch hunting knife under my poncho and I could probably stab the guy without him even seeing it but if I do I'm not getting away. And I *am* planning on getting away.

Then his cell phone rings and he pulls it out to answer. He yanks off his right glove with his teeth so that he can press the buttons more easily and that's when I can see he's got this deep cut on the underside of his second and third fingers. Maybe a week old, which would make it the right time.

"Yeah?" he says into the phone. "Sure, sure. You can drop it off tomorrow. No, no, it's cool—don't worry about it. Sure...all right." He makes another call and looks way up in the top tier of the stadium, right into the sodium lights practically. "You having a good time? I know it's cold up there. Don't worry, I'ma warm you up real soon, fact, I'ma *light* you up...sure I can talk like this. You like it, I know you do...we can leave at the start of the third quarter, you want. No, let's wait until then, it's a low scoring game so far. Sometimes Vinnie takes a half to get going...wait, wait, put Billy on, Billy? You want to come down here for a while? No? All right? Seat's pretty fucking good, man. All right. Keep your hands off her, you fucker. Leave some for me. All right, I'll see you in a while here."

It's him, I'm sure. The fucker who. I can picture him flipping through Jimmy's papers, I can see him holding him down on the sofa. And the whole time, I've got the knife in my hand under the poncho with a lot of spit in my mouth. But I do nothing.

At the end of the game, I let him get in front of me but I follow him. The Jets have lost, everybody hates him, the season is over, so far as the playoffs go. He's talking on the cell phone, I see. It takes a while to get out of the stadium, a sea of green ponchos. I switch one of my hats, for the hell of it. Outside it's cold and rainy and dark, the parking lot jammed. People are tired and disappointed, moving slowly. They know they have the traffic ahead of them. I follow him from the back, never taking my eyes off of him because of the green ponchos. Then I see he's meeting up with the girl and the other guy, which is good. I follow them from fifty feet back, with my head down. No problem. The traffic getting out of the stadium is insane, a line of SUVs with their lights on. Guys swinging flightlights with orange cones, nothing moving. My own truck is about two hundred yards away in the other direction but I'm keeping my eye on these three. They're in a good mood, I can tell by the way they walk. They reach one of the outer lots and get in a pretty nice customized van. The doors close, the lights go on. But no exhaust out the back, the engine is off. I'm thinking now, I'm ready, I've got all kinds of stuff in my backpack.

What I want, actually, is my truck. I want to have access to it. They're not going anywhere, I can tell, not real soon. The line of traffic is backed way up. But, just in case, I ease up behind the van, keeping my visor real low and make like I'm looking for my own car in the rain. I can hear they've got the music system on in there, but I don't look in the window. By now I have my tire-buster out, which is what you get if you weld a ten-penny nail to the head of a sawed-off sledge hammer. You lift the head, let it swing down, and you can drive the nail deep into a tire. You hit the side of the tire, not the tread, because the steel belting is much thinner there. I know, I've conducted experiments. So I look away and give the tire a whack. It goes in so fast, like a needle, no one should really notice the sound. And they don't. In fact, I can't see what's going on inside the van, because of the curtains, but I can hear the music and I can see that no one is in the cab.

So I walk quickly back to my truck, which takes five minutes, and when I get back near the van, I'm half expecting one of the guys to be bent over in the rain looking at the flat. But he's not. The space next to the van is empty now so I pull in, nice and close, the van to my left. Now I've got tools, wheels, everything I need. I check the van again. They're in the back, doing whatever. And the tire is half flat now. I have a little time, so, sitting in the cab, I pull out my electric razor and then I do what I planned all along, I cut my hair short, which takes maybe a minute, buzz, buzz, and then I change the setting on it and take my beard way down and then off, except for the goatee, like Jimmy had. It's fast and a little sloppy and I get hair everywhere that I'll clean up later. But it's a pretty good job. I'm about ten pounds heavier than he was and my teeth are a little better, like I said. But I get it pretty close. I'm paying brotherly homage here, too. I want to see their faces when they see Jimmy-me looking back at them.

Now I get out of the truck. I have the little gun—the popper, I call it—and the knife. I don't need much more. I stand next to the van's cab. Still that music. The passenger window is open six inches. Whatever they're doing, they don't care about getting rain on the seat. People are trudging by in the rain, they don't notice me. A few kids are throwing a football around about forty yards away, they don't see me. I examine the locks in the cab. The driver's side unlocked, passenger side locked. They have no idea. but I want to be careful. They've got the sound system on, that means the van's on the battery. The electric windows work. I reach in, find the button, and lower the passenger window completely. Then I get back in my truck and wait. It takes about five minutes but one of them, the balding guy, comes up and sits in the passenger seat. He give me a glance but I'm under my visor. He's smoking something and laughing.

"Naw, I'm taking a rest," he says.

I turn to him, my visor down now.

"You like the game?" I ask.

He doesn't seem to recognize me as Jimmy. "Ahh, man, fucking Jets," he moans predictably, then says, "Hey, weren't you sitting—"

That's when I reach out of my window, six inches from his, and fire. It's a direct hit. He has no chance, no thought, nothing. He jerks sideways, right down into the deep well in front of the seat, and doesn't get up, which is perfect. I know he's bleeding all over down there but can't see it. I lean out my window to check. He doesn't have any pants on, which is sort of freaky. Now I'm out of the truck and around the other side of the van, to the driver's side. I put my hand on the door handle. I can't risk messing with the window. I know the other guy is going to wonder what's going on. The boys are still throwing the football, haven't heard anything. No problem. Rain hitting my face, hard. Then the other guy comes forward in the van, saying, "Yo, Billy what the fuck you doing?" His voice is dreamy, relaxed. He's been taking something. "Billy, man, you sick?"

That's when I open the door. The cab light goes on. He looks up at me, surprised. His face is flushed, his shirt unbuttoned. He has no chance. The rain is blowing in.

"What?"

I get him in the left side of his head, but he jerks as I fire and I basically just get his nose. I need to shoot him again but I don't like the cab light being on and the little chime going. I close the door and hurry around the other side of the van and get him in the back of the head through the window. He's finished. Blood all over the inside of the cab, I admit it, but most of it low, none on the inside of the windshield. Both of them kick around a minute, fingers twitching, but then it's over. There is powder all over my gloves and coat, I know, but I'll dump them.

Now it's just the girl. I wait for a moment, for a stream, anything. Nothing, which is weird. I lock my truck, then open the van's sliding door. There she is, naked, on a big built-in mattress. I close the door. God, does she look good. She turns her head sort of dreamily.

"Oh, Jimmy," she says.

I didn't expect this, and pull the door shut quickly. It's dark inside the van. But I can see the baggies of pills over on the floor, all kinds of booze in a cooler.

"Finally you're *here*."

"Yeah," I say.

"Come on," she says, pulling at my pants.

I have to lay my gun and knife aside under my jacket.

"Come *on*, Jimmy." She her head back and forth, eyes closed.

"I missed you *so* much."

She has no idea. She's pretty far gone.

"Where *were* you?" she says. "I missed you so much."

"I got held up."

"I thought you *abandoned* me."

"No."

"I really, *really* did. You told me not to call, so I didn't."

"That's good." But I wonder if it's a lie.

"And you didn't call *me*."

"I was busy."

"I thought you'd *dumped* me and I knew you'd be mad if I called."

"It's all right now."

Her eyes are nearly closed. "I'm so-o-o happy. I knew you'd meet me, like we said."

I have my pants off. "Who were those other guys?"

"Just a bunch of jerks. Are they still here?"

"They left."

"Good."

She takes me with her hands and yes I was hard and I went right in and it was very nice. Nice as it gets. She twisted around and found a bottle while I went at it. "Oh, so good, so good, sweetie."

"All right," I said. I'm touching her breast but I can't feel anything much because I still have the gloves on.

"You're not jealous of those guys?" she asks.

"No."

"I just met them coming into the game."

"You did?"

"Yeah, just a few minutes before the game...they seemed all right and I was very lonely waiting for you."

"What's their names?"

"I don't know. Oh, oh. Keep—on."

"You got sort of lonely?"

"Yeah, yeah. You said you'd meet me at gate D."

"Right."

"I waited and waited."

"Okay. You don't have to wait now."

We went on for a while after that and then we were done, bingo-bango. I didn't really enjoy myself, but I liked the unexpected opportunity, if you want to know the truth. I didn't want to come, because of the DNA, but I couldn't help myself. I don't think she noticed much. She took another pill and rolled over.

"Are you boys done with me?" she muttered dreamily, "because I'm tired." Then she giggled. "Oh, it's you Jimmy, I forgot."

"It's okay," I said, wondering what to do next. I buckled my pants.

"Did your wife find out about the game?" she asked in a high voice.

"No, no," I said, guessing. "She thought I just had one ticket."

"That's nice."

Sailing on moonbeams. She rolled on the floor. "I don't mind if you boys want to come back," she said sweetly, her eyes closed.

Fucking DNA, I'm thinking. Even if it matches Jimmy's, it matches me, too.

"How'd you get to the game?" I asked, wondering if she had a car in the lot somewhere.

"You told me to take the Port Authority, Mr. Goofers, remember?"

"Oh, yeah," I say. "So you met these guys at the gate?"

"Yeah. Nice guys. I knew you'd like them."

"Today was the first time you met them?"

"Yes. Don't be so jealous."

They didn't kill Jimmy.

Poor mutts. He gave her the ticket ahead of time, never shows, and she gets flirted up by two guys with a van. So I had a problem. But with a girl like this, you have options. I know, I've dealt with them before. Miami is full of them, in fact. Most of them own a pair of heels and a suitcase full of cheap, expensive clothes and that's it. If they were truly beautiful, they'd be living in LA or in someone's condo. But they're not, and the rules of the market apply. Supply, demand. New product, shelf life, planned obsolescence.

I got her dressed and took all of her things, including the pills, and lifted her into my truck. She couldn't walk, and just slumped over in the seat and dozed. I checked the van carefully, very carefully, and got all of her stuff out. I'd never taken my gloves off, so no prints. But what about hair fibers? I used my little handheld car vacuum that charges off the cigarette lighter. Just a minute or two where I'd been. With the door shut no one outside could hear it. That would make all the difference. Within a few hours, the cops would be all over the van of course. But what could they find? Not much, I hope. Five years from now they'll vacuum a crime scene for skin cells and do the DNA match that way, you can be sure.

They could find the ticket stub to Jimmy's seat. I fished my hand into the pockets of the dead guys, found it on the third try. Then I remembered something else. The cell phones. She called one of the guys, asked for hot chocolate. He came down, she handed him the phone. That probably meant it was his phone. Then he called the other guy. There would be records of all these calls. But they didn't record that she was in the stadium.

"Hey sweetie," I asked her. "Give me your cell phone."

"I don't have one, Jimmy. You stopped paying for it, remember?"

"Oh, right, right," I said.

Time is passing. I want to get out of there. But I have to think about this. The cell phones will show they were in the stadium, calling each other. Nothing in that, necessarily, especially since it was a good hour earlier. As soon as I get her out of the van, there's nothing to link her to the two guys. Well, probably the parking lot had security cameras. I had to assume it. But what do they see? Sixty thousand people on Jets ponchos.

We got to Virginia by dawn and I got us into a little motel off I-95 that I like, just for a few hours. She was still whacked out. But so beautiful. I gave it to her again and then dragged her into the shower to clean her up. I was starting to like her a little. No wonder Jimmy ran around with her. Maybe there was a way things could work out. A girl like that just needs some stability, some regular affection. One time she said, sort of asleep, "You can do anything, just don't hit me again. Please don't." It was a dream she was having. I'd never hit her. It made me feel sorry for her. I looked in her pocketbook. Her name was Kim. When she started to wake up, I gave her breakfast and she asked for four pills. I gave her three. She took them eagerly, asked for a cup of coffee then passed out. I drove straight toward Miami, even in the daylight. She peed in her seat once and cried about it when she woke up but I cleaned her up in a rest stop and we kept going. She told me I seemed different and asked if I went to the dentist, but other than that didn't seem to know it wasn't my brother.

We spent the night in Edisto, Georgia, off the highway. It used to be a nice area. They've built up the area a lot in the last ten years, so it was easy to find a place to sleep. She didn't try to run off, because I had the pills. But I started to worry about the gun. It was a good one, yet I had to get rid of it. We passed some salt water marshes and I pulled over, found a stick, worked a hole in the marsh muck under the tide line and shoved the gun in there two feet down. Perfect, really. Salt water then air then salt water. It would rust away to nothing. I must've gotten rid of ten guns that way over the years. Then I stopped behind a restaurant and put everything in the fullest dumpster I could find: all my Jets stuff, the ticket stub, Kim's poncho, my gloves. In the morning I pulled through on the way out and the dumpster was empty. All Kim wanted was the pills. She asked for four again and I gave her two and a half. "Please?" No, I said. I tried to ask her about herself and she wouldn't say much, except that she once saw her mother and father get into a fight and her mother stuck a steak-knife in her father's thigh. I had to keep getting food in her, and frankly I also had to get her to sit on the pot, and wipe her as well. But she came back to life in the bed—it was strange and I started to see how Jimmy might have gotten a little addicted to her. And the fact that he'd been there before didn't bother me at all, to be honest. I had to hand it to him, he had a way of finding them. She would sort of lie there, nursing on it, if you know what I mean, and that does something to a guy, it gets deep in his head.

By the time we got about a hundred miles north of Miami—that part of the drive is a long stretch—I had her down to two pills on each shot, and I was thinking maybe I could get her cleaned up and have her around the house. Give it a couple of months. See where it might go. Thinking about this, how it might work, I said, "Hey Kim, who gave you these pills?"

She giggled. "Well, Jimmy, I actually have a little admission to make."

"What is it, sweetie?" I said.

She seemed real happy in the truck and hugged her knees. "Some guys came and found me in that new bar in Riverhead and said we'll give you a bag of three hundred specials if you tell us the security code to Jimmy's alarm system."

"How did they know you knew it?"

"They must have seen me sneaking in there, silly."

"They watched?"

"Yeah, a lot of people knew I've been coming over when Sharla is out, and the kids at school."

"What were their names?"

"I don't know."

I tried to contain myself. "What did they look like?"

"I can't remember, it was dark."

"You gave them the code?"

"Yeah. J-E-T-S, right?"

I sort of coughed. "Right."

"You don't mind?"

"No, sweetie, it's okay." Then I had an idea. "I think I've been kind of unfair to you, Kim."

"How?"

"About the pills."

"Really?"

"Yeah, two is pretty stingy."

"Can I have more?"

"Yeah, I guess so," I said.

"How many?"

I pulled over and looked in the bag. There were still a couple of dozen. "Six?"

"Oh, Jimmy! Jimmy!" she cried.

When I got to Miami an hour later I found a guy I know, Ramone, who is always looking for the right kind of girl for a guy who owns a big boat, a yacht actually, two hundred feet long, takes cruises. Pleasure cruises. I drove in and explained some of the situation. And that she was very willing. Ramone nodded constantly, he deals with this thing all the time. I showed him the bag of pills and he looked at them carefully.

"We can get more of these," he said.

Kim was tripping in the truck, lolling her head around and talking about butterflies. She sounded five years old. I also made sure to tell Ramone about how she nurses on it for a long time, and he heard that, knew that kind of eagerness was worth something extra. He pulled up her shirt and looked at her tits, looked at her legs, felt her hair, looked in her mouth with a flashlight. She was like a rag doll, didn't notice.

"How much?"

I figured my travel expenses and whatnot. "Ten thousand."

He counted out the cash. "The pills also."

"Right," and I gave him the bag.

She'd be on the yacht that night, he said, after they got her washed up and bought some new clothes for her. He burned her purse and identification in this special barrel he has out back, when he needs to incinerate things completely. She wouldn't be needing her driver's license anymore, not where she was going.

When I got home I sent the whole ten thousand to Sharla, for the funeral expenses, and then I cleaned my truck, repainted it, and sold it to a guy I know who needed one in Mexico. This was all a little while ago. I miss Jimmy, every time I look in the mirror, even though I grew my beard back. It's been quiet. Not much going on, this summer. I've started reading the sports page again. Who knows, maybe I'll catch the Jets down here when they play the Dolphins. It's a new season, and hell, I'm a big fan.

GONE DOWN TO CORPUS

BY DENNIS LEHANE

That Sunday afternoon, I go up the walk to Lyle Biddet's house and ring the doorbell. I'm hoping Lyle answers and not his mother or father, because I really don't want to think of him as someone's son. I want Lyle to answer the door so I can convince him, real friendly-like, that we're having an off-the-cuff celebration to commemorate our four years playing football together for East Lake High. I'll tell Lyle there are no hard feelings for him dropping that pass on the one and coughing up the ball on the thirty. No hard feelings at all. And Lyle'll follow me back down the walk where Perry Twombley waits behind the wheel of his Cougar with the Lewis brothers sitting in back, and we'll take Lyle on a little ride and find someplace real quiet and kick the shit out of him.

Ain't much of a plan, I know. Best I could come up with after five months of stewing on it, though, which again, ain't saying much. Only time I was ever much of a planner was on the football field, and that's over now, over and done, which is pretty much the reason we need to beat up on Lyle, the dumb fuck with the bad hands and all.

Lyle lives in this new suburb called Crescent Shores where there ain't no body of water, ain't no shore, ain't much of anything but all these shiny white houses that all look alike on these shiny white streets that all look alike, which is how come we got lost about six times trying to find his house until one of the Lewis brothers remembered there was a plastic squirrel glued to the roof of the Biddet's mailbox.

I ring the doorbell a second time. It's raining, the drops soft and sweaty, and there don't seem to be anyone around on the whole street. It's like they all left their white houses at the same time and drove off to the same golf tournament. So I turn the knob on the Biddet's front door and—I ain't shitting—it opens. Just like that. I look back over my shoulder at Perry. He sees the open door and his big grin lights up the whole car.

It's been three weeks since graduation. Fourth of July weekend. 1970. I'm eighteen years old.

My daddy fought in Korea. Only thing he ever says about it is that it was cold. Colder'n an icebox. He lost a finger to the cold. Lost half a thumb. In the summer, when everyone is hiding from the sun in dark rooms and under trees and tin porch awnings, my old man's lying out in the back yard with a cooler of beer beside him, eyes closed, chin tilted up. One time, my mother looks out the window at him and gives me a small, broken smile. "Damn," she says, "but he looked fine in a uniform."

Perry and the Lewis brothers park the Cougar a block over and then come back to the house, streak up the walk and inside, and I shut the door behind them. It's cool in the house, the air blowing from these vents cut high up in the walls, and for a minute we all walk around looking at the vents, marveling. Morton Lewis says, "I gotta got me a set-up like this."

His brother Vaughn goes, "Shit. We take just *one* of those vents, it'll be good enough for our whole place."

He actually climbs up on the couch, looks like he's fixing to rip one out of the wall, take it home with him. I can picture him a few hours later with the thing sitting in front of him on the kitchen table, trying to find a place for the batteries.

You put the brains of both Lewis brothers together and you still come up with something dumber than a barrel of roofing tar, but those boys are also tear ass fast and my-daddy's-a-mean-drunk crazy off the snap count, kinda boys can turn a starting left tackle into the town gimp, come back to the huddle not even breathing hard.

Perry says, "Nice house," and walks around the living room looking at everything. "Gotta bar too."

There's a small swimming pool out back. It's the shape of a jellyfish and, like I said, none too big, but we have a few drinks from the bar and then we all go out and piss in it.

That's what gets us going, I think. We go back into that too-nice, too-white house and the Lewis brothers have at the vents, and I push over a vase in the dining room, and Perry breaks all the knobs off the TV and pours his beer all over the couch and we go on smashing and tearing things for a while, drunk from the liquor, but drunk with something else too, a kind of hysteria, I think, a need to keep from crying.

If we'd won that last game of the season, we would have gone on to the divisional playoffs against Lubbock Vo-Tech. Only way college scouts see you if you grow up in a tiny shithole like ours is if you make it to the divisionals. And that's where we were heading, no question, until Lyle Biddet's hands turned to Styrofoam. He coughed up the ball twice—once on the fucking *one*—and North Park converted both of Biddet's gifts into touchdowns, left us standing numb and cold under a black Texas sky, the fans heading home, the lights shutting off.

My guidance counselor asks me a week later what I plan to make out of my life, what I'm fixing to do with it, what I plan to apply myself to, and all I'm thinking is: I want to *apply* my hands to Lyle Biddet's throat, keep squeezing till they cramp up.

Lyle, you see, never needed the divisional game. He was going to college no matter what. SMU, I hear. Nice school.

We've obliterated most of the first floor by the time the girl walks in. The hi-fi is in the swimming pool along with two shredded leather armchairs. The fridge is doors-open and tits-down on the kitchen floor. Potted plants are unpotted, the toilet's spilling into the hall, and don't even ask what the Lewis brothers added to the chocolate rug pattern.

So we're standing there, kind of spent all of a sudden, amazed as we look around a bit and see how much shit we managed to fuck up in forty minutes and with no one ever giving the order. That was the weirdest thing—how it just *happened*. It just sprung up, like it had a mind of its own, and that mind went apeshit and angry all over the Biddet's house.

And then the side door off the kitchen opens and she walks

in. Her dirty blonde hair is combed straight down but with two matching strands braided and hanging over her small ears. She's got white boots going up to her knees, and above that she's wearing one of those plaid schoolgirl skirts they wear in the private, Jesus schools, 'cept hers has got red finger-paint splattered on it and someone's drawn a peace symbol over the left thigh. Her T-shirt is tight and I can just make out a pair of hard little nipples pressing up against the tie-dye.

I've seen her a couple times before, when she was younger—Lyle's little sister, a year behind us. She'd gone to East Lake her first year, but then we heard rumors of trouble, a boyfriend in his twenties, a suicide attempt, some said, and the next year she didn't come back, got shipped to some place outside of Dallas, supposedly, locked up with the nuns.

She stops by the overturned fridge, looking down at it for a second like she isn't sure it belongs there, and then she looks up and sees us. She doesn't scream. For a second, I see something catch in her face. A word enters her eyes, and I know exactly what the word is: rape.

I see her throat move as she swallows it, and then she says, "You all done fucking up my momma's house? Or you just getting started?"

She's looking at me when she says it, and I can hear Perry and the Lewis brothers breathing real shallow-like behind me.

She ain't mad or nothing. I can see that. She ain't all appalled that we destroyed her house. In fact, as she holds her eyes on mine, I can see she's maybe thought about doing this herself once or twice, maybe came back here for that very reason.

I say, "You're Lurlene, right?"

She steps up on the back of the fridge, arms out for balance, just one toe up there, her other leg out in the air. She nods, looking down at the heating coils. "And you're Mister Quarterback man, ain't you? East Lake BMOC, all that shit?" She's looking at the fridge below her, a small smile creeping up her thin face, and she draws "shit" out in that Texas woman's way, makes it sound as wide as a field.

"Ma'am." I lift an imaginary Stetson off my head.

The way she's doing that balancing act atop the overturned fridge just kills me for some reason. There's four strange boys standing in her house, and the house looks like them boys rolled a grenade through it, but she's up there doing her ballerina act and somehow taking control of the situation by acting like there ain't really much of a situation to speak of. She just sucks the breath from my chest, I'll tell you what.

She looks out past my shoulder at the living room and whistles. "Dang. You all fucked this place *up*."

Terry stutters. He says, "We didn't mean to, miss."

She hops off the fridge, lands beside me, but keeps her eyes on Terry. "Didn't mean to? Boy, I'd hate to see what you could do, you had a *mind* to."

Terry laughs and drops his eyes.

"Any liquor left?" She moves into the living room and I follow. "Sure."

"I'd like me a tequila," she says, moving toward the bar, about the only thing left standing. "And then we can all go to work on the upstairs. What you say?"

Sometimes, after the sun's gone down and Daddy's been sitting out back all day drinking Lone Stars and adding some sour mash to the mix, too, he'll end up looking at his shitty house and sloping back porch and hard Texas dirt and he'll cry without a sound. He'll sit there, not moving or shaking or nothing, just sit rock-still his face leaking.

Says to me once, he says, "I'd known this was what it was all about, boy, know what I'd a done?"

I'm maybe ten. I say, "No, Daddy."

He takes a long pull on a can, tosses it aside and belches. "Died earlier."

We're up in Mr. and Mrs. Biddet's bedroom, taking a butcher knife to the big, fluffy, four-poster bed, just me and Lurlene. Terry and the Lewis brothers are in Lyle's room and by the sounds of it, they're tearing that place down to the fucking studs. For some reason, I'm not as mad at Lyle as I was when we came here, hell, as I was the whole winter and spring. I'm still mad, though. Madder than ever maybe. But it's something besides Lyle I'm mad at, something I can't put a name to. Something out there that hulks over the flat land like a dinosaur shadow, something bigger than Lyle and bigger than Texas, maybe. Something huge.

Lurlene's done tore hell out of all four pillows, and it hits me as the room fills with feathers, a blizzard of them swirling between me and Lurlene, sticking to her hair and eyelashes, me spitting them off my tongue—it hits me and I say it:

"How do we know when they're coming back?"

Lurlene laughs at me and blows at some swirling feathers and arches her back to catch some of the blizzard on her throat.

"They gone down to Corpus, boy. Hell," she says, drawing it out the same way she drew out "shit," teasing the word, "they won't be back till late Monday. They go every weekend come summer. Them and their precious Lyle."

"Gone down to Corpus," I say.

"Gone down to Corpus!" She shrieks and hits me with what's left of a pillow, the down spilling into my shirt.

Then she drops to all fours and crawls across the bed to me and says, "You think this is a rich house, boy?"

I nod, my throat drying up, her green eyes so soft and close.

"This ain't nothing," she says. "How'd you like to go to a house four times this size? Do four times the damage?"

Seems like I forget how to speak for a minute. Lurlene and her green eyes and too-thin face and body have slid into me somehow, under the flesh, under the bone. I'm about certain I've never seen any creature so beautiful as this girl with the butcher knife in her hand and that crazed laugh in her pupils. You can see hope living in her—anxious, lunatic hope, but pure and kind, too, wanting only to be met halfway.

She says, "Huh, boy? You want to?"

I nod again. Ain't doing much with myself anyway, and suddenly, I'm pretty sure I'll follow Lurlene anywhere she says. Bust up anything she wants. The whole goddamn world if she asks me nice.

'Bout five years back, we break down on Route 39, just me and my mother, and we're standing there in the white heat with the dirt dying of thirst for a hundred flat miles in every direction and Daddy's piece of shit truck gone gasping into a coma beside us, and my mother puts a hand over her eyebrows to scan the emptiness and she looks like any fight left in her just up and died with the truck. She looks like she can remember a time before she got where she is now, and and all those different who-she-could-have-beens fork out like trails before us, branching off and branching off into all that Texas dust until there's so many of them they just have to fade away to nothing or else she'll go blind trying to keep count.

Her voice is dry and torn when she speaks, and it takes a couple breaths to get the words out:

"Remember, Sonny, times like these—remember that somewhere there's someone worse off than you. You're always richer than someone." She tries for a smile as she looks over at me. "Right?"

Poorer, I'm thinking as we get back in the Cougar and follow Lurlene's directions to this other house. You're always poorer than someone. And that poor is a gate keeping you out of all the places other people can go. Only places you get to go are the shitty ones nobody else wants to visit.

Always poorer, I'm thinking, and then we reach this house Lurlene's directing us to, and I'm suddenly thinking, Maybe not.

Because whoever owns this house may not be poorer than anyone. Whoever owns this house may be the richest person in the world.

The front lawn is bigger than East Lake's football field. The house behind it is sprawling and beige with a red tile roof and it seems to spread itself from end to end like a god.

We come up to a tall, wrought iron gate stretched between two beige, brick columns that match the house. The gate is a good twenty feet high, and even with all the tequila-and-beer courage I got from the Biddet's, I can tell you I feel nothing but relief when I see that gate and realize we ain't getting in. I see it in Terry's face, too, even though he says, "So now what we do?"

Lurlene's sitting on the console between us, hunched forward, skinny arms wrapped around her knees. She takes a last swig from a bottle of Cuervo and hands it to Terry. I'm ready for her to say, "Drive through it." I'm ready for her to say anything. I might not like it. But I'm ready.

All she says, though, is, "Could I get by, kind sir?" and slithers over my lap and out the door.

She saunters up to the gate in her white boots and tarnished schoolgirl skirt, and behind me, Vaughn Lewis says, "I'm fucked up."

"Me, too," his brother says.

I look at Terry. He shrugs, but I can see the booze swimming in him, making his blood lurch and squiggle, his eyelids thicken.

Lurlene finds this box sticking out of the column on our left. There's numbers on it, and her fingers dance over them and then she's heading back to the car as the gate begins to open, just starts sliding back into the bushes behind the column on our right. Lurlene hops in and sits in my lap, tosses an arm around my neck and looks out through the windshield as the gate goes all the way back.

She tells Terry, "Time to put it in 'drive.'"

There's a picture of my parents taken just before they got married. It's 1949 and my daddy's wearing his uniform. It's all neat and sharply creased, and his hair is short and slicked back, and he has all his teeth. He's beaming this white, white smile, and holding my mother so tight with one arm that she looks about to bust in half. She's smiling, too, though, and it's a real smile. She was happy then. Happier than I've ever seen her. She's young. They're both young. They look younger than me. Behind them is a chain link fence with a sign on it that says, Fort Benning, GA. My mother's dress is white with a pattern of what looks like black swallows on it, those swallows soaring across her body.

And, man, she's happy. She's happy, and my daddy has all his teeth and all his fingers.

Lurlene gets us in the house the same way she got us through the gate. Her fingers dart across these numbers on a gizmo beside the front door and then we're inside.

We walk around for a while. Ain't none of us, except Lurlene maybe, ever seen a house this big. Ain't sure any of us knew there was a house this big. The front hall has two staircases that meet in a curve up top. It's got a chandelier the size of a fucking Cadillac and all these vases that're taller than any of us including Terry, and the walls leading up the staircases are lined with paintings in gold, frilly frames.

On the second floor, there's a ballroom, Lord's sake. And past that, a room with a long bar and a pool table twice as big as the one in the Biddet's house with these leather sacks for pockets. In the guy's study there's a desk you could sleep on and never worry about rolling off in the middle of the night. There's another bar in there and bookcases lining the walls and the ceilings go up a good fifteen feet and there are ladders on rollers for the bookcases. I go up to that desk and there's a picture of this guy with his wife and two kids and another of him on a golf course and another of him, Jesus Christ, shaking hands with Lyndon Baines, himself. The King of Texas. Man who walked away from the Big Job and said, Fuck it. I ain't no President. I'm a Longhorn. You all fight the war on poverty and the war 'gainst the yellow folk, I'm going home.

I say to Lurlene, "Who *are* these folks?"

Lurlene sits up on the corner of the desk. She picks up the picture with the guy and LBJ. She holds it by the corner in one hand, her wrist bending back, and for a second, I think she's going to throw it across the room.

She puts it back, though. Right where she picked it up from exactly. Maybe it's all the dark oak in there or the red-wine, leather chairs, or all those thick book spines staring down at us. Else, maybe it's just LBJ staring out from that photograph, at us, but I know all of a sudden that we ain't going to touch this room. Ain't going to do a damn thing to it. The rest of the house, maybe, but not this room.

Lurlene says, "I go to school with the daughter."

I look at the pudgy guy with LBJ. "*His* daughter?"

"She was my friend at Saint Mary's." She fingers the hem of her skirt. She looks up at the high ceilings and shrugs. "She ain't my friend no more, though. She ain't nothing but shit."

She hops off the desk and I can see that her eyes are wet, not much, but wet just the same, and a little red. She places her palm on my chest as she passes and gives me a peck on the cheek.

"Come on," she says. "Let's go downstairs. See how much destruction your friends done."

My graduation, my mother gives me twenty dollars she's managed to tuck away. She tells me to go have some fun, I been getting too serious.

Daddy gives me his old truck. Same one broke down on my mother and me that time. Says to me: she's all mine.

I spend a week patching that old bitch together, blow the whole twenty dollars in junkyards on hoses and bushings, a distributor cap.

The afternoon I get it running, I take a few of my father's Lone Stars and chase a red sky across miles of scrub gone purple with the dusk. I pull over in the middle of all this nothing, and I sit on the hood, and I drink down those beers one after the other until the world's gone dark around me. And I wonder what the fuck's going to become of me. I wonder what I'm supposed to do now. Got me a useless truck and a useless high school diploma. I should be like my parents were in that 1949 picture, all smiling and hopeful and shit. But I ain't. What's waiting for me out there, out past the dark and the whole of Texas, ain't nothing I'm looking forward to. And what's waiting behind me don't amount to anything neither but what stole those smiles off my parent's faces.

I lean back on the hood. I look up at the stars. I look up at the black, black sky. It's so quiet. And I think about what my daddy said about how he would have died earlier had he known what the world was going to bring. And I sort of get that now. I sort of do.

To die. But not by my own hand. And not by some yellow man's neither. But somehow. In a big blaze that'll light up the dark sky. Something like that.

Coming down the stairs, me and Lurlene are wondering just what the other boys have been getting up to, imagining a big rich house turned into a squatter's shack in the fifteen minutes we've been gone, but when we turn into the living room past that gigantic entry hall, we find Terry and the Lewis brothers just standing around, fidgeting, and I can tell by the cushions on the three different couches in there that they ain't even tried to sit down. They just been standing there the whole time, hands in their pockets or wiping against their jeans, and the moment I walk in, Terry says, "We don't like it here."

I say, "How come?"

He shrugs, his eyes wide. He's kind of crouching a bit, shoulders tensed like he expects the ceiling to come crashing down on him. "Don't know. Just don't. Ain't no place to set."

I look around at all the couches and antique chairs. "Ain't no place to—?"

"We just don't like it," Vaughn Lewis says. "We just don't like it at all."

Vaughn, too, is all tensed up, his eyes darting around, like he expects something with teeth and claws to charge him.

"We're fixing to go," Terry tells me.

"I want to look around some more," I say, though I'm not sure I do.

"Come on," Lurlene says. "We got some damage to do!"

Terry shakes his head. "Ain't wanna touch nothing in this here house."

I look at Vaughn and Morton. They both look ready to dive out the window.

And I can feel it, too. Ain't nothing here but an empty house, but it's some mean house. Some big, mean, icy house. Too clean, too gleaming, ready to swallow us all.

Terry says, "We gone git, son." He steps up to me, meets my eyes. "Got to git. Got to."

I say, "Okay. Git then."

"You coming?"

I look at Lurlene. The hope in those green eyes has gotten bigger and more desperate.

I say, "No. You boys git along. I'll catch up."

"You sure?"

I meet his eyes and nod. "We'll see you."

They each give Lurlene a shy nod as they leave, but they can't get out of there quick enough. Seems a half second after they close the front door behind them, I hear the Cougar roar out of there.

"The gate," I say.

Lurlene shakes her head. "You on the inside, it opens by itself as you approach it. You on the outside..." She shrugs and walks around the living room looking at stuff.

I wander into a den and open up a gun cabinet. I look at all these beautiful shotguns with carvings on the barrels and in the stocks, but I don't touch them. I go to the next cabinet and look at the handguns. I find one I like. It's a black Walther with a bone white handle. Fits in my hand real nice. I drop the magazine into my palm, even though I can tell from the weight that it's loaded. I slide the magazine back in. It's the first thing in the house I've touched, and for a second I see my mother with her hand over her eyes as she looks off across miles of scrub and dead land, and I put that Walther behind my back and walk out of the room.

Me and Lurlene wander the house for the next hour and I don't think we see but half of it. She shows me the scars on her wrists at one point, tells me it wasn't but a "cry out." Still, she says, all that blood on the bathroom tile. Like you never saw, she says. Like you'd never want to.

We find a bedroom that's got its own TV and a walk-in clos-et and dolls piled to the ceiling atop this wide dresser. There's a hi-fi in there and pictures on the walls of Davey Jones and Bobby Sherman and Paul McCartney, and I know we're in the girl's room, the one who used to be Lurlene's friend.

We stand in the doorway and I say, "You want to bust it up?"

And Lurlene says, "I want to."

I start to walk in. "Then let's—"

She pulls me back. She sags into me. She says, "No," in a sad crush of a voice.

I hold her as we wander around some more and eventually work our way back downstairs to the kitchen. There's a staircase off the kitchen, kind of tucked away by the pantry, and we follow it down. We find a bedroom down there with a tiny bathroom and it's own small kitchen. About the only small things I've seen in this whole house. The walls in the bedroom are bare, but there's women's clothes in the closet. Not the kind of clothes you expect to see in a house like this, kind of threadbare, Woolworth labels and the like.

The bed is small, too, and we lie down on top of the covers, and for some reason, I feel comfortable for the first time since I entered this monster. I lie there with Lurlene and after a while she says, "How come we couldn't do nothing?"

"I don't know."

"How come we didn't even *try*?"

I say it again: "I don't know."

"She talked trash about me at school," she says. "Told people I was cheap. Made fun of my clothes. Said I was common." She slides an arm across my chest and holds on tight. "I'm not common. I'm not shit."

I kiss her forehead and hold her.

"You still gone beat up Lyle?"

"No," I say.

"Why?" She gives me those green eyes and they seem bigger as they look down into mine.

I get a picture of the jungle for some reason, a world of green leaves, dripping. I see John Wayne pointing to that little yellow kid in *The Green Berets* and telling David Janssen, "That's what we're fighting for," and I think how I don't have no fight left in me. I think how John Wayne is full of shit.

I pull the gun out from behind my back and place it on the bed beside me, wonder what'll happen if we hear the sudden turn of a key in the front door lock upstairs, the rich family coming home and us down here hiding in the bed like a pair of big bad wolves waiting for Goldilocks. I wonder what I'll do then. Make that pudgy man in the picture go get one of his shotguns maybe. Make that pudgy man draw. I don't know. I know that at the moment I hate the pudgy man more than I hate Lyle.

And, yet, it was Lyle's house I fucked up. And I know I ain't going to do nothing to the pudgy man's house except wait down here with his gun. Why that is, I can't rightly tell you. But I feel ashamed.

I see my daddy out in the back yard, his face leaking, and I see my mother with that hand over her eyes, and I see the red sky I chased in that shitty truck. I see John Wayne in the jungle and LBJ in that picture and Lurlene standing up on the fridge, ballerina-like, and I see Lyle dropping that ball on the one, and those stands gone empty of fans under the black sky, and I think how it would have been nice for someone besides my dumb, drunk daddy to have told me that this is it. This is the whole deal.

"Maybe we should go down to Corpus," I say.

Lurlene curls into me. "That'd be nice."

"Just go down," I say. "Disappear."

Lurlene's hand runs over my chest. "Disappear," she says.

But we don't move. We lie there, the house quiet all around us, the quiet of a sleeping baby's lung. We listen for a sound, a click, a generator's hum. But there's nothing, not even a bed creak as Lurlene shifts her body a little more and places her ear to my chest and pulls my hand between her breasts. I can't feel her heart beat, though. Can't feel my own, either, my chest gone as still as the house as she lies against me, listening for the sound of my heart. Waiting and listening. Listening and waiting. For the steady beat, I guess. The dull roar.

NO THING

BY MIKE LUPICA

This is pretty much how it all occurred, how I ended up this way, come up on this kind of surprise ending, leastways for now, to my football career. I say surprise just on account of everything that led up to today and made me, Trumaine Ward, me of all people, once the poster nigger for everything *bad* in the world except the price of gas, the hot boy of Super Bowl Week.

I been telling my story all week, over and over 'till I nearly run out of saliva, riffing like some old jazz man won't take the fucking horn out his mouth, but, hey, one more time can't hurt. .

Anyways, where am I going, this wide-awake on Super Sunday morning?

Over to some church? Tell my story of salvation and redemption to a bunch of holy rollers'?

They gonna give me any publicity when we all through thanking the baby Jesus?

Shit, all week long, I been as high on pub as I used to get on the pipe.

Telling it one more time is probably a good way for me to get the whole story straight, use that *clarity* they always say I got when I look up the field with a football underneath my arm.

It started right up, first thing out the bus Tuesday morning, ten o'clock sharp, what they call Media Day at every Super Bowl, when they got right to it with me, at my own little booth on the 20-yard line. Like one of them set-ups at the carnival where they throw a ball at you, try to knock you into the water. Only in my case they were just trying to dunk me into the same old shit.

This time it's all right, though.

This time, they want me to come up smelling like a fucking rose.

"Trumaine," some sportswriter says, "did you watch the Super Bowl the last time you were in rehab?"

Not even giving me a couple of kiss-ass questions to warm me up, ease my way into it. Hit me right away with it, *pow*, like it was my first carry of the game, take it right up the gut and get popped by the middle linebacker, no gain, second and ten.

Not, what's it feel like being here, Tru? Not, who you think is gonna win, you guys (the Eagles) or the Raiders? Not even, How's that knee of yours you banged up in the NFC championship game, Tru?

Right to the shit.

But I was expecting it, wasn't no thing.

So I say to the guy, "You're talking about my last 28? Over there to Hazelden? I got to watch the second half, Rams vs. Titans, one that ended on the one-yard line. I'm with the rest of them in group, after I finish up my chores."

Guy stays with it.

"What chores?"

I give him a big smile now, showing off the only gold I didn't sell off when things got a little out of hand for that brief period which I'll tell you about, when my finances got more fucked up than they should have.

"What, I got to write your whole story for you?"

The guy, fat even for a sportswriter, said, "How about just the first couple of paragraphs to get me going, and I'll try to take it the rest of the way."

Like we was buddies. Now I go, "Shit, you sound like one of those bad girls I used to run with before I got myself back on the straightaway."

Gets me a laugh.

Guy still brings me right back.

"We were talking about the chores? At Hazelden?"

"Sunday was my kitchen day. I cleaned up after lunch and dinner with my man Essix, was a personal trainer before he got on the pipe."

"E-s-s-e-x?" the guy says.

"*I* before the x. That's how he told us in group the first day, it seemed important to him. Essix with an *i*."

"He have a last name?"

"I just always knew him as Essix, right up until they found

him that day in his room when he didn't allow up for breakfast."

Nobody laughing now.

What time I got here now, by the way? Nine-thirty. Nine hours to the kick exactly.

Still don't seem like enough.

"Dead?" the fat sportswriter says, all business now.

I want to say, no, the front desk at the Rehab Ramada just forgot to give him his wake-up call, yeah, he was fucking dead.

"Overdose. No one ever did figure out how he got the heroin in there, who smuggle it in for him. Essix, he was living on the street before some of his old trainer customers did one of those intervention deals? One where a bunch your friends gang up on you, smack you around before they face you up to being sick 'stead of just high all the time. Or maybe he just wanted to die in a nice, clean place, 'stead of in the park."

I looked up at all of them now, not just the fat boy scribbling away but all of them, knowing I was giving them all one of those angles they all loved, me and that poor motherfucker Essix, how some people make it from rehab to the Super Bowl, the way Mr. Trumaine Ward did, and some ended up like Essix the trainer, Essix with an *I*, deader than disco.

Now another guy in front, TV guy, hair spray-painted to his big head, hair red as ketchup, says, "You think you'd ever make it here?"

I give him my serious look, very serious nigger now, way I would when I'd give them some story in group, making Essix and the rest think we were all in this together. That I wasn't just in the program, that I was *with* the program even though I never really was, because even when things would get out of hand time to time, as I mentioned, I knew I wasn't like the rest of them.

That using, especially using to the *extent* I did, was never no thing with me.

"On that Super Sunday we talking about?" I say. "I was a better bet to end up like Essix."

Tuesday, that was. I mentioned it was Tuesday, right? Media Day? Raymond James Stadium, Tampa, with their pirate shit all over the place, on account of the Bucs play their home games there. Seems like five minutes ago I'm sitting there in my little booth, doing what I call my Piety Sobriety Rap, telling them about that last 28, meaning 28 days on the inside...goddam, the whole damn Super Bowl week going by so fast it's like some movie somebody was fast-forwarding all the way until here, Super Sunday morning, me sitting here, collecting myself.

Reviewing my situation, so to speak, one last time.

Of course now I wanted everything to slow down, the way it did on the field sometimes, when only I seemed to be going full speed, and everybody chasing me looks like they're wearing them tittyboy flip-flops some guys wear when they come out the shower.

Some of my boys on the team sometimes, saying they wake up Sunday morning and want to play the game right now, get it the fuck *on*, especially if it's a Sunday night game like the Super Bowl is, want to play it at nine, ten in the morning, just so's they didn't have to wait around all day.

Not myself, Trumaine Ward.

Not today, anyways.

All week, even playing the hot boy, finding different ways to tell my story, give them all the salvation and redemption bullshit they can handle, I want to hurry up, get to today, play the damn game. Now I just want everything to slow the fuck down, a little bit, anyways.

How can it be nine forty-five already? I ain't even got you past Tuesday yet.

Wish it was still yesterday, tell you the truth.

Truth according to Tru.

Some of the other players, ones who'd been here before, told me on the plane coming down, there was two separate deals, you know that, right, Tru? Super Bowl Week and then the Super Bowl game. There's always the star of the week, the best quote, one drew the biggest crowds, first when they set you up at the stadium, then Wednesday and Thursday, some conference room at the team hotel, all of us sitting at our own tables, answering the same questions we did on Tuesday over to the stadium. Like rehab, it was, now that I think about it, everybody getting together at the start, then breaking up into smaller groups. But everybody always seeming to tell *the same fucking story*. Anyway, the week leading up to the game, that was one deal. Then on Sunday, somebody else would come up star of the game, be the *hot boy*, one who walks off with the MVP trophy, the one says afterward, I'm going to Disney World or some such.

Like I say, I walk away with the week leading up, hands down. At breakfast every day, one of my teammates on the offense, Antawn Barkley, our tight end, usually, or Bijou Dallas, my blocking back, holds up the paper, points to another story about me and says, "There he is again, first page of the sports section again, get out his way, boys, runaway nigger." Fatboy the Reporter, very first day, must have been playing with me, knowing I wasn't just going to write his story, I was going to write everyfuckingbody's.

Friday morning, Bijou says to me, "Ooh, tell me again, Tru, how you climbed out the gutter and got so good and *clean*."

My agent, Dicky Hartnett, who'd stayed with me through it all, the worst of the shit, saw it all coming before we flew down from Philly, Sunday before this one here.

"Tru, you're the thing these assholes like better than a free lunch," Dicky says.

I ask him, what is that, and Dicky says, "An easy story. One about the comeback kid. Back from the depths." Dropping his voice so he sounded like one of the television boys. "Almost back from the grave." Laughing then and saying, "One like they eat like it's ice cream."

"Guarantee you," Dicky says, "somebody will try to go see Darryl Strawberry over at that rehab place in Tampa they got him in now. Wait and see. They'll say you're the Darryl of pro football, only difference being that you came back, you never had that last slip that finished you for good."

Slip, I thought.

Sounding funny almost, like it's a cartoon show, like, oh shit, there goes Tru again on one of them fucking banana peels.

"Slip tacklers now, that's all I do," I told Dicky.

"You were lost," Dicky said.

I said, "Now I'm found."

Part of our little routine.

"Trumaine (Amazing Grace) Ward," Dicky said.

"Amen," I said.

When's chapel, anyway? *Shit*. I miss chapel? No thing. I'll pray for my sins right here.

You think on all kinds of shit when you're wide awake earlier than you wanted to be on Super Sunday morning.

Eight-and-a-half hours to the kick.

Darryl. Fucking Darryl. He never came all the way back. Essix? Never even made it to the second week at Hazelden. That basketball player, Roy Tarpley, whatever happened to him? Michael Ray Richardson, he ends one of the first marquee junkies in the NBA, he ended up being a star in European ball, Italy or Spain or some such, they used to always have me and him in the same television retro-spec-tives. What is it our coach, Matt Corcoran, likes to say? We're all of us just running around dodging raindrops. Matt said he ate too much, even after a couple of what he called heart procedures, not wanting to call them fucking *coronaries*, which we all know is what they were. Other guys, up and down our roster, trying to get off the juice—which is what I'd always called steroids—or just trying to stay one step ahead of the snoops from the league, showing up with their little testing bottles, looking like they want us to fill them with perfume, looking to ring up another fucked-up nose tackle that put on fifty pounds of muscle between last year and this and wants everybody to believe it just on account of he's got a personal trainer now and watching what he eats, he only putting the good into his body 'stead of the bad.

Some guys still go out every night of the week and got shitfaced, like the oldtimer players did in the old days.

That wine is the way I started before I got on the cocaine, which became my drug of choice, before I finally broke into the clear.

Listen up now: This is Amazing Grace Ward, coming to you on Sunday morning, *Super* Sunday morning, talking some good shit now, sending out his message of hope about the grace of God.

Oh, they write me up good now, after all the years, when I was at the head of the fuck-up list, right at the top, head nigger out of all the bad boys who had messed up their careers and their lives, ones like Len Bias ended up dead, or the ones like Darryl who sometimes said they wished they were.

My agent Dicky drove me to Hazelden that last time, the last 28. I'm officially out of the league a year by then, after the Chiefs cut me. Even the Raiders, our opponent tonight, even they wouldn't give me a shot, and everybody in the league knew they'd sign somebody right out of lockup, they thought could help them win. There was a couple of other teams, I can't remember whether they was in play before my first four game suspension, for the first time, or the year I got after that. Even now, after all the telling, you'd think I'd have it down by now, when I was in, when I was out, whether I was at Smithers in New York or Hazelden or out there with the movie stars and such at that Betty Ford. So much shit, that's the problem. Anyway, he'd told the Chiefs, swore up and down, I'd kicked the thing. It was bullshit, of course, he knew it and I knew it, maybe even the Chiefs knew it. Was only a matter of time before I blew a test, even knowing the snoops were going to come around like every other day. After the snoops busted me I stayed around Kansas City for a while and then somehow I end up over to my cousin's place in Tampa, pretty fucked up that time, even I have to admit that, and Dicky come to get me.

All the way across Florida I ask Dicky why he was being so good to me, you can't take four percent of 28 days.

Dicky gave me this long speech about everything I had and everything I lost and how much talent for this game I'd been blessed with and how young I still was and what a good heart I had and finally says, "You're sick, Tru."

I say, "I know, I know."

He was like every counselor I'd ever had, you only shut them up by telling them what they wanted to hear.

I should call Dicky up right now, his hotel right around the corner, wake his ass up, even though he told me he was going to sleep until noon, after he left me last night he said he still had so many more parties to go to, he was starting to wonder if this was just about a football game or the fucking Presidential Inaugural.

Even Dicky never did think I had a prayer of ever making it back to the big game, this kind of Sunday.

Oh, he talks a good game now, talking being the agent boy's game, saying the only two who believed in me was me and him, and sometimes not even me. But we both know he's just playing, but I shocked him the way I shocked the world.

Showing them all I could be a great player again, and something even better than that:

A good boy.

Hell, yesterday afternoon, some hotel over in St. Petersburg, over to the water, they give me one of those Man of the Year Awards, on account of all the charity work I'd been doing, also on account of how my story inspired so many others to believe there's always a way out. They were right about the charity time I put in, no shit. Hospitals, treatment centers, schools, even a couple of prisons. If I'm not practicing or working out or looking at more goddam game film, I'm out there making another appearance, followed by a camera and the Eagles p.r. guy, like I was another famous asshole trying to good-work himself into heaven.

Should of gone to see Darryl this week.

Where was it the two of us got high that time?

Goddam, I'm all over the place this morning I should be getting Frequent Flyer miles.

Must've been in spring training, up in Vero, when he was with the Dodgers that time .

The fuck was I doing in Vero?

Even some of what you want to remember, you can't.

I should eat.

Reminds me, I told Coach Matt Corcoran the other day, "Man, was a time I could out-eat you."

He says, "No way. Look at me, for Chrissakes, it's like I add on a new wing of me every season."

I say, "Was after the Chiefs cut me loose. Don't you ever watch television? They got the pictures to prove it. I look like one of those fat boys Eddie Murphy played in them Professor movies."

Man, I was a treat back then, deciding to stay there in Kansas City like I mentioned after the Chiefs cut me on account of by then I didn't have nowhere else to go, at least presently, eating at Arthur Bryant's almost every night, like I'm trying to set the world's barbecue record, my counselor at the time—doing outpatient, not another 28 saying to me, "Go ahead and eat all you want, just don't go out and wash it down afterward, that's always started the progression for you in the past, hasn't it Trumaine?"

Like I couldn't handle one drink.

I ended up looking like Oprah.

Like I say, I got the pictures to prove it, me looking like somebody inflated me with fucking helium. Television guys still love showing me at this golf tournament in Kansas City one time, my Oprah period, not knowing the only reason I'm even there, letting people see me like that is because some asshole'd actually given me an appearance fee to show up, this being in that period I might've mentioned when I was selling shit off, having to borrow a little from friends, just to get over, on account of most of the money being gone,.except for what Dicky'd put away in one of those accounts I couldn't touch until I was between 65 and dead. When I was living at the Y briefly. But it was just part of the deal, at least for somebody like me, like some dues for all the fun I'd had in my life: You pay and pay and pay.

Do the crime, sometimes you feel like you never stop doing the goddam time.

Thursday, the last formal session with the press, sitting at my table in the conference room, some guy says, "How long is it for you now? Sober, I mean?

"Be a year and one month on Sunday," I say. "Provided I get to Sunday. I'm not even through today yet."

The guy laughs, like it's some kind of inside junkie joke, part of the rap, part of the material, not really giving a shit one way or the other, knowing the only day that mattered to him was *his*, today, right now, the part of today I was spending with him, filling his notebook the way I'd filled everybody else's since I got off the team plane.

I say, "Where you been, man, dead or in Europe?"

He says, "What's that supposed to mean?"

"I thought everybody with a press pass'd done me by now," I say.

You get the beat, right? See how the system works? My life before I got back on my feet, back up there on the straightaway, when I was pissing everything away because I couldn't piss in the man's bottle, I was one kind of copy then.

Was another now.

Wasn't no thing to them, either way.

Good nigger or bad, either way, it don't make no difference to them.

Ten-thirty now. ..

Eight hours to the kick.

Phone's ringing again.

Don't these people know I'm thinking here?

God*dam*, they even did an hour-long special on me the other night, Friday night I think it was, on that ESPN Classic. That show where they go through the fifty greatest athletes and then the next fifty, and just kept going. Like that there. The host explaining that when I came out of Florida State everybody thought I was going to be the next Jim Brown. That there were people thought I was gonna rush for two-thousand yards a season every season, the way guys used to go for a thousand. That I was gonna make people forget Brown and Gale Sayers and Eric Dickerson and Barry Sanders and O.J.

And know what?

I thought the same goddam thing.

I was built like an outside linebacker, six-foot-four and two-hundred-and-forty pounds and that isn't the best of it, best of it is I could run like the anchor nigger on the 4 x 100 in the Olympics. Win the Heisman fucking Trophy twice, freshman and sophomore years. Drafted No. 1 by the Dolphins before what should have been my junior year, come right out and led the league in rushing as a rookie, then the next two years after that. Though I rightly can't remember much of Year No. 3, even looking at the specials and the highlights and such, on account of that being the first year I got on the pipe a little bit.

More than a little bit, tell you the truth, some of them wild-ass parties, some of them situations you could get yourself in.

Oh man, some of them clubs.

Party all year and I still get twelve hundred rushing yards, fourteen TDs, even if those numbers fell off a bit from the year before.

And when I'm out there like that, everybody knowing who I am, saying, Come over to our table, Tru or, Stop by the house later, Tru, there's some people I think you'll find interesting, which always means pussy and dope, you want to know why I don't get caught, even when everybody in town seems me trying to put most of South Beach up my nose?

On account of they didn't want to catch me, is why.

On account of I was Trumaine (Amazing Grace) Ward, is why, and all they wanted to know was what I did between one and four on Sunday, or four and seven, depending whether or not it was a late game on CBS or not, the rest of the time they didn't want to know what they didn't want to know.

Couple of times my rookie year, Ed Halsey, our general manager, guy who drafted me, good guy, calls me in and says, "Tru, if there's anything you ever want to talk to me about, I just want you to know I'm here for you."

I just say. "All I want to talk about is gimme the fucking ball."

"Every once in a while we hear things," he says.

I give him my big smile and say, "Hear what you hear, baby. Then watch what you watch on Sunday. And then you know what you hearing ain't no thing."

And after that I'd go right back to sleeping through meetings sometimes and skipping practice sometimes—they'd tell the press that Tru was working on some of those back spasms again, thank the Lord they only bother his ass on Tuesdays and Wednesdays, not when we getting ready for the kick on Sunday— and ignoring the rest of the shit, the *baggage* so to speak, that came with having Trumaine Ward on your team, knowing he had to blow off a little steam sometimes, party a little bit when the rest of the boys, the good boys on the team, was home reading their playbooks and whatnot, knowing that with somebody like me, you had to take on the whole package.

You fucking kidding me?

If *O.J.* was still playing after he went Benihana on his wife and that waiter and got off the way he did, not guilty right across the board even if everybody on the goddam planet knew he did it, so much of a blood trail it looked like that Telestrator deal Madden draws his pictures over the replays on, you think somebody wouldn't've given *him* the ball again, told *him* to run his nigger ass to daylight like nothing ever happened?

What planet *you* from?

The contract was as plain for me as it was for other guys who came before, whose names I don't have to mention, the fuck-ups who used to be in the papers as much as me and the message was do whatever you want to do, other than cutting your wife's throat maybe, just don't get caught.

Don't get caught on Sunday by the other team and don't get caught by nobody before the next Sunday.

Which is what happens to me my fourth year and puts Amazing Grace Ward on a road you do have to call amazing now, one took me where it took me, good and bad, bad mostly, one 28 after another, series of bad breaks and mostly being in the wrong place at the wrong time you ask me, finally ending me up here, seven hours and forty-five minutes before the kick to the Super Bowl now, tired of walking from one end of this suite to another, tired of walking to the balcony sometimes, then back in to look at the clock again, thinking on everything that brought me to what the press all week kept calling my defining moment.

Makes me want to laugh now.

Where was I?

Oh yeah.

Getting down to it now.

Still talking that good shit.

Was about to tell you about how everything would've been fine for me if I don't get my ass arrested my fourth year, arrested twice, once for driving with a suspended license, the kind of shit Dicky the agent's suppose to stay on top of, and the other time, in that crack house, on account of having to go find Marvin, who once again fucks me and don't bring the merchandise, the *goods* so to speak, and so I finally have enough of his shit and go looking for him and it's just one of those cases I mentioned previously, being in the wrong place at the wrong time. Or maybe it was a setup, which I always suspected, somebody *knew* Trumaine Ward was gonna be in the house, working down the organizational chain from Marvin, able to get myself fixed up with some pipe before I drove back to that big place I was renting at L'Aventura.

Shit. All that time, beating the tests, getting tipped off by the trainer usually, knowing the snoops don't want to catch me, they'd rather make an example of some no neck in the defensive line with zits all over his back begging to get his ass rung up on steroids. All that time staying ahead of the law of the league, only now I get busted by the real law, sitting there in the back room of what Marvin swore up and down and on his momma's grave was a safe house with DuWayne, who'd fixed me up and those two girls, Shirrelle and Sharrissa, when they kick the door in and realized they hit the jackpot, like they won the goddam Florida lottery.

Was like I was in the clear, behind the defense, and decided to bring my own self down. But only on account of Marvin, you understand, none of it happens if you could ever count on fucking Marvin.

Even then, they don't throw the book at me.

Which means if you're a big enough star, even the law looks the other way, long as it wants. So I get probation and suddenly there I am, doing my first 28, sitting there in group when I know I should have be in the running backs meeting, listening to some rich punk from the upper West Side of New York 'stead of one of my coaches, punk telling about how his parents don't understand him, they don't love him even though they think they do because of all the BMW's they give him, whoo whoo whoo, what choice did he have but to start shooting up when he was fifteen or whatever he was?

From the start, first day, no shit, I always got the same thought inside my head:

What am I doing with these *losers*?

My whole career, see, I knew I could stop anytime I wanted to, get myself clean every single time I knew the snoops was coming around. (And you don't really believe in that random testing shit, do you? *Listen to me:* The only reason some of the no-necks get caught and busted for four games or whatever is on account of them being dumber than the guy without his shirt in the top row of the stands you see late in the season when it's snowing in Philly or New York or someplace.) Knew I could get myself clean when we got close to training camp, no thing, just by playing a little more golf than usual. One time on the radio, just playing, I tell the guy interviewing me I can do better with golf than I could doing another 28, and right away somebody writes in the paper maybe there should be a Trumaine Ward Pitch and Putt Rehab

Center, where if you put your ball through the windmill on No. 18 you not only get a free round but get to declare yourself clean of your addictions.

Even got a laugh out of me.

I had it *down*, is what I'm trying to say.

I had a system was *working* for me.

Would go play myself some golf when practice was over, play till it was dark, carry my own little stand-up bag sometimes, make sure I was so yard-dog tired when I was done I didn't even want to think about going out or even getting laid. And mostly it worked fine to me, with those few exceptions I mentioned. Only now, you understand, I had to do the 28 like all the other losers can't get a handle on their lives or their drinking or their using. And that wasn't my biggest fuck-up as it turned out, as I would discover later, my biggest fuck-up was making myself into a permanent suspect.

Like I hadn't lost no step on the field, just off it, and every little thing I did the rest of my life, a traffic ticket or getting into some beef with some asshole on the golf course or getting my picture taken with a couple of girls at some club would get people thinking I was high again.

Oh, I learned the Piety Sobriety Rap real fast, don't worry about Trumaine. God grant me the serenity and all the rest of it, change the shit I can, but always thinking to myself that the only two things needed changing in my life was one, taking the car keys that night when I shouldn't've and two, letting Marvin, who was *suppose* to be my friend, who was *suppose* to be somebody I could count on and reach on his goddam cell or beeper any time of the goddam day or night or so he *said*, on account of the boy was more wired up with gadgets than the telephone man's truck, get under my skin so I had to go looking for him, which is why I end up someplace I wouldn't've if my thinking was clear, if I had that clarity I mentioned going for me.

Just on account of it was one of those nights I let the general pressure of *being* Trumaine Ward, of being me, of carrying the goddam team on my *back* the way I did, get me to the point where I needed a little something to fix me up, then get me leveled off or whatnot.

Marvin drove up to West Palm from Miami one Sunday when I was at Hazelden, wanting to make things right, and the whole time we're talking, I'm thinking how everybody in my group, all the counselors at this place was like the home office for the 28, ought to hear what he's saying to me, on account of he keeps saying, "Tru, when you bust out of here, don't worry, I'll always be there for you, whatever you need, my brother."

Already talking about me getting back to down and dirty soon as I was clean.

No thing.

Phone's ringing again, hotel phone, not my cell, which means nobody I want to talk to, those people know to be calling on the cell.

Nearly eleven now.

Seven and a half to the kick.

Maybe I should go back to sleep for an hour, set that wake-to, sometimes a little nap after I'm up too early is the best sleep I get.

When I get out of rehab that first time, I say to the press, "You've only got so many Sundays in your life."

This after I serve the four games the league gave me on top of the 28 they give me at the time.

I say, "Trumaine Ward, who you all call Amazing Grace, he been showed a way to walk in the light on account of the grace of God, and the only thing gonna be dirty with him ever again is his uniform on your Sunday afternoons."

Then I give them the part about how many days I'd have soon as I got through today.

Starting to wind down now.

Might as well finish what I started.

Go the distance, so to speak.

Since I'm telling you the whole story, giving you the whole plot of the movie and whatnot, I have to tell you that what went down on account of Marvin that night wasn't the end of it.

Five years of shit is what it was the beginning of.

Five years in and out of football, out mostly, bouncing around, out of shape mostly, finally out the game for two years straight even if I was anything but straight, which is why everybody had such a good laugh when it came out I was going to try and come back one more time, ho ho ho, look who thinks he's got some ball in him, the famous rehab nigger from hell.

After, this was.

After I get picked up at that Super Bowl over to Miami, where I was under the impression they was *suppose* to be trying to bust the players in the game the night before the game, not somebody just in town to party with the partygoers and have a little fun.

And after I lose all my money, which of course everybody wants to blame on the dope when they should've been talking to that thief Harold, Harold the money man was *suppose* to be watch it for me.

Is the team brunch eleven or eleven-thirty?

I'll call Bijou.

"All those millions," one of those ESPN guys says the other day, doing one of those touchy-feeling interviews, leaning in like he wants to go down on me, "all those millions gone, how could you blow that much money on dope, Tru?"

"Why don't you ask that shitweasel Harold, if you can find him in whatever non-extradite country he and his fat ass and his fat girlfriend are living in now," I say back to the ESPN guy, making him do that little throat-clear deal they do when you say something you know is gonna make air on the twelfth of never, the guy telling me after if it was HBO, where you could say just about anything, he would've gone with it in a minute, giving me a big-guy handshake, thanking me for my *candor.*

Where was I?

Them five years.

Anyways, after all the other shit, finally there's the one everybody says is the big one, on account of it looking like the last straw or some such, which is me getting arrested that time for vagrancy, even though that one was a *total* fucking mistake, another example of me getting screwed, I just fell asleep at that bus stop...even after that, I *still* come back.

That was my last 28, which I think must've broke the world's record for 28's.

"You're still in denial, Trumaine," a girl in group says, pointing her finger at me. "You finally end up in the gutter and you still don't think you have a problem. God, that's pathetic."

"Aren't you sick and tired of being sick and tired?" another girl says, giving me another one of those cute lines they like to give you in all the piety sobriety books.

And I hold my mouth, wanting to get out of there, but thinking, The only thing I'm sick and tired of *listening* to bitches like *you*.

Work out on my own at first. Don't tell no one. Oh, they all ask later, were you shocked you still had your legs? And I wanted to say, I was putting the shit up my *nose*, not on my fucking *knees*. Dicky begs and begs after that and they finally give me a shot in that NFL Europe, last spring it is, like it's some kind of pro football probation, or maybe just a halfway house, thinking they're throwing me a bone, only I get over there and get my ass into game shape and start running through those losers and second stringers over there like they're traffic cones. Telling them what they wanted to hear, like always, telling them that football's my therapy now, fuck golf, football is the only treatment was ever gonna work for me, telling ones who don't know shit I was *cured*, even though real junkies and drunks know there isn't no such thing.

But here's the deal: They believed it.

Believed it on account of they wanted to believe it, for the same reason in the past they didn't want to know what they didn't want to know.

When they see I can still play, still help somebody, they want the shit to just go away, so somebody could hand me the ball again, and there wasn't no point in me bursting their balloons, telling them it was never no thing, I was just working a little extra now keeping myself under control, on account of all *I* wanted was the ball in my hands again, get off the blocks again in that first step they all still talked about, get to that hole before the others could.

The Eagles are the ones who took the chance, though Dicky said when I got back from Amsterdam we had us more options than that, the Eagles were just the ones gave us the most whip-out up front, didn't try to jack us around with incentives and all what they gonna give us on the back end.

Was eleven-thirty for the brunch, I remember now, brunch right after chapel, coach telling us last night we could sleep in, we wanted.

Like we was gonna be able to sleep late on a day like this.

Anyway, I go with the Eagles and they get me splitting time and touches with D'Ontae Pearl the first couple of weeks, only it doesn't take long for me to dust his back up ass and after that it's all me. All you, Tru! People found out that's what the offensive linemen started yelling when I was in the clear. *All you, Tru!* Eight straight hundred yard games. Cover of *Sports Illustrated* before the Redskins game for first place in December.

"Back from the Dead," cover says.

Test out clean all year.

Maybe I *should* take a nap.

Test all year, clean every time, on my way to seventeen hundred fucking rushing yards and would've made two thousand if I got D'Ontae's touches in September.

Twenty touchdowns in the regular season, three more the championship game, up there in Lambeau Field, Green Bay, frozen-food section of football.

Talking my shit like a champ the whole time, telling them what they wanted to hear about what I been through, how I got to where I was.

Keeping what I really thought inside, like always, until I want to *explode* sometimes, when I'd read something or hear them on the radio talk, acting like they *know*, like they're the ones done one 28, then another.

Then another after that.

Them calling *me* a junkie, on account of us all being so *modern* now, and I'm suppose to take it, stand there grinning, shuffling my feet like some oldtime movie nigger.

Wanting to fucking scream sometimes, *Don't you people understand?*

It was never no thing!

But I play the good boy instead.

Goddam, I'm tired.

I *know* I shouldn't've gone out last night, Saturday night before the big game of them all, but *goddam*, I *couldn't* walk this room no more after the team meeting, it was the fucking Super Bowl we were playing, I needed to get some *air*, just be with people for a while.

Get out myself a little while, you understand?

Figured I could make it back before curfew easy.

Shit, I could *always* handle one gram, wasn't nothing more than like one drink for me.

One to ease my pregame jitters and whatnot.

'Till one led to another.

Way it always did.

Was a party Marvin said we had to go to, Marvin saying was still early yet.

No thing.

Didn't I read somewhere how Joe Namath himself went out the night 'fore he won his Super Bowl?

Somebody knocking at the door now.

"Marvin, is that you?"

No answer.

"Marvin?"

How long ago the boy leave?

Promising he'd bring back with something would level me off, get me through the day, 'till it was time for the kick.

Get myself up off the bathroom floor.

Thinking, how'd I end up here?

Saying, "I'm coming, Marvin."

Unlatching the latch, opening the door.

"Where you been, nigger?" I say to Marvin.

Who's giving me these bug eyes.

On account of what's behind him, two cops behind him, along with Ed Halsey, our general manager.

And this big white dude from NFL Security bringing up the rear, crewcut guy, Marine-looking guy, the chief snoop, one who give us the talk on Media Day about avoiding places this week, type of places we might run into what he called your undesirables.

What's his name?

The snoop's, I mean.

First cop goes right past me, to where I left the rest of the rock and pipe and whatnot there on the coffee table.

Marvin says, "Tru, I didn't have no choice but to give you

up, swear to God, it's like they was waiting for me."

I say to Ed Halsey, "This ain't what it looks like."

He says, "Yeah, it is Tru. It's exactly what it looks like."

Staring over there at the shit on the coffee table with this sad look on his face, like somebody just died.

"What about the game?" I say.

He says, "There isn't going to be one, Tru. Not for you."

Quiet for a second before he says, "Ever again."

"Trumaine Ward," one of the cops is saying now, "you have the right to remain silent..."

Which is a relief, if you think about it.

I mean, not having to talk about none of this no more.

THE EMPIRE STRIKES BACK

BY BRAD MELTZER

"Think they know it's coming?"

"Not a chance."

"You sure?"

"Did you hear what I said? Not a chance."

"Even with the threat we sent?"

"That wasn't a threat," I clarify, checking the connections one last time. "All we did was tell them to watch their backs."

"And you don't think that's a threat?" Matthew asks, already starting to sweat.

"Oh, it's definitely a threat," I clarify. "But it's a nice one."

"Like sending your girlfriend Hershey's Kisses on Valentine's Day," Ezra jumps in. "You really like her, so you wanna tell her, 'Hey, I care enough to send you some free chocolate.'"

"That's exactly right," I agree. "Just like Hershey's kisses— and not just a few of those bite-size ones. I'm talking one of those oversized Mother's Day ones that comes in the big box and feels like a paperweight. Hot diggity. I can practically smell the tin foil."

Sitting on the edge of his perfectly-made bed in the small bedroom, Matthew shakes his head with parental contempt that goes well beyond his twenty years. Everyone has his role to play, and when it comes to Matthew, well... every group needs a worrier.

"You sure this is a smart idea?" Matthew asks. "I mean, think about it, Ryan—all this for a stupid prank?"

"A prank? You think this is just a prank? You wound my heart," Ezra says, holding his chest like he's been shot. "First of all, it's not a prank; at MIT, it's a hack. Second, it's not just a hack. It's a test... nay, a veritable challenge to our honor, young Matthew."

"It's a rite of passage." I agree without hesitation. "Like drinking your first beer... like losing your virginity..."

"... like learning to tweeze your unibrow," Ezra adds. "It's our fate, Matthew. It's up to every graduating class, and this year's no different. Destiny beckons."

The words may sound over-melodramatic, but they're true. Since 1865, the annual Harvard-Yale football game has been the ultimate college rivalry. Sure, there are others: Michigan-Ohio State; Alabama-Auburn; and the oh-so-traditional Army-Navy game. But even the oldest of those only goes back 111 years. Harvard-Yale goes back 135. For the Ivy League alumni, *The Game* means a hobnobby weekend filled with fur coats, Bloody Marys, and pathetically ostentatious old-boy caviar tailgate parties (as if these people would ever lower themselves to eat a hot dog). For Harvard students, it means another day where they play out their fantasies that they're at the center of the universe. And for those of us across the river at the Massachusetts Institute of Technology—myself and my housemates included—it means yet another year to put the Cambridge snobs back in their place.

Ignoring the neatly stacked pile of laundry on the floor, I lean over Ezra's shoulder and watch him type the final coordinates into Matthew's laptop.

During the Harvard-Yale game of 1990, a flare erupted in the end zone, calling attention to a wire attached to the goal post. When officials pulled the wire, a giant MIT banner unfurled and waved in the wind. At the Harvard-Yale game of 1982, right after Harvard scored a touchdown, there was a loud explosion on the 46-yard line. As the smoke cleared, a giant black weather balloon—with 'MIT' painted on it—emerged from the turf and inflated midfield. From a hole in the ground, prankster history was made. The next day, it was written up in the *New York Times, Time* magazine, and most important to the group of MIT geniuses who pulled it off, *Rolling Stone.* For MIT students around the world, it was the single greatest hack in scholastic history. That is, until now.

"How we doing?" I ask Ezra as he continues to pound at the keyboard.

"Almost there..." he answers, his eyes focused on his monitor. "If you guys can just stay quiet, I'll—"

The door to the room flies open and bangs into the wall. "Who wants 1803 notes? Get 'em before they go online!" Stully shouts as he bursts across the carpet. He tosses his backpack on Matthew's bed, then kicks off his shoes, launching each one against the back of Ezra's chair.

Ezra turns around just long enough to shoot him a sideways

glance.

"So we famous yet?" Stully asks, hurling himself onto Matthew's bed.

"We would be," I shoot back. "But we keep having these unexplained, self-absorbed interruptions."

Stully reaches into his backpack and pulls out a notebook with *"They're smart: We're smarter"* sticker on it. "Are you being, sarcastic?"

"Okay, here we go," Ezra announces, turning back to the laptop.

The three of us crowd around the machine, reading over his shoulder. *Welcome to TelSat. Please enter downlink coordinates.*

Hacking is the easy part. So was finding the right broadcast coordinates. The only hard part was convincing Matthew's dad to let us piggyback the signal onto one of TelSat's satellites. It pays to go to MIT. Of course, it pays even more when your housemate's dad is chief technology officer and everything can be done with a phone call.

"Read me the front hall code for the UMass game," Ezra calls out.

"Will someone please tell me how this actually works?" Stully asks as Matthew reads the coordinates.

"It's just like pinball," I explain as Ezra punches in the UMass codes. "The originating Harvard-Yale TV signal starts at the Yale Bowl, then gets bounced up to Satellite A, before getting beamed back down to Boston's local cable channel. Lucky for us, Satellite A is a TelSat satellite. So by putting in a standard time delay—usually reserved for preempted events—we can intercept the Harvard signal long enough to insert a little of our own... original programming."

As I say the words, all of us grin. It's every MIT student's dream: throughout Boston, thousands of Crimson fans will turn on their TV sets for their beloved Harvard-Yale match-up—but instead, all they'll find is a live broadcast of UMass facing off against MIT. It makes the weather balloon look like a poor-man's whoopie-cushion. Oh, baby, geeks rule.

"Hurry up," I call out, checking the clock on the VCR. "Four minutes till kickoff."

"Gimme a sec," Ezra says, putting in the final coordinates.

Matthew looks like he's about to wet his pants. "Are you sure we should—"

"Yes," all three of us say simultaneously.

Ezra's fingers glide across the keyboard. A small box appears in the top righthand corner of his computer screen. The digital image slowly emerges, and the colors quickly become crisp. Within seconds, there's a perfect digital feed of the Harvard and Yale football captains presiding over the coin toss at mid-field. The referee points to the Yale side and the Eli fans scream wildly for the home team.

"Here we go," Ezra explains as we watch on his monitor. "Welcome to back hall satellite television—even more direct than DirecTV." He hits another few keys and four words appear on-screen. *Baker's Field—Platform: Audio.*

" ... and it's another cold November day as the Elis elect to receive," the announcer says as his voice echoes through the computer's small speakers.

"Almost ready..." Ezra says, his voice rumbling down the runway as he enters a second set of coordinates.

In the left corner of the screen, a second digital box opens, this one showing the MIT-UMass game that started only a few minutes ago. I stare down at our guys in the silver helmets with the giant red letter "T" on them. "Go, Mr. T!" I shout, never knowing any of their names. As a team, we're slower, smaller, and weaker than just about everyone else out there, but our marching band—often copied but never cloned—is so damn smart they're illegal in six states. Take that, Einstein.

"Okay, put on the TV," Ezra says as I flip on the once-broken television that we found at a garage sale. When we brought it home, it took Ezra twenty-seven minutes to rewire the insides and make it work perfectly. It took another twelve minutes for him to splice the wire that runs outside our house so we get cable and all the dirty movie channels for free. But it doesn't take Ezra's Electrical Engineering & Computer Science degree to tell us what happens next. As I click to Boston's local broadcast. we see a larger image of what's on Ezra's computer screen. The Harvard and Yale teams line up for the kickoff, the crowd roars with as much excitement as an Ivy League crowd can muster, and in our group house at MIT, Ezra puts his finger on the veritable trigger. As soon as he presses the

'Enter' key, the Harvard-Yale game of 2001 will fly off into space, and the MIT-UMass game will cut the proverbial line and take its place.

"Gentlemen, for those of you who are about to die, I salute you," Stully announces.

"Will you just push the button," I beg.

On the twenty-yard line, the Harvard kicker raises his hand and signals for silence. The crowd is on its feet, banners and old-fashioned pom-poms waving in the air. The kicker rumbles forward, winding up to boot the little pigskin ball. And just as his foot is about to make contact—just as the crowd's ready to explode—Ezra pounds the 'Enter' key, and all across Massachusetts, thousands of TV screens go completely black.

"Houston, we've got ourselves a real kick in the ass..." Stully says.

"What's happening?" Matthew asks.

"It's working..." Ezra promises, staring down at the remote link for the satellites on his computer. *Downlinking complete— uplinking in progress.* With our mouths gaping open, Matthew, Stully, and I huddle in front of the TV like ten-year-olds watching Saturday morning cartoons.

Ten seconds go by and the screen's still black.

"When's it gonna—?"

There's a high-pitched tone as a rainbow of colorful vertical stripes appear on screen. "We are currently experiencing technical difficulties. Please stand by."

"What is it? What's wrong?" Matthew asks.

"Relax," Ezra answers.

"But there's no—"

"Just give it another minute..." Ezra says, lost in his computer screen, which is still showing the Harvard-Yale game in one corner and the MIT-UMass game in the other.

"And the Yalies will take it on the thirty-nine yard line," the announcer says, his voice still audible from the computer.

For thirty more seconds, we stare at the vertical stripes on the TV.

"We are currently experiencing technical difficulties. Please stand by..."

I can't help but look at Ezra. "Are you sure it's not...?"

"I'm positive," Ezra insists. Forever the gambler, he adds, "If it doesn't come on in sixty seconds, I'll eat my sneaker."

With three quick beeps, Matthew, Stully and I simultaneously start our digital stopwatches. Welcome to MIT.

For one minute, all three of us stare at our wrists.

"Uh-oh, looks like we have a loose ball..." the announcer says from Ezra's computer. "And it is—fumble Yale. Harvard takes over."

Stully beeps. Matthew beeps. I beep. The TV screen is still on the color bars.

"We are currently experiencing technical difficulties. Please stand by..."

"So d'you want a side of underwear with that sneaker?" Stully asks.

Clicking furiously at the keyboard, Ezra is starting to panic. "I don't understand...it should've already bounced down..."

"You sure you entered the right coordinates?" I ask. I'm trying to sound unconcerned, but Ezra sees right through it. He knows he's in trouble. We're all in trouble.

"Maybe I beamed it to the wrong place..."

"Whattya mean, the wrong place?" Stully asks.

"Oh God—we're dead," Matthew moans.

"Just find out where it went," I warn.

Another minute passes as Ezra scours through the original TelSat coordinates. I read over his shoulder. UMass went from Transponder 16, straight to Transponder 23. It doesn't make sense—it should be working.

"We are currently experiencing technical difficulties. Please stand by..."

The telephone screams through the small room.

Stully runs to pick it up.

"Don't touch it!" I tell him. Stully stops mid-step. I turn to Ezra. "This isn't funny anymore."

"Put it back the way you found it," Matthew demands. "Now!"

"I'm trying," Ezra says, his fingers pounding at the keys.

The phone rings again.

"We are currently experiencing technical difficulties. Please stand by..."

"Just turn it off!" Matthew shouts.

"Relax!" Ezra begs.

"Don't tell me to relax!"

"Guys," Stully begs. "This isn't the time for—"

"We are currently experiencing technical difficul—" The voiceover gets interrupted.

And then, something happens.

On the TV, there's a hiccup of light...

"There it goes!" Ezra shouts, pointing at the screen.

Sure enough, a nanosecond later, the TV screen blinks, and we're staring at the Harvard and Yale football teams in their respective huddles. They line up at the thirty yard line. The play's about to start.   "We're okay," Ezra says. "See? It's all okay."

Matthew stares at the screen, his fists still clenched. They slowly loosen. He wants to believe we're safe. But he has to see it for himself. In the corner, the phone finally stops ringing. "   A   n   d Jankowicsz goes to throw..." the announcer begins. "He fades back..."   "I told you," Ezra says. "I told you it'd be fine."

"I don't understand," Stully says. "What about the UMass game?"

"Forget the UMass game," Matthew interrupts. We should just be thankful it's all back in place. I don't know how I let you talk me into—"   "Oh, looks like we have a loose ball..." the announcer continues. "And it is—fumble Yale. Harvard takes over."

Raising an eyebrow, I turn to the TV screen. "Wasn't that..."

"... the same play we heard two minutes ago." Sully agrees.

All four of us lean close to the TV. On screen, the fans are cheering; the coaches are pacing; and the Harvardians are jumping up and down, celebrating Yale's turnover. Still, something's off...   "Well, it looks like fourth and nine for Harvard," the announcer's voice squawks from the tiny speaker in Ezra's laptop.   Following the noise, we look at the digital feed on the laptop. There, it's fourth down and Harvard's about to punt. On TV, it's first and ten, and Harvard just took possession. We check again. From laptop, to TV, then back to laptop.   "It's like the game on TV's a few minutes behind the..."   My eyes go straight to the game-clock at the bottom of the TV screen. 13:42 to go in the first quarter. Then I look at the clock on the laptop. I have to squint to see it. 11:07. "It's   almost three minutes behind," I say. "The   signal   probably   just   got delayed, then came back to its original destination," Ezra points out.   "Well, that's just perfect," Stully says. "What an amazing prank... I can see it now: Hey guys, guess what we did? We tried to preempt the game, but instead—you holding on to your knickers?—we actually delayed the thing three minutes in the one way that no one watching would ever notice!" He lowers his voice a few decibels. "Isn't that like telling a joke without a punchline?" His voice goes back to normal. "Absolutely! Now who wants to be the first to call us losers?"

"Guys... you should see this." Ezra says, still locked on his computer.

"Maybe we should just get 'Kick Me' tattoos, and save the world the paper and scotch tape," Stully adds.   "Guys..." Ezra continues. "You really should see this."   "What's to see? It's a football game," I tell him. "And not the one we wanted."

"I know, but you should—"

"It's the game, Ezra—the prank sucked—get over it," I add. He's still playing zombie, lost in the screen. This time, though, his voice is all business. "Guys, we can make money on this." A l l three of us freeze.   "Excuse me?" Stully says.   "I'm serious," Ezra replies. "Think of what we have here: it's a perfect way to make some cash."

"What're you talking about?" I ask.   "Look at the TV—the game's going on in New Haven, but back here on the laptop, we've got a three-minute head-start on everything that happens. So if Harvard scores a touchdown..."   "... we'll know it three minutes before anyone else does," Stully says with a grin. "It's like seeing the future."   "The three-minute crystal ball," Ezra agrees.

"Whoa, whoa, whoa—what're you saying?" I ask. "You're gonna call up Vegas and squeeze in a last second bet?"   " A n d that's such a bad idea?" Ezra asks.   "First of all, it *is* a bad idea. Second, before you put it all on black, you can't bet on a game three minutes before it's over."   "That's not true," Stully says.

"You can bet on anything you want," Ezra agrees. "I see them do it all the time—the coin toss... the first completion..."

"You can even bet on a single field goal," Matthew interrupts. It's the first time he's said a word in over five minutes. But from the thin smirk that's spread across his face, it's clear he's no longer worried about a harmless college prank.   Right then, all eyes turn to me.   "It's the chance of a lifetime," Ezra says. "We'll call the guy I bet the Patriots games with. He'll make a mint."   I shake my head. "It'll never work."   "What're you talking about?"

"We may have the head start on TV, but what about all the people listening on radio?"   "The only radio is on the college station, which only gets picked up in Cambridge. Downtown, they get the TV simulcast," Ezra says.   "C'mon," Stully adds, putting a hand on my shoulder. "It's like free money. No one knows—no one gets hurt." I look to Matthew hoping to find the voice of pessimistic reason. He's still wearing his smirk. "If you're in, I'm in," he promises.

It's hard to argue with complex adolescent logic like that. "You really think it'll work?" I ask Ezra.   "Are you kidding?" he sings. "We can't lose..."

Twenty minutes later, the score is still tied at zero. Harvard has the ball on the fifty, and we've come to realize that by the time a one o'clock game starts on a Saturday, all the local banks are closed.   "That's it!?" Ezra asks. "That's all you could get? Three hundred and thirty-two bucks?"   "And   seventy-two cents," I point out. "Whatttya want me to do? ATMs max out at three hundred each."   "I'm in for three hundred and fifty-eight," Stully says, slapping his money on top of Matthew's desk. "Three hundred and forty-six," Matthew adds.   "And I got a cool five hundred and sixty-two," Ezra brags. He swears it comes from his big win on the Colts game, but I know he just made it up to calm me down.   "So what's the grand total?" I ask.   Stully and Ezra race to do the addition. There's only one thing worse than competitive friends. Competitive friends who're good at math. "One thousand four hundred and ninety-eight," Ezra says first. "And seventy-two cents," Stully points out. As always, Matthew's the first on the hesitancy express. "Is this going to work?" "All we need is a start," Ezra promises. "Just enough to buy us some confidence." He reaches for the phone and the three of us are silent. We're seniors at MIT. Chaos theory, we can handle. Bookies are another story.

"Are you sure you trust this guy?" Matthew asks Ezra. "Like my own brother. I've been with him every week for the past four years. He's small time, but he gets the job done." "Whatever we do, let's just do it quick," Stully says, staring down at the laptop. Only three quarters to go. "The last thing we want to do is run out of time."

Seven digits later, Ezra's leaning into the speakerphone, waiting to speak to Mr. Bookie, or Bookieman, or whatever his name is.

"I'm Alan," a strong voice answers in a meaty Boston accent.

"Hey, Alan," Ezra says, trying to sound like they're old friends. "How're you doing today?" "Who's this?" "It's Ezra," he says, offering us a playful smile. None of us smile back. "Why you callin' on Saturday?" the bookie asks. "Pats don't play till tomorrow." "Yeah, well... we've got some friends over from Harvard and they've got this bet they wanted me to ask you about. I said you wouldn't take it, but—" "Just tell me the bet," Alan interrupts. Typical bookie—eyes always on the prize. "It's stupid," Ezra explains. "One of 'em thinks he's a psychic or something. Anyway, they wanna bet that Yale's gonna fumble in the next five minutes." As Ezra says the words, he carefully pauses. Just like we practiced. There's a long silence on the other line. The bookie knows something's up. "And how do you know this guy?" he asks.

"Buddy from high school. His dad's a bigshot at Fidelity—I grew up with him in Newton..." I nod at Ezra. Nice going, bro. Drop the hints of money and let him come to you. "Listen, I told him not to waste your time," Ezra adds, perfectly smooth. "I'll just have him find someone who can—"

"Five minutes real time or five minutes on the clock?"

"Real time," Ezra says, never sounding overexcited.

"And you'll vouch for him?"

"Absolutely. He may be a moron, but he's *my* moron."

That's all the bookie needs to hear. Money's still money—especially when it's backed up by a regular client. "So how much does he wanna bet?"

"Depends on the odds," Ezra says. "Whattya giving?"

"On a Yale fumble in the next five? Tell him I'll give three to one."

Ezra covers the speaker, pretending to relay the numbers. "He says three to one. How much you willing to lose?"

I glance over at the cash that's sitting on Matthew's desk. If it's going to look real, we have to start somewhere. "A thousand," I call out.

"A thousand," Ezra relays.

Once again, the bookie pauses. He may be small potatoes, but a bet like that is a full meal. "And you're sure you know this guy?" he asks Ezra for the second time.

"Trust me," Ezra says. "He's good for it."

For the next five minutes, we stare at the TV as Yale struggles to move the ball up field. On fourth and long, they're forced to punt. They never get it back. And they never fumble. Of course, to us it's old news. We knew it four minutes ago. That's why we placed the bet in the first place. Like my dad used to say, sometimes you have to lose to win.

As the clock hits the five minute mark, the phone rings through Matthew's small room.

"This is Ezra," he says, picking up the speakerphone.

"Y'know, for smart guys, your friends ain't too bright," the bookie says with a song in his voice.   "I told him not to bet it," Ezra says with fake disappointment. "But that's the problem with Harvard boys—they don't listen to anyone but themselves."

"Whatever you say," the bookie adds. "When do I get my cash?"

"I'll have him run it over at the end of the game—but to be honest, he may still have another few bets in him."

"Fine by me."

Ezra looks our way and grins. Those are the magic words.

"So what's the new bet?" the bookie asks.   Ezra once again covers the speakerphone. "Hey, Karnac—he wants to know if you've got some more Do-Re-Mi to burn."   "One last bet," I call out. "I got a good feeling about which team's going to make the next field goal."   "He wants to bet on who makes the next field goal," Ezra relays. "Can you cover it?"

"How 'bout a figure first?" the bookie persists.

I turn to my housemates for one last check. There's no going back on this one. Everyone puts up five fingers. Matthew puts up four.

"Five thousand," I say.   "Five grand," Ezra relays.   "A n d who're you picking?" the bookie asks through the speakerphone.

"I'm not sure yet, but we'll call you before it happens. You still up for it?"   "You're covered," he says. "I'll give you eight to five if you can pick it five minutes ahead of time." There's a cocky twang in his voice. Of course, it's the first thing they show you in *The Sting*. Convince 'em it works, then reel 'em in.   "Sounds good over here," Ezra says.   But just as he's about to hang up, the bookie adds, "Hey, Ezra, you're not yanking me along now, are you?"

"No... not at all," he shoots back, forcing confidence into his voice.

"Because I'm not a schmuck," Alan insists. "And I'm not about to get my ass burned by one of those last-minute bets where your roommate the kicker nods to you on the TV and tells you he's gonna shank it on purpose so you can—"   "Alan, I'd never do that to you. Besides, we're picking who'll make it—not who'll miss. It's impossible to predict."   It's hard to argue with the logic. Still, Alan has to cover his ass. "So you'll back this guy up for the money?" he challenges.   "Don't worry—we'll cover it."

"I'm sure you will," the bookie says in full Boston accent. "You've seen enough Scorsese movies to know what happens if you don't. Now who's Matthew Hollister?"

Matthew's face goes white as the bookie says his name.

Crap. Caller ID.

"H—He's... he's my housemate."

"You call it whatever you want—I just want a valid phone number," Alan explains. "Speak to you soon." There's a click and he's gone.

"Well... I think that went well," Stully says.

None of us answers. Our eyes are already back on the game.

As the second quarter winds down, the score's still tied at zip, Yale has the ball on its own thirty, and Matthew's ready to vomit all over the carpet. "Just calm down," I tell him. "It'll be fine."   "Fine? You think this is fine? Do you even realize how many laws we're breaking?"

"How many?" Ezra challenges. Matthew thinks about it. "A lot. At least four... maybe five. I mean, just by delaying the broadcast, we're messing with the FCC. The FCC! Do you know what they can do to us?"   "Absolutely nothing," Ezra shoots back. "We're not talking the CIA here. It's the piddling FCC. They're Washington bureaucrats. In fact, they're so nonexistent, I bet you don't even know what FCC stands for."

Matthew doesn't hesitate. "Federal Communications Commission."

"Ohhh. I can already feel the terror in my heart. Here comes the Federal Communication Commission—everyone hide your pirate radios..."

"It's not a joke, Ezra."

"Are you kidding?" Ezra asks. "This isn't like skyjacking the SuperBowl and replacing it with early episodes of *Sanford & Son*—

it's a three minute delay on an Ivy League football game. Can you say it with me? Ivy League Football. Translation: Yawn, yawn, and more yawn. No one cares, Matthew—and even if they did, no one would ever notice. So sit back, relax, and stop worrying."

By the time half-time hits, we're so glued to the mini-screen on Ezra's laptop that my eyes start to sting.   "Have   you   even stopped to think about what would happen if we win ten grand?" Stully asks behind us. "Do you have any idea what that buys us?"

"I'm starting with a nice steak dinner..." Ezra begins.

"And then some shopping for a surround-sound system..." I add. "And maybe one of those flat-screen monitors..." Matthew adds, clearly warming up.   "And then a butler!" Stully shouts. "A butler just for us! And not one of those snooty ones like Richie Rich has—I'm thinking something robotic, and interactive, and *bullet-proof!* Like the liquid metal guy in *Terminator 2*—he changes shape, hangs out with you, and makes you look insanely cool all at the same time! I'd be like, *'C 'mon, T2, let's head out to the bar and find ourselves some Boston College girlfriends.'* And then he'd be like, *'Yes. Let us.'* And I'd be like, *'Yeah, T2, you know how to party!'* Ohhh, how sweet would that be?"

"Pretty darn sweet," I say.

"And not the least bit delusional," Ezra adds.

By the end of the third quarter, all we can muster is silence. With seventeen minutes left to play, we now understand why no one watches Ivy League football in the first place. Seven fumbles, six interceptions, fourteen dropped passes, and the worst coordination since... well... since the last time *I* played football. No one has been within field goal range for a full two and a half hours.

"What if there's no field goal?" Matthew asks. What if it just comes down to a Hail Mary in the endzone?"

"There's no way," I tell him. "The field goal's coming right now..." On screen, Harvard's on the fifty yard line.   "Third   and ten... Bertani fades back to pass..." the announcer begins. "He's got White open... The pass is off... White bobbles—but he's got it! White's on the forty... the thirty... the twenty..."

"Tackle him!" Stully shouts as soon as Harvard hits field goal range. "... the ten... *Touchdown Haaarvaaard!"*   The   crowd explodes, the band starts to play, and in our room, all four of us are

deadman silent. On the computer screen, Harvard lines up for the extra point. On the TV, three minutes earlier, Harvard's still on its first down. "Maybe we should call the bookie now and change the bet," Ezra suggests.

"What're you talking about?"

"This could be the only score of the game—we should call him up and put our money on Harvard scoring in this possession."

"And you don't think that'd look suspicious?"

"I don't care how it looks. All I want is our cash. Now pick up the phone and call."

"No. No way," I tell him.

"What do you mean, *no way*? Ryan, this isn't the time to be stupid."

"It isn't about stupid—it's about common sense. You heard the bookie the last time around: he already raised an eyebrow when we asked him about the field goal. And now you want to call him up and put money on the million-to-one shot that Harvard—the team that couldn't buy a touchdown—is not only about to score, but is about to do it during the exact possession that you've picked? He'll be so creeped out, he'll never pay the bet, and we won't see a dime."

"Yeah, well... if we just sit on our hands we're not gonna see a dime either."

"How about just calling up and betting the extra point?" Stully asks.

"It's too easy. The payoff'll be minimal, and then we've blown our one shot," I explain. "It's an Ivy League game with a full quarter left—trust me, when it gets to the end, we'll get our chance. Don't change the plan midstream."

Ezra shakes his head. "I say we put it to a vote. All for...?"

He's the only one to put up his hand.

"Against...?"

Matthew and Stully follow my lead. Three against one. Safe vs. sorry.

"You better hope you're right," Ezra threatens. He's got a tone in his voice I've never heard before. I turn to Matthew and Stully, but both of them have their eyes on the floor. That's how it always is with money—everything gets personal.

Two minutes into the fourth quarter. Yale fakes its punt and runs seventy-two yards for a quick touchdown. The home crowd at the Yale Bowl bounces up and down like popcorn in the stands, while blue and white pompoms gyrate in wild celebration. Ezra shoots me a look and tries to pick the fight all over again.

"All you have to do is—"

"Don't say it," I tell him.

"But if we—"

"It's fine," I insist. "Now that it's tied up, someone'll definitely kick a field goal." It's a ridiculous statement, and the moment it comes out, all three of my housemates look at me skeptically. During sophomore year, we all took Statistics. I'm not fooling anyone. But right now—if we plan on playing it safe—all we can do is wait.

During Harvard's next possession, they have the ball for two minutes and twenty-seven seconds, then fumble on third and short. Yale picks it up and keeps it for three minutes and thirty-two seconds, which is exactly when they throw their fourth interception. After that, it goes back and forth two more times. Harvard has it for three downs and punts; Yale has it for three and punts. With each chance of possession, Matthew, Stully, Ezra and I inch closer toward the tiny computer screen. We're huddled, shoulder to shoulder. None of us wants to deal with overtime. With two minutes left to play, this is it. Starting on their own twenty-five yard line, Harvard barrels down the field with three quick running plays—the last one, a twenty-yard quarterback sneak. Bertani slides like a baserunner just as three Yalies are about to flatten him. Now it's first and ten on Yale's forty-four.   "Ten more yards." Ezra whispers to himself, his eyes on field goal range. "Just ten more, baby..."

As the Harvard team lines up along the line of scrimmage, the Yale fans are on their feet, screaming. *"Deee-fense! Deee-fense!"* The referees step back. The quarterback leans in for the snap. And behind me, Matthew's grip tightens around the shoulder of my shirt. *Hut!* With the snap, helmets collide, fans cheer, and the Harvard quarterback spins around for a by-the-book hand-off. Racing straight up the middle, the running back tucks his head down and plows forward. He gets about two yards before he smacks into the human brick wall otherwise known as Yale's fattest linebacker. With an audible crunch, the Harvard running back comes to a dead stop—but the ball keeps moving... *"Fumble!"* Ezra shouts. Before Ezra can even finish the first syllable, the ball bounces up the field, bobbling, between two Yale defenders who can't seem to get their hands on it. Like a bad NFL blooper, the ball tumbles along the ground as college football's worst athletes scramble after it. Within seconds, the players pounce, and a dog-pile of bodies smashes together in a crimson, white and blue blur.

"Who's got it?" Matthew demands. The referees blow their whistles and everyone in the stands is on his feet. One by one, the players roll off the pile. But it's the Harvard players who are celebrating. "Harvard holds onto it!" the announcer clarifies as half the stadium erupts into cheer. They're not the only ones. Stully tackles me from behind with a bear hug. The ball's now on Yale's twenty-six yard line. Thanks to the fumble, there're only fourteen seconds on the clock. The score's tied. Harvard has to go for the field goal. "Get that bookie on the line!" I yell at the top of my lungs. Ezra grabs the phone as the Harvard kicker rushes onto the field. It's a forty-three yarder. If this were Michigan-Ohio State, it'd be a cakewalk. In the Ivy league, it's a longshot, even with the wind at his back. Still, Harvard needs the points. As the kicker lines up, all four of us are holding our breath and sharing the same thought: No matter what happens, we've got our field goal—but with a kick this long... the bet won't pay much if he misses it. For real cash, we need to go against the odds. Which is why we need him to make it.

"C'mon, jock-off," Stully begs. "Show 'em why they let you in the school in the first place." We press in even closer to the computer screen. The glowing images fade into pixels. Ezra's sweating hands strangle the neck of the phone.

Matthew shuts his eyes. "Tell me what happens." W i t h twelve seconds left... there's the snap... The kick is up...

"And it's goooooooood!" announcer shouts as Ezra and Stully jump around the room. Forty-three yards, straight through the uprights. My mind floods so fast, I can barely do the math on the odds. Hurry!" Matthew yells. Wasting no time, I kill the volume on the computer, and Ezra dials the bookie's phone number. All we've got is a three minute head start. "Everyone quiet!" I insist as it starts ringing. Sharing the receiver with Ezra, I look down at my watch. Two minutes, forty eight seconds. "C'mon—pick

up," Ezra mutters.   It rings again, but no one's there.   *Where the hell is he? He said he'd be—*   "I'm Alan," a voice answers. "H—Hey, Alan, it's Ezra. My Harvard boys with the—"

"I remember," he interrupts. "What's the bet?"

"Harvard," he blurts. "Five thousand that Harvard kicks a field goal in the next five minutes."

"And you're sure about that?"

"Absolutely," I say.

There's a short pause as I hear him scribbling. "So the one that's about to go up?"

"That's it—all on Harvard."

I look down at my watch. Two minutes, eleven seconds to go.

"You got it," Alan says. "It's in the book." With a click, he's gone.

"What'd he say?" Stully asks.

"Nothing," Ezra replies, flushed with newfound adrenaline. "He asked if it was the one about to go up... I told him that's the one we wanted."   "*About to go up*?" Stully asks, confused. "How would he possibly know that? It hasn't been transmitted yet."

My eyes glance over at the TV, where I see what everyone in Boston is watching.

According to the broadcast, Harvard just got the ball. It's first and ten. The field goal doesn't happen for another two minutes. A cold chill licks the back of my neck. *What the hell is—*   "Ryan, get over here!" Matthew says, still staring at his laptop.   O v e r his shoulder, we crowd around him and watch the small digital screen, where the Harvard-Yale game is over, and all the Harvard fans have rushed the field to celebrate. It's a madhouse of activity as the crowd pours out of the stands and into the endzone. College kids, players, and overaged alumni are swarming in every direction.

But what's got Matthew's attention is the banner that the Harvard cheerleaders are holding up above the crowd. In stark crimson letters are the words, "Congrats Seniors—Class of 1999!" "Class of '99?" Stully asks.   Oh, God..   "Turn up the volume!" I bark at Matthew.   ... and quarterback Jeff Bertani has quite a lot to be proud of..." the announcer rambles on.

Ezra looks my way.   "Matthew, how fast can you bring up Harvard's website?" I ask, my voice shaking.   With a click of the mouse, and some hunting and pecking at the keyboard, we're at www.harvard.com. "Do a search on the name Jeff Bertani!" I insist.

"I don't underst—"   "Just do it!"   Within seconds, the screen clicks over to a photo from the website. *Quarterback Jeff Bertani '99* it says across the bottom.   It doesn't make any sense... '99... He graduated two years ago... So how could he be playing this y—?   "*And it's gooooooood!*" the announcer's voice echoes from our television, where the broadcast has finally caught up with what we watched on the computer screen. Like before, the field goal sails the full forty-three yards. Like before, the overjoyed crowd rushes onto the field. And like before, the cheerleaders hold up their *Congrats Seniors—Class of 1999!* banner. But this time, as we rewatch the final minutes of the broadcast, white letters scroll up the screen as the theme from *Star Wars* starts playing:

Episode V:
The Empire Strikes Back
Hope you enjoyed
Fair Harvard's '99 victory.
Sadly, it's not as entertaining
as a blimp on the fifty-yard line,
but it's better than
watching those annoying little Ewoks.
(Honestly, who doesn't hate those bastards?)
May the Force be with You,
Your adoring, frothing fans
at the Harvard Lampoon

P.S. Stop stealing cable—
piracy's wrong and it's against the law.

Staring in shock, I watch the words scroll toward the top of the screen. I'm already grinding my teeth.   The phone rings and Ezra dives for it. "Who the hell is this?" he asks, hitting the speakerphone.

"I'm Alan," the bookie says. "Now is that gonna be in small bills or large ones?"

THE ARCANE RECEIVER

BY CAROL O'CONNELL

Gas station maps only featured the routes that were paved, and so those few feckless travelers in search of Arcane were dependent upon the humor of strangers along the way. Old timers, who knew all the jokes about that little town, could point them down the dirt road that led to it. "But not through it, mind you," the old men would say, "though there's no chance your car could run out of road. You'll walk the last ten miles if you don't carry but one spare tire." And then came a time of remarkable change, and the old men amended their directions to say, "The town of Arcane could've blown clean away with no harm done and no souls missed—if not for the mighty Bobby Hanson."

The high school senior was fair of face and form, and best of all, he was an apathetic paranoid. When the Hanson boy was on the run, he believed that people were after him, but he did not care. His head never swiveled round to see who might be gaining on him, and he was not spurred on by fear. No one had ever laid a hand on Bobby, and it never occurred to him that anyone could, not before he made his touchdown—the boy was that fast. He also had a talent for making other boys believe that they were better than they knew. And against the odds given by small-time bookies, he led the sturdy sons of farmers and ranchers into a winning streak that cut a wicked swath across the entire state.

The lone heretic among the good Christians of Arcane, a man who also passed for the town's idea of an intellectual, ventured the opinion that God had a second son, and He loved Bobby Hanson best. The librarian, Willa Sue Gunther, who was also a lay preacher and chief of police, said, "We'll just see about that." Her words were pure prophecy, for she had no way to know that, as she spoke, a rusted old Ford sedan was driving down the road to Arcane. The car's engine sputtered and died inside the town limits, stranding a tired woman and a ten-year-old boy who would soon eclipse Bobby Hanson.

There was one more stroke of God's wrath (as Willa Sue Gunther would come to see it). The only waitress in the only diner had sprained her back that morning and hung a HELP WANTED sign in the window, where the two strangers would see it the moment they stepped out of the exhausted Ford. That day, the diner also began a winning season, for the new waitress was easy on the eyes, though her small son was not. (In time, the whole nation would see one damn ugly baby picture, the only existing portrait of Roscoe May, beneath the headline, "Beauty and the Beast.")

The Hanson boy was truly a beautiful sight on the afternoon of the last home game. The frosty vapor of his laughter was the closest thing to a cloud on that cold winter day. The sky above the running boy was clear and blue, and some said Bobby flew like an angel those last nine yards before the bang. Louder than a firecracker or any other innocent noise, the sound was alien and shocking, even to the experienced ears of the deer hunters in the stands, but it never slowed Bobby's glory run in the final minutes of play. He scored his touchdown, then turned to face the astounded crowd—and their silence. The other players were as still as trees planted on the field. And then he saw the blood streaming down one sleeve of his uniform.

Back in Arcane at day's end, Bobby was one very tired teenager. He had been trucked over forty-eight miles of rough country in his father's pickup, then spent an hour in a clinic, where a doctor, who had never seen a bullet wound, kept saying, "I'll be damned," as he irrigated, then dressed,the bloody fissure in the boy's right arm. When the young football star returned to his hometown, reporters from every corner of the state awaited him with cameras and bright lights. He shyly told them, "It's only a flesh wound," for those were the doctor's words. His father slapped him on the back and said that John Wayne would have been proud. Bobby endeared himself to the journalists, drawing smiles all around, when he asked, "Who is John Wayne?"

On the way home to the ranch, father and son made a stop

at the police station, which was also the public library, where Willa Sue Gunther pinned on her gold badge to announce that she had switched jobs for the moment, and then she said, "I caught the shooter." Willa Sue's massive girth could have hidden two of the rancher's cows, but when she stepped aside, Bobby was staring at a slender, pretty woman with a frightened look about her. The new waitress stood close to her son, who called to mind a small white monkey with the sickly pallor of a shut-in. The little boy's ears were the size of a chicken-pot pie cut down the center and stuck to the sides of his head. And thick eyebrows joined together to overshadow tiny eyes no bigger than the points of bullets seen head on, oncoming—*firing*.

Bobby Hanson took a step back.

The rancher, Robert Hanson Sr., was shaking his head, deep in denial, as Willa Sue Gunther explained that the waitress's boy had shot his son. "He's only ten for God's sake." Willa Sue went on to say that it was a man's Christian duty to forgive poor little Roscoe May and not make a fuss about this.

The waitress's son trained his tiny bullets-for-eyes on Bobby Hanson. The child never uttered a sound, but he did move his mouth, and though Bobby was no lip-reader, he was certain that the little boy had formed the word *bang*. Every good instinct of a healthy young athlete said, *Put this freak away, and never, never —*

His father made the decision to drop the matter.

"Turned out well," said Mr. Hanson, when his son received offers of scholarships from every college and university in the state. "Payback for Christian charity." The rancher rolled his head back to look up at all the stars in heaven, then said, "I'll be damned if a certain somebody doesn't have his eye on you, boy. It seemed that everyone in Arcane was a prophet.

Early in September, Bobby Hanson moved a hundred miles south and made the cut for a university football team. Unlike other freshmen, he was not overwhelmed by the larger, more deadly players of college ball; they could never catch him. He had the fastest legs in six states—until the day he stopped at a local restaurant and saw the mother of Roscoe May working behind the lunch counter. The tired pretty woman jumped a bit at the clang of a tin fork hitting the floor and, again, when the drawer of the cash register slammed shut. She saw Bobby, recognized him, and he thought that she would surely cry. Her eyes were brimming, begging, *Please don't make trouble for me.* He nodded to say he would leave her in peace, and then he did. On the following day, he ran faster than ever. A local sportswriter claimed that the Hanson boy could outrun a bullet, but that reporter had no gift for prophecy, not in Willa Sue Gunther's league.

It was the last week in November when a bullet brought Bobby Hanson down, and the game was called before halftime. The shooter was never found, but he *was* identified. "At first, I thought it was a monkey," said one witness. "White as a maggot," said another. "It was Roscoe May," said Bobby Hanson. Three minutes before the police arrived, Mrs. May and Roscoe had abandoned their home in a trailer court. Mother and son disappeared in the dust of the back roads, and no one was chasing them. Detective Wayne explained why there would be no manhunt for a minor child: Roscoe May, now eleven years old, would only receive a reprimand for attempted murder. "So, even if we got lucky and found the gun," said the detective, "what's the point?" The man made it clear that the case was closed when he handed Bobby the bullet. "Here, son—a souvenir. It came from a handgun. Don't that beat all? Most people couldn't have made that shot with a rifle. Well, at least you know the boy's gone. And he won't be back—I can promise you that much."

Bobby Hanson was becoming a bit of a skeptic- He stared at the bullet recently dug from his young body, then decided to transfer to another school as far away as a slew of new scholarship offers could take him. This last shooting had garnered national attention for his talent as well as his wounds, and an Ivy League football team was now an attainable dream.

That next September, a prestigious northern university enjoyed a phenomenal surge in ticket sales. A full scholarship precluded any thought of giving up the sport, but such an idea had never occurred to Bobby, for he loved the game and played it with deep grace, body and brave soul. He was slightly less beautiful, but only by two bullet wounds, and faster than ever. The track coach begged him on bended knee to become a long-distance runner, but Bobby turned the man down. Football was his game, the only game that mattered.

When the young sophomore ran onto the field with his teammates, he was welcomed by the roar of grateful fans who believed this new player would lead them out of the darkness of a three-year slump. Bobby Hanson never heard their cheers, all for him; with perfect concentration, he searched the crowd for a pale monkey with a gun. Well into November, he thought he saw the boy in the stands, just a glimpse of maggot flesh and pie-sized ears. The chief of security, unable to find Roscoe May on any stadium camera, advanced the theory that Bobby was seeing things. "Just nerves, son. It'll pass."

During the final game of a winning season, Bobby Hanson dodged a bullet. The shot went wild as a fan struggled with a twelve-year-old boy for possession of a handgun. This time, Roscoe was captured. His mother was found three states away, working as a waitress in a roadside diner. Mrs. May signed a parental waiver to give a distant court authority over her son, for she had no plans to travel north. The policeman who had interviewed her said that she took it well when told that it might be years before her only child would be released.

A court date was set, and Roscoe May bided the waiting time in a facility for youthful offenders where Bobby Hanson was his only visitor. The child sported a winter sunburn from his time on the open road as a runaway, and this made Bobby wonder about the previous paleness and the jittery mother. Had the waitress always known what she had raised? Had she locked the boy up, hidden him from the light of the sun, the eyes of her neighbors—and the police? Had mother and child been on the run when they had driven down the dirt road that dead-ended in Arcane? Bobby would never know, for he never asked. He had only one pressing question, "Why do you want to kill me?"

"I'll never shoot you dead," said Roscoe May, and that was all he would ever say for the remainder of his childhood. At the age of thirteen, he escaped from the juvenile facility, stealing a gun on his way out the door. "He was such a quiet boy," said the warden. "Scary as shit, but not a discipline problem," said a guard, when both men were interviewed a month later. For thirty days, no one had thought to warn Bobby Hanson that his personal shooter was at large. A sportswriter discovered the escape while researching a story on the predictable winner of the coveted Heisman Trophy. When Roscoe's jailbreak became a media event, scalpers outside the stadium received record sums for tickets to a college game, and every seat was filled.

October was the season of ghouls.

Bobby scanned the stands, his eyes traveling from face to face, unable to tell the sports fans from the people who had come to watch him die. And it never entered his mind that he should refuse to play the game. One newspaper man failed to see bravery in this; he called it defiance, as if this were a bad thing, and his column suggested that what happened that day—well, Bobby Hanson was begging for a bullet; he had it coming to him.

Roscoe May shot the great hope of college football, and the bullet did a world of damage this time. The Heisman Trophy went to another player on the day that Bobby's shooter went to trial. Though juvenile records were sealed, all of Roscoe's prior acts were national news, and a judge had decided to try him as an adult. The jury set a record, delivering a guilty verdict in four minutes, twenty-two seconds, according to a sportswriter's stopwatch.

Bobby Hanson continued to move through life with uncommon grace, though he walked with a limp. He took a job at a local television station, then quickly worked his way up to a major network and became the country's highest paid sportscaster. He was still beautiful, and the cameras loved him so. Bobby really shined in football season; his passion for the game crackled through lenses and television screens, infusing the fans with exhilaration and wiring them up to electric anticipation of games to come. He also wrote a nationally syndicated column, and the great talent of college football proved equally gifted as a journalist. From September to January, even his rivals admitted this: whether writing a column or calling live action from the announcer's booth, Bobby Hanson was the best thing that ever happened to the only game that mattered.

On Roscoe May's eighteenth birthday, he was transferred to an adult prison, then released at the age of twenty-three. The press corps turned out in force for the ex-convict's first interview. There was only one notable absence among their ranks.

The world had changed over the years that Roscoe May had spent in jail. A new breed of players had broken away from the sports columns to make front-page headlines defending charges of drug addiction, drunk driving, murder and rape. Roscoe May, also a new age sports celebrity, was surprisingly unchanged. He was quite small for a grown man, five feet tall, if that. And perhaps he was uglier, thinner now, but his skin was as pale as ever.

All the journalists at the prison gate were hoping that the shooter would finally break his long silence, and three of them fired off the same question simultaneously, "Why did you do it, Roscoe?"

The agile little man climbed onto the hood of a car and crouched there, looking out over the crowd of faces turned toward him with great expectation, and then he said, "Shooting Bobby Hanson is what I do."

The first reporter to regain his wits said, "You mean—he's like—your *job*?"

"Yeah, I made him what he is today." And every reporter who still relied on an old-fashioned notebook wrote down these words—as if they might be true.

Bobby Hanson winced, then slugged back a beer, his fifth, as he watched the televised interview at the prison. The world made more sense to him now that he was willing to bow to the absurd. At last, he understood why Roscoe had said to him, "I'll never shoot you dead." Shooting the star from Arcane would always be the pale monkey's career, and that fact was spelled out for the whole country in the bold type of headlines. And, just to be certain that everyone *got* the message, the film of Roscoe May's interview was played on the nightly news — night after night.

For ten days following the shooter's release, television executives were jazzed, stoned, *drunk* on viewer ratings that were going through the roof and over the moon. Never had so many people tuned in for the evening news hour that ended with Bobby Hanson's sportscast. A single show had captured the entire audience, coast to coast, and advertising segments were selling for obscene amounts. The excitement of anticipation mounted every day until the tension was almost unbearable, exquisite—sublime.

Primetime. The most watched crime victim in America was on camera when the shooter rushed out from the shadows behind the bright studio lights. Though Roscoe May had the advantage of a drawn gun, Bobby Hanson was still a superbly coordinated human being. He drew a revolver on the little man and shot him through the head, *shot him dead.*

People talked about that gunfight for years. Bobby had finally given America the live action, the blood sport and sudden death that it had craved for so long.

What a show.

And now they could all go to hell.

The American hero, perhaps the last one, retired on the following day and disappeared from public life. Bobby Hanson's countrymen were devastated and deeply saddened by the end of exhilaration and anticipation. United by grief, a nation mourned the death of Roscoe May.

THE END OF INNOCENCE

BY ANNE PERRY

The soft wind rippled across the fields and stirred the heavy elms at the far end of the pitch. It was the 5th August, and far too early in the year for a rugby match, but by October all the young men would be in France. Yesterday the Kaiser's army had marched into Belgium, and England was at war. In the next few days the men of all the villages in Northumberland would have joined their regiments, and a local derby would be impossible, a thing of dreams. Joseph was thirty-nine. He would not bear arms, but he would go as chaplain, follow where the men went, wherever that might be.

So this match mattered: it was pride, tradition, the last time it would be played by these men. The world was changing, probably forever. This golden afternoon, however absurd to play rugby now, would sit like a jewel in the memory through the dark days to come.

Everything must be right: the places for the old men, the women and children to sit, tables for the refreshments, a proper area set aside for the carts to park. It was always a match played with passion, even ferocity, but village pride, as well as good manners, demanded that hospitality be the best that could be offered.

He saw young Alan Trubridge walking over towards the goal posts, the sun glistening on his hair. He waved but Alan did not see him. He looked anxious. No doubt he was concerned about his father who was still very fragile since the loss of his leg. He knew more about war than other men because of his profession as a military engineer. He had seen enough death in the Boer War to have a better idea than they of what lay ahead. What words of comfort were there that Joseph, or anyone, could offer? There was only comradeship and the knowledge of loyalty.

Actually Alan's thoughts concerned a debt he was hard-pressed to pay, and about which he could tell no one. His father's dependence was a secret he could share with no one at all, not even Dorothy, in fact especially not her. How could she regard John Trubridge with the old respect if she knew how he had cried out in pain after his terrible surgery, and the morphine he had needed just to make it through the night? Injuries like that were beyond her imagination, or anyone's who had not seen them.

She had not sat up all night with him as Alan had, watching the delirium, the sweats, the dry retching and the agony of body, the shame and the fear.

They had had to let the resident hand go, and have Mabel come in from the village by day, but always leave by nightfall. Alan had managed on his own, cleaning, laundering, mopping up so no one else would know.

John Trubridge was better now, still gaunt, and the shadow of pain was there in his eyes, but his dignity was back, his belief in himself and in some purpose, even on crutches. The addiction to the morphine was gone, but the debt for it remained. Thank God at least he had no idea how much that was. Alan had borrowed it from Will Harrison. Now that war was a reality, he would have to pay it back a little each month out of his army pay, and trust to God he would not be killed before it was settled.

But then everyone was going with that trust for one reason or another. There were even those like Dorothy's twin brother Ernest, who thought they might all be home by Christmas. It would be good if he were right!

He was standing doing nothing, staring at the goal posts. They were perfect. He should move on and check the other end. The sun was hot. Hope it was cooler by this evening for the game. He started to walk over the short, level grass.

Should he wait until Christmas before asking Dorothy to marry him? Was that the fairer thing to do, fairer to her, at least? Would it make parting easier, rather than leaving her betrothed to a soldier, feeling an obligation that might prove restricting? It smacked a little of emotional pressure, as if he were saying 'I'm going to war, be faithful to me, even though I can't offer you anything but letters now and then, probably full of pretty wretched news.'

He could see her standing over on the far side of the pitch, with half a dozen others, the sun on her fair hair, the breeze ruffling her skirts a little and making the soft fabric cling to her body. His heart ached for the beauty of her.

Blanche was standing a couple of yards away, darker, without the laughter or the charm. They had called her 'Prof' at school, not always kindly. Blanche's love for him was an embarrassment he would rather not think about at the moment. Not that she was obvious about it. She had too much dignity for that, but he could not help seeing it in her eyes. Probably most of the village knew how she felt, and that he had only ever loved Dorothy. They were made for each other.

He quickened his pace until he caught up with Joseph.

"Good afternoon, Reverend," he said with a smile. "I think everything is just about ready." He squinted a little as he stared across the grass. "Should be a good match."

"I hope it'll be cooler by this evening," Joseph replied. "And it is still light until nine o'clock. I can't think of anything better than to have the two villages come here together."

Alan glanced at him, but Joseph was staring into the sun also, shielding his eyes from the brightness, and perhaps from being observed too closely. The minutes were racing by. How soon this would become only a memory as they walked into the darkness. A curious thing, time! It passed with a relentless, measured tread regardless of anything man could do, and yet all its volume depended upon what you did with it. These bright hours which were now the present would become caught like a fly in amber, never to be forgotten, and never recaptured. He cleared his throat.

Joseph stood quietly as if he knew Alan wanted to speak to him.

"Er... Reverend..." Alan began.

Joseph pushed his hands into his pockets. How could he look so relaxed? He would be leaving in a day or two, just as they all would, and he had a wife and two young daughters. How would they manage without him? He didn't have to go.

Joseph turned from gazing at the young women, moving among the light tables ready for cakes and sandwiches this evening. He smiled. "You want to see me?"

Alan felt the color warm in his face. "Am I so easy to read?"

"I would be in your place," Joseph replied.

"I want at least to ask her before I go," Alan explained. "But is it fair? To her, I mean. Does it place an obligation on her, just to make me feel... I don't know... as if I have someone? I think it might matter terribly... in France."

"I think it might," Joseph agreed. "But mostly I think you should ask her, and let her decide."

"But if I do, then I've already placed her in a position where she has to accept and tie herself, or else refuse," Alan pointed out. "And she might feel obliged... because..." he tailed off unhappily. He wanted to ask her so much he could not set his emotions aside. If he didn't ask her before he left, perhaps something would happen to him, and then she'd never know how he felt.

"Alan," Joseph said firmly. "Don't take from her the right to make her own decisions. Just don't press her if she won't commit herself, but remember that if you don't ask her, then she cannot say anything at all. Don't rob her of that. She may want more than anything else to tell you how she feels."

Alan relaxed, the tension slipping away inside him. It seemed so simple. It was what he needed to do. He looked across the green of the pitch and lifted his hand in a wave. Dorothy waved back, smiling.

"Thank you," he said to Joseph. "Of course you're right. I'll see you this evening." And without hesitating any more, he ran across the grass to join Dorothy. They would walk home for lunch together, it was barely two miles.

He nodded to Ernest and Chris Eaves, then he fell in step beside Dorothy, linking his arm in hers, deliberately not catching Blanche's eye. He did not want the discomfort of seeing the loneliness in her. He started to walk.

"I think we'll win this year," Dorothy said cheerfully, keeping up with him. "Everyone's got a terrific spirit up. Ernest says we've never been better."

"It would be a good note to go out on," he agreed, then instantly regretted it. "Sorry."

"Don't worry," she said quickly, tightening her arm on his. "No one believes it'll last very long. Ernest says that when the Kaiser sees we mean business, he'll back down. We probably could have had the match by New Year anyway, but it'll be good now, regardless."

He looked at her face in the sun. Was this the time to ask her? He might press too hard, make her feel as if she owed it to him, for all the wrong reasons. And yet when would he ever be able to ask her and not feel the emotion well up inside him like this and take control.

"Dorothy…"

She turned to him. Did she know?

But before he could say anything more, Ernest came running up from behind them, his face flushed and a look of unmistakable irritation in his eyes. He slowed his pace and fell into step with them.

"All ready?" he asked, looking at Alan. "We'll beat the socks off them this time. Hope they take it in good part. We'll all be comrades in arms in a few days. By the way, I don't suppose you know anyone who'd like to look after my car for me, do you? Not much use to me for the next few months, and I paid a fortune for it! Overpaid, actually. Bit of daylight robbery if you ask me. But that's Will Harrison all over." He gave an angry little gesture. "I should have known better than to buy anything from him. He's an absolute outsider."

"Never mind," Dorothy told him, linking her other arm in his. "You said yourself, it won't be long."

"We don't know that!" Alan said quickly. "Best prepare ourselves."

"Oh, come on!" Ernest said cheerfully. "We can beat the Kaiser's boys any day. Where's your patriotism, old fellow? Put a bit of heart into it!"

"I just think we shouldn't take it lightly…" Alan began.

"Don't be such a misery!" Ernest chided him. "We'll win the game this afternoon, and we'll win the war this year! All it takes is guts and a little belief in ourselves." He turned to Dorothy. "Isn't that right, Dot?"

"Of course it is," she agreed, her eyes bright. "Come on, Alan! We'll be fine. You'll see."

Alan forced himself to smile at her and nod his head. They reached the village church and he stopped for a moment while they went left, then when they were around the corner and he could not see her any longer, he went right towards his own house.

His father was in the sitting room in his armchair, his eyes closed, the newspapers half folded on the floor beside his foot. In the bright sunlight the lines were cut deep in his face and his skin had a papery quality, as if it might tear if anyone pulled it too hard. Still, the hollow grayness of constant pain was gone, and the hands in his lap were loose, not clenched.

He opened his eyes as Alan came in. He smiled. "All ready for the match?"

"All ready," Alan conceded cheerfully. "Feel like coming? I think just about everyone from both villages is going to be there. Ernest will take you in the car, if you like?"

"I'll think about it," the older man replied, and Alan did not press him. That was their understood way of saying that he did not feel well enough, or did not want to face the well-meaning questions and the awkwardness of people who are kind, but have no idea what to say to someone who has been ill more profoundly than they can imagine, and endured physical pain they do not know. Somehow the empty trouser leg embarrassed them, they did not know whether to look at it, or look away, say anything, offer to help or not.

"Ready for lunch?" Alan asked. "Bread and pickle, and the rhubarb pie, so Mabel said. And there's cream."

"Sounds good."

Alan looked at his father's face, then at the newspaper on the floor. He was on the brink of asking what was in it, then changed his mind. Let them have at least one meal without thinking about war. It lay behind everything they said, an awareness of the lifetime's familiar objects in the room, the silence in the village street beyond, the drone of bees in the delphiniums in the garden and a dog barking somewhere. It was all so normal, and so immeasurably precious. Why do we value such things so intensely only when they are a danger? No use in asking.

He turned and went into the kitchen to fetch the meal from where Mabel had left it set out on a tray.

They had only just finished eating when Will Harrison appeared. He was a big man with a handsome mustache and hard blue eyes. He greeted John Trubridge cautiously, inquiring after his health, then turned to Alan.

"All ready for this evening?" he said heartily. "Got to make the day one to remember, eh?" He glanced at the tray, then at some neatly folded papers on the bureau in the corner. He looked at Alan with a bright smile. "Perhaps we could talk outside, and not keep your father from his work. I know how important it is, sir," he added.

The older man nodded gravely, but there was a faint flush of pleasure on his face. "By all means," he conceded. "After all, it's a village derby. These things matter."

Alan followed Will through into the kitchen, then with surprise into the back garden beyond.

"Better private," Will said conversationally, walking up the lawn towards the plum trees a good fifty feet from the sitting room window.

Alan experienced a curious sinking in the pit of his stomach. He knew when Will spoke that it was going to be about the debt between them.

"Such a lot of money," Will said lightly, but there was a tension in his body. "Does your father know how much?"

"No!" Alan moderated his voice. "No. And I would rather he didn't."

"Yes," Will agreed. "I imagine he would feel very badly. Rather strips one of dignity, not to say the natural desire to keep one's illness private, and the difficulties of it, of course.

Alan was embarrassed, and in spite of his gratitude for Will's help, annoyed that he should mention it in such a way. It was intrusive. "I'll pay you back every month, as I can," he said quickly. "I'll have my army pay reverted to you."

"I imagined you'd say that," Will nodded. "It's not as if your father were dependent on you. After all, he's a pretty good military engineer. Rather a special man, in fact."

"Yes," Alan said decisively. "Very special, actually."

Will smiled, but there was no warmth in it. "Ernest thinks the war is going to be over by Christmas. But then he was always a trifle facile in his opinions."

"I've heard a few people say that," Alan replied. "I'd imagine it's what they want to think."

"The reality's going to be very different." Will was still looking at him speculatively, as if trying to read his thoughts. "But even if it doesn't last long, there will be a lot of men killed."

"Of course," Alan said sharply.

"And you could be among them," Will pointed out. "Hope not, of course, but we have to face reality."

"Any of us could." Alan felt a shiver run through him.

"So I'm afraid your army pay month by month isn't going to be sufficient, old chap." Will shrugged. "I'll need rather more than that."

"I haven't got any more..."

"Well you have, actually."

"No I haven't! I sold everything to pay for the morphine before I came to you. Good heavens, do you think I'd have come to you if I could have raised it any other way?"

Will's eyes were very level.

"Not what I meant. Just a small favor you could do me, and I'd call it evens."

That should have been a tremendous relief, and yet looking at the hard glitter in Will's eyes and the set of his heavy shoulders, it was not. Alan felt unmistakably afraid. His mouth was dry when he spoke. "What?"

"Put a spot of laudanum in your father's night-cap tonight," Will said very clearly. "And leave the keys to his safe in the dish on the mantelpiece. Make sure you stay in your room. A spot of laudanum for you too might not be a bad idea."

Alan was horrified. He knew that there were military papers in his father's safe, things that would make a difference to England's success in the war. A man a yard away from him on the lawn, with the August wind in his face off the fields, was asking him to betray his country! For a minute his breath would not come.

"I can't!" he gasped. "That's... it's..."

"A very practical solution to your troubles," Will finished for him with a tight smile. "Think about it, Alan, but don't take too long. It needs to be tonight. After all, old chap, consider the alternative." He glanced towards the house. "I can see that you don't like the idea, but at least it will be nice and private. No one will ever know about it but you and me. The other way... rather messy, you know? You off to France, to live or die... your father left here to face debt and embarrassment. In fact I don't think 'humiliation' would be too strong a word. Anyway, give it a bit of thought. I'll see you after the match. Oh... and leave the back window open." He started to stroll gently down the grass. He pointed to the window nearest the wisteria. "That one, I think. Make sure you get it right, there's a good fellow. I don't want to be messing around trying one after another. And Alan..."

Alan stopped. His mouth was too dry to speak.

"Don't think of calling Constable Riley over from Hadfield for me. If you do, I shall have to tell him I was coming to see your father, who had left the window open for me..."

"No one would..." Alan started to say.

Will smiled. "Believe me? Oh, but they would. It all makes excellent sense. A weak man, addicted to morphine, bought it illegally, got addicted to it, into debt! Finally reduced to selling his country to pay for it. He sent for me. I didn't know what he wanted... until too late. Very believable, old chap. And make no mistake, I'll tell them." He shook his head. "I have no intention of letting you stitch me up. Try anything like that, and I'll ruin him. Sordid end to a distinguished career." He opened the kitchen door. "Don't bother to show me through. I'll find my own way out. See you at the match!" He walked through the sitting room. "Good afternoon, Mr. Trubridge. Don't suppose you'll be coming to the game this evening, sir. But we'll trounce them, it'll be one to remember."

Alan did not hear his father's reply. His head was swimming. Minutes ticked by, or perhaps it was only seconds. He knew he must do something, but either course open to him was hideous. He could not sacrifice his father to ruin and despair, nor could he betray his country. Will Harrison had left him no way of escape. He had thought of all the paths by which Alan might evade him, and blocked each one.

He must get away from the house before his father suspected anything. He must not know. With a smile on his face that felt ghastly he went through the kitchen and into the sitting room. "I'm going to see the Reverend," he said without meeting his father's eyes. "Will wants a favor from me, and I need to talk to... to the Reverend about it. I'll be back for early supper."

"Yes, of course. Are you all right, Alan?"

He smiled, only a quick glance upwards. "Yes, of course. I'm fine."

"It's not the match worrying you, is it?" That was only half a question. "Dorothy?" His father's voice was gentle. They had never discussed their feelings a great deal. It was sometimes too revealing, usually unnecessary. They understood each other well, and had been close in instinctive knowledge since Alan's mother had died nearly twelve years ago. The sharing of a pleasure, a poem quoted, a piece of music, a good discussion on anything that mattered, philosophy or a rugby match, all said more than bare words. Companionship was its own explanation. He would miss that more than anything else he would leave behind.

With his throat tight he answered. "Only a bit. I'll speak to her this evening, after the match, I expect. I'll see you later." And he went out into the street and walked briskly back towards the church and the Manse beyond.

He passed half a dozen people he knew and either waved or called a hasty greeting. He could not entertain any kind of conversation today. He reached the gate and saw Christopher, since early school days his closest friend. He was coming out of the churchyard opposite. If he went to the door he could not avoid him. They knew each other too well to hide anything. It was Alan that Christopher had turned to when Will Harrison had stolen his first love, and then thrown her aside when he was bored. Christopher had never forgiven him for that. None of them had ever seen Eleanor since, or known what had happened to her.

Alan turned away from the gate and walked on briskly, as if he had purpose. Anyone seeing him would assume he was going back to the pitch, presumably he had forgotten something.

Chris was not the only other one to dislike Will. Fred Mundy had no love for him either. He blamed him for some cruel gossip that had circulated for quite some time. Jim Wallace from the Hadfield village had never forgotten the golf match in which he believed Will had cheated him out of first place, and the prize that went with it.

Would this evening's game be a last chance to settle some old enmities before the infinitely greater tide of war made them brothers in arms against a different enemy, one whose wages were not village squabbles, broken dreams or broken hearts, but the terrible reality of broken bodies buried in the mud of a foreign land?

These petty grudges were absurd. Even to think of them at all would be idiotic, were it not that it was a way to keep sane. The future was too big even to look at. Concentration on a single anger was bearable.

He turned and walked back towards the Manse and went straight up to the door and knocked. It was answered by the minister's wife and she was too wise, now of all times, to ask what a young man wanted with the Reverend. She simply showed him into the study and left.

"Sit down, Alan," Joseph said, frowning a little. His voice was soft, as if he knew trouble before it was spoken. He had a strong, gentle face with very dark eyes. The bookshelves behind him were filled with well-used volumes, every one ready to fall open at his favorite passages. There were far more than scriptures or studies of theology. Even at a glance Alan could see poetry, the Greek legends and stories of classical and renaissance Italy. The largest space not covered by books held a portrait of the poet Danté.

How Joseph would miss this haven of thought and collected beauty of the ages when he left home for the fields of France! And he was going because he believed it was his duty, and to fight for what he loved, in his own way, by sharing the life of the men and giving them what comfort he could. At least he would walk beside them every step of the path. Surely this was the ultimate way he proved that he believed what he preached every Sunday?

"How can I help you, Alan?" Joseph's voice cut across the turmoil in his mind. What could he say? He already knew at heart part of the answer. Whatever it cost, he could not leave the keys for Will Harrison. It was impossible.

He looked up. Joseph was waiting. He could not tell him. He must say something else, anything. What?

"Are you concerned about your father?" Joseph asked.

"Yes." That was the answer. "Yes. He's going to be... so much on his own. I don't know why I'm telling you. I'm sorry. It's not as if you would be here. There's nothing you can do. I suppose I just don't know how to take care of it. I feel... helpless."

Joseph smiled. "We're all pretty helpless at the moment. There comes a time when there's nothing you can do but trust in God and carry on the best you know how. I know that's not a lot of comfort now. I'm afraid it's all I have."

"I know," Alan said ruefully. "It isn't as easy as I used to think—merely black and white, right or wrong, and that's all there is to it."

"Is there something else, Alan?"

"No... no thank you. Thank you for listening to me. I expect half the village'll be here in the next day or two. I don't envy you trying to find something to say to them."

Joseph looked down at the desk. "It's the same thing for everyone, just trying to find the right way to say it for each."

"I'm glad you're coming with us—except I wish you were staying here too! Sorry. That sounds idiotic."

Joseph stood up. "No it doesn't. We're all going to wish we could be in more than one place. But for now, give the game your best effort and don't think of tomorrow yet." He offered his hand and Alan took it, and made his escape with the burden of decision still just as heavy in his heart.

Everyone from both villages was there for the match. It was an exquisite evening, the low sun golden on the grass, the wind barely rustling the elms against a stainless sky already glowing with the softness of evening, the warmth of color deepening in the west, shadows spreading deep. The crowd had gathered all around the edges of the pitch, women and young girls in their pale summer dresses, cottons and silks like so many bright flowers among the plainer shirtsleeves of the men. Children played on their own with hoops and balls, and one little boy was trying unsuccessfully to get a kite up in the still air.

Several groups of older men stood around, talking to each other seriously about the finer points of the game.

Alan gazed around him. He knew the world beyond. He had studied and traveled a little, but what mattered was here. It was these people he loved and who bounded all that was precious. He could see the roof of his own house in the distance, where his father was sitting reading. His mother was buried in the church-yard. Dorothy was over there in the crowd, and Christopher, Joseph and his wife and two daughters, the postmistress, Mabel who cooked for himself and his father and kept the house in order, Blanche and her father the schoolteacher, the shopkeeper, Chris's father the blacksmith, Dr. Kitching.

He must pay attention to the game. It was about to begin. Now of all times he must not let them down. The whistle blew and he plunged in as if victory here were all of life.

It was hard fought, at moments brilliant, at others clumsy beyond belief. Idiotic mistakes were made, and superb tries, men running as if their feet had wings. The scrums were violent, no mercy asked or given.

Just before halftime the score was eleven all.

They were in the scrum again, pushing, shoving, scrambling for position, feet everywhere. Alan felt a boot scrape down his leg, tearing the skin. He was hit heavily in the middle of the back and fell forward. There was someone half underneath him. He had no idea where the ball was.

He was shoved from behind and caught by a shoulder in the chest. He fell sideways and saw Will Harrison slip and crash heav-ily almost underneath him. He tried to stand up and was knocked from the left. Chris was beside him and then gone again. He lunged forward and regained his balance. The ball was gone. Will Harrison's head was in the mud below him, the pale skin of his throat and ear exposed. He hesitated only a moment, thinking of his father, the long nights, the pain, the whole village going to France, then he trod down hard on Will's neck, and turned away. He knew what he had done as he felt the bone crack. Is this what war would be like? Knowing the second it was over, and too late?

Someone had the ball and the scrum broke apart. He stag-gered to his feet. He must not look back. He lunged forward blind-ly and his legs buckled underneath him. The ground hit his chest, driving the breath out of his lungs. He must get up, look as if he were playing. Someone tripped over him and fell. He was glad of the boot in his ribs, the weight on top of him. They scrambled up together. It seemed like eternity before the whistle blew and there was a shout that something was wrong.

He turned round and saw the referee go over to where Will was lying motionless on the ground. He bent and looked at him, then rose to his feet. He seemed dazed. He swung around, looking for Dr. Kitching.

Slowly the whole crowd realized it was not just a man slipped or a broken leg. An anxious silence hung over the field as the doctor detached himself from the spectators, ran over and bent down to look. Alan recognized the dark figure of Joseph going over to join the little group. They were speaking together quietly.

It was only a few more moments before Kitching stood up and said that Will was dead. His neck must have been broken in the scrum. It was a terrible accident, but by no means the first of its kind.

Alan had never imagined he could feel so utterly alone. Cain must have felt like this, cast out of all he knew to wander the earth.

But Will would have betrayed them all, these quiet ordinary people Alan loved so much—and ten thousand other towns and villages like them all over the land.

He never doubted for an instant that Will would have said he had come because John Trubridge had sent for him, offering him secrets for money to buy morphine. God knew, enough of it had changed hands between them in the past! The police would believe it! How could they doubt?

Alan couldn't have done that! The betrayal was beyond him.

Dr. Kitching was addressing the crowd, his voice sounding thin in the fading summer evening. The light was already gold on the top of the elms. He was telling them Will Harrison was dead, and they should all go home. There was nothing more to be done tonight. He apologized, as if somehow it were his fault, then he turned to Joseph.

Alan did as everyone else did, walked quietly, bemused, back along the lane to the village. But unlike others, he walked alone. He hoped anyone seeing him took it for grief. They could never know the burden he carried that hurt inside more than bruises or broken bones, swelling until it filled all of him.

Will had no family for Joseph to tell, or try to comfort. Of course there would be letters to write, but that could wait until tomorrow. Rugby tragedies did happen. He had known of others, admittedly less serious, many broken bones, head injuries, even one that ended in paralysis. But death was not startling, merely an added burden of sorrow at a time when men and women were expecting far worse to come, and there were too many good-byes to be said.

It was about the time people would have been home from the game, had it run its full course, when there was a knock on the study door and Dr. Kitching came in, his face puckered with deep concern.

"What is it?" Joseph asked immediately, rising to his feet. "What's happened?"

Kitching sank to the chair on the other side of the desk, his eyes dark with weariness and distress. "I don't know, Joseph. I'm not sure how bad it is. I considered ignoring it altogether, but I don't think I can because there may be others who have received them as well." He was holding a piece of paper in his hand.

"What is it?" Joseph was puzzled.

"An anonymous letter," Kitching replied, passing it over. "It's pretty simple. It just says Will Harrison was killed deliberately— murdered in fact."

Joseph took the paper from him, surprised to find his hand was not shaking. "Murder?" he said with disbelief. "Who would say such a vicious thing? And..." He was about to add 'pointless' until he looked at the paper and saw that Christopher Eaves was accused and the rivalry over Eleanor given as the reason. It was motive enough, in most people's eyes. No one knew what had happened to Eleanor since, and Christopher had never loved anyone else in the same way. He had had a few slight romances but they had never grown to anything serious. The ghost of Eleanor came between him and any new sweetness and certainty. Joseph looked up at Kitching.

"You don't believe it's possible, do you?" Kitching's voice was high and edged with distress.

"No," Joseph replied with more decision than he truly felt. The whole world was changing. Young men were thinking of death

255

in a way they never had before. They went to answer the calls of duty and loyalty to all they loved, home, family, a set of ideals and a way of life. Some of them looked no further than that, and imagined it would all be over in a few months. Others, perhaps a little older or wiser, knew that no one experienced the violence, the terror and alienation of war without being irrevocably changed. Not everyone would come back, and among those who did, many might be maimed. Was this vicious letter some settling of old scores before the sunset of this golden age? It was a startlingly ugly idea, and he could not rid himself of it. "Have you any knowledge as to who wrote this?" he asked.   Kitching shook his head. "None at all. I don't even know if Harrison was killed on purpose or if it was a complete accident. I thought I'd go and look at him again, but I'd appreciate it if you'd come with me. I find this..." He stopped, choked for words to express himself. Joseph stood up. "Of course. We'd better go straight away."   He explained to his wife only that Kitching needed him and he was expecting to be gone a short while. He was aware how precious every hour was, but he had no choice, and she was accustomed to him being sent for on urgent matters he could not share with her. She said nothing except to wish them good-bye, but he was aware that she stood in the lighted doorway and watched them until they turned the corner and were no longer visible.   Kitching took him to his surgery where Will Harrison was lying, and lifted the sheet off his face. Joseph stared down at him. He had been a big man in life, full of confidence, even something of a bully, not a man Joseph liked. But lying here now, naked but for the covering of decency, he looked smaller and oddly vulnerable. Funny because now he was beyond all pain.

"You see?" Kitching said, pointing to the abrasions on the side of Will's neck where the skin had been torn by the rough sole of a boot.

"That could be accidental, surely?" Joseph asked, peering at it and then looking up at Kitching. "Isn't that how it would be if someone trod on him, without meaning to?"

Kitching pointed delicately to where the tears formed a slightly curving pattern. "That looks as if someone turned sharply, and that's what broke his neck, instead of only bruising him, or even knocking him unconscious."

Joseph followed his indication. "Couldn't it just as easily have been an accident?"

"Possibly, but it looks less like it. Why would anyone turn, unless they had the ball? And from what I could see, no one ran with it from there. In fact no one ran with it at all, until after Will must have been dead."

"But this doesn't prove murder, does it?" Joseph argued. "You can't hang a man on this."

Kitching pulled the cover over the face again. "No." He looked across at Joseph. "I'd be inclined to ignore it, if I were certain no one else received any letters like the one I have. But I can't be."

Joseph wanted to say something helpful, but it would have been a lie. The truth was ugly, and unanswerable. "We'll have to wait until morning. The village is a small place. If there is another one, and the recipient doesn't destroy it, as I think they should, then we'll soon know about it."   Kitching sighed. "I agree. Thank you, Joseph. I... I just didn't want to do this alone, I suppose. What a damnable thing, now of all times." He walked to the door and turned the light out. "You might as well go home, and get a decent night."

But there were other letters. By mid-morning the village was buzzing with accusation against Christopher. To begin with he was bewildered, then hurt. By lunchtime he was thoroughly frightened and had no idea which way to turn. He was an ordinary, decent young man who had grown up in the cottage behind the forge. He had been to the village school and believed that he had a secure place in the esteem of his friends, albeit a less privileged one than many of them. Now, without warning, it was shattered.   A l a n heard it from Ernest, a little after eleven o'clock. He dismissed it as rubbish. Ernest was quick and graceful, like Dorothy, but he had a sharp tongue and had never been especially fond of Christopher, thinking that he gave himself airs he had no right to.

Then he heard it again from the postmistress. She shook her iron gray curls as she fished behind the curtain for a rubber band. "I don't know what things are coming to. Nice young man like Christopher. Can't believe it's true, myself. But it's all over the place. You're his friend, Mr. Alan, you're going to have to stand by him, and that's no mistake."

Alan thanked her and walked out into the sun with his heart hammering in his chest.

Even as the thoughts were racing in his mind, he was walking towards the Manse. This time there was no decision to make. He could not say why he had done it, of course. That would defeat the whole object. If he could not think of another reason, then he would have to remain silent, and let people think what they would.

It was desperate, and yet in a strange, sad way it was a kind of relief. His father would be devastated, but perhaps that was always going to happen, whatever course he had taken. Damn Will Harrison. Hope he was in some kind of hell.

Joseph received him right away.

"They are saying that Will Harrison was murdered," Alan began as soon as the study door was closed. "And that Christopher did it."

"I know," Joseph replied. "I am truly sorry. I find it very difficult to believe. And I know that you and Christopher have been friends for years. I will do all I can to get to the bottom of it, I promise you, and to protect Christopher's name as much as I can. Or to stand by him should that prove impossible."

Alan let out a long sigh, and squared his shoulders. "Christopher didn't kill Will Harrison. I did."

Joseph was startled, incredulous. Then his frown eased out into sadness. "I know you count loyalty very high, Alan, and I admire you for it, but why on earth would you kill Will Harrison?"

"I... I quarreled with him."

Disbelief was plain in Joseph's eyes. "Over what, that you would kill him for it?"

"I can't tell you..."

"Alan..."

"I did! Believe me, Reverend, I am telling you the truth. I saw my chance in the scrum, and I took it." He closed his eyes, as if it could block out the remembrance which was inside him. "I put my foot on his neck and I turned it. You can't allow Christopher to take the blame for something I did. That would be intolerable! Surely you, of all people, can see that?"

Joseph smiled ruefully. "What I can see is a young man of

great idealism prepared to sacrifice himself to save his friend, perhaps believing that as the son of a distinguished military hero of the past, he may receive a gentler hearing on the matter that a young man whose father is the village blacksmith, and whose mother was a laundress. I see a childhood friendship grown deeper with manhood, where the stronger protects the more vulnerable, and perhaps pays back debts when the protection and the loyalties were the other way."

"But I did kill Will Harrison!" Alan said desperately. "Maybe I would lie to protect Chris, I don't know, but it isn't necessary. He didn't do anything!" He took a deep breath. "I came to you first, because I thought you would want to make sure justice was done, but I'll go to Dr. Kitching, and over to Hadfield to the police, if you don't."

Joseph glanced down at his hands, then up again. "I'll speak to Dr. Kitching, but I won't speak to the police. I can understand your loyalty, Alan, but I don't think you have thought this through very carefully. Consider your father, as well as Christopher."

Alan felt the blood leave his face. This was the sort of nightmare where every step he took was blocked. Every time he thought he had escaped, he began to run, and the way in front of him was off again. He rose to his feet, ashamed to find his legs shaking. What was battle going to be like if he was afraid simply standing here in his minister's study fighting against his own demons?

"Thank you," he said awkwardly. "But it won't change anything." And before Joseph could say more, he went out of the door and closed it behind him softly.

He told Dorothy what he had done because she raised the subject when they met in the early afternoon. He could not allow her to believe Christopher guilty, and it seemed she did so.

"You said what?" She stood in the sun in the quiet lane, her eyes wide and angry.

"I told the Reverend it was I who killed Will Harrison, not Christopher," he repeated.

Her face was flushed, her soft hair blowing a little in the wind. "For heaven's sake, Alan! What on earth are you thinking of?" She sighed impatiently "I know you feel a sort of loyalty to Christopher going back years, and that he looked after you when you were at school, and all that, and this is all very quixotic and I love you for it... but think of our happiness as well!" She bit her lip, aware that perhaps she had presumed too much, not the fact, but the speaking of it aloud, before he had. "The Reverend didn't believe you, did he?"

"No, he said not..."

"Thank heaven for that! At least he has more sense!" She pushed her hair back off her brow, smiling a little now as relief took hold. "It's all just silly gossip because people are—upset. Everything's changing so quickly, with the news of war, and knowing all of you are going away. People are jumpy. It's all so difficult, so uncertain. And we'll miss you dreadfully."

"Not half as much as we'll miss you!" he said with a rush of emotion. "And all this!" He looked around at the hedges with the last of the wild roses falling, and the ripening fields beyond, the great elms in the distance. It looked exactly like any other late summer.

"I know," she said gently, taking his arm. "But you'll be back soon, and everything will wait for you. Just don't say anything more about Will Harrison, and let Christopher take care of himself. It'll all blow over. I know they quarreled about Eleanor, and no one could blame Chris for that, but he wouldn't kill anyone, and they'll all realize it in a day or two, you'll see."

Could he tell her that what he had told Joseph was true? He had killed Will Harrison. Would she ever understand that? Could she put herself in his place and imagine the dilemma he had faced, the need to act one way or the other, choose between two wrongs, and do it in the space of a few desperately short hours? There was no time to weigh and measure, seek other alternatives.

"Alan?" She was regarding him quizzically, a half smile on her face. In her clear eyes there was no reflection of the turmoil he felt. She had given an answer to Christopher's problem in that he should face it himself. That excused Alan, and so also her. There was no more to be said. "Alan, darling, let it go," she urged. "We've only got another couple of days. Let's spend them happily. Give us both something to remember when we're apart. It's terrible that

Will is dead, but we can't alter it. Don't let it cloud everything else."

It was true. And neither of them had liked Will. But it could not be dismissed in a few words. However true part of them were, it was infinitely less than the whole.

"Come on!" she said, moving a little forward. "Let's walk up as far as the stream before supper. It's going to be another perfect evening."

He went with her, but the golden light held no warmth for him, and in spite of being beside her, he had never felt more alone.

Joseph did not believe Alan when he said he had killed Will Harrison. It seemed too obviously an attempt to save Christopher, born out of old loyalties. It was like Alan. The ties of love had always bound him very tightly, as long as Joseph had known him, and that was over ten years now.

He did not believe Christopher would have killed Will, in spite of the vicious way Will had destroyed his romance with Eleanor. But Joseph had discovered many times that there were darker and more complex sides to even the sunniest people, and sometimes shallower hearts where one had expected pity and strength.

It was a strange lie for Alan to tell, panicky and ill-judged. But then everyone's emotions were raw now. He must be profoundly worried about his father, who was still not strong. His long illness had drained him far more than most people in the village supposed. Joseph had seen the pain in his face, even the despair at times. Only Alan's selfless devotion had pulled him through.

And yet for Alan to have stayed when all the rest of the young men of villages all over the county were going to war, would have been an even greater burden. John Trubridge was intensely proud. He would have died alone rather than have his son remain at home in safety to look after him. It was perverse, difficult, but Joseph admired him for it. He could not count the times when visiting him he had looked away rather than see his pain, in order to leave him the dignity of pretending it never overcame him.

Joseph sat back in his chair and stared at the ceiling of his study. Who had sent that miserable letter to Kitching? And who else had received one and started the talk in the village? He had not recognized the ugly printing on the page Kitching had shown him, but then whoever had sent it had taken obvious trouble to disguise the hand. No one would willingly have been identified with such a contemptible thing.

He would like to know who it was. An honorable person knowing anything about Will Harrison's death would have come and said so, face to face. Only cowards made accusations to which they would not sign their names.

There were many men in the scrum who might have felt they had reason to hate Will, but who hated Christopher enough to accuse him without evidence? That was somewhere to begin. It didn't have to be anyone on the pitch, since they didn't claim to have evidence they could substantiate. It could be anybody.

Did they really believe it could be true? Who thought so ill of Christopher they would allow it to warp them into such an act? He thought of the people he knew, both men and women, probing in the painful places of his memory for the secrets he had learned one way or another, the weaknesses and private sins his profession had made him privy to.

They were so ordinary, the fears of loneliness and failure that beset us all, the embarrassment, the envy, the rejection, the dread of ridicule, the exhaustion of illness, the misery of poverty. So few of them were born of real viciousness, only confusion and a lack of understanding as to what really matters, and that they already had the power to alter things, if only they would use it with faith.

Perhaps whoever wrote that wretched letter already regretted it? It might be that somewhere within a couple of miles someone else was also sitting alone, wishing in despair that they could undo the last day and not set pen to paper. He wished that might be so, and they would be sorry enough to admit to it, and confess that the charge was untrue. That would take a lot of courage. But he thought with pity of the path that lay ahead of the person either shipping out to France to face battle beside the man he had betrayed, or staying here safely at home and watching the others go, and knowing it was too late ever to take back the words.

He wished he could find them and try to persuade them

tonight, but he had no idea who it was, not even if it were a man or a woman. Their spite would poison both places, and he would find it hard to forgive them for that.

Alan and Dorothy sat beside the stream watching it rattle over the stones, dimpled in sunlight, shadowed brown and green under the overhanging banks dense with grasses. It was the perfect place to ask anyone to marry, and Alan had intended to ask her this evening, but his mind was filled with Will Harrison, and the terrible decision he had made and carried through. He could not ask anyone to commit themselves to him, with this weight on his soul. He would far rather have been here alone, free to think, to try to explain to himself what he had done.

But whether he did that or not, he must help Christopher. He must find a way of making either Joseph or Dr. Kitching believe him, before they all left and it was too late, and that would be intolerable. He would have to invent another reason that they could accept, otherwise it would have to be the truth.

And yet doing so would expose his father's vulnerability and the magnitude of his debt, the very reason he had killed Will in the first place. There was an irony in that—perhaps even a kind of justice.

Dorothy was looking at him. She was waiting for him to propose to her. He knew it as surely as if she had said so.

His father would rather have died during that hideous operation and the long, agonizing recovery, than know that Alan had killed a man to protect his secret. If he had to tell anyone why he had done it, then lied as to a death, a murder, not just the village but the whole country would know. It would never be forgotten.

"Alan..." Dorothy's voice hardly penetrated his thoughts. "Alan!" she said more insistently.

He turned to face her.

"Are you still thinking about that wretched anonymous letter?" she asked, with an edge of impatience. "For goodness sake, forget about it! We've only got tonight and tomorrow left! Think about us for a while. You can't help Christopher. If he killed Will Harrison then justice will catch up with him, and you can't prevent that! If he didn't, then it'll all go away. Alan!"

"He didn't kill him!" he said sharply, angry that she should even consider it, and perhaps angrier still that she should speak so easily of justice as if it were an absolute and she understood it. Judgment was so difficult, far more than he would have imagined even a week ago. It was not always between right and wrong, sometimes it was between two wrongs, and no time to decide which was the worse. Any fool could choose when it was black and white. What about when it was gray and gray?

She was smiling at him now, a million miles away. What would she say if she knew it was he who had killed Will? 'Justice will catch up with you'? Would she understand why? Would she care?

He looked steadily at her fair face, beautiful in the evening light, and he saw expectation in it, certainty of herself and her beliefs. She was waiting for him to tell her he loved her, and she knew he did. He had done since they were both in school. But the words were not there. Will's death had separated them. He was no longer the man she knew. He had turned himself into someone else she could not love. And what was more amazing, he could not feel the same excitement, the warmth and the peace he had felt for her until only yesterday. Now she was a stranger with a beautiful face, and a mind that was as bright and shallow as the stream a couple of yards away.

"I know what you're waiting for me to say, and I can't." He met her eyes and saw the disbelief in them, and then the anger. "I have no right to ask you to commit yourself to a man in my position."

"And if I choose to?" she said roughly, fighting tears.

"You don't, Dorothy," he answered with a gentleness he had not known he felt. It was not passion, not tenderness, but a kind of remote regret, as if they had parted long ago, it was just that he had not understood it until now. Very slowly he climbed to his feet and looked down at her. "I've got to go and see if I can do something about Christopher. I'm sorry."

"Ernest says he probably did it!" she challenged him.

"Ernest wasn't even in the scrum," he replied. "But if he was the one who wrote the letters, then I wish to hell that he and I were not in the same regiment. I'd rather not face an enemy with him beside me."

She blushed crimson. "That's a terrible thing to say!"

"It was a terrible thing to do," he returned.

She stood up too, her cheeks flushed, her dress a little rumpled. "No it isn't! Not if Christopher is guilty, and Ernest thinks he is. So do I."

Alan found his throat tight. "And you can make a judgment so easily, and be sure you're right?"

"Yes I can! What's the matter with you? You've changed. Are you afraid of going to war?"

"Yes, of course I am!" he said bitterly. "Only an idiot thinks it's going to be a big adventure. We won't all come back, you know? It's not death or glory... it'll be boredom, exhaustion, fear, injuries and more boredom."

"Is that what your father says?" she demanded. "You shouldn't listen to him so much. It isn't like that any more. Just because he got injured in South Africa and then lost his leg later because of his wound, doesn't mean it's like that for everyone."

"There's nothing to argue." He moved a step away. "Christopher didn't do anything to Will, and I've got to go and see that people don't believe that he did. I can't go away leaving it. I'm sorry." And without waiting for her to say anything more he turned and walked away rapidly up the bank and across the rough grass towards the lane.

He would have to think of a way of saving Chris, without destroying his father, but the more he turned over every possibility in his mind, the deeper was his feeling of helplessness and despair. He was oblivious of the soft wind in his face carrying the perfume of the hay fields, or the song of the wild birds in the hedgerows. He almost bumped into Blanche before he noticed she was there. She was riding her bicycle and she dismounted immediately. His first reaction was irritation. He did not want to see anyone at all, but least of all her. The effort to mask his feelings and be civil was more than he could manage. He knew his face gave him away.

"Hello, Alan," she said quietly. "You look wretched..."

He drew in breath to snap back at her, anything to make her leave him alone. His world was in ruins and he was more deeply afraid of disaster that would destroy all he loved. There was no strength left to be kind. But she spoke before he had time.

"You must be worried sick about Christopher." She fell in step beside him along the narrow track, pushing the bicycle. "I don't think we'd normally be so quick to repeat stupid gossip like this, but everyone's frightened because we're facing the unknown, and we can't even do it together. Half of us will be left behind not knowing what's happening to those we love, while the other half go off into a situation none of us has ever faced before. I know people like Ernest are saying it'll all be over by Christmas, but we don't know if that's true. And even if it is, some will be killed. Even if it's only a few, those you love best could be among them."

It was the most reasonable remark he had heard anyone make so far, and the anger in him melted away. He looked at her face. It was quite calm, but the fear in her eyes was real. She was holding it in only with difficulty.

"Yes," he admitted. "I... I can't think what to do to show that Chris isn't guilty of anything. I know he still hurts over Eleanor, but he didn't kill Will."

She walked in silence for a moment or two, thinking hard. "Don't you think that if anyone killed him on purpose, it would be over something that happened just lately, rather than years ago?" she said finally, as they came to where the lane narrowed as the hawthorn hedge spread wide and low over the verges. "Why would he wait until now?"

Was it a glimmer of hope? "He wouldn't!" he agreed quickly. "Unless it's because we're going to war? And there won't be another chance."

She turned to look at him with level candor, her glance critical. "That doesn't make a lot of sense. If they both came back he would deal with it then, if he still cared. And if Will were killed it wouldn't matter. I can't believe Chris would want to do that now, before going, on the chance he might be killed himself." She pushed the bicycle wheel over a rattle of stones. "That just isn't the kind of person he is. If it mattered to him that much, he'd have done something years ago. But knowing Chris, he'd far more likely have had a fight when Eleanor went, not keep it until now." She stopped, as if there were something more to say, but she did not want to go on.

"What?" he asked. It was automatic. If she did not want to tell him then she wouldn't. The moment the word was out he wished he had not spoken. The sooner they reached the village and he could decently leave her, the better.

"Unless he just heard something about Eleanor in the last day or two," she replied. "Do you know if he did?"

"No." He was surprised. "Not as far as I know, and I think he'd have said."

"Maybe not, but you'd have seen it in his face," she pointed out. "He's pretty transparent."

"You're right!" He felt a wave of relief. "Surely people will see that?"

They walked a further dozen yards or so. The light was low and touched with gold, shadowing the lane completely. The evening air was sweet, and there was no sound but their footsteps and the slight squeak of the bicycle wheels.

"You can't take that for granted, Alan," she said, looking at him quickly, and then away again. "Most of us aren't thinking so very reasonably now. We're frightened. That does funny things to common sense, and I sometimes think to our better nature as well. Somebody wrote some pretty rotten letters. I don't even know how many, do you?"

The relief vanished. "No," he admitted. "But I know Chris didn't kill Will Harrison." He avoided meeting her eyes.

"Do you?" There was no inflection in her voice, certainly no challenge. She was asking him. The temptation to tell her the truth was almost overwhelming. At least he would no longer be alone with his monster. But he must not. It would be dangerous, and unfair to her. But he was also weary to the soul with lies.

"Yes, I do."

Now it was she who kept silence for a space. Far away on the slope of the hill a sheep bleated. Above the woods the starlings were circling.

"Then that means you know the truth," she said finally.

He waited for her to add that it was his duty to speak it, but she didn't He had no intention of looking at her. He did not want her eyes reading his feelings. She was too quick, too honest.

They were almost at the corner where the lane opened out

and joined the road to the village. Then he would be rid of her. He stopped, without knowing why.

"You can't protect everyone, Alan," she stopped as well, looking at him now without any pretense at the games people usually played. She was not a lonely and rather plain girl, and he was not a young man she was in love with, who had always preferred someone else. He was a young man going to war in a few days, and she was someone who had seen the anguish inside him and not turned away from it.

He did meet her eyes after all, and saw a courage there which was better than laughter or admiration, and just at the moment it was also better than love.

"If you don't tell someone the truth, you may end in protecting no one at all," she added. "I would go and see the Reverend, if it were me."

"I tried," he said with a twisted little smile. "He didn't believe me. He thought I was lying to protect Chris."

She looked down at the ground. She took a very deep breath and let it out slowly. "I'd have thought the only person you'd lie this hard to protect would be your father."

The fading sunlight seemed to shimmer around him. He could see every blade of grass at the roadside, the tiny moths fluttering and dipping. Did she know the truth?

"I'd go and see the Reverend if it were me," she repeated.

There was no escape. She was right, he would only end in getting everyone hurt. If he were the one hurt himself, there would be a kind of cleanness about it, even honor, if nothing else.

"Yes... I think I'll do that. Thanks, Blanche." He smiled at her. He meant it profoundly, and saw the color burn up her cheeks. She wasn't pretty, but there was something in her which was more than that, even beautiful. "Thanks," he said again, feeling awkward. Then he turned and walked quickly down the road towards the Manse, before he could lose the courage.

Joseph walked down the lawn towards the apple tree with Alan beside him. He was not really surprised to see him back. He felt helpless to do anything for him. All day the talk in the village had gone back and forth, one in accusation, one in defense, far too many repeating what they had heard or thought. It saddened him and made him angry, but even his indignation had done nothing to crush it, except within his hearing. He knew perfectly well that it had resumed the moment he was out of earshot. He had changed nothing, except to set himself apart.

Alan was deeply unhappy, but there was a different air about him. He had resolved upon something.

"What is it?" Joseph asked him when they reached the tree, already laden with tiny fruit. It needed another two months at least before they would be ripe. It would be a good crop, if the winds didn't take them.

Alan stared at him, his eyes pleading. "When I told you that I killed Will Harrison, it was the truth. I just didn't tell you why because it was to hide that that I did it."

Joseph was stunned. What could Alan Trubridge have to conceal that was worth even injury, let alone killing a man?

"I see," he said aloud. "And are you now going to tell me what that reason was?"

"Yes." Alan's gaze did not waver. "When my father was ill I got morphine for him. I got a lot of it, over time. More than Dr. Kitching or anyone else would give him. And he was ashamed of it. He believed a soldier should have the courage to bear any amount of pain without recourse to such things. And then afterwards it took him a long time to... to be able to do without it."

Suddenly a hundred small things became clear to Joseph. Shadows of memory fell into place and became understandable. "I'm terribly sorry," he said, and meant it. John Trubridge had been a good friend, a man he admired deeply. "Was your purchase of it illegal? Is that what Will Harrison knew?"

"Well, I suppose semi-illegal, yes. But I had to borrow the money from Will to get it. I couldn't not..."

"I understand. You don't have to explain. And you owed Will a considerable sum. Alan, for heaven's sake, couldn't you have found another way?"

Alan's face was white with misery. "I offered to give him my army pay every month until the debt was cleared, but he wanted it now, before we go to France." He swallowed hard. "He said he would cancel the whole debt if I left the key to my father's safe on the mantel shelf, and the sitting room window open."

Joseph was so shocked it took him a moment or two to repeat the words over in his mind and understand what they meant. How could it be true? How could he even contemplate selling his country, let alone blackmailing someone else into helping him? It was inconceivable. And yet even as he denied it, he looked at Alan's face and knew it was true.

"And if you did not?" he asked. He knew the answer to that also, but he had to hear Alan say it.

"Then he would make public my father's illness... and how he faced it," Alan said simply. "And if I'd told the police there would have been nothing they could do until he'd got in, then he would have said my father had left the window and the keys for him, for more money for morphine. I couldn't let that happen."

"No... no, I see that." Joseph agreed. He could see it. John Trubridge would have been ruined, very possibly even executed for treason. The son who had loved him could not bring that about.

"What should I do?" Alan asked.

"Nothing," Joseph said immediately. "Not yet."

"There's no time," Alan began.

"I know," Joseph cut across him. "The day after tomorrow we shall leave, and none of us will come back the same as we were. The innocence will be gone from us, and some of the belief. We will have seen things around us we haven't even imagined yet. And more than that, deeper and far worse, we will have seen things inside ourselves we didn't dream of." He lowered his voice. "And of course some of us will not come back at all. And our women will be different as well. All of them will be afraid for us, and some of them will mourn." He took a deep breath. "And I imagine some of those we leave behind will never understand how we have changed, or why."

"You mean like Dorothy?" Alan asked.

"I don't know. Do I?"

"I think so."

"Don't judge her too quickly."

Alan smiled, and Joseph saw in his eyes that the decision was already made. Whatever happened in the future, there was no going back on that at least. It was not a sudden change, only a sudden realization. He was not totally surprised.

"What are you going to do?" Alan asked, the edge of urgency back in him.

"I'm going to see Dr. Kitching. I think you should go home and prepare for traveling. Spend your last day with your father. He'll miss you very much. But keep your own counsel on this matter. Be brave, and kind to him. Let him believe there is nothing wrong except parting. You have the rest of your life in which to make peace with God for what has happened over the last few days. From now on you can be whatever you want, if you want it badly enough."

"But..."

"No 'buts'," Joseph answered firmly "Go forward doing all you can, and leave the judgment to God. You can't help anyone by telling this story, except as you have to me. It is better for everyone, including Will Harrison, if his death is considered an accident. I shall see to it that Christopher does not continue to be blamed for it, I promise you."

"Just... go?"

"Harder, perhaps, than confessing and taking the blame now, but of infinitely more service to your fellows," Joseph said. "We need you, Alan. You can't afford the luxury of sitting down in a heap of guilt. You must keep going, lengthen your stride, not shorten it. Now go home and be with your father. I'm going to see Dr. Kitching, and then I am going to spend tomorrow with my family too."

"Yes," Alan said huskily, but his voice was quite steady. "Thank you, Reverend."

"You're welcome. Will you tell my wife I shall be back in half an hour or so. I'll go the back way across the lane."

"Yes... and thank you."

"You already said that. Goodnight."

"Goodnight, Reverend."

"An accident?" Kitching said with surprise. "You walked over here at this time of the evening to tell me that?" Joseph sat down in the big leather armchair. "Yes, I think it's important that the village knows that before we all leave."   Kitching looked at him levelly. "What made you decide that now?"   Joseph smiled. "You have your professional confidences, Robert, so do I." "Was it anything to do with young Christopher, and Eleanor Cooper?" "Nothing at all." "And it satisfies your conscience?" "I can think of nothing better. It is not an easy answer, but some questions are too difficult. The questions between right and wrong are simple, it's the ones between one wrong and another that confuse us and test our judgment, and our compassion, and perhaps above all our courage. Let it be, Robert. Will Harrison died as a result of his own actions. Don't make a lot of other people suffer more than they already have, and will go on doing."

"Right you are, Joseph, an accident it was," Kitching agreed. "God knows, in a little while one death is going to be a small tragedy, by comparison." He stood up and walked over to the window. "The longer I live, the more I realize how much I don't understand. For example I can see young Alan Trubridge down there on the bank by the stream, and he's talking to Blanche Elder. I would have sworn he was in love with Dorothy, but that's not what it looks like from here. I've never seen such tenderness in his face."

Joseph smiled. "It's not a time for laughter and pretty girls any more. I'm afraid it's the girls with courage and strength who matter now, and will do until this is over, and perhaps long after that. Things are never going to be quite like this again."

Kitching turned back to the room. "I know that, Joseph. But there's still one more day of innocence left."

Joseph stood up. "And I am going to spend it at home. Goodnight, Robert, and thank you."

HOLLYWOOD SPRING AND AXLE

BY GARY PHILLIPS

I was trippin' about how Jefferson Street Joe Gilliam went out when my head bounced off the sliding glass door. That's what I get for bein' all nostalgic when my sorry butt should be on point. I'd like to play it off to the fact that on the flat screen TV Fox Sports West had a still up of Joe lookin' all Captain America in his Steelers uniform. Yeah, that would make my ego feel better, but it wouldn't be the truth.

Homeslice followed up his shove with a blow toward my gut. Hell, I was old, not Methuselah. I blocked his blow and feinted with a quick right to his head, then switched up at the last blink. I tagged his muscle powder sniffin' ass with a chop to his Adam's apple. That got this Warren Sapp wannabe gasping and just for giggles, I kicked him in the ankle just like I'd seen Chow Yun-Fat do in one of his early Woo epics. It wasn't as elegant, but it got extra large to buckle, and I earned some props with a straight right to his jaw.

"Damn, Rack, why you gots to all the time be Jim Brown'in and shit?" Biddy Truck squeaked. Biddy sounded like Mike Tyson after taking a few speech classes. What was even more of a crack-up, Biddy was black, blonde, and a woman. She was maybe a few years older than me but still had a build topped off with a prow of a chest that wasn't the result of artificial sweeteners courtesy of a Beverly Hills nip and tucker.

"Why you all the time got to be flexin' on me, Biddy? Don't we go back far enough that you know you need to stall this bullshit out on me?" I smoothed down my Alexander Julian tie and stepped around the clown down on one knee. Back in the day, I wouldn't have let up till the fool was flat on his back. But experience did teach you pacing, not to mention I didn't want to take a chance and throw my shoulder out-of-socket.

She gave me her Toni Braxton smile "I'm just testin' the boy, honey, it's never personal."

I glanced back at the curved bank of glass that overlooked the Pacific below the cliff of sand and rock. Her fly crib was in Newport Beach, and had been bought via all kinds of devious shit she'd pulled. But then, California let anybody be a sports agent. You had to have a license to work over dogs, but not people.

"Now that the prelim is over, you ready to talk business?"

"What you havin', Rack? Sparkling or stiffer?" She put on that diva glare at the hired help as he got himself upright. He stomped to the bar she'd had built-in out of volcanic rock.

It wasn't yet eleven A.M. "Ginger ale is cool."

"You know what I want." She was looking at me but telling him what to bring us. We walked into another part of the house all decked out in West African and Moroccan tones. Very soothing, and different than what it had been years ago when I'd been here for a *Sports Illustrated* party. What I really remember about that night was this model and part-time cheerleader pulling me into one of the bathrooms. She sprinkled crank on my johnson before she gave me a blow job that would have made Larry Flynt blush. Whatever her name was she was just another in a long line of chicks chasing the ghost train of stardom in this town. And I was willing to let her believe I was a conductor that could get her on, at least for a few hours.

"So what's Bronson offering?" Nefertiti-like she held out a dark red nailed hand and my man laid a glass of what I figured was V.S.O.P. on her. My soda he slapped down onto the coffee table, giving me a "next time it'll be different" narrow stare. He then wandered off to probably hit the iron to get all buffed for the next intruder he's—supposed to impress.

"Your price."

She enjoyed some of her brandy. "No haggling?"

"It's cheaper to make this thing go bye-bye, aw'rite? You know you got us by the jock, Biddy. The NXL's season kicks off this Saturday."

"You come with the cash?"

She knew goddamn well I hadn't. Just like I knew she didn't keep the item hidden at her pad. "Let's work out the particulars of the transfer, and I'll be Johnny-on-the-dot for the when and where."

"A million three?"

"To the peso."

"No fast moves?" She glided a hand on my thigh. "Still firm," she teased. "You got a few miles left in you."

"And a few brain cells." I reached over for my ginger ale and unscrewed the cap. "Because I'm curious, why'd you set the boy up?" I swigged some of my drink and kept steady on her.

She lifted padded shoulders. "Means and opportunity, that's all."

She could give vultures lessons. "So we doin' this?"

"Why so harsh, Rack?" She took another drink. "I might get insulted and shit, like you don't like my company."

"Yeah, we wouldn't want that."

"No, we wouldn't." And she downed the rest of her yak. She flirted and I reciprocated, and we made the arrangements. After that, I bounced. The chump who'd gotten froggish with me was skulking around out front when I lighted from the house. He had one of his over-sized kicks planted on the bumper of my vintage Jag X-KE.

"You don't get a tip for cleaning my windshield," I bagged.

Nice and slow he wheeled toward me. "You best not be coming back to Biddy's, hear?" He underscored his words with a jab of his finger into my chest.

I was gonna show him our first tussle in my favor wasn't an accident but then, I'd been that young and full of myself too. I laid my expensive marquee dental work on him and got in my ride. He saved face and I probably saved myself from wrenching my back.

On the 5 Freeway heading north from Orange County back to L.A., I found myself reflecting on Joe Gilliam more than I was focusing on the matter with Biddy. He and Willie Thrower—his real name, damn, who was QB in one game with the 53 Bears—Martin Briscoe and his one year with the Broncos, then in the American Football League, had shouldered all kinds of grief making the way a little easier for my turn in the bull ring in the early 80s. I had my share of hate mail and death threats, so I knew what these cats went through. Plus you had the coaches and owners in the NFL not saying it directly, but intimating that, you know, blacks just didn't have the mental capacity to be quarterbacks. The position involved too much thinking, memorizing plays and instant shifts of strategies.

And Jefferson Street Joe, who had one good half season with.the Steelers, died of a heart attack watching Monday Night Football. He had tuned in to a game where each team had a brother starting as QB—Steve McNair of the Tennessee Titans.and Anthony Wright of the Dallas Cowboys. Ain't that a blip?

Back in Santa Monica, I made my way over to the Watercourt Complex off Olympic and the offices of Artamus Bronson, esquire.

"I hate this." Artie balled up a paper napkin in one hand and tossed it onto the copy of *ESPN* magazine on his desk. On the cover was the flavor of the minute, Kenya McAdoo, the scrambling quarterback who'd taken Oregon State to the Rose Bowl and victory. And the cat who was the reason for our consternation. Artie unlimbered his baller's body from where he'd been eating a sandwich and came from around his desk where I stood.

"Hey, I asked you up front how you wanted to play this—playground or street." I drifted to the window and looked out.

"I know, I know." He adjusted his rimless glasses and blew out a whistle of frustration. "But I just couldn't take a chance on any hard head moves backfiring and this thing getting picked up by every sports and news outlet from here to Sydney. Even the hint of this surfacing so close to Kenya debuting with the Renegades would be dreadfully devastating."

Only Artie could say something like that with a straight.face and mean it. I jingled my keys in my pockets. "Kenya plays one, two years tops in the upstart National Xtreme League, maybe set a passing or QB rushing record, then you get him some real folding money with the NFL." I hadn't meant to, but I did sound.envious. "L.A. might even have a real team back by then."

Artie crooked his head slightly. "We all get to ride, Rack. Some of us longer than others, a learned man once told me." He clapped me on the shoulder.

"That sumabitch must of had a concussion when he said that, figuring he had all the time in the world."

"He still does." The counselor smiled and his mother's dimples appeared in his cheeks. "Now your girl isn't going to.double cross us?"

"She's a scorpion, Artie, but she takes a perverse pleasure in being good to her word. I deliver the dead presidents early tomorrow morning at the spot, and she'll turn over the vial."

"And I want you to destroy it as soon as you get your hands on it. Stomp it out of existence."

"Don't you want me to have it dusted? For piece of mind to.make sure it's the real deal with his prints on it?"

"I'm already in jeopardy of losing my bar card and license if it comes out I've had knowledge of, and actively participated in, the destruction of evidence in a criminal case. The less I know, the better."

I growled, "But it's okay for me to put my dick on the line?"

"Aw, come on, Rack, you know it's not like that."

I gave him a quick twitch of my mouth. But sometimes he wore my one good nerve. He was a Yale-trained lawyer, and acted like one now and then. "Look," I started for the door, "I've got a few things to see about before I make the run."

"I'll hook up with you round eleven tonight, then? At the Denny's on 6th?"

"Yep. and don't get cute?"

"What?" he said way too innocently.

"Don't try to help your client and hold back an extra hundred grand or so. Biddy can look at a piece of coal and tell you what carat diamond it'll be. She'll know it's off once she grabs the bag. Comprende?

"I got it." He winked.

Stepping into his outer office, another visitor was arriving.

"Hey," Tomas Bustamante crowed, "what up, old timer?"

"I got your old timer." I would have grabbed my crotch except the hottie of a receptionist was looking, and I didn't want her to think I was a middle-aged man with no home training.

We gave each other some pound and I kept on as he knocked and entered Artie's office. Bustamante, "El Robusto," had just signed a three year, ten million dollar contract with the Saints as their star linebacker. Artie had negotiated the terms and conditions, and served—like he did with most of his top of the line clients—as his financial manager too. That going back to get his MBA after his J.D. had sure paid off for the youngster.

I jetted, and made a few calls on my cell phone on the way to my next destination. I rolled to a joint on Manchester near the airport in Inglewood called Hill's Hideaway. It was named for a place back in the 30s when Central Avenue, The Stem, was the place for black life in L.A. Then it was a club where you could fall by and catch hot jazz by Satchmo or Duke Ellington when they came through town. Back in my headline days, this version had been the joint when I started as a QB for the Rams, taking over for an injured Vince Ferragamo. You could always find a big booty mama stuffed into in a tight mini to do the bump with, or the slow grind to a Delfonics cut.

Nowadays it was a hang out for semi-active players and hustlers, and retired bus drivers and county workers. Sure enough, I spied the cat I was looking for bullshittin' with some of his buddies over a domino game in the back.

"If I had your hand, I'd throw mine in," Cool Daddy Longstroke, aka William Hackett, teased after we'd said our intros.

"Say, can you spare a few ticks?"

"For you, yeah."

We strolled away from the others, including Sweet Willie T. It was legend in the hood Sweet Willie had once taken care of two crooked vice cops taking more than their fair bite out of him. Word was he'd tricked them into a darkened apartment down in Venice by the beach when it was still funky. The joint contained three Doberman pinschers whose vocal chords had been severed, and fed cayenne pepper for three days. No more problems.

"What you hear about Biddy these days?" Me and Cool Daddy sat across from each other in a booth. After beating cancer, his drinking was confined to an occasional lite beer.

"Damn," he chuckled, who'd have thought I'd live long enough to be your Huggie Bear?"

I shook my head. "I ain't fittin' you for a snitch jacket, playah. All I'm askin' is what do the drums say?" I didn't make the mistake of offering money, that would have gotten the Miller tossed in my face. "Help a brother stay up."

"This have something to do with your step-son?"

"It does," I admitted, realizing not for the first time that seeking information always involved showing part of your hand too. "What have you heard?"

He wiggled his mouth after a taste. "Biddy's been hurtin.' You know back in the golden age when she rep'd you and some other then up and comers, her conniving ways were needed. But the sharks and wolves have graduated school, Rack, and can understand a spreadsheet,not just the point spread. And it ain't like she was ever really let into the ol' boys club in the first place."

"True, true," I agreed.

He held up stubby fingers, diamond rings on two of them. "Atlanta office closed," He folded a finger, "New York connection dead," he folded down another digit, "and her last real money maker, Marcus Dupree, jumped to what's her name, the one that used to be with Artie."

"Carmen," I put in. Carmen Williams and Artie had gone to law school together, and did a stint helping poor folks at Legal Aid after that. Eventually they went out on their own to open a private practice office, and kept a home together. But things got nasty, and they broke up bitterly as partners in business and love.

"So she's looking to make one big score and get out," I concluded out loud.

"Wouldn't you?"

"Ain't we all? Thanks, man." I got up and put some money down for the bill. "Come on out to the Coliseum Saturday, let's catch the Renegade's opener." I was being optimistic, but you had to maintain your game, baby.

He squinted at me. "That the pretend league whathisname started, the wrasslin' dude?

"They got a network contract and ten teams including here. The cheerleaders are built like they stepped out of *Penthouse*, and about as dressed."

"But they're playin' now, in the spring," He tapped the table with one of his knobby fingers. "This ain't football season, Rack," he wheedled. "You know that."

"This is L.A., we don't have seasons," I reminded him. "And it is a free ticket."

"Naw," he decided, "I'm'a go see one of my old hos, see if

she'll take her false teeth out and gum my dick for an hour or two till I get hard."

"Right on." I thanked Cool Daddy again and made for the door. Because it was dark in there, I hadn't noticed this particular poster when I'd entered. But as a patron came through the front, a shaft of light sparkled across the walls. For a second I was disoriented until I realized it was me in my Rams uniform. But it wasn't one of those posed, I-just-been-to-the-hospital-to-see-little-Timmy shots.

In this one my uniform was dirty and there were grass stains on the sleeves and pants. I had dropped back and the ball was released in a text book spiral as Zeke Mobley, then the right tackle for the Vikings, was about to clock me. Printed underneath the faded colors in bold type was: Ice under Pressure, Erskine "Rack" Wilkens, Throws a Touchdown. It was personalized by me to Mary Hill, who'd been dead now some ten years. Last I knew, Zeke had gone broke from several bad marriages and goofy investments. There had been a collection I'd given money to so he could get yet another orthoscopic knee operation. I got out of there on the double.

Walking across the blacktop of the parking lot of West L.A. College in Culver City, I felt revived at the sights and sounds of the Renegades going through their afternoon practice on the football field. And it didn't make me blink seeing Carmen Williams standing around talking on her cell phone. There were a few other agents, agent-lawyers, agent and some other title on the other side of the hyphen also out and about.

I went past her as she clicked off. She smelled good, like strawberries and lemons, and her long braided hair shimmered. If she recognized me, she did a good act of not letting on. I spotted McAdoo going through his drills and went over to Drew Grodin, the head coach.

"Big time, what it be like?"

"Same old, same old." We shook hands. Grodin had been a rushing back for the old Cleveland Browns and the Baltimore Colts.

"You come to try out?"

"As long as I can take the oxygen tank with me into the huddle."

He snickered and I watched a series of plays. Grodin would blow his whistle and go out there to instruct the youngsters in what they were doing wrong, and emphasize what they did right. After ten minutes, the team took a break and I pulled McAdoo aside.

"It's handled, huh?" He took off his helmet.

"The kid had a broad chest, a 'v' for a waist and an earring that was a diamond studded dollar symbol. Corn rows descended from the bottom of his wave cap. He was twenty-one, and had been on the covers of several magazines, and in a photo layout in *Vanity Fair* with several pouting actresses. The million three Artie was advancing him to pay out on the sly was less than the NFL signing bonus the counselor was assured of getting when McAdoo's two-year NXL contract was up.

"Just about." Williams headed for the lot. "She say anything to you?"

"You ain't my mama," he huffed.

"But I am the motherfuckah who's got to hold your hand, Kenya. Now stop acting like the spoiled baby you are, and answer my goddamn questions."

"Hey, you can't—"

"I can do what ever the fuck I please. You want to call Artie and tell him to fire me, go ahead. It don't make me none. I'm not the idiot that handled the crack vial trying to get some honey to sit butt naked on my lap."

"Yo, Rack, chill, dawg," he said excitedly. He tugged on my arm to get us to stand further apart from the others. "Look, " he began, "it's just that I got a lot on my mind, know what I'm sayin'? I can't let this shit fuck with my program, thas' all. You know how it be."

It was if I were confronting the self-centered me of more than two decades ago. That because of the one thing I could do half-way right, and people would pay to see me do it, the world owed me all the toys and goodies. "So, did she say anything to you?"

"Carmen?" He lifted one side of his torso. "Jus' good luck and to let me know she was around, that's all. She chit-chatted with a few dudes, made em know she was the one, ya feel what I'm sayin'?"

I held back making a remark about him making sure he

stayed put with Artie. He couldn't be that dense. "I know I've asked you this twice already, but you're sure you can't remember anything else about this chick that handed you the crack?"

Grodin looked over at McAdoo and pointed at the field. He put on his helmet. "You don't know how bad I want to find that triflin' bitch. But nobody at the party says they invited her, and that name I overheard that night, you didn't turn up anything?"

"Candy ain't exactly an original alias, Kenya. And you being drunk and lousy with the description except you liked the way her butt felt when you rubbed on it is not all that helpful.

"Huh." He seemed genuinely perplexed and jogged back onto the field.

I hung around watching him and the team go through their paces. They players were mostly guys who'd been cut in the NFL, had come down from the Canadian Football or NFL Europe League, or out of small colleges that hardly got scouted. Some were walk-ons. And a precious few were like McAdoo, who though a talent, needed some toughening up.

The NXL was hyped as the hip-hop, rock n' roll alternative to your old man's NFL. The NXL's rules, to live up to its extreme sensibilities, didn't allow fair catches on kick-offs, a defender could put his hands on the receiver, and a no huddle offense was mandatory during the two minute warning. Rappers, rockers and wrestlers were investors in the league, and you couldn't turn on MTV, BET or VH1 without seeing one of them yapping about it. If he stayed healthy, McAdoo would get toughened in the pit, and his name would rise as the league's stock did. Ultimately, this would better position him for bargaining with the NFL. Say what you would, they were still the big dogs in terms of prestige, money and endorsement possibilities.

I was about to say goodbye to Grodin when my past slapped me upside my head again.

"Excuse me," this Renegade said, intentionally bumping into me.

"What? Ain't enough room here in the open for you to go around me?"

"Pussy." The dude grinned and went out on the field.

It hit me cold who it was. "He's the back up quarterback?"

Grodin was making a notation on his clipboard. "I was only half joking about you suiting up, Rack."

Jamie Hayes was the tow haired, blue-eyed Rhodes Scholar who'd taken my job when we were both on the Houston Oilers. I was on my last legs and he was the young gun. I resented him and made it known. He ignored the advice I tried to give him, what little I extended myself. But when I got cut, he'd stuck out his hand and it was my turn to ignore him. We hadn't seen or talked to each other since.

"He came to the open call we had," Grodin said. "It was just a P.R. thing that Dunn foisted on us to show that the NXL could be anybody's dream." He kept writing and Hayes took a snap. "But damned if he didn't have a few moves left in him." Hayes' pass wouldn't give Kerry Collins pause, but it reached its target.

"Fuck," was all I could articulate. I headed out and saw Carmen Williams was still around. She was standing near a burgundy Mercedes Sport rag top talking with Norris Dunn. He was the brain who gave us the 24/7 freaknik of high octane pro wrestling, and now was looking to do the same with the NXL. Nearing my car my neck tingled and peripherally I caught the both of them scoping me out. What was up with that?

The rest of the afternoon involved me doing some more checking into Biddy's financial situation, and trying to hunt down the babe who'd tripped up Kenya at the party last weekend. As Cool Daddy had hipped me, it seemed my girl Biddy was hanging on by her weave. The fine receptionist in Artie's office ran Biddy's address and social security number—it's a long story but back in the day when she was my sports agent I'd sneaked and found it out cause I'd suspected her of shorting me on my money—for me through a research service they used. Turned out Biddy had missed a couple of mortgage payments on that Xanadu of a house of hers. And had to stop renovations on a building she owned in town.

I also took a trip to the library. The A. C. Bilbrew branch was on El Segundo in Compton. Now what most people know about this small city next door to L.A. is it's the home of gangsta rap. And to listen to some of their songs, averages a murder every ten minutes. But like any place once you get past the drama, it's a study in contrasts. And this branch was the one in the system that housed extensive records chronicling the history and current events of the African American community.

Going through some *L.A. Sentinels* and *Compton Bulletins,* black weekly newspapers, on microfiche, I found a few items on Biddy and her dwindling client roster. I also looked through a stack of several national black magazines such as *Ebony* and *Emerge.* Yawning, the sun going down, I also went through a few *Savoys,* This was a trendy, bourgzie magazine aimed at black folk who want to be upscale or upmarket or what ever the hell we're supposed to be aspiring to these days.

I came upon a profile on Carmen Williams and read through eagerly. But all the puff piece revealed was that she was smart, beautiful and ambitious. A ten-year-old could have told me that. I was about to put the mag aside when I gloomed on this picture of Carmen in the mag being handed some papers by her secretary. It was one of those shots to show how busy and efficient she was. Yet her hair was just right and her elbows weren't ashy. Carmen was standing next to the other woman's desk, and each beamed vitality like they'd just been to a feel good seminar by Lyanla Vanzant. The name plate was visible on the chick's desk. It read: KHANDI LYNN.

Later, I met with a nervous Artie and copped the dough.

At our cars he said, "You be careful."

"Of course."

"I mean it."

"Thanks, weed hopper."

He hugged me. Artie hadn't done that since, hell I couldn't remember when. He'd had always been what you'd call reserved.

"You've always been there for me, Rack."

"It's what I do. But you're the only family I got, man. We're solid."

At 4A.M., I kept the appointment to turn over the money for the crack vial with McAdoo's fingerprints adorning it. I arrived at Biddy's building on Hyperion on the edges of Los Feliz, near Barnsdall Park where Sunset and Hollywood Boulevards come together. It was a brick three story structure that way back when must have had shops on the ground floor and apartments overhead. Judging from the expired notice to sell alcohol beverages pasted in one large window, it had been undergoing a division for a restaurant, and probably space for an over-priced coffee shop and gym offering custom colonics.

Up high on one side of the building, the layers of previous paint-overs had been sand blasted away. Revealed in the spill light from a street lamp was the faded words announcing a business that had once been an occupant: HOLLYWOOD BRAKE AND SPRING.

I'd been told to enter through a side door along a narrow passageway filled with wood and tall weeds between this building and the next. Crouching at that door I listened but couldn't hear anything. I crept around back searching for another way to get inside. Biddy's Lincoln towncar was there parked on a patch of gravel. There was a corrugated roll-up garage door at half-mast. I was peeping inside the darkened interior when Homebrew caught me slipping.

"What up, G?" A silver-plated gat shined in his hand. I turned around and he was happy to jam the barrel into my cheek. "Where's them big faces, bitch?"

"In my car. But I want to talk to Biddy first."

He wet his bottom lip and gave me a little chunk with the gun. "You ain't in no position to demand shit."

"I didn't bring the money, asshole. I've got to talk to Biddy."

This got him doing the bug-eye, then he back-handed me across the temple with the piece. I dropped, woozy like getting tackled from behind. I sucked it up and got off the ground, lurching forward slack jawed like a zombie as homeskillet backed out in the Lincoln. He was in the alley and driving away as I pitifully pounded on the trunk. He'd been alone in the car.

I went inside and found a room intended to be a back office. You could get to it quicker by the side door. Most of the sheet rock was up, and wiring snaked down from the exposed ceiling. Light was by way of a hanging drop cord that I'd turned on. Biddy sat in one of those old-fashioned wooden chairs, a bottle of her favorite near her on an upturned plastic milk crate. A styrofoam cup of the brandy was in her hand and resting on her thigh. Her tongue hung out, and her blonde hair was in her face. She was dead and gone.

Homedivision had been wearing gloves. Given there were

no holes in Biddy, I bet he'd strangled her She had probably been sitting here in all her royalness, sipping and waiting for me to make the delivery. He was behind her, maybe massaging her shoulders cause she demanded attention. It wouldn't have taken long; he had the muscles and meanness for the job.

The idea was I'd have gone through the door and it'd be dark, he'd bap me on the head with the gun, then book with the shekels. I'd be left stumbling and mumbling and the cops would be happy to track down some looser ex-football player who had finally gone OJ. But this wasn't about framing me. Though if he'd shot me, even the LAPD couldn't have ignored homebrew as a suspect.

The gash on my head hurt, and I realized I'd dripped some of my blood on the ground. Nonetheless, I wiped away my prints with my shirt tail anywhere I could remember touching, and got in gear. I only had two ideas where homefries was heading. I sure hoped I guessed right the first time.

Finally I wasn't a half-step behind, I was in the rhythm of the game, baby. The Lincoln came out of the underground parking structure, homeboy at the wheel. Too bad I couldn't have made like a real PI and followed him around in my car, but frankly, I had no idea how to tail anybody. I had stationed myself on the wall beside the electronically controlled gate, after I'd spied Biddy's hoopty parked in there through its bars.

Giving it the best Tiger Woods pivot of my hips, I swung the twenty pound pry bar up and at the car's windshield. The glass didn't explode but spider-webbed bad enough so he couldn't see straight. The Lincoln skidded across the driveway at a sharp angle and plowed into a thick palm tree. How Californian.

He didn't bother getting out of the car and blazed some rounds at me through the back windshield. I dove, using the vehicle for cover as his shots ripped through the car's body. One came out the rear quarter panel, right near my head and ricocheted off the sidewalk. They ain't building cars like they used to.

But homerun was desperate to get away and had to jet. He figured he'd be slick and came out the passenger side, gun ready. But like I said, I was on my J, I could see the whole field and anticipated my opponent's moves. I clipped his square head with the spoon end of the pry bar, and his dazed ass fell onto the ground. Quickly I was on him, my foot on the forearm of his gun hand.

"Zup, brah," I cracked and bent down to punch him twice in the face, sending him beddy-bye. My hand was swollen for three days after that but at that moment, I was too pumped to notice.

I looked around the Lincoln's back floorboards but was surprised not to see Khandi hiding there. This was her apartment complex, I'd had Artie's girl find her address through the research service they used. I'd reckoned on orders from Carmen he'd bop to his girl's pad, scoop her up, and bounce out of town. Her being a slick lawyer, and therefore an expert at twisting the facts, she'd put the blame all on him and her, once they were on the run.

Standing there as dawn began to flood the sky, and who knew how many cops swooping to the scene, I re-did my calculations. There was a thump, then another one. Popping the trunk with the key, Khandi was lying there in her Victoria's Secrets, tied up with lamp cords. I didn't think she and homeseizure were into S & M. One of the rounds had punctured her leg, and I tied a tourniquet around the wound after lifting her out.

Later, it was determined that Khandi and Le'Ron, that was homey's first name, had planned to double-cross Biddy all along. Biddy was up against it, and wanted money quick to split herself. She knew that Khandi and Le'Ron went around together and had him approach her with her scandalous blackmail scheme. Biddy knew there'd be all kinds of talent at the NXL party, and figured to hook one fish or another. Means and opportunity she'd said. It wouldn't take long for a fine number like Khandi to snag one of those cocks strutting around assuming a twist would have to be a fool not to want him. Hell, I used to believe that shit myself.

In exchange for me not implicating her, Khandi gave up the vial. They'd been smart. She'd applied super glue to her fingertips to obscure her prints. It was all McAdoo's after he'd handled it and she'd slipped it into a plastic baggie in her purse.

Let homebuy go on as much as he wanted to at his trial about the item, he wouldn't have any physical evidence. And what jury would believe him over her anyway? He'd come to snatch her to silence her and make a clean getaway. But now she could spin it as she didn't know what the hell was on his mind when he barged into her bedroom, using his key to her place to gain access. It was Le'Ron's dope after all, and everyone knew crack heads were unpredictable.

In court she'd probably wear a conservative, mid-length skirt and add the tears and horror of lying in that trunk at the right moments. Okay, I was a sexist, but don t tell me the jury consultant Carmen had-secured for her wouldn't be telling her the same thing.

"I still think your ex was involved," I said. Kenya couldn't find an open man and ran for a first down against the Destroyers. "I'm not a hundred percent sure all this wasn't really about sinking you, then she'd scoop up you're A list clients."

"You don t trust women." He had some of his beer and enjoyed the sun shining on us. We had sweet seats on the Renegades' bench on the sidelines.

I studied his profile for a few beats and said, "You're getting back with her, with Carmen."

"We're just going to take it one day at a time."

"Shit."

"Mom called me."

"How's she doing?"

"Same. She'd like to hear from you."

I didn't have an immediate reply. "I'll try, huh?"

"I know you will, pop."

And we smiled while the game continued.

GONE TO THE DAWGS

BY PETER ROBINSON

It was the penultimate week of the NFL football pool and Charlie Firth was ahead by ten points. Nothing could stop the smug bastard from winning again now. Nothing short of murder.

Such was the uncharitable thought that crossed the mind of Calvin Bly as he sat with the usual crowd in the local bar watching the Monday night game, St Louis at Tampa Bay. Outside, in the east end of Toronto, the wind was howling, piling up snow in the side streets and swirling it in surreal patterns across the main roads, but inside it was warm, and the occasional single malt between pints of Guinness helped make it even warmer.

There were six of them at the table, the usual crowd, all in the pool. Calvin was second, having come up with a complicated system of mathematical checks and balances that had earned him solid eights and nines all season, plus the occasional eleven, and behind him by six points was Marge, the only girl in the group. Well, woman really, he supposed, seeing as she was in her fifties. The other three Chris, Jeff and Brad, weren't even in the running.

"How's your mother Calvin?" Charlie's loud voice boomed across the table. Calvin looked away from his conversation with Marge and saw the sneer on Charlie's face, the baiting grin, the arrogant, disdaining eyes.

"She's fine, thank you," he said.

Charlie looked at his watch "Only it's getting late. I'm surprised she lets you stay out this long."

He laughed, and some of the others joined in, but more because it was the thing to do than because they had any heart for it. Truth be told, nobody really found Charlie's sense of humor funny. Vicious, yes. Cutting and hurtful, yes. But funny, no way.

Perhaps it wasn't worth murdering someone for two thousand dollars, Calvin thought, but it might be worth it just to clear the world of the loud-mouthed fucker. People would probably thank him for it. Three years in a row Charlie Firth had won that NFL pool, and he hadn't let a soul forget it. Twice Calvin had come in second, and Charlie wasn't about to let him forget that, either. The teasing would go on well into the baseball season.

Yes, if he got rid of Charlie, he would be doing the world a favor.

The Buccs threw a touchdown pass to take the lead in the dying seconds of the game, and Calvin shook himself free of his dark thoughts. Of course he wouldn't murder Charlie. He'd never harmed a soul in his life, didn't have the guts for it. It was nothing but a pleasant, harmless fantasy

Got that one, thought Calvin when the game was over, and Charlie had picked the Rams. He was still nine points ahead of the field, though, pretty much impossible to catch, and Marge was still six behind as they went into the final week. It had been a weekend of upsets—the Seahawks beat the Raiders, the Chiefs beat the Broncos and the Lions beat the Jets—but Calvin had come away with nine points.

"Say hi to your mom from me," Charlie called out as Calvin bundled up and headed out to clear the snow off his car. He didn't bother answering.

Calvin hadn't been home five minutes, was watching the news quietly on TV, when the banging started. Mother had a walking stick which she didn't use to walk with, as she rarely bothered to walk, but to bang on the floor of her bedroom to summon her son, calling out his name. With a sigh, Calvin hauled himself out of the La-Z-Boy and climbed up the stairs.

He hated Mother's sick room, the unpleasant smells—she never opened the window and didn't bathe very often—the way she lay there looking frail, hands like talons clutching the sheet tight around her neck as if he were going to rape her or something, when the very idea of her nakedness disgusted him.

"Yes, Mother."

"You were out late."

"It was a long game."

"Anything could have happened to me. I could have had a

seizure. What would I have done, then?"

"Mother, you re not going to have a seizure. The doctor told you yesterday your health's just fine."

"Doctor, schmoctor What does that quack know?" Her tone became wheedling, flirtatious. "Calvin, baby, I can't sleep. I'm having one of my bad nights. Make mommy some hot milk and bring my pills, Little Calvin. Pullleeeease."

Calvin went back downstairs and poured some milk into a saucepan, enough for two, as he decided he might as well treat himself to some hot chocolate if he was heating up milk anyway. As he listened to the hiss of the gas flame and watched the milk's surface change as it heated, he thought again how pleasant it would be if he had the guts to do something about Charlie Firth.

The man was insufferable. For a start, he was well-off and always made a point of letting you know how much his possessions cost, from the Porsche to his leather Italian loafers. Women, of course, just wouldn't leave him alone. He had a big house on Kingswood, prime Beach property—all to himself, as he had never married, probably because no woman in her right mind could stand his company for more than a night—and as well as winning the NFL pool, he had been his company's real estate agent of the year more than once. A success. And Calvin, what had he got? Nothing. Unemployment benefits. A savings account that was thinning out as quickly as his hair, a pot belly that seemed to be getting bigger, a hypochondriac mother who would probably live to torment him forever, a small, gloomy, draughty row house on the wrong side of Victoria Park. Nothing. Sweet fuck all.

Bubbles started to surface on the milk. Time to turn down his heat. Mother hated it when he burnt the milk. Before he had even got the mugs out of the cupboard he heard the banging on the ceiling again. As if the silly old cow thought banging with that stick of hers would make milk boil any faster. He burned himself as he slopped the hot milk into the cup, forgot about his hot chocolate and hurried upstairs.

In the light of the next day, killing Charlie didn't seem like such a good idea. Given Calvin's luck, he was bound to get caught, for a start. And, technically, Charlie would still be the winner. If you didn't phone your picks in on time, the Administrator assigned you the underdogs, and even with the DAWGS, as they were called, Charlie would still beat the field. He would be too dead to collect his winnings, of course, and Calvin supposed they would go to whoever came second.

The way the pool worked was every Wednesday before five o'clock you phoned in your picks, based on that day's point spread, to the Administrator, who ran the whole thing from his desk at one of the major newspapers downtown. You always got his answering machine with its curt message: "I'm away from my desk right now. Please leave your message after the beep." There were over a hundred people in the pool, at a hundred bucks each for the season, and in addition to the grand prize of $2000, there were also smaller weekly prizes. Calvin had actually covered this year's entry fee on one weekly win. Usually by Friday evening, a photocopy of everyone's picks, along with the weekly and accumulated scores, was faxed to Jeff, who made copies and distributed them in the bar.

Calvin liked to see which teams everyone else had chosen—especially Charlie—but this week he would miss it. On Thursday, he had to accompany Mother down to Fort Myers, where they would spend Christmas with their only living relatives, his Aunt Vicky and Uncle Frank, who had retired there seven years ago and were generous enough to help out with the airfare.

The Florida trip used to be the highlight of Calvin's year. Not because he liked the place. Three or four days was about all he could stand. It was too hot and too full of old people, or people who didn't speak English, as if Toronto wasn't bad enough that way. No, what the Florida used to mean to him was freedom, glorious freedom! Mother used to stay down there for at least six weeks, and as soon as she was "settled" Calvin was allowed to go home alone. God only knew how Vicky and Frank put up with the old bat, Calvin wondered, but they did. Now she was too worried about getting sick and not being able to afford US medical bills, so they were both returning on the following Wednesday.

That Tuesday morning at breakfast, Calvin checked the sports section to see if the spreads had changed since Monday.

He liked to do that, factor it into his calculations. Sometimes you could guess a lot just by the ways the spreads were changing. After that, his day followed its usual dull routine. He cleared the driveway of snow, did household chores, did some food shopping and took care of Mother. But Tuesday evening, Calvin had a date.

This was one thing nobody knew about him—at least, so he believed. Calvin had a secret girlfriend. Heidi. Probably no one would believe it if he told them that a pudgy, balding, boring fifty-one-year-old man like him could have an attractive blonde forty-year-old woman as a girlfriend. Sometimes he could hardly believe it himself. They had met six months ago in HMV downtown, both looking at the selection of show tunes. A common interest in film musicals led them to venture to a local coffee shop together, where they found they enjoyed one another's company immensely. A loner by nature—apart from the easy and informal gregariousness of the bar—Calvin found it hard to talk to her at first, but Heidi had a way of drawing him out of his shell. There was, of course, a big problem.

Heidi was married.

Slowly, piece by piece, it emerged over furtive meetings in the city center, first just for coffees, then regular lunches at Red Lobster, that Heidi was not exactly happy with her marriage. Her children had both left home, one to Winnipeg, poor sod, and the other to Southern California, so it was only a matter of time, she told Calvin, before the separation occurred. Until then, they had to be very careful and keep their relationship a secret. Her husband worked shifts for a security company, and this week he was working evenings. Calvin would go over to the west end, where Heidi lived, not far from High Park, and they would talk and make love until midnight, at which time he would dress and sneak out of the back door to where he had parked his car several blocks away.

That Tuesday, Heidi did not seem to be in her usual good spirits.

"What's wrong?" Calvin asked, after he had suspected her of counting cracks in the ceiling while they made love.

Nothing." she said.

"Come on. I can tell there's something bothering you."

"I told you, it's nothing. Leave it."

"Maybe I can help."

Heidi turned, propped herself on her elbow and looked at him. "I don't think I can go on," she said after a pause.

Calvin felt his chest tighten, his heart race. "What do you mean?"

"This. You and me. I don't think I can go on."

"But why?"

"It's not that I don't like you, Calvin." She stroked his cheek. "It's just...oh, everything, the lies, the guilt. Joe and I had a really long talk the other night."

"For God's sake, Heidi, you didn't tell him...?"

"No. No, of course not. What sort of a fool do you think I am? No, we just...well, he realized he'd been neglecting me and I realized I missed him more than I thought. We decided...you know... to try to make a go of things."

"Make a go of things?"

"Yes." She smiled. "We're going to start with a trip to Mexico. A sort of second honeymoon. We're going for new year's."

"B-but..."

"Oh, Calvin. Don't be upset. Please don't be upset. You had fun while it lasted, didn't you?"

"Yes, but...but I thought..."

"You thought what?"

"I mean, just now, even when you knew this, you...we..." He shook his head.

"Was that so unfair of me, Calvin? Just to have you one last time? Was that too selfish of me?"

"It s not that."

"Then what?"

"It just seems so sudden, so abrupt, that's all." Calvin sat on the edge of the bed and reached for his clothes.

"But you knew it had to end one day."

"I sort of hoped that when you and Joe split up, we might... you know..."

"Oh, Calvin, that's sweet. That's *too* sweet."

"I gather you didn't?"

Heidi lay back on the pillow. "I never thought, really, not

beyond the next time. I've hurt you, haven't I?"

"It's all right. I'll mend."

"I m sorry, Calvin."

"Don't worry about it. I'll go now."

"You'll be careful? Make sure no one sees you?"

"I'll be careful."

Calvin bent over to give her a goodnight kiss, as he always did. She turned her head and offered him her cheek. He kissed it lightly and found it surprisingly cool, then he went downstairs and sneaked out of the back door. He thought of making a lot of noise, but Calvin wasn't the type to draw too much attention to himself.

He was okay to drive, he told himself as he headed out of the nearest bar to which he had gone as soon as he'd left Heidi's —he'd only had two pints and a shot of whisky, and he felt in control. Sad, hurt, but in control.

The city crews had been through the neighborhood and the roads were pretty clear. He headed down Roncesvalles towards Lakeshore and the Gardiner, noting how quiet the roads were. Hardly surprising as it was going on half past one on a cold, miserable Tuesday evening.

It was all over with Heidi. He couldn't believe it, couldn't believe the callous way she had treated him. How could she? He had even fantasized a real life for them: restaurants, theatres, musicals, weekends together. Now this.

Almost home. He stopped at a red light. Nobody around. Glow from TV sets in a couple of windows. Christmas trees. Lights.

As he neared the next set of traffic lights, he saw someone come out of a bar alone and start to cross just as the light was changing. It was Charlie. There was no mistaking that expensive leather jacket, the hand-tooled cowboy boots. He was clearly a bit pissed, not falling down drunk, but definitely unsteady. And unobservant. Calvin was driving slowly enough to stop, but something, he couldn't say what, some demon, some inner compulsion, seemed to take control of him. A quick glance to make sure there were no other cars visible ahead or behind, nobody on the street in seeing distance, and almost unbidden his foot pressed down on the gas pedal as if it were made of lead.

Charlie knew something was wrong, saw it coming at the last moment, but it was too late to do anything about it. Calvin saw the horrified expression on his face, even fancied he saw recognition there, too, then the car hit him with a satisfying, meaty smack and threw him away from the car. Calvin felt the shuddering bump and crunch as he ran over the body. No stopping now. He sped off and turned the first corner, heading into the maze of residential streets that would eventually take him home, heart in his mouth, blood pulsing hard through his veins, but alive, alive at last.

Calvin didn't sleep at all that night and spent the next day in terror of the knock upon his door. The newspaper reported Charlie's death and asked anyone who might have seen anything to contact them. Calvin was almost certain that no-one had seen him, but there was still room for doubt, and that doubt bred fear. If the police came to check out his car, they would see the damage Charlie's body had caused to radiator and the headlight. They could probably even match paint chips from the body to his car; he had seen them do it on TV.

So terrified was he that he almost forgot to phone in his picks. Almost. At four thirty he picked up the phone with trembling hands and dialed the Administrator's number. Just as the answering machine cut in, Mother's stick banged on the floor above. He automatically held the phone at arm's length and put his hand over the mouthpiece, even though there wasn't a real person on the other end, and shouted up that he was busy and would be with her in a few moments. When he got back to the phone, he was just in time to hear the familiar beep. He began: "Giants, Broncos, Bills, Jets, Rams, Bears…"

The journey to Fort Myers on Thursday morning was a nightmare tor Calvin. Not because of the weather, though the flight was delayed more than an hour and the wings had to be de-iced. Not even because of Mother, despite the fact that she never stopped complaining for one moment until the plane took off,

when she immediately fell asleep. No, It was because he expected to be arrested at every stage of the journey At check-in, he
noticed two airline officials huddled to one side talking, and occasionally they seemed to be looking in his direction. Sweat beaded
on his forehead. But nothing, happened. Next, at U.S.
Immigration, just when he expected the firm hand on his shoulder, the hushed "Please step this way, Mr. Bly," the immigration
officer wished him and Mother happy holidays after barely a
glance at their passports.

Could getting away with murder really be that easy? Calvin
wondered when he disembarked at Fort Myers and found no
policemen waiting for him, only Frank and Vicky in the crowd
waving, ready to drive him and Mother back to the condo.
Nothing had happened. Nobody had come for him. He must have
got away with it.

Though the locals thought the weather cold and farmers
were worried about the citrus crop, Calvin found it comfortable
enough to sit out on the deck. As he poured himself a Jack Daniels
and looked out over the long strip of beach to the blue-green sea,
Charlie's murder began to seem distant and unreal. After a few
hours, and three or four bourbons, he could almost believe it
hadn't happened, that it had merely been a bad dream, and the
following morning, he imagined that when he got back to Toronto
and walked into the bar, they would all be waiting there, as usual,
including Charlie, flashing his winnings.

In the late afternoon Florida sun, how easy it was to believe
that snowy Tuesday night in Toronto had never happened.

By Christmas Eve, Calvin was already two games up, having
picked the Bills to beat a three-point spread against the Seahawks
and the Broncos to win plus seven over the 49ers on Saturday.
He'd lost the Giants-Jaguars game, but even with his system he
could never expect to win them all.

He was sipping a Jack Danlels on the rocks and watching
Miami against New England, hoping the Pats would beat the
spread, when during the halftime break came a brief interview
with a convicted killer called Leroy Cody, scheduled to be elec-
trocuted early in the new year. Instead of pushing the mute but-

ton, Calvin turned the sound up a notch or two and leaned forward in his chair. He'd read about Cody in *USA Today* and found his curiosity piqued by the man's nonchalant, laconic manner and his total lack of remorse.

The interview was a special from death row, Leroy in his cell in drab prison clothes, hair cropped close to his skull, no emotion in his eyes, his face all sharp angles.

"You shot a liquor store clerk for fifteen dollars, is that right?" the interviewer asked.

"I didn't know he'd only got a lousy fifteen dollars when I shot him, now, did I?" Leroy answered in his slow, surprisingly high-pitched drawl.

"But you shot him, and fifteen dollars is all you got?"

"Yessir. Sure was a disappointment, let me tell you."

"And then you shot a pregnant woman and dragged her out of her car to make your escape."

"I didn't know she was pregnant."

"But you shot the woman and stole her car?"

Leroy spat on the floor of his cell. "Hell, I had to make a last getaway. I don't have no car of my own. I had to take a goddamn cab to the store, but I was damned if I was gonna hang around and try to flag one after I done robbed the place."

"And you feel no remorse for any of this?"

"Remorse?"

"Regrets."

"Regrets? Nope. No regrets. I'm a killer. That's what I am."

"You regret nothing at all?"

Leroy smiled; it looked like an eclipse of the sun moving slowly across his features. "Only getting caught," he said.

Calvin's attention wandered as the commentator started to spear, and then they were back at the half-time show, catching up on scores. But even as he checked the numbers, part of Calvin's mind stayed with Leroy Cody. *"I'm a killer. That's what I am."* He liked that. It was honest, direct, had a ring to it.

Calvin tried it out loud: *"I'm a killer. That's what I am."* It sounded good. He let the fantasy wander, trying on his new self and finding it a perfect fit. "I'm a killer. That's what I am. Me and Leroy. Yeah, man." And if he was a killer, he could kill again. Why stop at Charlie? He could kill Heidi's husband. Could even kill that bitch Heidi herself, maybe make her beg a little first. He could kill...

There was no upstairs in the condo, but he heard the click-click of Mother's walking-stick on the tile floor before he heard her voice. "Leroy," she said (he was sure she called him Leroy), "are you going to just sit here and watch this garbage all Christmas? Why don't you come and play cribbage with the old folks for a while." Calvin sighed, picked up the remote, turned off the game and muttered, "Coming, Mother."

There were no cops waiting at the airport when Calvin and Mother got back to Toronto on Wednesday. It was over a week since Charlie's death, and still nothing to fear.

After settling Mother at home, against her protests, Calvin decided to drop in at the bar. As he had suspected, the usual crowd was there. Minus Charlie.

"Calvin," said Marge, patting his arm when he sat down beside her. Welcome home. You've heard the news?"

Calvin nodded sadly. I heard just before we left for Florida. It's tragic, isn't it?"

"I still can't believe it," said Marge. "He always seemed so..."

"Alive?" Calvin suggested.

"Yes. Alive. That's it. Alive."

"Is there any progress?" he asked the table in general.

"No," Jeff answered. "You know the cops. They've put it down as a hit and run, asked for the public's cooperation, and that's the last you'll hear of it."

"Unless someone comes forward," Calvin said.

"Yes," Jeff agreed. "Unless someone comes forward. By the way," he went on, "here's the final scores on the pool." He handed Calvin the sheets of paper.

Kelly, the waitress with the walk out of a forties *noir* movie, finally came over with his drink. Calvin desperately wanted to see the final scores, but he didn't want to appear too anxious. After all, Charlie's dead. So he sipped some beer, talked a little about his Christmas, and then, casually, glanced down at the sheets.

The first thing that caught his eye was his weekend's score:

five. That had to be wrong. Calvin had checked the same scores after the cribbage game and found he had nine. He had also won the evening game, the Raiders over the Panthers, *and* the Monday evening game, when the Titans had creamed the Cowboys. So how could he end up with *five*? He had *eleven*.

He turned to the column of picks and noticed scrawled across the line where his should be, the word "DAWGS." Charlie, of course, had got the same. It meant they hadn't got their picks in on time.

But Calvin *had* got his picks in, he remembered phoning them. It was late in the afternoon, four-thirty to be precise, but definitely *before* the five o'clock deadline. So what was going on?

"Calvin?"

The voice came as if from a long way. "Huh? Sorry. What?"

"Just that you've gone pale. Are you okay?" It was Marge, and her hand was on his arm.

"I'm fine," he said. "Must be...you know...Charlie...delayed shock."

Marge nodded. "I don't suppose it seemed real until you got back here, did it?" she said.

"Something like that. What's happening with the pool?"

Marge frowned. "Well," she said, "with Charlie gone and you forgetting to phone in...er...I won."

"You?"

Marge laughed nervously. "Well, don't look so surprised Calvin. I've been there with the best of you all season."

"I know. It s not that."

"What, then?"

"Never mind. Congratulations, Marge." Calvin knew he couldn't complain. Whatever had gone wrong here, however he had gone from eleven to five, there was nothing he could do about it, and getting upset about the result would only look suspicious.

"Thanks," said Marge. "I know it must be a disappointment, you being so close and all." She managed a weak smile. "I only beat you by one, if that means anything at all. It was my best week of the whole season. Twelve."

Calvin laughed. He couldn't help himself. "So what are you

going to do with your winnings?"

Marge looked at the others, then said. "I decided, well, we all decided, really, that I'd use the money for a wake, you know, to pay for a wake here. For Charlie. He would have liked that."

"Yes," said Calvin, still quaking with laughter inside while he tried to keep a straight face. "Yes, I think he would."

When Calvin got home he poured himself a large whisky and tried to figure out what had gone wrong. *Five*. The *DAWGS*. It was an insult, a slap in the face.

He cast his mind back to that Wednesday afternoon and remembered first that his hand had been shaking as he dialed. He had, after all, just killed Charlie the previous evening. Could he have misdialed? The first three numbers were all the same, and connected him to the newspaper the Administrator worked for. The last four were 4697. It would have been easy, say, to transpose the six and the nine, or even to dial seven first rather than four, given that he was upset at the time. He tried both and got the same message: "I'm away from my desk right now. Please leave a message after the beep." The only difference was that 7694 was a woman's voice and 4967 was a man's. So that was what had happened. In his disturbed state of mind, Calvin had dialed the wrong number. Why had it happened like that? Why hadn't he listened to the message, noticed the difference in voice and realized what he had done'?

Then he remembered. Just as he had got through, Mother had knocked on the bedroom floor for him. He had held the phone at arm's length and covered the mouthpiece, as you do, and yelled up that he was coming in a minute. He *hadn't heard* the Administrator's message, only vaguely recognized it was a man's voice on the answering machine, heard the usual beep and left his picks with someone else at the paper.

Someone who hadn't a clue what he was talking about.

Calvin held his head in his hands. *The wrong number.* All for nothing. He drank some more whisky. Well, maybe not *all* for nothing, he thought after a while. Hadn't he already decided that, nice as it would have been, he hadn't killed Charlie only for the money? Wasn't $2000 a paltry sum to murder for? More than $15, but still...he knew he had had more reason than the money. Winning the pool was a part of it, of course, but that wasn't to be. So what was left? What could he salvage from this disaster?

"I'm a killer. That's what I am."

The voice seemed to come into his head from nowhere, and slowly as the whisky warmed his insides, understanding dawned on Calvin.

"I'm a killer. That's what I am."

The sound of a heavy stick hammering on the ceiling above broke into his thoughts. He could hear her muffled yelling, "Leroy! Leroy! I need my hot milk, Leroy!"

Calvin put his glass down, looked up at the ceiling and got to his feet. "Coming, Mother," he said softly.

RUMORS OF GRAVITY

BY JOHN WESTERMANN

Dinner was at eighteen-hundred hours at Chez Nutmeg, a lavish hotel just off Constitution Plaza, one of the steel-and-gold towers recently erected as Hartford prospers without me. My day-tour patrolling the crumbling red bricks and frame-houses of the North End had just ended at sixteen hundred hours. I had plenty of time to do what I had to do and get downtown to see my former college teammates, class of 1993.

Actually cocktails were at six. The dinner honoring retiring offensive coordinator Jimmy Calhoun was set for seven-thirty. Details matter. I know that now. Dreams count, too. Determination.

I'm Police Officer Bobby Wilson, and tonight I'm going to dress up and party with the people I knew at my personal peak, guys named Townsend, Rexford, Arlon, and Whitney, and those are their first names.

I signed off-duty, hung my leather gun belt and rumpled patrolman's uniform on treble-hooks in my locker, and put on a gray Hartford PD sweatsuit, then headed downstairs to the precinct weight room, thinking just a light pump this May after-noon, add a little flush to my face. Stanley Martin was in there, fouling the air like a construction site, three hundred pounds of po-lice-andro-beef who could bench the entire offensive line from my college team. Stanley was shot in the leg once and didn't know it until he changed his pants at the end of the tour. He was work-ing the squat rack, his face contorted, preparing for future battles.

I nodded at him and hopped on the exercise bike, spun the pedals a while, staring at the bars on the narrow basement win-dows, then the black-fringed pictures on the wall of the two young cops who ate their guns last winter. A chill of recognition passed through me, so I turned my attention to the amateur col-lages of successive precinct dinner-dances, one dumpy wife wearing the same sad dress year after year. I recalled hoisting iron in the spiffy weight-room at Trinity, and the soon-to-be honored Coach Calhoun spitting his core philosphy in my face: "Harder, Wilson. One more rep. Because gravity, Wilson, is a vicious god-damned rumor, so don't never give up. You hear me? Never never never never." Nor was Coach Calhoun above using class warfare to motivate his troops. We were scrimmaging New Haven Community College, it was, "These gangsta kids gonna eat your preppie lunches." Homecoming against the Lord Jeffs of Amherst, and it was, "Ta,ke your shots at these pampered pukes while you can, boys; you know you're gonna be working for them." Jimmy Calhoun was regarded in New England as a gridiron genius, which may or may not have been true. Son of a bitch could stay on mes-sage, though. He deserved his dinner, and 1, for one, was glad he was gonna get it.

I climbed off the stationary bike and went once around the Universal-Gym, finishing with a set of dead lifts in perfect form so as not to wrench my back. I figured, no sense playing hurt. Before leaving the building I stepped into the precinct commander's office and mentioned gang violence brewing up north, tips I'd received on Latin King activity.

He muted his television set, and thanked me. "I'll swing some extra men up there. You want the over-time?"

I reminded him of my big-shot football dinner downtown, and he smiled sadly, perhaps that I could have attended a school as good as Trinity College and wound up working here, then he returned his attention to Market Wrap.

I jumped in my Blazer and headed for home, nervous, still not sure, and, once in my West Hartford studio apartment, I con-sidered staying home, backing out of everything. I flopped onto my futon and faced my wall of fame, such as it was. I imagined how little a woman, any woman, would think of my life, of joining it. Between my police academy diploma and a good-samaritan plaque from the Rotary was a picture of me and Maggie Maynard and Kevin Connelly hoisting brews in front of the Bacchus mural at Alpha Delta Phi. Kevin was the starting quarterback then, and my best friend on the team, a good guy drunk who soon lost his roster spot, then everything else. He never showed up anymore.

Six years out, and Kevin was already on the list of lost alumni the school sends around. I alone represented the outlaw faction now, and tenuously at that.

So why go at all?

Coach Jimmy Calhoun once told me he was sorry he had recruited me. I told him that was something we agreed on, something to build on. The only time he ever smiled at me was when I told him I was leaving college to join the police force, that I'd knocked up my high school honey.

Why suffer an evening of dramatically lowered self-esteem, the one non-graduate from a team that conquered New England, the working-class stiff? I mean, seriously, not one of my teammates has a boom-box or a kitchenette, unless they are on his yacht.

Maggie Maynard-Rucker will be there, that's why I'm going.

Because her perfume stills clings to my imagination, and her voice still echoes in my soul. We had a year together as freshman, like no other year of my life, or hers, I suspect. We have a chance for that again.

I don't have a room at Chez Nutmeg for this gathering of eagles because I don't need my name on any lists—not because I'm broke, which I am. Most of my old teammates were here from out-of-town, the heart surgeons, the pre-maturely gray lawyers, the guy who owned a piece of the New York Islanders. Three of them have graciously sent business-like notes to my apartment, indicating my welcome at their hospitality suites, promising 'round the clock booze for the aging warriors.

I checked my black plastic cop-watch, and realized I should hurry. I wanted to arrive at the hotel early, not to bond, and not because I haven't done my homework. I know my city from high to low, top to bottom. The home-field edge is mine.

I showered, shaved close, and got dressed, then sat on a stool in my kitchenette and wiped down the envelope I'd received from Arlon Rucker's office. I plucked some marijuana buds and a pre-rolled joint from my personal stash and used a hemostat to nudge them inside the envelope, then used the hemostat to close the envelope and slip it in the inside pocket of my navy blue business suit.

I checked my look in the mirror by the only door. My wedding/funeral suit was lumpy over the off-duty revolver on my hip; and my ties have always sucked. I'm sure they'll snicker at me behind my back. Typical tackle. Slow for his age. Whatever they say is probably accurate. I know the drill. Tonight the stars will bond with stars, bench-warmers will sit with bench-warmers, and the outlaw will celebrate alone.

Like I goddamned, son-of-a-bitch cared.

I yanked off my tie and went with the shiny black t-shirt under my suit. Now I was large and dark, the way I ought to be, ready for war in the trenches. I locked the dead-bolt behind me, walked downstairs to the parking lot, and it dawned on me as I climbed into my polished black Blazer that if we all strapped on the pads and played some ball right now, I'd kick ass. I've stayed in shape, and I was always a starting tackle, captain of my high school squad. In college our best player Big Ed Grissom did what I did, so I rode the pine and got drunk a lot with Connelly. And this was Division 111, student-athletes, small potatoes. Maggie eventually broke up with me, and found herself a starter. Then afternoon practices meant only drudgery, play after play lined up against a guy who could kick my ass and didn't mind doing it. Game-hits don't hurt, at least not on game day; practice punishment is swift and certain, thudding car accidents in the red New England mud, bruises on bruises, and a look at life through the ear-hole of your helmet. Big Ed won't be coming tonight, of course, because Big Ed went home to New Hampshire after graduation and drove his pick-up off a cliff.

Heading downtown against rush-hour traffic on Route 1-84, I recalled last year's affair honoring the retiring equipment manager. It had been Men Only that night, maybe a hundred of us at Mather Hall on campus. Lots of scotch, cigars, and bonhommie, the poor bastard weeping when they handed him his Bantam plaque, then going around the room and naming without hesitation everyone present, grads from three decades, until he got to me. Then the dopey old duffer scratched his hairless head with the wire-less microphone. "Uh..."

"Bobby Wilson," I said, my face on fire. "l left school early."

"That's right. The army, right?"

"I joined the cops."

"Right. Well, those were happy times, boys. Why, I can remember once back in '71, when Electric Bob climbed the chapel drain-spout and damn near fell to his death..."

Yada, yada, yada. Oh, my peers will condescend to talk to me tonight. Everybody has such good manners these days. My cop-stories amuse them, but no one is sorry they didn't join the force with me. "Am I Commissioner yet?" they want to know. "What seems to be the hold-up? Captain? Nothing?"

"If I told you, I'd have to kill you."

"Oh, something hush-hush," they decide for themselves.

I am nothing.

Tonight the wives are coming, and I don't have one of those either, not anymore. She lives on my salary on eastern Long Island, which makes visits a nightmare of fog-bound ferries and clogged highways. Six year old Robert calls me Officer Daddy, when he calls at all. I wonder where he heard such a phrase. No, I don't. Maggie, I believe we can save each other.

Maggie wrote to me in the aftermath of my divorce, encouraging notes filled with warmth and longing, and the phrases haunt me as my sorry life ticks away: "Sometimes none of us get it right the first time out." Or: "Sometimes, Bobby, what looks like solid gold is junk." And: "It should be easier to change our minds. You know?" I felt her terrible pain and easily translated her message: She wanted me back. Enough already of Arlon Rucker from the class behind us, a strapping mulatto who looked too much like Derek Jeter. Arlon wound up All-New England quarterback, married Maggie, and slithered off to some Caribbean med school. He is a plastic surgeon now, with a great pair of hands, they say. I protected Arlon and those valuable hands whenever I got in the games, usually when the late Big Ed went down with a hammy. I'll bet Arlon's forgotten that. I'll bet he never sees me coming.

At five-forty-five I descended from the interstate to downtown surface streets and cruised past the arched entrance to Chez Nutmeg. I parked my truck near a hydrant, half a block away, fanned my PBA cards across the dashboard, and locked up, thinking, Oh, the perks of police work. Shameful what we servants carry home.

I ducked into the Starbucks on the opposite corner and ordered straight coffee, then commandeered a counter stool near a window with a view of Chez Nutmeg, the crawl of taxis and limos arriving under its burnished awning, the uniformed doormen rolling brass luggage racks to-and-fro. I welcomed the caffeine blast, and felt in my gut the way I did before a big game in high school, when how I performed really mattered.

I admit that I blew it with Maggie the last time. She had told me as much when she said goodbye in my dorm, making it all my fault, blaming my drinking, my quitter mentality, the huge chip she thought I carried on my shoulder. Maybe.she was right. Or maybe she only thinks she was right. I'm willing to let her think she was right.

From my perch I sipped my coffee and watched older stars like Barry O'Brien and Mike Hoskinson show up together with women I recognized from past reunions. George Sutherland had himself a new pretty wife, and the Doerge brothers came solo, thank God. I could do this.

I carried my styrofoam cup from the store, crushed it up, then bent low to jam it down the storm drain outside. Leave no unanswered questions. That was the secret. I might, had I not been thinking so clearly, carelessly tossed it into the ring of sculptured yews around the base of the hotel, or handed it to a doorman who might then remember I had been in Chez Nutmeg three nights prior. Dumb things. Get you needled.

I dodged the busy staff and pushed through the revolving glass doors, entered the atrium lobby with my defenses on high-alert. Six years of urban police work, I can mask my feelings anywhere, but seeing my Maggie with that phony Arlon might crack my resolve. I might get shortsighted. And it was now or never, at least in the movie I was watching.

I spied Doctor Rucker working the old-boy circuit in the corner of the open-air lobby bar. Maggie rested dutifully on his arm while Arlon chatted with men who had played in the days of leather head-gear and high-topped cleats. They were captains of industry now, of medicine, Wall Street, everything. At least lieutenants.

Maggie wore a simple black dress and pearls, chaste high heels, and a dazzling rock on her finger for camouflage. Maggie saw me over Arlon's shoulder, and there was a sudden sparkle in her eyes for me, I just knew it, another coded communication. Her dreams have been mine, lo these seven lonely years.

I nodded to her, and weaved through the milling crowd like a nimble half-back, approaching Arlon from behind, fighting the impulse to clip him.

"Thanks for the invite," I said to her, touching her tanned bare shoulder lightly. "It's great to see you again."

Arlon heard my voice and spun away from the codgers. He wore tiny wire-rimmed glasses now, and he removed them as he leaned between us. "Sure thing, Bob-o. Make sure you stop upstairs later. We'll reminisce."

God, I hated that half-wit nickname. Everybody always had to say his name properly, you know what I'm saying? He was always so proud of himself. So cocky. "Sure," I mumbled. "Whatever."

"I mean it."

"Cool. Thanks."

Maggie squeezed my flexed-cord arm and smiled. "You look great, Bobby. Younger than when you left school. You've lost weight, or got taller. "

And cracked up four police cars, got shot at twice, grew a handlebar mustache, and shaved it off, lost both my parents, my wife and son, my house in New Britain, so mu.ch you have missed. "I'm in decent shape, I guess. Hell, I have to be. We don't have referees out on the streets, you know. No one to blow a whistle. No huddles. No time-outs."

"I thought you people were the referees," said Arlon.

"Been down from your marble tower lately?"

Arlon smiled patiently at me and squeezed the nape of Maggie's neck.

I turned away from the obviously unhappy couple and scanned the crowd for familiar faces, maybe someone I'd forgotten who still liked me, who had not noticed my downward spiral. I pretended to recognize a pal and moved off, then hit the opposite end of the bar for a double Bloody Mary. I needed the vodka to soothe my growing fears. This was happening, whether I wanted it to or not.

For the next ten minutes I sipped my drink and worked the perimeter, avoiding conversations, getting my money's worth.

"Hungry, huh?" one redheaded waitress asked as she held out a tray of stuffed mushrooms.

"Starved. Thank you," I said. "Plus, anyone who has ever been to a wedding knows the cocktail hour has the best food."

"I was married once," she said wistfully.

I backed away, kept my eyes on Maggie and the man she wanted to leave. No one noticed me, I'm sure. Big as I am, I can blend.

The lobby lights dimmed twice, and the burnished doors to the Nutmeg Ballroom fanned open. We dutifully filed inside, and I sat with boisterous strangers from five years prior to my class, thinking I was right to load up on cocktail franks and stuffed mushrooms, because the prime rib was gray and tasteless, a chore to choke down. However, my view of Maggie's left flank was exquisite, offering me her contours, bare shoulders, her down-cast mouth as she sipped from her water glass and nibbled at her fish. Arlon virtually ignored her throughout the dinner, though he glanced at me through his buppie glasses from time to time, as if he sensed my desire for his wife, or what was coming.

The man sitting directly across from me noticed the by-play, and said, "That's Arlon Rucker, isn't it? Man, I remember, he was good."

"Of course he had all damn day to throw the ball, me and Big Ed Grissom kicking tail up front. You could have done what he did. Trust me."

"Big Ed's dead, right?"

"Gone but not forgotten," I said, raising my glass.

A metal pinkie-ring tapped against an open mike. The head coach had made his way to the lectern and stood now in front of a gold-on-navy TRINITY banner, ready to bore us to death. "Football, ladies and gentlemen, builds strong minds, strong.bodies and strong character. It brings young men closer to God, or Jah, or Allah, or whatever deity we may be playing for at the moment."

All around the ballroom eyeballs rolled north and two loud-mouths hooted.

"Hah! Just kidding," said the coach. "Wanted to see if you boys were awake." Then coach got pre-game serious and bowed his crewcut head, asked for a moment of silence for Grayson Talbot, class of '39. Robert Watkins Miller, '55. Duane Abdul Hassan, '74, and Big Ed Grissom, '93. "Great men gone too soon," he said. "Playing for Trinity's squad in Heaven...Thank you, folks. And now, the reason we've all returned to alma mater, let's have a warm Bantam welcome to our guest of honor, Coach Jimmy Calhoun."

Even I got up and clapped as Jimmy Calhoun limped to the podium during the rousing ovation. Of course, I could have given his dopey speech as well. Never give up. Gravity is a nasty rumor. Jesus loves the running game. Blah, blah, blah. The moment I'd been waiting for.

I made eye-contact across the room with Arlon Rucker and gave him the arched eyebrow, the one that had always meant it was time to hold an emergency meeting of the doobie squad. His handsome brown face broke into a thoroughly disarming smile. All, apparently, was forgiven. The bonds were re-established. Hike.

"You old dog," he said, low-fiving me when we met in the lobby. "Still doing herb, even on the job."

I said, "Nothing really changes, right, Doctor?"

"This ain't a set-up, right? You're not going to arrest me and try to run off with my wife?"

I smiled, and said to Arlon as the elevator door slid open. "You must already be high." We rode eleven floors up in silence. Nearing the twelfth, I said softly, "I miss football, Arlon. Nothing else has come close."

Arlon glanced up at the floor-indicator. "I hear ya, brother."

The door opened, and we stepped into the hallway opposite the ice machine and a row of vending machines. I grinned at Arlon and got down into my stance, ready to pass-block.

Arlon barked, "Blue. Twenty-One. Blue Twenty-one. Hut. Hut."

Damn, but I could almost smell the grass, the sweat. On the second hut I exploded off the line and charged down the carpeted hallway, growling. I broke-down at the door next to Arlon's corner suite, spun left, and delivered a forearm shiver, hard enough to spring open the door and bend the jamb.

Arlon, who had jogged up behind me, said, "Whoa, Bob-o Easy, big guy. Let's not trash the place."

I stepped back into the hall, admiring my handiwork.

"Come on, before anybody sees us." Arlon tugged me to his door, swiped his key-card through the lock and led us into his three-room suite.

"Hold it," I said. "People will be coming up here after dessert, right? Better for both our reputations we don't stink the place up."

"Good thinking."

I smiled. I couldn't help it. I patted my breast pocket."Let's hit this bomber on the roof."

He closed the door to his suite behind us and we found the Exit sign over the stairwell, and climbed to the top landing, where the night wind raced in past a steel door propped open by a brick. A small sign taped to the door said the solarium was under construction, due to open in August.

"Watch your step," I said, leaning outside. "It's dark out here."

Arlon hovered close to my back as I circled the empty jacuzzi and ducked behind an elevator shaft to escape the wind. There, touching only the edges, I opened the envelope he'd sent me filled with my loose weed, and a joint. I plucked out the joint and passed it to Arlon, who suddenly had hotel matches in his hand. Arlon cupped his hands against the wind, struck the match, and lit up the jay, hit it twice, passed it to me and the matches to me.

"You got enough in there to leave me some?" Arlon asked when he had finally exhaled. "I can't exactly cruise my homies anymore."

"Must be rough. Sure. Keep it." Arlon was always such a mooch, so entitled. He tucked the envelope inside his jacket.

I walked from behind the elevator shaft to the chest-high wall at the edge of the roof. He followed me like a dog, so I handed him the burning joint and he toked twice again, stared out over the city, the play of lights on the Capitol rotunda.

"How's Maggie?"

"A pain in the ass, trust me, just like all the other wives."

"How are those team vacations you guys go on?" I asked.

He grunted, "Nice."

"You guys ever talk about me?"

He blew the smoke away. "We talk about the NASDAQ."

I motioned that he should take another hit, so he did.

"Arlon, when did you get so uppity?"

"Around the two million mark, okay? Jesus, Bobby, you know you graduate, you grow up...It doesn't become you, being bitter. People have noticed."

During the sermon on the roof the joint had gone out in his precious hand, so he passed it back to me, his servant, to re-light. I took it and paused, then gazed south, first toward our beloved alma mater, the gothic outline of Northam Towers and the white stone chapel dominating the southern horizon. Then I turned and pointed north, from whence we heard multiple sirens howling. "That's where I work," I said.

"I did my residency at Penn. You don't have to tell me about the ghetto, Bob-o"

I grabbed my crotch. "Bob on this."

Arlon's eyes flashed anger, then by the light of my struck match he saw that I was smiling, just busting his horns. He laughed once and squeezed my neck. I took one more small toke and went to pass him the joint but clumsy me, I dropped it to the warm tar roof.

"Typical lineman," Arlon said. "Hands of stone."

"My bad. I got it." I bent over, but instead of retrieving the glowing roach, I wrapped my hands of stone around Arlon's slender ankles. His socks were nylon, hose, girls call them. I felt his Achille's tendons contract as I did one last deadlift for the day; and Arlon must have thought I was kidding, or had things under control, a net, something, or that gravity really was just a nasty rumor, because he didn't even scream until he was halfway down to the landing I had always planned for one of us.

I crouched behind the parapet and took two deep breaths of sweet night air, then lay flat on the roof and waited, hearing nothing more than a tarpaulin flapping in the wind. At thirty seconds I risked a peek over the parapet. Nothing. No lights. No hue and cry. Two minutes later I looked down again. Nothing.

313

Perfect.

I stayed on my hands and knees as I skirted the Jacuzzi, then rose and dusted off my suit. I walked down one flight of stairs, where it took me but seconds to enter the busted suite next to Arlon's, find Jeffrey Barnwell's wallet in the dark and toss it from his balcony after Arlon.

Perfect.

I can imagine what you're thinking, but this was not about race, okay. This was about a woman who deserved to be saved, and true love that never dies. Plus, I was only into killing the white half of Arlon, the greedy half. If the world is now shy one soul brother doctor, I'm truly sorry, it couldn't be helped.

Naturally, I took the stairs all the way down to the ground floor, seeing no one, not even a security camera, although the wiring was in place at each landing; ya gotta love new.

The commotion was just beginning in the lobby as I arrived. "A body," someone yelled. "In the bushes. They've called the cops."

I was perhaps the tenth alumnus to arrive at ground zero, but the first Hartford cop. I hung my shield from the breast pocket of my jacket, and stood a little taller. "Everybody stay back," I said. "Touch nothing. I need to preserve the integrity of the scene." Arlon had augered head-first into the soft New England earth between two chest-high yews, and you could have parked a bicycle between his legs, at least I could have.

People, of course, noticed the white seersucker suit. "That's Arlon Rucker," they said. "I don't believe it."

"By, God it is," I said. "Jesus."

Word spread, and within moments Maggie Maynard-Rucker arrived at the scene, saw what had happened to her husband, and fell shuddering into the arms of Cal Costello, this loser from the class ahead of mine.

"What happened?" she cried. "He got up to go to the mens' room." Maggie stole another glance at the body and cried harder, probably from the shock of it, and Costello was running his hands over her back.

I flashed my shield in Costello's face, and took Maggie by the arm. "Police business," I said. "We need to do this for Arlon.

And don't look," I said, showing her my strength. "Remember him at a better time." Then I selflessly led her inside to the hotel security office and away from prying eyes. Before I went back outside I got her coffee, tissues. She would be just fine. I would see to it, and I told her so.

Detective Horace Blight had caught the squeal, and he rolled up in his black Caprice, all fat and grumpy and pale.

I leaned in his window open.

"Wassup, Wilson? What do you got?"

I nodded at the roof of Chez Nutmeg. "Jumper."

"Jackass." Blight meant the jumper, not me. He said he was already reeling from a busy night, and his car seat was covered with half completed forms on prior cases. "Plus, two Kings just got waxed in the North End on a drive-by, right in front of a stake-out team. Now what's up with this guy?"

"A guest at the hotel, at the college football reunion," I said.

"I hate conventioneers," said Blight. The big detective hauled himself out of his car and walked into the garden and bent over the body. "Damn," he said under his breath, "you could park a Harley up his ass."

"I'm hip."

Detective Blight picked carefully at the clothes, found Arlon's wallet in the rear pants pocket, the other wallet on the ground near his great right hand. Arlon, of course, also possessed an envelope with his professional logo on it, said envelope filled with loose marijuana.

I knelt next to Horace Blight, nudged his elbow and looked up at the balconies. "You don't think he was going room to room?"

"I know I don't carry two wallets."

"He didn't need the money, I can tell you that. Big-shot doctor. Guy led a charmed life."

"Doctors go nuts, just like everybody else."

"Maybe he never really felt like he fit in," I ventured. "Maybe he never even liked us."

Horace Blight stood up and stepped out of the flower bed, lit a cigarette, blew the smoke away from me. "Who knows what evil jerks..."

I laughed and shook my head in sorrow, a move they ought to teach at the police academy. Just then reinforcements arrived in an explosion of flashing lights, dingy squad cars with additional detectives, two uniforms for crowd control, an ambulance that would not be needed, a morgue wagon that would.

"Better men than me are here," I said.

"You want me to put you present?" asked Horace. "Pick up some overtime?"

"Who needs the aggravation?" I said. "I'd rather go back inside and dump a stiff one."

"Then you're gone." Detective Blight showed me his back, faced his team of specialists, and divided up the assignments, the searches of the roof, the dead man's room, the separation and canvassing of witnesses, the collection of any physical evidence, fibers, blood, semen, that sort of thing. He was looking at a long night of the obvious, I prayed, not much of a mystery at all. He would find the dead man was drunk and stoned, a victim of bad risk management, his own room entered with his own key-card just moments before he plunged from a neighboring balcony, the damaged door jamb of the neighboring suite, the purloined wallet near his person, his corporate dope stash, not a pretty picture, and not that hard a puzzle: typical marauding guest.

"So get lost, already," Horace Blight said over his shoulder. "You were never here."

My expertise no longer needed, I backed away from the bushes and ducked under the crime scene tape, a man with a future. I wandered inside again, through the lobby crowded with sympathizers, headed for the security office, where I would assist my Maggie with the advent of widowhood, the details of sudden death; and damn if I didn't bump into Jimmy Calhoun. So I hugged that old coach, with real tears in my eyes, and I thanked him for teaching me to never never never give up.